CHASING COLUMBUS

A novel in the History Detective Trilogy

by

David J Andrews

Also by the same author

Lobster Calypso

Endeavour's Legacy

The History Detective Trilogy

1. Chasing Columbus
ISBN– 978-1906658-00-7

2. Bahamian Rhapsody
ISBN– 978-1906986-76-6

3. Khan's Legacy
ISBN– 978-1909271-92-0

With thanks to Jenny.

For her patience, understanding and support.

"If stories come to you, care for them and learn to give them away where they are needed.
Sometimes a person needs a story more than food to stay alive."

Artic Dreams – Barry Lopez

To be ignorant of what occurred before you were born is to remain always a child. For what is the worth of human life unless it is woven into the life of our ancestors by the records of history.

Cicero

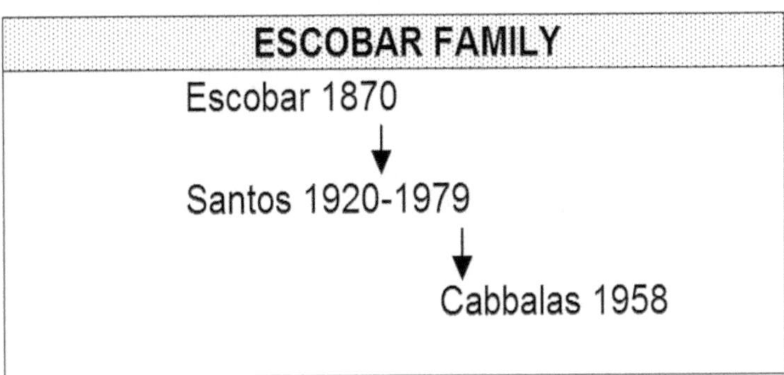

ESCOBAR FAMILY
Escobar 1870
Santos 1920-1979
Cabbalas 1958

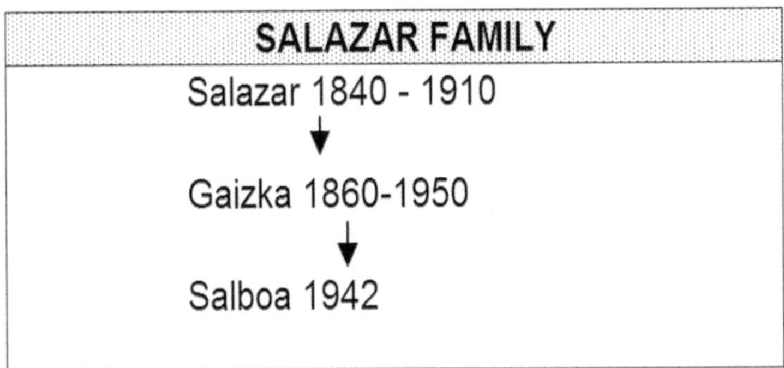

SALAZAR FAMILY
Salazar 1840 - 1910
Gaizka 1860-1950
Salboa 1942

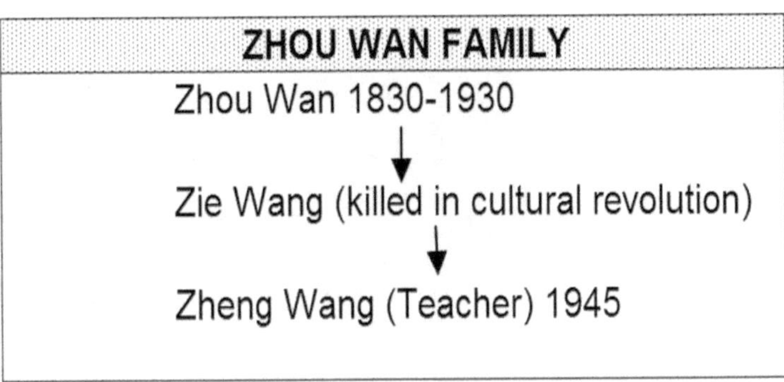

ZHOU WAN FAMILY
Zhou Wan 1830-1930
Zie Wang (killed in cultural revolution)
Zheng Wang (Teacher) 1945

Prelude

1492 San Sebastian,
La Gomera.

The small island of La Gomera nestles southwest of Tenerife in the Canary Islands, a mixture of eerie crags, steep green terraced hills and a small population. In 1492, that population was no more than a few hundred souls eking out a sparse existence in the hills. This represented the western edge of known civilisation and many believed that not far to the west of the island lay the end of the world and a drop into oblivion. To other, more enterprising adventurers, the west held the promise of limitless wealth just waiting to be claimed. An increasingly popular view was that the quickest way to the vast riches of the Orient lay west, not east as had previously been believed.

No one believed this more than Christopher Columbus. He knew that discovery of a quicker route would mean fame and fortune and he was determined that this destiny should be his. All he had to do was convince a wealthy backer that he was right and he could achieve his life's quest and personal dream to be an Admiral and owner of a vast new empire. He even had a map; the Martellus map, especially revised and redrawn to prove the virtue of his claims to potential investors,

Columbus was a tall unprepossessing man with a serious countenance and a mass of once red, now white hair. Closer inspection of his blue eyes and aquiline nose revealed an intense man on a mission. Determined to raise the money required to mount a western expedition, he spent many soul-destroying years petitioning the travelling court of Queen Isabella and King Ferdinand around Spain. Because of this dogged pursuit to find funding, his dour countenance and distinct lack of humour became legendary amongst courtiers and staff of the royal household.

Despite his assurances, arguments and pleas, Columbus struggled to convince Queen Isabella of the strategic importance of his proposed voyage, all the while secretly worrying that the Portuguese would get to the Orient before him. He knew that King Joao of Portugal was committed to exploring the eastwards route and would do so with his own expedition as soon as it was viable.

Columbus consoled himself with the thought that, as a nation, the Portuguese had less money than their richer neighbour and would be unable to mount a full expedition for some time. Even more worrying was his fear that the Portuguese would discover that he was travelling with copies of their maps that he had 'borrowed' from the Prince Henry 'School of Navigation'. Mindful of these potential threats, Columbus renewed his efforts to convince Queen Isabella to support him. To help him achieve this he and his brother Bartholomew adjusted the Martellus map to make what many believed was a shorter route via the east appear to be an almost impossible journey.

The modified Martellus map succeeded in winning over Queen Isabella who was looking for a diversion after the final defeat of the Moors at Granada. The Moors, Islamic invaders in Andalusia, had been forcibly removed and for the first time Spain was united as a Christian country. Peace had been hard won and Isabella aimed to keep it that way.

With great relief, Columbus put to sea at Cadiz with much pomp and ceremony and huge excitement from the large crowd gathered on the quay. His fleet consisted of three ships, the *Santa Maria*, the *Nina* and the *Pinta* with ninety men aboard. The voyage went well at first and Columbus used the time to instil discipline into his officers and men. He was well aware that this needed to happen at an early stage of the voyage because rumour and superstition was running rife amongst the uneducated sailors, who were convinced they were on a journey to the end of the world. Unfortunately, sudden squalls caught them unawares and the *Pinta* suffered rudder breakage that could not be repaired at sea. It forced the ships to land on the tiny volcanic island of La Gomera, the second-smallest of the Canary Islands in the Atlantic Ocean off the coast of Africa.

As the ship came in sight of land, Columbus stepped down into his small cabin and made ready to disembark. Although frustrated at having to break his journey, he realised that nothing could be done until the rudder was fixed. He consoled himself with the thought that at least he would have the company of the lovely Contessa Beatriz de Bombadilla who was now the acting governor of the island, following the death of her tyrant husband. He had been having an affair with Beatriz since the tragic early death of his wife. He found her a charming companion with the additional benefit that she was a great friend of the Queen. Beatriz relied heavily on the Queen's patronage, she had no title of her own and wanted to maintain the position in society she had reached before her husband's demise.

Columbus stared hard at the island as they slowly entered the small harbour at San Sebastian, the capital and main port town for the island, shouting orders to pull alongside the rickety pier. He watched absent-mindedly as the sailors went about their tasks, torn between his desire to see the Contessa again and raging against the twist of fate that had brought him here. Desire won and the lovers' reunion was joyous, rekindling the relationship they had enjoyed whilst following Isabella's travels around Spain.

Days later the ships carpenter put the final touches to the *Pinta's* rudder mechanism and tested it. He had fitted a new rudder blade and Columbus idly wondered how many other problems the aged ships would incur on the long journey ahead. Not for the first time did he wish that he had newer and larger ships for the voyage. He made an effort to smile as he walked amongst the sailors, after attending mass at the Church of the Assumption in San Sebastian, ever conscious of their superstitions and dread of the unknown. As their leader, he knew he had to set a good example by looking fearless and unconcerned by the epic journey.

The final evening before departure, the three small ships, each about seventy feet long by twenty-five feet wide, lay rocking lazily at anchor. Columbus watched the sun set for the final time over the island from the terrace at the Torre del Conde, home of Beatriz. He smiled at her fondly, knowing that she endured a difficult existence on the island. The locals still did not accept her; a legacy from the harsh rule of her hated husband, and rumours of her many love affairs, they called her '*la Cazadona*', the huntress. She read his thoughts. "I wish I could go back to the mainland permanently."

"Maybe there is a way," replied Columbus quietly.

"What do you mean?"

"When I return from the voyage I will have the title of Don as a Hidalgo and also money so we can live in Spain." Beatriz looked uncertain. "But the Queen will take any treasures you bring!" she exclaimed.

"Technically I am allowed a tenth of everything I bring back, but that only applies to that which I declare." Columbus looked away, not catching her eye. "But, what happens if you don't declare everything?"

"Best you don't know the details."

"It would be wonderful to live in Spain again, especially now that it is free of the Moors." Beatriz replied wistfully. "Not only will we be wealthy but the Moors will never again invade our beloved country," replied Christopher, standing up. "They even invaded this island! The Church of San Marco here was originally a Mosque!" Indignation flared in Beatriz's eyes.

"I blame them for spawning your husband."

"The Count Hernan Peraza made my life hell and was rightly accused of taking a local princess as his mistress," agreed Beatriz

"They say her family ambushed him and murdered him in cold blood, is it true?" queried Columbus, intrigued. "They did me a great favour, he treated me like dirt." Beatriz flushed at the memory of the cruel Count. "It has made you the de-facto ruler of this island," smiled Columbus. "You have the approval of Queen Isabella. She understands your plight."

"I want more Christophe! This is no place for a woman alone! I want recognition in Spain and a place at The King's and Queen Isabella's court."

"Tomorrow I will set out to cross the ocean and make you the richest woman in Spain," he smiled. "You may die." Beatriz could not keep the sadness she felt out of her voice. "Listen, my love, there is no danger of us going off the edge of the world," whispered Columbus conspiratorially. "Your men are worried." She turned troubled eyes upon him, seeking reassurances she felt sure he would be unable to give. "The world is round. I have the map to prove it."

"What map?" confused now, Beatriz quizzed her lover. "Paolo Toscanelli the famous cartographer gave me it! It was part of the reason for my expeditious marriage to Felippa Pestrello the daughter of the Governor of Porto Santo. He became friendly with me the same year, thirteen years ago. It's his ideas I am beholden to!" Columbus found it hard to keep the excitement from his voice, even though he knew it must remain a secret for the time being.

"What ideas?"

"That the land to the west is closer than anyone realises. He has given me detailed maps of the western Atlantic including the island of Antilla."

"But the seamen are worried. They are fearful for their lives; they think they are on a journey to certain death! You should tell them." Beatriz was near to tears now. "Do you think I can disclose to anyone that I know what awaits us? Of course not! For it would only serve to damage my claims. I want to go down in history as the discoverer of the new world not a follower." Columbus sought to find the words to convey the importance of what he was saying. "So people have been there before you?" Beatriz whispered incredulously, finally understanding what her lover was telling her.

"Exactly, now let's talk no more of it." Columbus turned away, making it clear that he would say no more on the subject.

"Priest!" shouted Columbus to a small wiry man dressed in the sombre robes of a priest approaching them, "Pray for us, I want no ill winds or bad luck on this trip. You need to make sure of that."

"As I am going with you sire I have every reason to pray to the Almighty for success." Zarco nodded fervently. "I wonder why you want to come with us at your age?" replied Columbus looking at the older man and noting his strange slanting eyes for the first time.

"I have my reasons."

"Tell me your reasons, old man." Columbus shivered as a cool wind blew across his face. Something about the man concerned him. "You wouldn't understand." Zarco shook his head slowly. "Try me." The response was terse, betraying the unease he continued to feel. "I live for the future, for people who believe that man cannot drive his own destiny." Zarco started hesitantly.

"That is God's role." Columbus cut the old man's speech dead, fixing him with his cold blue eyes.

"I am God's servant. My father was famous in Portugal for colonising Madeira. I too have my goals, different goals."

"I'm only concerned with my voyage, and will need your God's help, see to it."

"If it is God's will, it will happen." Zarco nodded again, his face hard and unreadable.

v

"Where do you come from Zarco?" asked Beatriz also noting the strange eyes. "A holy place in the mountains, a place where the keys to mankind's knowledge are held." The old man continued to gaze into the distance. "Weighty matters," replied Columbus frowning. "If your father was Portuguese, why should I trust you?"

"The matters of man's soul are weighty sir," replied Zarco. "They require faith, have that in me and you will succeed, without it you will fail."

"Indeed," replied Columbus making a mental note to watch this man. "I want no trouble with the crew Zarco, just look after my spiritual needs."

"What's wrong?" hissed Beatriz as Zarco walked away and Columbus turned to her frowning. "Why did you speak to a priest like that?"

"Zarco reminds me of the Portuguese," replied Columbus deep in thought. "Ever since I stole their World Maps I have to be careful who I trust."

"But your brother Bartholomew stole the maps, what is there for you to fear?"

"I may not have stolen them, but he was under my instructions and sold copies for a large profit in Italy. Still, whatever happened I have to live with my deeds and it was worth it. Thanks to Toscanelli and Martellus I know the Orient is only two thousand seven hundred and sixty miles from here not the nine and a half thousand miles that everyone else believes. Even the Emperor of China thinks so."

"God will look after you." Beatriz reached for the crucifix at her neck as she raised a silent prayer to bring him back to her safely. "Yes and Zarco," replied Columbus, his voice heavy with sarcasm as he watched the small man, now a distant figure, walk slowly towards the ships. "Come." He strode purposefully back into the house. "We leave on the early tide so best I leave you soon." He looked hard at the Contessa, a stunning sight with her long black hair tumbling down her back, before pulling her close to him one last time. She was so like the other Beatriz in Spain, his acknowledged mistress, he mused. Pushing thoughts of the other equally beautiful Beatriz aside he concentrated on saying his goodbyes properly. He was a lucky man.

After ten days, sailing the crew fearfully waited to see whether they would drop off the edge of the world. Bound together in terror, as the days passed without incident even the most superstitious amongst them began to realise that it wasn't going to happen and settled down to the monotony of life onboard a ship in confined spaces. Twenty-six days later, and in a state of dehydration and hunger, the small flotilla was in trouble. Columbus, in a state of despair, and convinced that his calculations were wrong felt his spirits rise as he finally heard the longed for shout, "Land!" After weeks of staring death in the face, it seemed that their prayers had been answered. Columbus himself was the first to disembark from the *Santa Maria*, breathing thanks to the Almighty, convinced he had landed in Japan. It was in fact a small island in the Bahamian island chain, which he named San Sebastian. The native people of the island greeted his arrival as if he had come from the moon, a God to be honoured. They gasped in wonder at seeing people in such strange clothes, carrying what they believed to be magical sticks. This initial joy would eventually turn to bitter regret that the Spanish had been welcomed on their arrival, after the tribe was destroyed through a lethal mixture of disease and maltreatment.

For Columbus the important thing was that he had found land and with it the riches he craved. He made his way carefully through the many reef islands where the trusting natives honoured him with gifts. In exchange for trinkets, such as nails, he claimed treasures of gold and silver until the ships holds were brimming full and becoming top heavy and unstable. It would soon be time to return to the East in triumph, although he still had not found the 'special' treasure that he intended not to declare, which would assure him the wealth he desired.

Leaving the large island of San Dominica the expedition headed home by way of the island of North Bimini, an island that already had a reputation for providing eternal life simply by swimming in its spring water. The crew spent a few days collecting the by now usual gifts of gold and silver, but Columbus was still looking for something special. He was taken aside by the native King and together, with only a few of the King's most trusted soldiers, they walked for over an hour inland through the jungle until they reached a secret place where to his surprise he saw primitive but effective smelting facilities for iron and gold.

His interest piqued, the King led him through into a secret chamber and presented him with an object that made his eyes widen in amazement and awe. It was a symbolic gold cross nearly a metre high with a large diamond at the front and many smaller ones on the back alongside strange writing symbols. This was special and he knew it. This was the special treasure that he had been looking for that would enable him to keep his pledge to Beatriz.

He thanked the King effusively and bestowed on him all manner of trinkets in return, knowing that nothing he could give would compare with the beautiful cross. Taking the object, concealed in a cloth, he carefully lifted it, groaning at its weight. Unable to carry the dead weight far, he enlisted a soldier to help him and saw the avaricious glint in the man's eye when a corner of the cloth covering came off. The soldier would later die in mysterious circumstances, as would all who came into any form of contact with the Cross.

What Columbus had not noticed was Zarco following them into the jungle, the Priest's hidden face betraying all his emotions. He gave thanks to his own God and made his own plans. For Columbus, the return journey was perfect until disaster struck. His flagship the *Santa Maria* was wrecked on a coral reef at La Espanola (now Haiti) and he realised he would have to leave men behind whilst he sailed home on the *Nina*.

Leaving a small garrison on Puerto Rico Island, Columbus and his reduced fleet returned to adulation in Spain after making a secret stop in La Gomera to share his good news with the Contessa and ask her to hide his most precious treasure. Whilst he celebrated his new status in Spain by meeting the Queen in Barcelona, Zarco quietly returned to La Gomera and assembled a group of loyal men; a private army for his allegiance was not to Columbus. He visited the Contessa and earnestly told her that it was essential that he take the Cross, as Columbus had no rightful claim to it. Zarco explained the story of the many crusades of Prince Henry of Portugal, or 'The Navigator' as he was known. Zarco had been a Knight Nobleman in the Prince's service.

After the conquest of Ceuta in Morocco, Prince Henry founded a naval school and launched numerous successful crusades. By the time the Prince died in 1460, the Portuguese had explored the coast of Africa down to Sierra Leone and discovered the archipelagos of Madeira, the Azores, and the Cape Verde Islands. During these crusades, Prince Henry had amassed much wealth. He had captured African's, taking them back to Portugal as slaves and stolen many African treasures, including the Cross, from the rightful owners. With the burning eyes of a zealot, Zarco stressed to Beatriz that it was now vital to return the cross to its home, for it was more than just a cross; it was a nation's future. He then surprised her by explaining her late husband's duty and role in this divine mission.

The Contessa remained unmoved by Zarco's arguments and refused him; as far as she was concerned, the cross was the key to her future with Columbus. In the dark of night, Zarco and his men broke her door down and stole it from the terrified Contessa's bedroom where she had hidden it for safekeeping. Outraged, Beatriz exercised her right as Governor of the island, ordering soldiers to find Zarco and his followers and bring back the cross. The soldiers intercepted the fleeing group at San Sebastian, capturing them all bar Zarco who amazingly escaped.

Fleeing to the town Zarco found an ideal hiding place to deposit the Cross, along with something far more important to him, something that if found would have meant his immediate death, and something that in time would spread around the Spanish world. He alone knew the real meaning of the Cross-and its secrets. His last act before leaving the town for good was to record the hiding place and pass the details to a trusted sea captain heading for the West. Having escaped the Contessa's men, again disguised as a priest, he made his way into the lush forests in the island's hinterland.

There in the mountains, near the highest peak Alto De Garajonay at over four thousand eight hundred feet, Zarco spent the last years of his life joined by a small band of like-minded brothers. Communicating across long distances by the whistling language 'Silbo', they remained safe from the Contessa and her soldiers. A reliable friend executed his dying wish and the secrets of the Cross and its hiding place was gone. He had completed his task, others would now see to its completion.

Columbus and Beatriz scoured the island without success, even taking a pilgrimage up into the mountains. For Columbus, three more voyages followed and increased his wealth, though he lost his fancy titles. However, he went to his grave still believing that Cuba and the other Caribbean islands were part of China. Beatriz remained on the island, unhappy but finding solace in the arms of a succession of lovers. Queen Isabella never knew or suspected Columbus of the grand deceit regarding the cross, which remained hidden. It was a deceit that would come back to haunt the human world four hundred years later.

March 2008
Holiday Inn, Pudong, Shanghai

For the umpteenth time Guy Tresanton looked around the crowded conference hall of the Holiday Inn, realising that a lot more people were present than he had first thought. Pangs of fear gripped his stomach and waves of adrenalin flooded his body, making him feel giddy as his eyes flickered down to his opening speech. This was it; four hundred people sat expectantly in front of him and his was the opening speech for this first conference in Shanghai. Everything looked perfect; Pudong was chosen as the location for this important event as from its development in the 1990's Pudong had emerged as China's financial and commercial hub. He tried to put thoughts of escape into Puxi, the older part of Shanghai, to one side as he looked through his notes and for what felt like the hundredth time went over his opening words. This was his show, the big one. After months of preparation, he finally had his company's entire Asian supplier base in front of him. They were here for a reason; his company needed them, but if his plans were to come to fruition, he needed them even more.

Guy took off the gold-framed glasses he used for reading, pushing back his unruly sandy hair that had a tendency to hang in waves over his face. Over six feet tall, with light blue eyes and a slightly freckled face that looked as if it had a perpetual frown of concentration, Guy gave the appearance of an over indulgent school master. He looked younger than his forty-seven years with a boyish grin that lit up his face, instantly banishing the frown. However, despite an athletic spring to his step from daily tread-mill and weight training, Guy's slumped shoulders currently gave him a careworn appearance. The truth was he was at the end of a long relationship and a single future beckoned which was not appealing.

Shuffling his papers to re-focus his mind Guy could see his entire Chinese sourcing team sitting on the conference chairs, with expectant faces waiting for him to start speaking. Amongst them, he could see his local Sourcing Director, a tall slim man called Sam Ling. This was their show, as important to them as him, four months in the planning and it had to succeed as his proverbial neck was on the line. IPT Impact Technologies, his employer had been nominally in the region sourcing products for many years but only recently, under his stewardship, had they become serious in purchasing high technology medical components for their own Swiss and England based factories. He had fought against prejudice and outright obstruction to get this far; including battles with his own boss a humourless Swiss Finance Director called Manfred Christ.

IPT, had until recently, controlled the niche biotech market for high technology valve systems. Complacent of their position in this specialist field, IPT had been shaken to find themselves the subjects of serious low cost Asian competition. The initial response had been to ignore it, confident of their brand leadership and expecting that it would go away. When this strategy did not work, a maverick owner had appointed Guy on the basis that something needed to be done. Unfortunately, in the conservative Swiss business world the maverick owner did not last long, especially as his actions had been against the wishes of the board. This left Guy without the support of the man who had recruited him and fierce resistance from the rest of his colleagues at IPT to his sourcing work in China.

Guy was convinced that the only way to save both him and the Chinese team was a show of strength at this conference; seeing it as an opportunity to demonstrate the effectiveness of his business plans and the excellent work he and the team had done so far. His nervousness returned, as he knew that in the audience there were half a dozen senior Swiss managers waiting to watch him fail and prove their doubts correct. Guy was determined to disappoint them. The 'Winterthur Mafia', as he called them, sat unsmiling in the front row seats all in the same black suits.

Guy ignored them. He was on the verge of a major breakthrough in building a credible supplier base with innovative ideas. This would put them ahead of the competition and well placed for the next decade. The only problem was, the suppliers were high technology specialists and he was the salesperson. Minutes to go and Guy looked around again, seeing Manfred right in the centre of the front row with an expression that said, 'this had better be good.' Guy clenched his teeth, this was his one chance, he thought, blow this and he could kiss the job goodbye. The man did not like him and had been looking for ages for an excuse to get rid of him. Guy prayed to whatever God was watching over him as the lights dimmed that he would not give him that reason. His legs felt like lead and his chest was thumping. He saw the large professional camera outfit in the corner as its light turned green, it was time. He forced a smile and gripped the lectern harder.

"Ladies and Gentlemen, welcome to IPT's first Asian Supplier Conference." He felt himself shaking as he said the words but concentrated as the first of his PowerPoint slides appeared on the large screen behind him. He waited until his Chinese colleague translated his opening remarks. He stammered over a couple of words and tried to tell a poor joke, which fell flat on the inscrutable Chinese audience in front of him and even flatter on the Swiss Mafia. He took a long gulp of water and stumbled on through the presentation trying desperately to gain fluency. Time passed interminably slowly as he made his way through the prepared slides. He finished the water and smiled wanly as a girl replaced the glass and he took a sip.

"Your technology is fundamental to us and this is not about us saving money but working with you as partners," he continued. "We expect the highest standards in our trading as we are signatories to the United Nations Trading Compact." He froze as his vision suddenly started to blur, shaking his head and making a mental note to get his eyesight checked. He started on the next slide waiting whilst the translator caught up and groaned as he felt his head sway and his legs start to buckle. What was happening to him? His mouth dried up, he could not speak. He grabbed the glass of water and could not hold it he was shaking too much. He saw the impassive gaze of the audience waiting for him as if suspended in time, his eyes drifting to Manfred where he could see the beginnings of a familiar frown. His mind started to free wheel, the room spun around and he lurched forwards. There was a scream somewhere in the background as he collapsed to the side taking the podium with him as his world went black.

"Where am I?" Guy groggily came to in a side room, struggled to sit up, and looked around him. "You collapsed, we brought you in here," replied Sam, his face showing concern for his business colleague. "The conference, what's happening?" Guy wanted to know as the memories of his collapse flooded back into his muzzy brain. "It was cut short, Manfred announced an early meal." Sam announced flatly. "Is he still here?"

"He's gone, said he had to get back to Switzerland, said you would know the reason why," said Sam quickly. "It's over isn't it?"

"I'm finished," groaned Guy sitting up and feeling nauseous. He slumped back down, so much for treating people with respect. "You fainted," uttered a voice beside him. He looked around and saw a small bespectacled man. "I'm the hotel doctor; you passed out probably through tension."

"It was the damned water, there was something in it," shouted Guy trying to sit up again. "Check the glass Sam! Go and see to the team!"

"It broke as you fell to the ground; you took the podium with you," said the doctor. "I was drugged, I'm telling you. There is no other explanation." Guy put his feet gingerly on the floor trying to stand up. His arm was badly bruised and he felt like his ankle had twisted during the fall. "It's quite common in moments of extreme stress for the body to shut down as a defensive reaction," said the doctor reassuringly, "It's nothing to be worried about."

"Worried about?" Guy exploded, "It's just cost me my job, that's all," he shouted at last managing to stand up. "You should rest for a while," interrupted the doctor packing his equipment away. "Take these pills twice a day; they will slow down your pulse, calm you down."

"I don't need calming down!" roared the reluctant patient as a woman opened the door. "Who the hell are you?" he glared at the newcomer. "My name is Elsie, I'm the Sales Director for DWT, one of your suppliers, are you alright?" her hesitation in the face of his anger was apparent. "As well as can be expected." With bad grace, Guy tried to pull himself together to respond to her polite enquiry. "May we talk in private?" Elsie said and sat down in the chair recently vacated by the doctor. "I guess so." Guy sat back down and felt a little better, though in no mood for gracious platitudes. He subconsciously pushed his hair backwards. "What can I do for you?"

Elsie hesitated and looked around to make sure that the doctor had left the room before whispering, "That was a first warning."

"What?" Guy's eyes opened wide in astonishment, this was the last thing he expected her to say. "The water was drugged; you were targeted to teach a lesson."

"What lesson?"

"Stop exploiting our people. You think you are doing our people a favour but you're not." Guy was astounded. "We provide employment, isn't that a good thing?" he puzzled aloud. "You are encouraging people to grow greedy, ruining our environment." Elsie's face was inscrutable as she delivered her message, leaning back in her chair with folded arms to ward off any argument. "Hardly all my fault, besides I probably don't have a job now so it hardly matters and there are many companies doing far worse than me." Guy was poignantly reminded of his own dire situation again. "I'm glad that you didn't get hurt in the fall Mr Tresanton. We don't want to hurt people only give them a shock."

"This is about more than saving Chinese workers, what is it?" asked Guy looking at her quizzically. "Nothing else Mr Tresanton," replied Elsie looking flustered. "Good day." She abruptly stood up and left.

Later, Guy sat in the hotel St Regis in Pudong looking out of the window, his discarded BlackBerry on the floor. The email from Manfred had been curt and economical with words as always; *Unfortunate event, role no longer viable please return to make suitable arrangements.* Swiss speak for termination no doubt, and not a word about his health. Not even a polite enquiry. Well, thought Guy adrenaline cursing through him once more, sod them, he would resign. He would not give them the satisfaction of firing him.

Anger propelling him across the room, he decided to check out the other odd event of the day and grabbed the phone, calling the number for DWT. He soon found out that no one called Elsie had ever worked there; it was clear that the woman he had met that afternoon was a fake. What was going on?

As he sat musing over this latest revelation, his mobile phone rang, the tinny sound breaking through the tension in the room. He looked at the screen with surprise; it was his mother in England. She never rang him on his business phone.

"Guy, it's your father." His mother's voice sounded etched with fear.

"What about him?" Guy ran his hands unconsciously through his hair in agitation, whilst trying to sound calm for his mother. "He's missing."

"Missing? How? Where?" The words came out in rapid succession as Guy grappled to understand what he was being told. "In Hong Kong yesterday, the police rang. Oh Guy, I don't know what to do, are you somewhere near Hong Kong?" The tears in her voice were clear even at this distance and Guy felt wretched with the desire to comfort her. "Leave it with me mother, tell me what happened."

"A boat trip in the harbour after his lecture, on one of those so-called 'junk' boats; you know the ocean sailing boats? He never returned and hasn't been seen since." Her voice broke off again. "The police?" Guy asked without much hope. "They don't know much more."

"Is there anything, try and think."

"I can't think of anything else. The police want to question you."

"Me?" replied Guy puzzled. His father was an eminent psychologist much in demand. "Why me?"

"I don't know. A junk was found abandoned, but it wasn't registered anywhere. Someone had tried to set fire to it."

"All right mother, leave it with me." Guy dropped the phone. How much worse could things get? He rang Sam's local secretary. "I need the first flight to Hong Kong." He slammed the phone on the bed and made his way through to the bathroom.

Kowloon District
Hong Kong

He sat stony-faced in the small police office as the police officer called Jack Hwang went over the story again. A small man with a balding head and piercing eyes, Hwang looked at Guy impassively and repeated what he had told Guy's mother. "The junk was stolen."

"Anything else?" even to Guy, his responses were sounding increasingly short tempered. "His room is empty; everything is gone almost as if it was deliberate. Tell me Mr Tresanton, was your father depressed?" Guy shook his head vigorously. "Impossible! He was a man who dealt with other people's depression!" he said hotly. "Don't start thinking this was suicide, there is no way. I suggest you get out there and find him."

"I need to know your recent movements," replied Hwang sternly.

"What am I a suspect now? I don't believe this." Exasperated and sweating in the heat of the confined room, Guy fought the urge to lash out at the diminutive police officer regarding him sceptically across the desk. "My job is to check all possible options." Hwang shrugged. "Then get after whoever stole that junk! Surely, you have fingerprints. They must be all over the deck!"

"You should co-operate Mr Tresanton. My job is to check all avenues. You are one of many suspects and your attitude needs to improve."

"Are you threatening me?" Guy shook his head incredulously. "I don't threaten people, Mr Tresanton. Just answer the questions and everything will be fine. Are there people who would want your father out of the way?" Hwang shifted in his chair and leant forward, as though inviting confidences. "Look, I have been to hell and back over the last two days and you sit there as if we are discussing an Agatha Christie film!" Guy spat. "Of course there isn't anyone who, as you put it, '*wants my father out of the way*'! He is a psychologist, not a gangster!"

"Was there a large inheritance for you Mr. Tresanton?" Hwang's monotone response cut through Guy's rant. "Go to hell!" shouted Guy heading for the door and wandering into the hot noisy streets in a daze. In the space of a few short hours, he had lost his job, his father and now he was a chief suspect. Things couldn't really get much worse.

Still smarting with anger from his confrontation with Hwang, Guy found an Irish bar he knew in Kowloon and started to drown his sorrows in pints of Guinness. Admitting to himself that alcohol was probably a bad idea, Guy felt the stress of the evening dissipate into a relaxed melancholy, as he talked to an Aussie whose view of the world bordered on anarchistic. Drink followed drink and suddenly Guy felt the world start spinning again.

He returned to consciousness to find himself in a dubious looking room lying stark naked face down on a grubby table with a young woman attacking his back with coarse hands. It started to take on a surreal air as he peered over his shoulder through an alcoholic haze; was he drugged again? Realising he was in a massage parlour he tried to relax as the girl professionally worked the knotted muscles in his shoulders. Concentrating on the journey her strong fingers made up and down his spine, he drifted back into unconsciousness grateful for the embrace of darkness.

Abruptly he stirred as a movement of cold air unsettled him. He opened his eyes, the world around him was spinning then floating and the girl was gone. His lustful thoughts about her readily dissolved as he blinked at the ephemeral shapes in front of him. "Dad!" he tried to shout as the familiar grey haired face of his father appeared out of the mist. The face ignored him; it seemed to turn with a wan smile as he shouted again and mouthed words towards him.

"*Remember what I taught you,*" he thought he heard. "Dad, I thought you were…," he stopped dead as he saw a shape behind his father. It looked like a dragon, which started to slowly materialise into an aged stern looking Chinese man. "He has seen too much."

"He is a chosen one, he cannot be removed," replied his father. Guy felt like a spectator at his own trial. "He must be removed," repeated the Chinese man sternly. "Guy, go far away from here, and never return," whispered his father urgently. Guy could not speak, he squirmed and tried to move his arms; was this reality or was he dreaming? He tried without success to move his arms; perhaps he was dead. Was this what death was like? "Be quiet old man," scolded the Chinese man. Guy cried out in anguish, but no sound came out as his father started to fade away and then the police stormed into the room roughly pushing him off the table and against the cold wall.

May
north eastern Bermuda

The hot afternoon sun was sinking fast as the lone diver made her way gingerly along the rock formation on the opposite side of

Harrington Sound. Facing towards the large, natural Castle Harbour, the area faced directly onto the Atlantic Ocean. An experienced scuba diver, Jacqui Oleson was the archetypal blue-eyed blonde-haired woman. In her early fifties, she was a legend in the diving community for her ability to manage the most difficult of dives. A divorcée, she and her daughter, Leila, lived on the island, running a scuba diving school on the more popular west side at Little Sound in the Southampton district. In their spare time, their joint passion for diving saw them spending many hours exploring the local reefs. They were always on the lookout for unusual sites for their customers, particularly amongst the vicious reefs that ringed the island providing a veritable ships graveyard.

Jacqui thought she knew the Bermuda waters well after thirty years of diving, but this afternoon she was feeling puzzled, very puzzled. The two women were spending a precious afternoon off on a dive further east than usual, exploring an area usually avoided by even experienced divers due to the harsh underwater currents. Jacqui had told her daughter to wait for her on the launch as she went down alone for one last dive of the day. Now, swimming along the sheer rock face her frown deepened as she reached the darker levels, the water getting murkier. Genuinely puzzled by what she could see, she tried to call Leila on the radio, but to no avail. As the visibility reduced, her slim figure narrowly missed catching the rocky outcrop. With a growing sense of unease, Jacqui wished she was not diving alone; she and Leila were a team, instinctively knowing where the other was and she was missing her badly on this dive.

Moving uneasily through the water, Jacqui admonished herself; it wasn't just the hope of finding a new and exciting dive for prospective customers that had led her to this strange place. She had also heard rumours about treasure supposedly hidden in the water on this side of the island. Her common sense told her that this was probably just a local fantasy, but it was well known that the unusual geological structure of Bermuda created deep cave systems, perfect for hiding things, and many of the caves were unexplored. Normally, she ignored gossip but the rumours were persistent and she had her own suspicions.

She knew that another diver had gone down very close to where she was searching now and been injured. He had left the island without talking to anyone but she knew that this was where he had been the day of his accident. It was rumoured that he had seen the treasure during his ill-fated dive and Jacqui was intrigued. Now, alone and feeling increasingly uneasy Jacqui began to question for the first time her decision to break her own personal rules and dive alone. The truth was she hadn't wanted Leila exposed to any potential danger.

Making her way carefully forwards, Jacqui frowned behind her mask at the odd colours in the water; this was not right, nor was the absence of marine life. She checked her watch; by her calculation, she had forty minutes of air left, which gave her only another five minutes to look around. She kicked out and swam deeper, astonished by the brightening light in the distance, she could have sworn that it was an artificial electric light. She could now see the murky ocean floor no more than three metres below.

The hard ancient rock stared at her as if it had eyes challenging her right to be there, dark and forbidding. She shivered involuntarily as she switched her torch onto its strongest beam, glad again that Leila was safely onboard the boat. She looked upwards into the rocks, startled by the strength of the strange light again. Momentarily blinded by the strength of the beam Jacqui blinked and shook her head to clear her vision. Intrigued by something so bright this deep under the surface of the ocean, she swam towards it and then saw that it originated from inside an overhang of rock. As she entered the cleft, she started swimming upwards for about ten metres until she entered a cavern and fresh air.

The only explanation that Jacqui could think of was that the cavern must be the result of an air pocket created by pressure differences. Further, ahead she could see a large pool of water, separated from where she was by a rock barrier. She swam closer, curiosity overcoming her natural instincts to get out of the cavern as quickly as possible. The pool of water on the other side of the natural barrier was about three metres wide. Pulling herself partially out of the water, she saw something dull glistening on the barrier edge. Looking closer she saw that it was a diving mask with reddish brown stains on its Perspex cover that looked suspiciously like blood. She shuddered; it had to belong to the injured man. He must have come down here. The blood worried her, it worried her greatly and again she contemplated turning back but again curiosity overcame her fear.

Disconnecting her mouthpiece to save precious oxygen Jacqui looked around. The whole cavern was about fifteen metres in diameter and bathed in an eerie glow emanating from an adjacent cavern. She lifted herself totally out of the water and slid across the barrier and into the pool recoiling in shock, as she tasted the water… fresh water! Unable to believe what she had found Jacqui stared in amazement; she was inside a cave complex under the sea, an ideal place for smuggling. The caverns flow of air from above must provide enough pressure to keep the sea at bay even though she was well below sea level. Lifting her radio again Jacqui tried to get it to work, desperate to share her news with Leila, but it was dead. To be honest she would have been amazed if it had worked; radio waves could not possibly penetrate the cave structure.

She looked around trying to decide what to do next, her sensible side telling her to head upwards, her sense of adventure telling her to keep going. Adventure won and consoling herself that at least she wasn't using precious oxygen, Jacqui decided to find where the light came from. Hopefully Leila would not get too worried.

Calculating that she must be at least a hundred and fifty feet down in the rocks, she walked into the fresh water that came up to her chest. It was extremely cold but her wet suit was protecting her so far. Stepping through a small opening, she entered the next cavern and stared into the light gasping as she did so. My God! she whispered to herself, ahead of her lay a veritable Aladdin's cave of treasures. Then she gasped again in shock.

"You shouldn't have come here, you really shouldn't," came a voice. She spun around to her right and saw a man holding a gun pointed at her. "I didn't mean to," she replied, her eyes drawn to what he had in his hand. Revulsion flooded over her and she retched losing her balance as she did so.

"Come here," gestured the man. She stood up and waded forward as if in a trance, this was her worst nightmare but unfortunately, she was not asleep. "You attacked that man didn't you?" she trembled, realising she was in deep trouble. "Drop the oxygen tank, you won't be needing it," growled the man, his voice quiet but full of menace. Jacqui dropped the tank, terrified at parting with this familiar lifeline, and walked towards him, stepping out of the water as she did so. "Who are you?" she was standing six feet away, and avoiding going any closer to the cold metal gun in his hand. "Take your diving suit off?"

"What?" Jacqui stuttered. "You heard; I said take the diving suit off," snarled the man. "Okay, okay," she said struggling with the zip on the tight fitting suit and shivering as she peeled the protective layer of rubber off. Eventually she wriggled out of it and stood there feeling very vulnerable in her bikini. "What is it you want, who are you?"

"I am the ruler of this kingdom and you are a trespasser." The man sneered at the terrified woman, "You should have waited until you were invited. I would have invited you. I like nice girls, but you have seen too much."

"I haven't seen anything." Jacqui hastily replied, trying to stop her teeth chattering with cold and fear. "You've seen everything. Now take the rest of your clothes off." Her captor's cold eyes burnt into her. "No, this has gone far enough." She screamed as he fired the gun, deafened by the noise of the bullet hitting the rocks above her. "All right," she shouted in fear realising with horror that he was deadly serious. "You look good," he smiled and she cringed in fear as she saw him come closer. The fear turned to a primeval scream as she felt the gun touch her skin.

CHAPTER 1

Buttermere Lake,
English Lake District

Blackie Silver cursed aloud as he stumbled across the car park, staring balefully across Buttermere Lake whilst wondering where it had all gone wrong. A large, heavy built and balding man in his mid-sixties, his florid face belied his predilection for copious amounts of brandy. With a large grey moustache, one eye slightly off centre and a passion for modern jazz he cut an eccentric figure in the neighbourhood. To the locals he was a sorry looking but familiar sight, forever stumbling around trying to find his battered Land Rover. He owed his status, as owner of the largest house for miles around, to his nouveau riche class-loving father Sebastian Beckman. A short stocky bull necked man, Beckman had arrived in the British Isles after the Second World War as an Austrian refugee. A dour, unsmiling man he had quickly married an equally dour English woman called Janice Silver and taken her name.

The Silver's had found the ancestral pile near the village of Buttermere in the Lake District; a place called Hogthistle Hall overlooking Buttermere Lake with the Haystacks fells dominating the skyline to the southeast. The house was a wreck but Sebastian's fortune soon restored it to its former splendour. Their first offspring was Josef, nicknamed Blackie due to his childhood habit of being permanently dirty. Three years later, a daughter Elizabeth followed and Janice threw herself into the role of lady of the manor with the appropriate airs and graces. To all intents and purposes, a refined lady of impeccable lineage, persistent local rumour had it that one side of her family came from common seafaring stock. In reality, Janice was the daughter of Claire Silver, who tragically drowned during the sinking of the liner *"Lusitania"* by the German navy at the start of the Second World War.

At eighteen Blackie discovered the delights of the local pub and brandy, his excesses culminating in a car crash that killed a local horse, causing him to lose his right eye in the process. Worse was to follow, five years later his father and mother were killed in a car crash without leaving a will. At the age of twenty-three Blackie inherited everything much to his sister Elizabeth's horror. Unable to persuade Blackie to share the estate, she resorted to the courts and failed. Bitter and filled with hatred, she left Buttermere, later meeting and subsequently marrying a young psychologist. Blackie proceeded to spend money prodigiously on drink and gambling until the exasperated family solicitor, Thornberry, warned him he was on his way to becoming insolvent. Something had to be done to resolve the situation and that something was a woman.

Constance Hershey was moderately pretty and subject to a domineering mother, Ivy. With money, but no status, Ivy's sole role in life was to force Constance into a decent marriage. This game plan was hindered by the embarrassment of an illegitimate child, the result of an affair between Constance and an itinerant sailor. At Ivy's insistence, her grandson had gone to live anonymously with his father's family in the Caribbean shortly after his birth, and had no further contact with his mother's family.

At Thornberry and Ivy's instigation, Constance agreed to meet Blackie. What she saw repelled her as much as the estate appealed, so putting her finer feelings aside for the opportunity to live in such a vast house they married in indecent haste. Instantly Blackie's immediate monetary problems were gone. Both marriage partners felt that they did not have exactly what they wanted from the marriage, but at least Blackie now had someone to look after the estate. Bored with her husband's drunken behaviour Constance duly took a firm hold of the estates finances and leased some of the land to local farmers to create steady revenue back into the Silver coffers. Relieved, and well aware that his wife found him somewhat lacking, Blackie was free to head back to the bottle.

Then one evening came a fateful call that changed everything. Blackie, half-drunk and alone in the house, took a long distance phone call from an agitated young man claiming to be Constance's long estranged son, Joe, living in the Caribbean. Recovering from the immediate shock of discovering his wife had a son; Blackie quickly learnt that Joe was in financial trouble. Unable to tell if the young man was genuine or stoned he listened, intrigued by a long tale of hidden Caribbean treasures that followed the man's monologue bemoaning his debts. However, even this wondrous story of riches did not detract from Blackie's rage at Constance's deception and after she returned that evening to a furious husband, their estrangement started. Two weeks later Blackie embarked on a monumental drinking session.

The next day, after a long liquid lunch, Blackie drove unsteadily back alongside the lake to The Hall determined to clear the air with Constance. It was early evening as the old Land Rover, grunting and rattling more than usual, pulled up in front of The Hall. Blackie staggered out still the worse for wear and saw a light burning in Constance's private suite. He fell through the front door, stopping dead in his muddy tracks across the flagstone hall at the sound of a piercing high-pitched scream. "It can't be true!" he heard Constance's voice sob. "Constance?" he called to her, there was silence. He staggered across to the stairs and tried again, "Constance where are you?" From away to his right he heard a muffled noise and the sound of a window hurriedly opening. Constance saw Blackie and wailed. "My son, Joe!"

"What is it?" growled Blackie, panting heavily. "He's dead," she wailed. "Killed whilst diving, they say it was an accident."

"Who told you this?" Blackie's face clearly showed the confusion he felt.

"He's been murdered! I know it, someone attacked him."

"Attacked, how?" asked Blackie grimly. "With a knife! I spoke to him after you did, he said 'they' were after him and would try to kill him," the words tumbled from Constance's anguished mouth. "He was going to come and see me. They wanted to know what he found." She continued. "Who are *they*?" asked Blackie, hearing a noise again. Someone was in the house; Blackie was convinced of it. The sound of glass smashing in the distance broke the moment. Blackie lumbered across to the window and peered out, quickly spotting a small wiry man staggering across the lawn.

"Bloody hell!" Blackie cursed loudly. Storming downstairs into the kitchen, he grabbed his old hunting rifle. Through the open window, Blackie heard the man curse in a foreign language, before ducking out of sight.

"Come out or I shoot," he roared, incandescent with alcohol fuelled rage. In the distance, he heard a horse neigh and his eyes caught a movement to the left of the greenhouse. The bastard was making a break for it; spinning around Blackie fired at the retreating backside and was rewarded with a shout of pain. "Don't kill him," yelled Constance rushing up behind him. "Who was he?" Blackie spat back over his shoulder, reluctant to take his eye off the intruder. "A Spanish gentleman called Matarife," replied Constance. He brought me the news."

"And what else, eh?" Blackie's eyes narrowed as he sneered, "He seemed to know his way around this place."

"How dare you!" shouted Constance. "My son is dead and all you can do is make wild accusations! Leave me alone you useless drunk!"

Blackie lowered his gun and sought refuge in his drinks cabinet; it really was all too much. Cursing again as the familiar liquid fire of the brandy warmed his throat and belly he felt his head start to spin again. Listening to the sound of his distraught wife sobbing upstairs, Blackie swore, knocked back a whole cut glass tumbler of brandy and collapsed unconscious onto the sofa. He regained consciousness about two hours later in pitch darkness. Glancing at the old clock on the mantelpiece, he saw that it was two o'clock in the morning. Shivering in the gloom he realised the electricity was off and he was freezing. Jumping up he grabbed a candle and a box of matches left next to the open fire. He lit the fire and slumped back down onto the couch, letting the warmth permeate his body as he dozed back into a fitful sleep.

He awoke gasping, choking and coughing as he jerked awake. He saw an inferno of fire around him. Roaring in pain, Blackie staggered drunkenly out of the house and up into the hills behind The Hall, conscious that something was very wrong.

Nearly an hour later he fell into a stream before passing out again. He presented a fearsome sight on the side of Sour Milk Ghyll, his head throbbing. He stumbled back down the hillside, the moonlight glinting off his bald-head, eventually reaching the small village of Buttermere and hammering on the door of the Bridge Inn. It was his local and he took great pride in its plaque commemorating a visit from Queen Victoria and Prince Albert. "You! Where the hell have you been?" roared Jake Scowcroft, the landlord, from an upstairs window, peering down onto his bedraggled customer. "We've been trying to contact you. Everyone is looking for you!"

"I need a drink, Jake." Blackie mumbled through dry, cracked lips. "You need to get home Blackie, that's what you need to do, your house is on fire; I've called the fire brigade. They're on their way!"

"Bugger!" growled Blackie sobering up instantly as he remembered with blinding clarity what had been bothering him. "My wife's in there."

"What? I'll give you a lift, you're in no fit state to walk back alone," said the dishevelled Scowcroft opening the front door.

Blackie swore aloud as they drove to the bottom of the drive, got out and saw The Hall. The place was an inferno; outside on the gravel drive the fire brigade stood together hopelessly shaking their heads. Constance would have had no chance. Getting hold of the shocked landlords arm, he pushed him back into his car and demanded that he return to the pub. Sneaking the keys to his Land Rover out of his own pocket, he thanked the fact that he had been too drunk to put the vehicle in the garage earlier. Turning the key in the ignition, he sped off after Scowcroft, keeping the lights off until he had turned the first bend.

"They'll find you," said Scowcroft as he seated a bemused Blackie in the Inn, passing him a large brandy before settling himself down to hear Blackie's version of the evening's events. "You need to go to the police and plead manslaughter on diminished responsibility. I can vouch for how much you had to drink even before you left here," he continued, amazed to find himself at the centre of such a dramatic situation. "I'm not going to prison." Blackie stated flatly, shaking his head to emphasise his words. Scowcroft shook his head. "I don't think you realise the enormity of what has happened, man, you're in big trouble. Your wife is almost certainly dead and the house is razed to the ground. The finger of suspicion will point at you. Plus, even if you are telling the truth and you didn't set fire to the place, there's someone who knows the true state of relations between Constance and you. You have to admit, it doesn't look good."

He poured a strong black coffee and set it down next to the brandy glass, motioning Blackie to drink it. "I am telling you, it wasn't my fault," retorted Blackie angrily. "It doesn't matter. You shouldn't have left The Hall. You should have told the fire brigade you were there. The police will arrive there in a matter of minutes, count yourself lucky they were elsewhere tonight and you missed them. I can't believe you have dragged me into this."

Scowcroft shook his head and scowled at Blackie. "Poor Constance, whatever she did, she didn't deserve this."

"I need to get away." Blackie cut across the landlord. "How? They have helicopters and spy satellites," replied Scowcroft, "You would do better to go and face up to it"

"There is someone I can call," whispered Blackie to himself and slunk out to the Gents to find some privacy.

Swiftly returning to the bar, Blackie sat back down and drained the last of his brandy.

"Insurance job?" said Scowcroft an idea dawning on him.

"What do you mean?" Blackie puzzled.

"Make them think you burned also! That's the way I would do it. Your solicitor, that old chap, can then direct the money to you abroad."

"A new life in the sun," muttered Blackie cautiously.

His inspired telephone call had been long distance and seeing a glimmer of hope of escaping he became re-energised as adrenalin took hold. He had to move fast; the police would already be on their way here. "Thanks for the help Jake, see you sometime." Leaving the landlord speechless, he banged out of the door and jumped into the aged Land Rover; it was not registered on the roads so he doubted anyone would have records of it. With a bit of luck he would become a non-person. Plans began to form in his mind, knowing that his emergency long distance contact was already arranging the supply of a fake passport and other items.

Inspector Weckman stared impassively at the scene. A local policeman of many years' experience, he had been caught at the other side of the Lakes on a hit and run accident when the first news of the fire arrived. By the time he got there, nothing much of the old hall was left. It was only now, the following morning that the fire had burnt out enough for forensics and uniformed police to start the slow process of exploring the ashes. After noting the absence of Blackie Silver, and following a conversation with a foreign man claiming to have information regarding the cause of the fire, Weckman concluded that this case might well develop into a murder enquiry.

Two days later a stooped figure dressed as a minister of the cloth, sporting a false greying beard and wig, boarded a P&O cruise ship leaving Southampton docks for the Caribbean. Intent on his disguise, Blackie did not notice the diminutive man on the liner's other side who glared down at him before limping into the crowd of passengers. The man, called El Matarife, looked coldly across at Blackie; if he had his way, the Englishman would be dead already but he had his orders. A short, lightly built man El Matarife had trained as a jockey in his youth. The loss of a finger following a bad fall ended his promising career in that profession and he now worked in the world of private protection and surveillance. He glanced across and sighed; tailing the shambling Blackie should be easy money.

The Caribbean Sea
5 miles south west of St Lucia

The steady sway of the thirty-six foot Southerly 135 RS cruising yacht was extremely therapeutic, especially enhanced by a gentle breeze that traversed the deck and wafted over its only occupant. The harsh mid-day sun shone down onto the sails as they fluttered searching for wind to give them life. Guy looked around satisfied and stretched out lazily enjoying his yacht. He had named it *'Hidalgo'*, meaning noble in Spanish, for no other reason than a need to have something noble in his itinerant life.

He checked the Southerly with a practised eye observing the slight movements in the sails and relaxed feeling the sun's rays warm him. Knowing that the onboard computer was steering the craft better than he could was a great benefit, enabling him to sail alone most of the time. Even the sails were raised and lowered by powerful electric motors. She was a marvel that he had fallen in love with the moment he had seen her in a second hand boat sale in Barbados, a rich man's plaything no longer of interest.

It had been four months since Guy left Hong Kong under threat of a prison sentence. Arrested for alleged improper conduct with a massage girl and obstructing the course of justice, he was given an ultimatum to either pay a hefty fine and leave the country immediately or stay and be charged. He had been glad to board the midnight flight back to England, convinced that the police would never find his still missing father. On his return, he sold his London flat, said goodbye to his mother and bought a one-way ticket to the Caribbean. Finding himself in Barbados at the boat sale, he was immediately drawn to the beautiful *Hidalgo*, attracted by the stylish lines, the large stateroom and onboard computer systems. Overall, she was a very comfortable boat, with six foot three inches of headroom in the main cabin. Another outstanding point was the swing keel that allowed him to beech her when the mood took him, it was lowered and raised by a hydraulic ram at the touch of a button. Twin rudders and three spacious cabins added to the overall delight. What little money he had left he blew on a frenzy of drink and debauchery with any girl he could lay his hands on. Feeling let down by life Guy was determined to enjoy himself.

Guy's answer to his increasing depression was to drink more and more; preferring constant intoxication to sobriety until his drinking companions finally ran out of patience and he ran out of money. The only earner left was chartering out *Hidalgo* and when this failed, he turned to the even more lucrative trade of contraband running. This latter career path had started with a journey last month south to Venezuela to pick up a collection of pirate DVD's for distribution on the American market. The boat's speed made it an ideal smuggler's craft and reduced the chances of being caught. If chased he could get speeds of up to thirty knots out of her in a force ten to twelve gale.

However, his mood and despondency still did not improve and he gradually progressed to mixing alcohol with soft drugs. In his more sober moments, Guy knew that he was slowly losing sense and purpose; he knew it, but he just couldn't get himself to care. He reached crisis point when the precocious daughter of the local police Inspector Pollard, alleged that she had become pregnant by him. Despite the pregnancy being no more than a scare, he was aware that Pollard would never forgive him; he was a marked man.

Despite his mental anguish, Guy felt at one with nature and ironically looked physically better than before. Formerly pale and freckled, his skin was now bronzed and healthy looking, despite his habitual drinking and his sandy coloured hair had gained lustre and was even more unruly than before. He had also just discovered the fascinating world of classical music. Dependent on his mood he veered across the whole spectrum from Gustav Mahler, when severely morose, to Mozart when feeling buoyant. He supposed it was a sign of his increasing years and maudlin tendency to wallow in sentimentality but the music seemed to suit his new life. However, despite these changes he still veered towards the view that the whole world was against him. What he really needed was someone else in his life because above all he was lonely.

Feeling the gentle undulations of the sea as the waves slapped the bow with increasing frequency; Guy gathered speed to seven knots. He raised his head lazily to check the horizon and then slipped back into a semi-comatose position. As far as his eyes could see, the sea was empty, no one interfering with his own personal paradise. His was a life of extremes; highs such as today on *Hidalgo* feeling renewed in body and spirit, followed by lows as the alcohol took effect and self-destructive urges overcame him. He supposed he was going through a mid-life crisis as he had come off the treadmill of life. No ties, no debts, no regrets and above all a new determination to work only for himself.

He sat up and stretched, ducking down as he entered the cabin and eying his slim figure in the mirror. There was no doubt his health had improved dramatically and he had lost weight. Gone were the worry lines, the bags under the eyes and the inability to sleep without tranquillisers. His new philosophy was simple; he owed the world and society nothing. His mother Elizabeth had taken his departure very badly, following so soon after her husband's disappearance, and had retreated into semi isolation in north Yorkshire. They had only been close through his father and now that was gone. The only problem for Guy was the re-occurring dreams and night terrors that had become increasingly vivid. Many nights he woke terrified in a cold sweat as he tossed and turned, sure the Chinese man was there in the cabin. Maybe his father had been trying to warn him.

Energised by a great gust of wind that crossed her bow, *Hidalgo* suddenly jumped, increasing the speed to ten knots. Guy grinned with pleasure, a smile that tightened as he noticed a vessel heading his way. Who the hell could that be? he thought tersely, then grabbed his binoculars and groaned. It was a speedboat gaining fast on him and coming out of the shadow of St Lucia's twin pitons. He didn't like it, such speed usually meant trouble, either pirates or the police. Both were bad news.

He grabbed his shirt and a cup of coffee and sat resigned on deck watching the boat approach. He frowned further; it was the police, not the obnoxious Inspector Pollard colloquially named Grasshopper because of the way he rubbed his large hands together, but Santo, his sidekick. Guy called Santo 'Cricket' owing to the strange clicking noise emanating from his mouth. He took over manual control and went into the wind whilst lowering the main sail and starting the engine.

"Guy Tresanton! Got an urgent message for you," yelled Santo above the sound of his boat's engines. "What's wrong with the radio, Cricket?" Guy made it clear that the disturbance was unwanted. "Your radio isn't working and don't call me that." Santo snapped, not for the first time. "No doubt you'll fine me for that too," replied Guy secretly pleased that he had upset the man. "What's the message?"

"New visitor, our records show he's related to you." Santo looked delighted to be the bearer of troublesome news. "I don't have any relatives and anyway why's that a police matter?"

"Man's got a police record," smirked Santo, "wanted by the police in England for larceny. Has the same surname as you."

"How do you know all this?" Guy was puzzled now. "That's police business." Santo puffed himself up pompously. "Come on Cricket, you must have more than that to come all this way to find me." Guy could see Santo hesitate, as if trying to work out how much he should say before replying, "We were tipped off."

"So why didn't you arrest him?"

"We couldn't find him at the airport. He must have been disguised or slipped past us off a cruise liner." Santo looked disgruntled at this admission. "And Grasshopper automatically thinks I'm part of the conspiracy!" Guy exploded, "He must be embarrassed! First major event to ever happen round here and he blows it! So, what does he want from me?"

"We need your help to find him. Man is called Silver, your mother's maiden name. Her brother we believe." Santo struggled to look as though this was a request rather than a demand.

"A long shot. I am not convinced."

"Do you deny having an Uncle?"

"Grasshopper sees this as his chance to get me," replied Guy wondering if it could possibly be his Uncle Blackie, his mother Elizabeth's hated brother. Surely not, he mused, according to his mother her brother was a man far too stupid to have an international police record.

"Boss wants to see you now. I'm to take you back with me." Santo conveyed the message anticipating trouble. "Bollocks!" Guy shouted, "Unless you have a warrant I'm staying here Cricket."

"He won't like it."

"Tell Grasshopper that as far as I know there is no crime by association in these parts much as he no doubt wishes there was. Even if this man is my Uncle I have no desire to meet him, tell him that."

"Have it your way," replied Santo revving the engine. "He won't like it and get your radio working. It's dangerous without one."

"I'll do that, and you tell Grasshopper what I think of his idea of law."

"Take care Tresanton, he will find this man."

"I bet he does. It is the biggest thing that has ever happened to him on this island. He'll be wetting himself in anticipation of all the publicity. An international case is everything he has ever dreamed of. Well, I have a piece of advice for him. Check out the informer first. Why would someone want to shop someone else unless they gained from it? People don't do things for free."

"Perhaps."

"And another thing, if you had a photograph of the man you should have been able to spot him even in disguise."

"We don't have a photograph."

"Goodbye Cricket,"

Guy swung the wheel to port and *Hidalgo* again caught the wind on the Genoa. He looked at the retreating police launch grimly as he raised the main sail and re-engaged the automatic system. The visit had spoilt his good mood; he went down to see to the radio set. If his dammed Uncle was on the island then it could only mean that he was looking for Guy, and probably money too. Whatever happened it appeared that his lifestyle was about to come to an abrupt end. Tinkering with the radio, he recalled that his mother would have nothing to do with her brother, Blackie. Despite the fact that she lived in the Yorkshire Dales, literally an hour's drive away from her old family home in the Lake District, her hatred of her brother stopped her ever visiting.

Three hours later at sun set Guy dropped the sails and anchored in a small bay off the island's south end. He lay on *Hidalgo*'s teak deck and thought of his father's words in the dream. *"Remember what I have taught you."*

For the umpteenth time he went over all that his father had taught him. There had to be something special. He had mentioned his strange experience in Hong Kong to others and always been greeted with wry smiles. No one, including his mother, believed it had been anything other than an overactive imagination, or hallucinations, bought on by mind-altering substances. Perhaps they were right; perhaps the Aussie had drugged him. He poured himself a cold glass of Chardonnay and went down below to lie next to the chart table and think. His eyes were inadvertently drawn to a book on his single bookshelf about the sixteenth century explorers.

A moment of revelation hit his mind and it all suddenly came flooding back; his father teaching him passionately about the early explorers, the race to understand latitude and far more difficult, calculate longitude. He remembered his father's enthusiasm for the subject, their trips to the museums of Drake, Frobisher and Captain Cook. He even remembered a personal favourite, William Dalyrumple, an unheralded earlier explorer.

His father was trying to get him to concentrate here, he was convinced of it, but why? He contained his excitement and brought himself back to reality. He made a decision; he would stay at sea for a couple more days. This would be a wise move, allowing him time to clear his head and plan what to do next and his Uncle, if indeed he was here, time to stew. Besides, he thought to himself, it would be smart to keep his distance from Grasshopper.

Later that evening he motored around to a hidden and remote cove on the quieter south-eastern seaboard of St Lucia. With Vieux Fort settlement visible on the mainland, he soon fell into a deep sleep. Without warning, the familiar dreams came back so clearly that he physically shrank down into his narrow bunk. He desperately wanted to attack a menacing form coming ever closer but his eyes would not open.

As usual, he dreamt of the same Chinese man that he had seen behind his father in Hong Kong, a tall stooped figure staring wordlessly at him. The man raised an arm and pointed an accusing finger towards him, his eyes cold and hard. Guy sat up terrified and sweating as the figure faded into the distance, his last image was that of a poor Chinese girl, her arms upraised looking imploringly at him. As always in the dream, he tried to help her but could not. Awake now, but still shivering with terror, he padded across the cabin to get a drink; there had to be some meaning to it all but what? He stared out of the porthole across the quiet bay watching the moonlight make strange shapes on the seawater, the dull shape of Maria Islands on his starboard side.

The first light of dawn broke in the bay, a new day dawned and with it the horrible feeling that his temporary idyll was ending. Perhaps it was a sign that he had to confront life again. What on earth had his Uncle done in England to have the police chasing him across continents, and who the hell was the police informer? He sighed and started to raise the sails, it was time to confront the world again and stop running.

Present Day Tay Ninh Vietnam
Forty miles from the Cambodian border

The tall, aged Chinese man exuded an aura that demanded attention and that most people found unsettling. His appearance alone commanded respect; at slightly under six feet in height, with a shaven head and hard, unyielding dark blue eyes his wiry body stood ramrod straight. People often guessed that he was in his seventies, but was actually only sixty-five; this miscalculation was probably owing to the cold, hard nature of his countenance. His domain was a twenty-acre site, a kilometre outside of the village of Tay Ninh. He seemed to glide over the ground rather than walk in his long black gown, a technique he had learned over time and found added to his presence.

His people knew him as the 'Teacher', and like all teachers, he had his pupils or disciples. Over sixty of them lived in a compound; the females dressed in yellow robes, the male in green. The compound, known locally as the 'commune', was only a kilometre outside Tay Ninh, but it could have been on a different planet. He had chosen the area carefully, as Tay Ninh was the centre of an international religion found only in Vietnam called Caodoism. This faith believed in the reincarnation of great figures in world history; effectively a fusion of Catholicism, Buddhism and Confucius. It suited the Teacher to have such a devout movement nearby, for it disguised his own activities brilliantly.

Who would question his own movement when a much larger and more auspicious one existed next door?

The locals left the commune dwellers alone, largely because his followers couldn't speak Vietnamese, using instead Mandarin or sign language to communicate. The villagers were understandably wary of the commune; uneasy traders never smiled but left immediately provisions were purchased. Rumours abounded of prisoners being tortured, ritual sacrifices, weird chanting and orgies. Sometimes the local boys dared each other to go closer, but a seven-foot metal fence with barbed wire on top surrounded the commune. Not even the most daring youth could get to the top, so instead they came back with inventions to prove how brave they had been. Inside the commune, there were three brick buildings of different sizes, each with tiled roofing. A single-track road led to a single gate and the only users were the people inside. Occasionally a large black Mercedes with darkened windows would sweep up to the compound, containing the teacher.

Some villagers moved their families further away from what they considered an evil force, whilst others turned to their own gods for protection. Since the war thirty years ago, it had been easy to denounce troublesome neighbours; even children had done so, denouncing them to the Vietcong and their leader Ho Chi Minh. Now, with a new more liberal and capitalist President, the government was following the successful lead of their northern socialist neighbour China and encouraging individual enterprise. None denounced the commune or the Teacher for he was too powerful. Had they known what was really going on inside the compound they would have left all the quicker and thanked their gods for a close escape.

Not far to the south east of the commune there was consternation by the local authorities in Ho Chi Minh City when the commune people arrived at local museums and libraries offering to buy artefacts and books long buried in their ancient vaults. It was disturbing because the current museum keepers had not known such texts and artefacts existed. History under the Khmer Rouge officially ceased to exist with the destruction of surviving artefacts ordered. Rather than destroy all signs of the past, however, some enterprising museum owners had merely put them out of sight until the next regime. They figured there would come a time when they could sell the books at a tidy profit. Higher authorities tried to stop the process but as always with large amounts of money, the new individual museum keepers found creative ways of ignoring them and the flow of historical texts and artefacts continued unabated.

Inside the commune, the Teacher looked around at the familiar rolling countryside where he summoned his key disciples every day for exercises. If the villagers could have seen them they would have noted how all looked at the Teacher fearfully and with respect. The Teacher had learnt from his beloved grandfather the simple maxim that men and women were easier to lead by fear. He came from ancestors who had always ruled, it was their destiny. Now, people flocked to him, spellbound by his message and in time, he planned, they would come in hundreds and thousands. He was the only one with the gift and knew that at last the time had come. The other pieces of the jigsaw were in place. Everyone would learn to call him both the Teacher and the saviour. Now it was time to start the lessons

CHAPTER 2

As he approached the Marina on the north west of the island, Guy stared across at Pigeon Island to his left. The small island consisted of only forty-four acres, but was witness to most of St Lucia's momentous historical events. Somewhere, in the back of his mind, Guy recalled that the British Vice Admiral Rodney had used the island as his Caribbean naval base. Ahead, he could clearly see a large dark building, the residence of Grasshopper. Guy looked around, certain that he would be getting a visit from Police Inspector at some point; it was part of the ritual since his affair with the man's daughter had ended two months ago.

He turned his mind to more pleasant thoughts; he loved the beauty of this island, its greenery, unpredictable climate and most of all its great sailing conditions with steady, strong winds. He entered the shallower waters, admiring the pure blue water in front of Pigeon Island as it rippled on the white hull of *Hidalgo*. He was coming in voluntarily after Cricket's surprise visit; on reflection he had decided it was better to face the situation head on, even if it meant a face to face with Grasshopper. The Inspector rightly suspected him of smuggling valuable artefacts. On two occasions, he had almost been caught, dumping the cargo overboard to avoid capture. Even with these set-backs the work had created a tidy profit, and he was sorry that increased police attention had resulted in it drying up for the time being.

In the distance, he saw the familiar figure of Grasshopper aboard a police motorboat, fortunately heading north away from him. Thanks to his own irresponsible behaviour with Grasshopper's wild daughter, he was closely watched and his every movement scrutinised.

Guy scanned the skyline again as he turned right into the narrow marina dropping the sails, storing them, and putting the fenders out. He approached the last few metres on the diesel engine past a permanently sunken schooner, its masts sticking out of the water as a dire warning to all who passed. He glided slowly in, scowling as he always did at the grotesquely painted bright blue hotel to his right, an eyesore for certain, but very St Lucian in its style. In fact, in a strange way, he was getting to like it, which probably meant that he was starting to belong here.

He tied the boat up, idly wondering if his uncle would choose to make an appearance today. He mentally calculated that he could turn *Hidalgo* around in about a day ready to meet his next charter. That would avoid his uncle for a further week. He might even persuade a local girl, Isabella, to come on the trip with him again. He needed a crew; someone to cook and help with entertainment. Deciding to take advantage of Grasshopper's absence, Guy scrambled ashore and walked over to a nearby shed to retrieve his antiquated motorbike. Kick starting the small Suzuki he headed out of the marina complex and turned south, before heading eastwards towards a ramshackle old house on the coastline. The house, outside the tourist resorts near the town of Dennery, was another reason why Guy had chosen to make his way to St Lucia.

Purchased by his maternal grandfather, Vincent Silver, it had originally been the home of a sugar plantation overseer. His mother had told him about the abandoned, wooden house, in happier times and he now used it as a safe haven when Grasshopper was on the prowl. Nestling in a poor area of the island, it had stood empty for years, barely habitable but perfect to use as a secret refuge. Before Guy arrived, a neighbour had been using the house as a shelter for his animals, convinced that no one from the Silver family would ever claim it back. Guy had literally had to fight his way through the door, past cobwebs and a nauseating smell of animal waste.

As he accelerated the small 200cc, Suzuki through the islands hinterland, past large banana plantations, it suddenly struck him that the old house was exactly where his uncle would head. Blackie was one of the very few people who knew about the house, and had probably headed to St Lucia for the same reason as he had. He looked instinctively in his mirror and saw a slight movement far away behind him, a car. The police were following him; he should have expected nothing less, the disappearing launch was clearly just a ruse to lull him into a false sense of security. He would have to take a detour route along smaller roads. He accelerated sharply before turning right onto a small track road, climbing higher into the central spine of the island. He headed directly east, past more banana plantations and a small shantytown, before negotiating a tight left turn up a small dirt track. Stopping at the tree line, he looked back and saw a familiar black car about a mile back from him in a cloud of dust. It was Cricket's car, he was still following him. He grimaced and turned off the track altogether, slowing down as he approached the edge of a dense forest before swerving into the undergrowth onto a forest path he knew well and that eventually came out above the house in Dennery. He motored on into the forest, the path narrowing to a metre wide, and ducked as a large branch narrowly missed his head

The forest became gloomier as he headed into its depths, the sun starting to fade and a light rain falling. He was now deep in the rain forest near the Errard plantation, keeping his eyes peeled for snakes or large spiders and slowing down to avoid the worst of the rain coming off the branches. Twenty minutes later, he emerged onto the east coast and headed slowly down a rough track to the house that stood overlooking the sea.

Taking the precaution of cutting the engine and pushing the bike round the back out of sight, he looked carefully for signs of life. He had *Hidalgo*'s flare pistol with him for insurance. Seeing nothing unusual, he went into a small wooden shed and retrieved the key from a small ledge above the window. Guy made his way over to the house and opened the front door, shivering as the cold, musty air hit his lungs from the damp atmosphere inside. Kicking aside a mountain of junk mail, he walked through into the main lounge, stopping suddenly. Someone was in the house; he could sense it.

"I've got a gun so come out slowly!" Guy yelled as the door to the kitchen swung open, and he tensed ready to defend himself.

"Hope you don't mind, let myself in, family home and all that." Said a brandy sodden voice. "Uncle?" Guy stopped in surprise at the cleric who stood in front of him. "Elizabeth's boy, I presume." smiled Blackie stepping forwards. "Good to meet you. Never saw much of you, your mother and I…" he tailed off, clearly struggling to find words. "You robbed her blind." Guy replied, surveying the older man shrewdly. "Now, what are you doing in that outfit, and how the hell did you get in?"

"Everyone helps a man of the cloth." Blackie slyly motioned to his clothes, "The taxi driver spoke to an old man next door, one look at me and he opened the front door." "That would be the same man that used to let his animals live here." Guy was momentarily amazed.

"Thought it was a bit ripe."

"Well I suppose I should say welcome, but you could have warned me."

"No time my boy." Blackie nervously glanced around.

"The local police are after you." Guy made it sound like a statement rather than a question, offering his Uncle no opportunity to dispute the fact. "How do they know I'm here?" asked Blackie frowning, his one good eye narrowing. "An informer, I've already had a visit."

"Damn, that's bad news."

"So why are you here?"

"Spot of bother in England, need to lie low for a little while until it gets sorted." Blackie waved his hand dismissively as he spoke as if waving away his current troubles. "Until what *'gets sorted'*?" Guy's voice filled with suspicion and distrust. "Few insurance arrangements, that's all," said Blackie giving Guy a brief version of recent events. "I knew about the family home here so thought I would take advantage, knew you were here also. Thought it gave us the ideal chance to become acquainted and make up for lost time. I must say the old shack's looking a bit careworn."

"It's not been looked after," replied Guy grimacing.

He did not need this now. Grasshopper would have a field day if he found them both together. "This small spot of bother?" he continued sarcastically, putting the small flare pistol away, "Interesting way to describe your house burnt to the ground and your wife dead. Whilst we are at it, why was your stepson murdered?" "No idea, told me he'd found something of great value. I just need to lie low for a few days until I get sorted out, let things calm down." Blackie glossed over recent events. "Calm down? You have to be joking; the police sent a launch out to my boat this afternoon, you're hot property. Were you followed?"

"I don't believe so. I came in on a holiday cruise in this disguise, even had a couple want me to marry them."

"So the police in England have lost track of you but someone has deduced that you are here." Guy shook his head it didn't make sense. "Did you tell anyone you were coming?"

"Only that old blabber mouth Scowcroft; he owns my local pub, will talk to anyone. I shouldn't have told him but I felt beholden."

"Grasshopper will track you down."

"Strange name, I can stay in disguise."

"Do that." Guy stood up, as if to leave. "Well, I can't stop you using this place, it's yours anyway. I usually sleep on the yacht, if I still have one."

"Why's that?"

"Grasshopper is looking for any excuse to get me, long story."

"And I'm an excuse."

"You are. So tell me the real reason you are here, you haven't a hope in hell of collecting any insurance and I should think there's a murder warrant out for you." Guy made one last effort to try to find out what had heralded the arrival of his errant uncle. "Maybe there is, but I was drunk, I'm not a murderer and I have to find a way to clear my name. My stepson was on to something big before he was murdered, I am convinced of it. Serious money, need to find it, I'm broke otherwise," replied Blackie, realising that he would now have to share, his nephew was tougher than expected.

"What and where?" Guy was more interested now.

"Don't know 'where' that's why I'm here. As to 'what' it's a treasure, I'll tell you later about it. Will you help?"

"We need to eat." Guy was practical, as ever. "There's no food," replied Blackie. "I looked."

"I brought a fish", Guy told him, switching the old electric cooker on and clearing the table. "Make yourself comfortable, there are two bedrooms upstairs whilst I get this cooking."

"Thanks."

"What exactly do you have with you in terms of money?" asked Guy as they sat later at the old oak table in the kitchen. "Two thousand dollars. I dare not use credit cards."

"Well at least you've thought of that," replied Guy looking at his Uncle Blackie properly, now divested of the beard and clerics collar.

He looked a wreck, a ruddy drinker's face criss-crossed with age lines, a baldhead and one eye that looked in a different direction to the other. He had never heard anything good about this man; certainly not from his mother, who had made sure he knew about the family rift and Blackie's drink problems. Now it seemed he was barging in on his new life. Grasshopper would have a field day! There was only one answer, he had to get Blackie out of here as soon as possible, or leave himself. "This treasure is it real?" he said finally, to cut the silence.

"Real enough to get my stepson Joe killed."

"That could have been for drugs or a mistake."

"He told me what he had found, and I believe him because of what subsequently happened." Blackie thought back to the urgency in the young man's voice when he had spoken to him.

"What exactly is this treasure?"

"A valuable iconic Cross. Have you ever heard of the Tucker Cross?"

"No!" Guy shook his head to emphasise his words.

"Worth millions, went missing in Bermuda off a Spanish galleon in the sixteenth century. Well, this is the Columbus Cross, similar but larger. It became legendary in the fifteenth century. It's worth an absolute fortune, beyond value actually."

"Columbus, as in Columbus the explorer?" asked Guy thinking back to his father's words. "Yes, that Columbus." Blackie looked surprised at Guy's obvious interest. "Trouble is no one knows where it is, only that it's here in the Caribbean."

"Big place, so where are you going to start looking?"

"Here in this house, there has to be a veritable cornucopia of information. That's the interesting thing in all this."

"What is?" Guy said sharply.

"I vividly remember talk of this treasure in my childhood. It always seemed very romantic and appealed to me as a boy. Your mother and I come from an illustrious line of Silvers, going all the way back to Jack Silver in the nineteenth century. He and his son Vincent Silver were responsible for bringing this Cross to the Americas, or so I've been told. There has to be a link don't you see?"

"Where was your stepson when he was attacked?" Guy was very interested now.

"If I knew that, do you think I'd be hunting around here?"

"If you're right then someone else is clearly after the same treasure."

"Probably." Blackie concluded sadly.

"Definitely the same person who grassed on you to the police." Guy continued with his theory.

"Correct."

"Well it sounds to me like a fool's quest and I, for one, have better things to do!" Guy summed up his feelings swiftly, "Uncle, if you are staying you can clean this place up for a start, I have work to do!"

"What sort of work?"

"Sailing chartered trips."

"I need your help," said Blackie, "you are family after all."

"Am I? What you did in England is your business, but putting my livelihood at risk is my business. What the hell do you expect me to say; welcome dear Uncle, this is the best thing that has ever happened to me?" sarcasm dripped from Guy's voice.

"Give me a couple of days; that is all I ask. Just a couple of days to let me see what I can find." Blackie's gruff voice took on a wheedling note. "Providing the police don't find you first," replied Guy coldly.

"They won't, but I need your help."

"Look, let's get this clear. I'm tolerating you, not helping you. There's not a single damned reason why I should help you. You are asking me to put aside years of animosity, just to support some damn fool quest for an imaginary treasure!"

"There's nothing imaginary about it! That treasure is real and it is here somewhere."

Changing the subject Guy said, "My mother is on her own now, did you know that?"

"Your father?" For a moment what looked like regret passed across Blackie's face.

"Disappeared in Hong Kong presumed dead." Guy said it quickly, defying further questions. "I'm truly sorry. Despite what you think, I used to like your father. He was a clever man, a scientist even if it was a science I little understood."

"Anyone trying to psychoanalyse you would have fun," replied Guy sarcastically.

"The estate was mine, not your mother's."

"Not sure how you worked that one out, she had a legitimate claim to a share."

"I had no money for drink." Blackie said honestly.

"Always the victim!" Guy's patience was beginning to wear thin.

"That's not how it was!" Blackie's voice boomed out in the small room.

"Well, this is how it is now, Uncle. Do what you will but keep me out of it. As for your drink problem, you will have to go without."

"Took precautions on that front my boy, brought my own brandy, want some?"

"No, and for the last time stop calling me your boy!"

Guy rose early the next morning and set off back to the marina, on the Suzuki, grateful to see *Hidalgo* still riding at anchor. He topped up the boat's fuel tank with diesel and bought provisions for his trip. Once on board his beloved yacht, he started to relax as he always did. Taking a leisurely lunch, he had just finished stowing ropes when he heard a familiar gruff voice. "You were told to report to me Tresanton."

"Am I under arrest?" asked Guy coldly, looking across at the large form of Grasshopper. The man was only a little over five feet tall with short, crew cut red hair. An unattractive man, he had permanently moving grey eyes and a face that went very quickly red when angry. "No, but I need questions answered."

"Then I didn't have to report to you," replied Guy coldly. "Not unless you have changed the law around here."

"Where is he?" asked Grasshopper climbing onto the *Hidalgo* with difficulty.

"Who?" Guy feigned nonchalance.

"Your Uncle."

"I have no idea, did you lose him?" Guy continued.

"Don't play games." Grasshopper snapped.

"So you lost him?"

"He's wanted on murder and larceny charges, coupled with probable intent to defraud. If you are hiding him, or obstructing my enquiries in any way, you are committing an offence." The small man puffed himself up to deliver this piece of police information.

"Wouldn't you just love that?"

"Yes, I would. Where is he Tresanton?"

"I told you, I have no idea."

"And I told you, I don't believe you. Where did you go last night?"

"Over to the east of the island." Guy motioned with his hand in the general direction.

"Another girl?" Grasshopper's face started to turn red.

"That's none of your business Inspector."

"Most things on this island are my business. I don't like you Tresanton, never did, even before you met my daughter. People I don't like I find out more about."

"What's that supposed to mean?"

"Interesting time you seem to have had in China recently. You were in trouble with the Hong Kong police, a potential rape charge."

"Not proven."

"Doesn't need to be as far as I am concerned. Tresanton, I know you for what you are, a charlatan and a crook. I will get you one day and when I do you will go to prison so quickly your feet won't touch the floor." Grasshopper's face was now puce with suppressed rage. "If you have quite finished I have work to do." Guy forced himself to meet his enemy's eyes. "I will be back, do I make myself clear?"

"The only thing clear, Grasshopper, is that you intend to persecute me. I guess that means I will have to talk to my colleagues in the consulate. As for your clumsy attempts to stitch me up with an Uncle I have never met; I do not intend to respond to your attempts at victimisation, much as you would like that. Now, if there is nothing else, please get off my yacht." Turning away, Guy made it clear that he had ended the conversation. "No one is above the law Tresanton. Every move you make I will know about, including everything and everyone on this boat."

"Go and issue some parking tickets!" replied Guy, seething with anger as the large bulky man clambered down to the marina.

Finding he could no longer concentrate, Guy walked down to the small marina office to find Barry, an old ex-pat South African, who never seemed to leave his chair. "Trouble with the big man, eh?" greeted Barry, who had obviously seen the recent confrontation with Grasshopper. "He's an oaf!" exploded Guy, clenching his fists with pent up aggression.

"He's trouble; suggest you get away for a while."

"An American couple are due in tomorrow, I need a crew." Guy ran his hands through his hair in his familiar gesture, "I'm desperate to get away Barry, but I need more charter work, or some lucrative transport deals."

"I'll have a look around for crew and charters. See what there is, but you're too hot for the transport deals. No one is going to take that risk, word's out, charter work only, I'm afraid."

"Thanks, Barry."

Still unable to relax, Guy headed off back to the house on the bike, taking the circuitous route and checking for followers. Again, he had the uneasy feeling that someone was watching him but could see nothing. He found Blackie sitting on the floor poring over some old papers.

"You've been drinking?"

"No time for that. Look, these are the original papers establishing the Silver's sugar plantation in the late 1800's; they switched to bananas later. They talk of a man called Jack Silver who ran a charter yacht company in the nineteenth century; must be in the blood, eh, or is it history repeating itself?" he smiled. "I'm a Tresanton, not a Silver." Guy pointedly responded. "You're a Silver, boy, make no mistake. Now, it says here this Jack had a rival, a Spaniard called Salazar, who disappeared after the two fought in the Canary Islands. As I told you before, Jack had a son called Vincent; my own great grandfather, Vincent Silver.

"How can you be sure this Vincent was your great grandfather?"

"It's in my mother, your grandmother, Janice's papers. She was orphaned, along with her twin sister Marie, when Vincent's only offspring Claire Silver was killed in the Second World War. She told me many times about Vincent, his wife Veronique, and a great family secret. There is no doubt that Vincent is the key to what I'm looking for. I have just got to find it! It's here somewhere I'm convinced!"

Guy was astounded by the excitement in Blackie's voice, compared with the morose man he had met earlier. "Have you eaten, or just drunk all day?" He asked sarcastically.

"Wait a minute!" exclaimed Blackie suddenly, lifting up an old newspaper cutting. "It says here, that Vincent Silver arrived in St Lucia in the late nineteenth century with his wife Veronique. It talks of them buying a house in Soufriere and rumours of an iconic treasure, a Cross that mysteriously disappeared. Bingo!" His one good eye lit up. Guy, his mind preoccupied with what they were going to eat and looking with distaste at the empty bottle of brandy, merely said "Really?"

"There's got to be more stuff here!"

"Boxes of stuff in the loft," replied Guy looking at his Uncle's bloodshot eye. "You've been drinking all day haven't you?"

"Elixir of life my boy, this is bloody thirsty work! Anyway, I can see you've had a few lately, judging by the empties, so don't preach."

"You'd better control it."

"I don't need you preaching. I need help with this, boy, this could change everything."

"Perhaps I don't want to change."

"Nonsense, you can do better than this."

"By stealing from someone else and getting involved with murderers? Forget it! I'm happy with what I have, or rather what I had." Guy shook his head ruefully.

"Too late for that, like it or not you're involved."

"Don't push me; I've just had a hell of a discussion with Grasshopper who is convinced I have you hidden away. I don't know why I am hiding you, just find what you are looking for then get the hell out of my life," snarled Guy looking into the cupboard. "I'm going to get ready for tomorrow."

"Sorry you feel that way. What's happening tomorrow?"

"I'm going away on *Hidalgo*. I have an early hire the following morning and need to get her ready." Guy went upstairs and collected his gear as he heard Blackie banging about in the loft, the occasional curse filtering down through the ceiling.

Finishing his preparations, Guy stopped to eat a sparse meal of tinned sardines and bread before sitting down to listen to the local radio. He must have dozed off when he was stirred by a cry of satisfaction. Blackie came banging down the stairs, gripping a dusty old notebook. "Says in here that there's a safe in the house, clear as day," he yelled. "Have you a safe here?"

"Not to my knowledge," replied Guy, puzzled, as he watched Blackie tear around all the old rooms checking the walls. "Must be under the dammed floorboards," continued the old man lifting rugs.

"I assume you will put everything back as you found it when you've finished wrecking the place?"

"Come on boy, I can smell it, help me."

"For God's sake Uncle, what part don't you understand when I say I'm not interested."

"Ah, this is it, beneath here," said Blackie grabbing an axe and completely ignoring his nephew's protestations.

"Wait a minute." Guy snapped. "Don't stop me now boy, I can feel it," replied Blackie, swinging the axe and smashing floorboards. "It's here, the boards are a different colour, see." He hammered away and finally broke through into the under floor. Feeling around he jumped up excited, "There's a box down there! It has a knob on it, must be a safe! Come on give me a hand."

"All right, if it shuts you up," groaned Guy helping the old man lift out an ancient black iron safe. It was extremely heavy and had obviously lain there for many years.

Despite his reservations, Guy was now intrigued. "Only problem now is how to open it." He said.

"True, I need the numbers of the combination. Is there any way you can break this open by force?" Blackie looked across at his nephew. "Not a chance, it's solid. Do you know any likely numbers?"

"Let me see," said Blackie, thinking hard. He tried various birthdays and then started guessing at the years that may have been significant to Vincent. After half an hour, he gave up and stared disconsolately at the box. "There has to be something that is known only to the family." He sat down and concentrated for about fifteen minutes, then reached out and slowly entered a number. With an audible click, the safe opened and he whooped with joy.

"What was the number?" Guy was interested in how his drunken relative could have worked it out. "I recall my mother talking about grandfather's nickname for Veronique; I converted it to numbers, as in A + 1, and it worked."

"What was the nickname?"

"They both loved the sea; he called her 'Porpoise'," smiled Blackie looking into the safe and revealing a leather backed notebook. "Just what I've been looking for!" he shouted, trembling with excitement. He stumped across to the old kitchen table and started to read. The diary cover was in immaculate copperplate handwriting headed,

'*The diary of Vincent Silver 1920.*' Underneath the title were the hand scribbled words, '*Treasure or Nemesis?*' Guy frowned at the cryptic words as his Uncle animatedly skimmed the first pages. "It's a load of boring stuff about a sea voyage in an old sailing boat called *Calypso*. It talks about a Spanish rogue called Salazar, and a challenge of nations. Damn," Blackie broke off, "The words then go into another language."

"Here, let me have a look," said Guy. "It's in Spanish, don't speak a word myself, but could get it translated."

"Bugger! Look inside the back cover," said Blackie lifting his head, "there's a sketch, which has to be it."

"What?"

"The Columbus Cross, yes, it's got the single large diamond at the front. My God, this is it my boy. He had it after all. Now where the hell did he put it?"

"There is more to this story, I am convinced. Now come on, spit it out."

"Well, Queen Isabella of Spain claimed Columbus stole it from her," Blackie put the diary down and picked up his glass of brandy, resigned to telling Guy what he knew.

"Your stepson found it, didn't he?" Realisation dawned on Guy.

"Not quite, but he knew where it was. The answer is in these pages so we need to get reading."

Cadiz,
Spain

The tall Spaniard named Salboa drew attention as he walked past. With his long flowing grey hair, goatee beard and obligatory red shirt he was accustomed to receiving attention. Now in his late sixties, six feet tall with coal black eyes and permanently tanned skin, exuding confidence as he strolled into the headquarters of 'Alhambra Lines' shipping company.

Based in Cadiz, Salboa had built up the business from a small two-freighter company, to one that dominated the South America to Spain and Europe freight routes. The company had grown into a considerable success and, for a time, he had been one of the richest and most desired men in Spain. However, recently he was plagued by rumours that his shipping lines were involved in shady Latin American deals, involving drugs and guns. There were also innuendos about his private life and missing persons. There was no proof, but there was no disputing that his company had suffered. As lucrative orders were lost, he was forced to sell some container ships, and now it was rumoured he was in deep financial trouble.

Salboa curtly acknowledged the secretaries and made his way to the main lift, beckoning for his aide Joel Mendez. The small, harassed clerk joined him and they rode the lift to the third floor. Salboa strode out and across to his large desk indicating for Mendez to take a seat. "Tell me" he demanded curtly. "More trouble." stammered Mendez passing over the latest report, his hands trembling. "We lost the Peruvian timber account."

"Very disappointing." Salboa's eyes did not betray his true feelings, their dark impenetrable depth capable of reducing opponents to shivering wrecks. "We are out of cash." Mendez stuttered.

"We will survive." Salboa assured him. Mendez, reaching for another paper, continued nervously. "The repayments are starting to crucify us," he said. "We need to look for credit protection."

"Leave it to me," said Salboa pushing a button.

"But we need to do something."

"I told you I'd take care of it, Mendez. Tell the creditors we will pay them. Now go, you're annoying me."

Turning away from the frightened clerk, he growled to another man entering the office, "So you survived your ordeal in England?".

"Nearly killed me, the idiot." Responded Matarife angrily, ignoring the retreating Mendez. "Bloody gunshot in my calf."

"He still believes that he set fire to the place and killed his wife, I trust?"

"Yes."

"Good. It serves our purposes." Salboa folded his hands together in satisfaction.

"The fire took hold faster than I expected, only just managed to escape before the whole place became an inferno." Ignoring Matarife's narrow escape, Salboa continued, "What did the woman's son tell her?"

"She went into shock when I told her he was dead."

"You were supposed to seduce her and find out more. Why tell her that her son was dead?"

"I wanted to shock her, hoped she would confide in me, after all I had seen her twice before and she was most accommodating."

"Bloody stupid thing to do," growled Salboa. "You nearly compromised the entire operation. Now, because of your damned incompetence the idiot has disappeared. Do you know where he is?"

"Yes, he's in St. Lucia in the Caribbean. I told the police there."

"What?"

"They are doing our work for us."

"That's the last thing I want. My God, I am surrounded by idiots and incompetents." Salboa exploded, holding his hands up in frustration. "They will keep him on the run." Matarife tried to explain his plan. "Give them a false trail; we track him ourselves from now on. Understand?" Salboa barked his instructions. "Yes," nodded Matarife miserably.

"So you killed the only person who knew something?"

"He wouldn't talk."

"Finesse you idiot, how did he die?"

"Heart failure, we weren't to know. My men may have misjudged his tolerance to pain after his encounter with the madman."

"And where is this madman now?"

"We don't know exactly."

"Idiot." Salboa repeated himself, amazed at the incompetence of the man he was paying to do this work. "I have served you loyally for many years Salboa. I will not fail you." Matarife assured the irritated man in front of him, accompanied by a slight bow of his head. "You'd better not. It's time for me to get involved, we have to act faster. I want vengeance for my father. We are flying to St Lucia now by private jet. Call ahead to get the yacht ready."

Tay Ninh,
Vietnam

The Teacher looked around calmly and raised his arms to indicate his followers should gather close. He watched silently as they did so, content that they would obey his every word. He nodded to Yen Lie, his second in command, a sturdily built Vietnamese woman. She ruled the commune to his exacting standards with hard discipline.

He was ready to educate them all a little more, enough to keep them believing and wanting more. "The time has come to reclaim what is ours, to put right any misconceptions and ensure that our people gain their just recognition. The principles of our movement are recognising and changing what is wrong. You alone are capable of this, and through me, have the power. Our philosophy is about finding truth; understanding what really happened in history. Then we take that truth and use it to our advantage."

"We always do as you say Teacher," intoned Yen Lie, messianic in her faith in him.

"I will now talk of the great explorers of the Chinese dynasty in the fifteenth century who discovered the world, long before western adventurers. I speak of the year 1421 when Admiral Zheng He and his great global expedition set sail, rounding the Cape and discovering the Cape Verdi islands. I speak of him then sending his lieutenants; Admiral Hong Bao to Brazil and South America before Magellan, and Admiral Zhou Man to Australia and Antarctica."

"This is all very interesting, but where's the proof?" asked a tall, willowy female in the front row, her distinctive long red hair flowing over her yellow robe. "There is much proof," smiled the Teacher, making a note to talk to the girl afterwards. She deserved special attention and would share his bed tonight. He recalled her name was Sabine, an American girl from Texas. Pretty with blue-green eyes, she had a strong enquiring mind and he detected a ruthlessness that he needed. He knew she was from a poor family in America and that she had been a private dancer until she arrived at the compound. Without doubt, she was one of the most able followers in his group, ready for promotion and a key role in the future movement. "In Mexico, they have found ancient Chinese Junks. In Peru, there is a village that speaks Chinese. Linguistics, clothes and artefacts, are all evidence that Chinese colonies were set up in California as well as Peru hundreds of years ago. I have seen maps drawn by a cartographer in Guadeloupe in 1424, sixty eight years before Columbus got there, maps drawn by the Chinese."

"Great news indeed," agreed Yen Lie.

"Correct," replied the Teacher.

Sabine hadn't finished asking questions just yet. "How does this all fit with our mission?" she asked "We are many races, not just Chinese. I don't understand why you only talk of Chinese achievements."

"It's not about race but about truth," explained the Teacher, "Western knowledge says that Europeans discovered the known world, finding new civilisations whilst Asia was in a barbaric state. Well, the opposite is true as you now know."

The Teacher smiled at the rapt attention he was receiving; he had known this news would be well received. "Consequently history has been misrepresented; our aim is to correct that misapprehension. Unfortunately, recent generations of Chinese were not so enlightened as the earlier dynasties and destroyed much documentation. However, as I have indicated enough remains to prove that Chinese adventurers discovered the known world from India, to America and Australia."

Sabine, realising she had been given an opportunity pressed her advantage. "In what way does this benefit us?" she asked. The Teacher wanted questions; she was ambitious and determined to take her rightful place next to him. She would then take care of Yen Lie. "We are all excited by this Teacher, please give us details." Sabine pleaded, fascinated. The Teacher smiled and told them. "The Chinese explorers left valuable items behind when they went around the world. Think of it; we have an entire movement of people long before western records began. We have DNA records showing Chinese ancestry in Mexico and the Caribbean for instance, providing the keys to finding great treasures and great power. The rest will be revealed at the appropriate moment. In the meantime, you need to ready yourselves for a great mission. We are not alone in this quest; there are many who will help us, many different cells connected only through myself. There are those who are scared of us, scared by what we can do. You must all be vigilant."

"Teacher, the Chinese explorers, why did they not colonise and control the countries they discovered?" asked a different voice. The speaker was a small shrew like man called Zie Lai. He was the acknowledged senior male of the group and looking to reassert his authority over Yen Lie and Sabine. "They chose to keep moving, spreading the message. You are all very privileged people as you have been chosen to fulfil this and more." Zie Lai nodded, as did Yen Lie. Both made mental notes to discipline Sabine. "You all have your jobs to do, see to it that they are done well," continued the Teacher resuming his familiar harsh expression. "Sabine you may come with me. Do not forget we will succeed only through your total obedience, with that we will succeed beyond your wildest dreams. Our march to destiny has begun."

"Of course," smiled Sabine, looking triumphantly at Yen Lie and Zie Lai. She was sure that they had mistaken her for a harmless American, to be manipulated in the same way as they did her fellow Americans in the commune. What they did not understand was that she was as ruthless as they were, and fully intended to use this to her own advantage. She had grown up the hard way in San Antonio, Texas in a poor family where she had learnt to stand on her own two feet early. Finding out about the Teacher after an aunt inadvertently let slip that her cousin was in the organisation, Sabine had made up her mind to follow too. Not that she had ever met the girl in the commune. She had no compunctions in doing whatever was necessary to achieve her own aims, and this included using her feminine charms to manipulate others. As far as she was concerned, sex was a weapon that she used to her advantage, no more than a bodily function, and she never let emotions take control of her. Now she had a supreme chance and she would not fail.

CHAPTER 3

At almost sixty years old, Beatrice de Rock was a formidable woman. At the best of times, she resembled her auspicious surname; at the worst of times, she had a temper that reduced even the most officious person to a humbled wreck. She stood surveying the remains of her new, but crumbling house near Soufriere in southern St Lucia. A little over five feet six tall and weighing nearly fifteen stone, Beatrice was a successful, second-generation American French clothes designer. Unfortunately, the sudden death of her mild mannered artist husband, Bernard de Rock, had coincided with the collapse of French fashion in America and her collections had gone out of fashion with a vengeance. She regarded it as fate.

Left alone at the age of fifty-eight, with a bankrupt business, she had decided to return to her French colonial roots. The house in St Lucia had belonged to her family a long time, in fact since the days of French ownership of the island, some two hundred years before. It stood a little over two kilometres from the Fond Doux estate, famous to tourists as the site of a successful uprising against the British by the locals two hundred years ago.

Since her mother, Marie, died some fifteen years ago the house had been unoccupied, apart from occasional rentals to French artists. Descended from a dynasty of strong women, including her maternal grandmother, Claire, and great grandmother, Veronique, Beatrice was proud of her ancestry and happy to take on a house that no one else in the family wanted. Despite the family history, the old house was currently a bottomless money pit, but Beatrice had ideas, that she was determined to make work. Her plan was to open a French boutique on the island that would appeal to the nouveaux riche from France. She could see it now, a completely new collection to launch at the Paris Fashion Shows, an eclectic mix of Caribbean and French. Unfortunately, her main problem was that she had no capital and needed to find some quickly. That was the other reason she was here; she had received a strange phone call telling her to come to the island quickly because she had a family claim to a great hidden treasure. Although she was initially dubious, the man had sounded genuine and Beatrice had decided to take this chance to start life afresh.

Beatrice's adopted daughter, a Chinese girl called Rose Ling, was also going to live in the old house. Rose's adoption was not traditional; ten years ago, the girl's mother had contacted Beatrice unexpectedly asking her to adopt her daughter. Beatrice had initially refused until the woman had explained that she had known Claire, her maternal grandmother, and would pay her for the favour. Despite her initial reluctance, the adoption had turned out to be a blessing. Much loved by Beatrice, Rose was an intelligent and articulate young woman. The only problem was that now Rose had grown into a pretty twenty-year-old, Beatrice felt she could no longer keep pace with the girl's needs. That was another attractive reason to come to St Lucia; Rose was interested in the story of hidden treasure and Beatrice hoped that the mystery would keep her occupied.

"Breakfast, is ready," Beatrice shouted up the stairs. "Thanks," replied Rose, walking nimbly down the stairs. Despite her young age Rose's face had an enigmatic quality that made it look as if it held a thousand secrets, or so Beatrice thought. She could not quite make up her mind if Rose did indeed have secrets, or if she was imagining it. Either way, she was starting to feel inadequate in the face of the girl's undoubted intelligence. "Morning, Aunt Beatrice," smiled Rose indulgently as she helped herself to a slice of toast.

Rose had excelled in languages and sciences at school, with top marks in all her exams. Beatrice had assumed a conventional career using these skills would follow, but it was the last thing on Rose's mind. She had made it very clear that she wanted to be a police detective, which in Beatrice's opinion was hardly a suitable career. She thought it was a dangerous job, and worried about her mixing with gangsters and criminals. Rose listened politely as she did with most of her Aunt's advice, before heading off in her own direction. She had long ago realised the limitations of her Aunt's world and was excited to move to the house in St Lucia. She was profoundly grateful to Beatrice for bringing stability to her life after some emotionally difficult times, but now she needed more excitement. Despite her traumatic childhood, she was by nature a happy character, always seeing a bright side even when one didn't exist. She hoped the move, with talk of hidden treasure, would provide an opportunity to develop her detecting skills.

Unknown to her aunt, Rose had recently developed a passionate interest in researching her Chinese heritage. In addition, also unknown to Beatrice, she frequently suffered disturbing dreams, which she was unable to understand or explain. Rose did not think these dreams were connected to the loss of her parents. She had last seen them in China at the age of ten, and had few memories of them now. She knew that they had lived at Wuhan, an industrial city in the heart of China on the banks of the Yangtze, famous as the place where Mao Tse Tung had started his famous swim

She even found it hard to recall their faces since the dreadful night she had been called into the headmistress's room and told she would never see her parents again, as they had both been killed in an accident. There had never been a shortage of money for her education and she had received the best, so Rose had always presumed that her parents had left her well provided for in their will. However, neither she nor her aunt knew what had actually happened to her parents, and once Rose turned eighteen the money stopped.

Rose looked at herself in the hallway mirror; her green eyes assessed her short, glossy black hair that swung in a collar length bob and she knew that she was pretty in a classical way. However, Rose had little interest in such things unlike most of her female friends. A little over five feet in height, she was usually described as a tomboy, preferring the rough and tumble of sports to more traditional female pursuits. She excelled at games of all sorts, taking up martial arts and joining the Army Cadets as she grew older. Having finished her education, she was now a Police cadet, ready to enrol in the police force when she had finished her training. However, that would have to wait until her Aunt was settled into her new life and she was currently taking a sabbatical from her studies.

Today, she found herself very intrigued by Beatrice's conviction that there was more to discover about the house, with its hidden secrets and rumours of an eventful past.

"So have you dug up any skeletons yet, Beatrice?" she asked with a smile

"Not yet, but I will. The caller said it's a diary we are looking for." Her aunt's voice came back to her from behind a pile of old boxes. "Written by your mysterious ancestors?" asked Rose taking another piece of toast. "Yes, though I've found nothing as yet, but it's here Rose, I can smell it. Besides, we've only being here two days, give it time."

"Time to apply my detective skills then!" Rose said, knowing that it would provoke a reaction from her aunt. "Absolutely, but I wish you'd get those silly ideas out of your head Rose, there are better things you can do with your life."

"The answer is always in the detail, first thing they teach you," continued Rose ignoring the familiar comment. "I'm going to look upstairs."

After a whole morning without success they turned their attention to the upper rooms and then, finally, after not finding anything of note, the attic. With difficulty they both climbed up the ladder and Beatrice cursed as she hit her head on a low beam, she wiped it with her hand, and it came away black with dust. "Bloody hell, it's been a long time since anyone was up here," she said, sweating as she shone a torch through the gloom. Boxes lay in front of them as they started demolishing layers of packaging materials. Moving forwards, Beatrice stumbled and lost her footing, falling down onto an old crate heavily. It splintered apart. "Help me," she muttered pushing herself upright. "Get the torch."

Rose shone the beam at the broken case, "What's that?" she said, her interest caught by something inside the broken crate. "Looks like a decorative box," grunted Beatrice. Rose leaned forwards and lifted out a small, square box covered in red leather. She felt the lid; it was jammed on. She took it across to the stairway to see it better. With a grimace, she levered the lid hard and smiled in satisfaction as it finally came away. "Well done Rose, what's inside?"

"Hard to tell," replied Rose lifting out a leather parchment. "It's an old document," she said, and handed it to Beatrice. "It's written in French, I can't understand a word," grumbled Beatrice. She put it to one side, gasping as she noticed an old green leather-bound notebook at the bottom of the box. She peered at the name on the cover, "Veronique Silver." she read aloud. "There's a note inside!" she continued excitedly and then her voice dropped with disappointment. "It says the diary sits in a safe within the house. Well, at least we are making progress I suppose."

"Logical place for a safe is downstairs," said Rose and followed by Beatrice headed down. "let's go down and look around."

She went through all the rooms and ended up in the main lounge, next to the fireplace. "I've a feeling it's in there!" she said to Beatrice as they looked at the large open fireplace. "Looks like I'm going to get dirty," she said as she reached in and felt around. Lifting her hands higher she felt an unusual ledge above the actual grate area and lifted a torch. "There's something here Aunt, I can feel it." She shone the torch and looked harder, "There's a safe!" she shouted exultantly.

"That's it then, well done Rose, can you open it?"

"No, it's locked, we need a combination."

"Here, let me see," replied Beatrice taking Rose's place and grimacing at the black soot that covered Rose from head to foot. "Be careful its edges are sharp," said Rose standing back and trying to get some of the soot off her. She watched as Beatrice grunted and cursed on her knees with her head up the chimney. The sight would have been comical if it had not been so serious. Finally, there was a roar of triumph and Beatrice emerged covered in soot but grinning and clutching something in her hand, a book. "This is it Rose!" said Beatrice. "Her diary, if this doesn't sort out my problems, I don't know what will."

"How did you crack the code?" asked Rose admiringly.

"Recalled my mother mentioning the pet name Veronique had for Vincent and converted it to numbers, it worked."

"What was the name?"

"Shark," smiled Beatrice.

"There's not much in here that I can understand, it is all in French," commented Rose, opening the book in clouds of dust, whilst Beatrice tried to clean herself down, "It's very faint and hard to read."

They both sat down eagerly in the lounge chairs, Rose still clasping the book, "Still can't see much!" she exclaimed with disappointment, "A dead end after all that. Hold on there is something scripted on the back in English." Beatrice moved closer so that she could see,

"To my beloved Veronique from Jason Silver, St Lucia — 1910"

"Perhaps there was still a Silver living on the island then? It's the only lead we have," replied Rose looking at the words. "We need to get it translated into English; I only speak Spanish, which doesn't help us, don't you speak some French?"

"None I'm afraid, only English."

"Time to practice my police training, I'll be back later," said Rose grabbing a light coat. "If you don't mind I'll take the hire car!"

She drove down to the local police station in St Johns in the hired Fiat Uno. Looking carefully she was disappointed and surprised to find that there was no one of that name in the Islands records. In desperation, she tried calling her training colleagues in Chicago, begging them to use their database. Still nothing, puzzled she looked around as a police officer walked in clicking his tongue. "Can I help you?" asked Cricket, as he walked over smiling. "I'm looking for a record of someone with the name 'Silver'. I need to know if there are any are located on the island." Rose told him, glad of his offer of help. "Any particular reason?" asked Cricket trying to conceal his surprise. "It's linked to the house my aunt and I have just moved into in Soufriere."

"Miss, you are in luck, there is a Mr Silver here on the island; met him yesterday as a matter of fact, though he doesn't go by that name."

"Can you tell me where he is?" asked Rose excitedly.

"Classified information I'm afraid." Cricket clicked his tongue loudly as if to underline his words. "Surely it can't be a matter of life or death!" smiled Rose. "It would really be very helpful to me," she continued flirtatiously, eyes flashing under her thick, shiny fringe. "I guess there's no harm in it," replied Cricket flushing under his collar. "He sails a boat called *Hidalgo*, you should find him at the marina. He doesn't like to be called Silver though and he's a bit of an oddball."

"Thank you very much officer." Rose smiled nicely, showing dimples in her cheeks.

"No problem Miss, as you are new perhaps you would like me to show you around the island sometime?"

"That would be nice, I'll let you know," said Rose hastily heading for the exit.

Guy slept badly that night, having another of his 'Chinese nightmares' as he now termed them. He awoke early in a cold sweat and left the house careful not to wake the snoring form of his Uncle and reached *Hidalgo* just as the sun was rising. He began to make ready to leave. The island was becoming too crowded for his liking; it was time to get away. He spent the morning working on boat maintenance, particularly the ropes and engine. He could not afford any problems when far out at sea. Just as he was taking a breather on deck, he saw a couple of people approaching in the distance and groaned aloud thinking it was Grasshopper again. Then he noticed that these people walked rather than waddled and were female, therefore potential charter customers. "Can I help you ladies," he shouted down from the cockpit, ready to be charming. "Mr Silver?" asked Rose.

"You've got the wrong person," replied Guy and started to turn away, all thoughts of being charming gone.

"Tresanton then," said Beatrice. "If that's what you call yourself."

"Who wants to know?" Guy's voice was filled with suspicion. "Well, are you?" Beatrice barked, obviously losing patience. "Perhaps." Guy gave an evasive reply. "Well are you going to invite us aboard or not," demanded Beatrice staring at him. "That depends. Are you looking for a charter?"

"I just want to talk." It was Beatrice's turn to look evasive.

"Got to be business, my time is valuable."

"It is business," snapped Beatrice.

"Come aboard then," sighed Guy turning his head and then cursing as a familiar car screeched into the marina.

"Tresanton," shouted a burly man inside an ill-fitting uniform, heavy jowls quivering as he jumped out of the car. "Hello Grasshopper, nice to see you, but as you can see I'm busy at the moment. Could you come back later?"

"Don't get cute me with me Tresanton." Grasshopper looked as though he was likely to explode at any moment.

"What can I do for you this fine morning, officer?" Guy said with a fake smile.

"The name is Chief of Police Pollard to you Tresanton. Excuse me ladies I need a minute of this man's time."

"No problem," replied Beatrice smiling at the man. "I think we met the other day."

"Yes we did Ma'am. I showed you the way to your new house. You were lost if I recall." Rose smiled back at Cricket who was busy watching the drama from the police car. "Such a nice man," whispered Beatrice to Rose. "You must come over next time you are down in the south of the island."

"I will do that Ma'am, now if you will excuse me."

"Okay," said Guy. "I admit I should have had the radio working."

"It's not about that Tresanton. You're up to something."

"Really and what might that be?" Guy screwed up his face, as if concentrating.

"Your Uncle, where is he?"

"I've not met anyone claiming to be my Uncle, in fact until your officer told me the other day I had no idea I had an Uncle. If he comes by I'll let you know."

"Don't get cute with me I'm watching you carefully."

"I don't know what I have done to deserve all this special attention."

"You know what, leave my daughter alone or I'll finish you. Don't think I don't know what you are up to with that fancy yacht of yours."

"Your daughter came with me of her own free will; in fact she told me lots of interesting information about you. Like the fact you are never at home."

"You've been warned Tresanton, the next time I will act."

"Not what I would call a helpful, caring police force," said Guy coldly.

"I don't call corrupting an innocent young woman very helpful, Tresanton," hissed Pollard.

"Innocent?" laughed Guy. "Perhaps if you spent more time with her instead of overseas, you'd realise she isn't innocent and is crying out for attention."

"If I find you've being harbouring a criminal."

"Just what exactly has my Uncle done?"

"He's wanted by the British police, that is good enough for me," growled Grasshopper getting back into his car with great difficulty. "What the hell are you looking at?" he snarled at his colleague. "Nothing," replied Cricket putting the car into gear and dragging his eyes away from Rose.

Guy turned his attention back to the new arrivals. "So what can I do for you ladies?" he asked. "You can answer some questions," replied Beatrice inviting herself aboard and sitting down heavily at the chart table with Rose on the other side. "Your family name is Silver?"

"It's my mother's maiden name, not that she wants to use it anymore." Guy replied quickly.

"Why ever not?" Before he could answer they were interrupted by a familiar voice, booming "Hello," that cut the conversation dead. "Here comes the reason why not. A family feud," replied Guy groaning inwardly. What are you doing here?" he asked as Blackie stepped aboard in his clerics outfit. Guy had to admit that the disguise was very effective. "The police have just been here for God's sake!"

"Saw them and avoided them," replied Blackie. "I've been here for over an hour watching and observing. Now can you introduce me to your friends?"

"My Uncle," growled Guy.

"But I thought you hadn't seen him?" queried Beatrice. "Selective memory. Wish I hadn't seen him, it's different." Guy deadpanned. "But he has a criminal record!" replied Beatrice, agitated. "They've got the wrong person," replied Blackie smoothly. "Case of mistaken identity that I'll resolve later. So, what can we do for you ladies?" Blackie continued, "I'm not really a cleric, just comes in useful."

"I don't approve of taking the cloth in vain," said Beatrice frostily.

"Needs must, I'm afraid," said Blackie sitting down. "Very well, I guess I will have to put up with it," replied Beatrice. "Now to business, I think we can both help each other so Rose and I have a proposition." "For whom, me or my Uncle?" asked Guy.

"Both if you are the Silvers we are looking for." The older woman said shrewdly guessing that both men would be interested.

"We are, so what exactly is this proposal?" asked Blackie. "We shall have to trust you," replied Beatrice, looking across at Rose for confirmation as she did so. "We found an old diary in our house attic and it has a reference to your name."

"Really," Blackie's interest quickened, "an amazing coincidence!"

"Why?

"Because we also have an old diary, in fact here it is. There are clearly forces at work from above," smiled Blackie.

"Exactly the same as ours," replied Beatrice examining the green leather book in Blackie's hand. "Exactly the same outside," replied Blackie. "Unfortunately ours is written in Spanish."

"And ours in French! As you say an amazing coincidence," said Beatrice frowning. "Too much of a coincidence," said Guy staring at the two books. "Perhaps there is someone behind this," said Rose looking at the others. "Why do you say that?" asked Guy taking an interest in the Chinese girl for the first time.

"It's obvious isn't it. Two books lying hidden away for years and now we all arrive here and suddenly find them."

"My great grandmother was the wife of one Jason Silver, see the inscription here," continued Beatrice. "The name of our great grandfather," confirmed Blackie and then added suddenly. "It's the treasure," they all looked at him. "Sorry Guy but we need to share our knowledge or we will get nowhere! After all, we are all related. Point is that there is well known knowledge in our family of a magnificent Golden Cross called the Columbus Cross. Been talked about for years in fact."

"We have similar rumours in our family," admitted Beatrice. "It's beginning to make some sense."

"Perhaps I can help," replied Rose. "The way I see it is that someone is manipulating us all to get to this treasure. Why it has suddenly become an issue I have no idea but they are hot on its trail, and have found out about our respective ancestors and the part they played in bringing this Cross to the Caribbean."

"My step son called Joe claims to have seen it before he was murdered," said Blackie dramatically. "Murdered! My God!" exclaimed Beatrice. "And there are others after it?"

"What else do you know?" asked Blackie.

"Nothing," said Rose.

"Hardly adds up to a lot does it?" said Guy, ever the sceptic.

"I think it's quite a lot, actually," replied Rose coldly.

"Circumstantial, as my friend Grasshopper would say."

"Perhaps, but you have to admit it's intriguing, my boy!" said Blackie.

"Just let me get this straight," replied Guy looking from Beatrice to Rose. "You say that you have just found a similar diary to ours, and that they cross refer to each other. Why have we both only just found these documents?"

"I admit it's unusual," replied Beatrice.

"As I said, someone wants us to find these items." Rose repeated.

"Why?" Beatrice was troubled.

"To do their dirty work for them!" exclaimed Guy.

"It doesn't change the fact that we have a great opportunity," said Blackie. "There's a treasure out there waiting for us. All we have to do is find it."

"A fool's game," replied Guy. "It just doesn't ring true." Blackie remained firm. "I see it as the chance of a lifetime, and I for one intend to do something about it before someone else does. This is our inheritance not someone else's and we should work together to succeed. After all there's more than enough to go around and blood is thicker than water," he finished, red in the face. "More importantly as I understand it from all the copious reading I did yesterday," he continued, looking at Guy, "both our families go back to a common grandmother one Claire Silver, the only child of Vincent and Veronique Silver. Unfortunately, she died when the *Lusitania* sank, but not before having twins, my mother Janice and your mother Marie, Beatrice. The twins married on different sides of the Atlantic, so here we are; the first reunion in fifty odd years. That calls for a celebration, I reckon."

"Absolutely," said Beatrice, "we're all in this together including you Mr Tresanton."

"You have absolutely nothing else to go on," replied Guy angrily. He did not have much time for this bombastic woman, or his dammed stupid Uncle. "So what exactly do you suggest we do?" Blackie asked Beatrice sensing a similar level of interest. "Look for it of course!" replied Beatrice. "A fifty/fifty split if we find what we are looking for, agreed?" Blackie nodded his head vigorously. "Agreed," he said and attempting again to interest Guy urged him to do the same. "Come on Guy, this is the chance to find a fortune and tell Grasshopper where to go." Guy was not to be moved.

"Not much I can do to stop you wasting your time, just don't involve me," he said adamantly.

"You don't strike me as the type to ignore a challenge," said Rose, looking at Guy quizzically. Guy leapt up defensively, "What's that supposed to mean?"

"What I said. This is a real chance for us to avenge our ancestor's loss but we need your help."

"I suggest we start by searching both the houses. That's the first thing," said Blackie. "I have a charter tomorrow," replied Guy coldly. "I am happy with my life as it is Uncle, that's the difference between us. This will only lead to heartache and trouble."

"Well at least one of you is up for it," observed Beatrice. "We'll work with your Uncle. There's only one problem now."

"What's that?" asked Guy.

"How do we know that you won't go off and find the treasure without us?"

"Oh for goodness sake!" replied Guy, exasperated. "No one has any idea where it is!"

"We need to translate the diaries first from Spanish and French; which by the way is clearly an attempt to throw us off the trail. Do you know any French?" asked Beatrice hopefully to both men.

"Yes," replied Guy flatly. "And I speak Spanish," replied Rose. "So we swap the diaries and work together," said Beatrice grandly with a flourish. "I have a charter tomorrow so it will have to wait, though God knows why I am even contemplating doing this, "said Guy wearily. "That is assuming that you will let me take the diary away." He directed this last comment to Beatrice, who had been clutching her diary close during most of the conversation. "It can't wait," replied Beatrice flatly.

"I'll translate the diary in my spare time over the next couple of days, if I get some help with the charter."

"What sort of help," asked Beatrice?

"I need someone to take care of the passengers, cook meals and ensure they are looked after, *Hidalgo* looks after herself."

"We need to check the houses for other clues," said Beatrice coldly. "I'll go with you," offered Rose, "but not as a dogsbody."

"I should think there's little chance of that happening," observed Guy.

"What does that mean?"

"You are very opinionated and strong willed." Guy looked defiantly at Rose.

"And you are like a bear with a sore head."

"That's splendid then," said Blackie rubbing his hands. "There's nothing like a bit of friction and competition to make things happen faster. I'll expect results within a few days."

"Expect all you like Uncle, the charter comes first."

"Your Uncle and I will thoroughly search the houses," continued Beatrice firmly.

"You might think I am small and insignificant Mr Tresanton but I assure you I can pull my weight," said Rose staring coldly at Guy. "Never said you couldn't," replied Guy. "Extra help is always useful especially, as I've lost my regular help. "I won't let you down, Mr Tresanton."

"It's Guy, please."

Four hours later Rose retuned alone to *Hidalgo* carrying her worldly belongings in a large bag that she stowed expertly in the forward bow cabin. "Sorry about earlier," said Guy "I didn't mean to sound rude."

"I can handle it," replied Rose.

"Your mother is a determined lady."

"She's not my mother," explained Rose. "My real parents died some time ago, she is my guardian, or Aunt, as I call her."

"I'm sorry."

"There's no need to be, Beatrice can be overbearing but she means well."

"Let me show you the ropes, we need to sail on the evening tide."

"Where do we pick up the charters?"

"Down the coast at an exclusive resort near Castries called Marigot Bay, the place where Dr Dolittle was filmed a few years ago. They are an elderly American couple who own their own villa and pay well and besides it's only for three days."

They sailed at first light with the American couple called Jack and Nancy Dalton. The winds were light and the sail work not too arduous. Jack and Nancy wanted to concentrate on fishing which left Guy time to set the autopilot and try to translate the diary. He soon realised that his French was not as strong as he had thought. On the third day, the wind picked up a little and he beckoned to Rose. "Good time to get used to the sails in case we head further afield in the near future. Do you think you can manage?"

"Don't patronise me, Mr Tresanton. I've had military training in the Army Cadets and can look after myself"

"Guy, please."

"I'm going to call you the Bear because all I get from you is growls; you're like a bear with a sore head."

"Thanks and you're like a little Viper always ready to snap to the attack," replied Guy coldly.

"There we are then, code names."

"Very well Viper. Just remember, in a sailing boat despite what you may think, I have to be dictatorial, the wind doesn't wait until we've had a debate. We used to use it in management training sessions as the prime example of democracy not working because of harsh external forces."

"Guess so."

"You heard of grinders."

"No."

"Well basically they're the ones who do the hard work turning the winches here for the main and Genoa sails."

"Thought you had motors for that."

"I do, but as with navigation, you cannot assume they will always work. So we need to know how to read a chart and also how to manually lift the sails in time to get them to work."

"Confession time Bear; I have been to sea before on an army training exercise in a tall ship, so I do know what to do."

"You cheeky rat Viper."

"Viper with a forked tongue," she smiled. "That's no way to talk to a lady."

"Ladies don't lie."

"This one does, you really do come from another time Bear. When men were men and all that chivalrous crap."

"Well, as a matter of fact I do believe in chivalry and holding the door open for ladies, but there aren't any here."

"Wow, we really are going to have fun."

"You're in my chivalrous world now so you'd better get used to it! Now, get hauling on the main sail winch. I want it up in two minutes!"

Later they sat in the main cabin and relaxed enjoying the break, Jack and Nancy had gone ashore.

"Guess it's time to start deciphering the diaries," said Guy. Rose agreed. "On my list of to do," she said. "Beatrice will have something to say if you don't get it finished." "Did you just come along to keep an eye on me?" Guy asked her. "Both, probably." Rose decided to be honest about her motives. "Do you really believe all this treasure stuff?" asked Guy.

"You have to believe sometimes in the hopeful things."

"Mine is right here. I've had enough of working for other people."

"What happened?" Rose looked interested, sure that there was a story behind the man's gruff exterior. "Long story." Guy looked pensive for a moment, and then began again, "My father disappeared in China at the same time as I lost my job due to a poisonous, lying Chinese woman."

"So that's why you don't trust me!" Rose gasped.

"No, I do trust you, this one drugged me," Guy explained in detail what had happened at the conference in China.

"I'm sorry I didn't know. A truce then?" Rose held out her hand to emphasise her meaning.

"A truce Viper," Guy took her small hand in his, "Except when I get annoyed at you! I like this life sailing from one day to another with no fixed idea what's going to happen. I don't want to lose it."

"I can understand that."

"Do you?"

"Yes."

"I get bad dreams."

"What sort of bad dreams?"

"Chinese nightmares I call them," replied Guy watching Rose's sunny face cloud over. "What's the matter?"

"I get exactly the same, always an old Chinese man who is beckoning to me."

"How strange," replied Guy, explaining what had happened to him in Hong Kong. "This is starting to get weird, almost as if it were pre-ordained." Rose looked thoughtful. "Perhaps it was," she said. "What do you think's happening here?" replied Guy quietly. He was not alone now in his suspicions, there really was something going on. "I don't know," she said, "but we need to be very careful. People can go mad in these situations."

"You're right, look if it's just you and I then I will help all I can, there has to be some link along the line, I just wonder where."

"I think someone, probably a Spaniard, is manipulating us," replied Rose quietly. "Only I don't know how or why." Guy looked surprised at the idea. "A Spaniard?" he said. "Yes, it was a Spaniard who called Beatrice, told her to come here, that's the reason she came chasing a dream to fund her next business empire." Guy looked thoughtful at this information. "Blackie was the same; he had to leave England in a rush, so perhaps the events were connected." He told her. Rose changed the subject swiftly. "Let's get to the diaries and later I want you to teach me to navigate."

"I agree," replied Guy feeling strangely elated as if he was starting to live again with a purpose.

The next day passed easily and Guy began teaching Rose the principles of seamanship, while Jack and Nancy were occupied fishing. Guy caught the smiling glances from Rose as the overweight American couple clambered around deck and then sat for hours staring at the lines with no catch. A poor haul of fish did not seem to bother them. Fortunately, the winds were not too strong, barely getting over ten knots, although Guy was comfortable in most weather conditions. Rose proved herself a very capable crewmember taking to the life like a duck to water. Guy found himself wondering more and more about her; she was intriguing, however he could sense a deep melancholy. "What made you come here?" He finally asked. "I want to be a detective and Beatrice wanted help. She would struggle without me." Rose answered, comfortable enough with him now to be truthful. "She wants this treasure badly." Guy mused. "Ever since she got the phone call, she does. Now, enough about me, what about you, how about the mystery Bear, any relationships?" Guy shook his head. "Finished just before the other wonderful recent events in my life."

"I'm sorry."

"No need to be."

"True, having spent time on *Hidalgo* I can see why this new life appeals to you."

"I have being working on the diary." Guy told her with a smile. "Beatrice's great grandmother was quite a person; she talks about the day when she met my great grandfather."

"Your great grandfather writes poor Spanish as if using the language to deter snoopers."

"My French isn't that great."

"Anything more?"

"Not yet."

"Let's finish them tomorrow night when we drop the Americans off. I'll cook you one of my special meals whilst we are at anchor in Marigot Bay," Guy promised.

In Soufriere Blackie sat down exhausted. They had ripped both the houses apart and found nothing. Beatrice too was frustrated, particularly when Blackie resorted to drink claiming it made him think better. She needed this treasure badly, very badly, and had found it hard to think of anything else since the midnight phone call. The Spaniard had convinced her that what he said was true by his knowledge of her grandmother's personal details. She stood up, glanced with distaste at Blackie, and went for her coat. It was time to find Rose and see what they had discovered.

Marigot Bay was moonlit and peaceful with the sky full of stars as they finished eating. "Lovely meal," said Rose taking the dishes down to the galley. "I'm impressed Bear. Now what have you found?"

"There's a long description of a football match and men called Salazar and Escobar," said Guy as they settled down. "I've still only got half way through, but it's pretty innocuous stuff. They talk a lot about taking walks together for instance."

"It's the same in your great grandfather's diary. We have to be missing something." Rose suggested. "Or looking in the wrong places, or for the wrong things."

"Could be," agreed Guy and then going off at a tangent asked her what had happened to her parents. "I have frequent nightmares about them." Rose told him sadly, looking at the coastline. "Let's change the subject; it's too painful for me."

She turned towards the sea dimly recalling memories of a childhood in south East Asia with her father. She had not really understood what had happened to them, but now perhaps it had significance, was it an accident or was it more sinister? She saw her father clearly in her dreams but perhaps now was the time to cleanse herself and put it behind her. "We're not getting very far with the diaries are we?" she said quickly, breaking her thoughts. "Not really," replied Guy, sensing her sadness. He reached down to an old large oak box. "What's that?" asked Rose. "It's an old compass," smiled Guy. "My father gave me it many years ago. I used it to learn to navigate with and have kept it ever since. I guess you could call it a family heirloom." Rose admired the silver inlay on the box. " It's beautiful," she said. "It must be very old" Guy smiled, "It is," he said. "Over two hundred years; my great-great-grandfather, Vincent's father was a sailor. Guess you could say it's what got me interested in sailing in the first place. Still prefer to use it than the GPS systems. It's made of brass with a glass dome and set in the oak box, very accurate, though it has a wide variance for magnetic north to real north." Rose looked puzzled. "What do you mean?" she said. "Your first navigation lesson," replied Guy. "True north is the curse of mariners world-wide, that and calculating longitude." He broke off realising that she was no longer paying attention to him. "What are you looking at?" he asked her. "There's something inside the compass dome," said Rose excitedly. "Look." Guy tried to see where she was pointing. "Where?" he asked her

Rose reached inside the dome and felt around below the graduation marks. Her small fingers managed to lift a small escutcheon plate next to magnetic north. "Good grief! I never realised that was loose!" cried Guy in amazement. "I saw it move," said Rose. She reached under again and managed to dislodge a small metal strip. After a great deal of manoeuvring, the strip came out of the compass. "That must have being there for years, probably why magnetic north has always being so far off," theorised Guy, still in shock. "Looks like it," agreed Rose. "The property of Jason Silver," she read out. She turned it over. "It has some cryptic words."

"What do they say?" Guy was intrigued. *"All Saints, Devils Isle, Rodney, Cockburn'* she read aloud.

"What on earth does that mean?"

"No idea," replied Rose with a shrug.

"I wonder how long that's been there."

"A long time, I would think, it must have come loose. Did you drop the compass recently?"

"It took a knock the other week," admitted Guy. "Knocked the radio to the floor and it hit the compass. When I was trying to fix it I dropped the wrench onto the compass and it fell sideways, that must have knocked the metal strip free."

"I wonder what Devils Isle means?"

"Got it," said Guy triumphantly. "Rodney is Rear Admiral Rodney, made his name here at the Battle of All Saints defeating the French."

"Devil's Isle and Cockburn?"

"Has to be an island with a British Admiral present but there's hundreds out here," said Guy thoughtfully and starting to yawn. "That wine is going to my head."

"Suggest we both sleep on it," said Rose also feeling sleepy, "must have been powerful wine."

That night the dreams came to both of them as the water lapped against the hull of *Hidalgo*. Rose had a vision of her father in the distance smiling at her as she tried to speak to him. She tossed, turned, and then lay awake thinking. Guy saw the familiar face of the enigmatic Chinaman frowning at him as he came closer. Unlike Rose, he settled into a deeper sleep and felt himself drifting into another world.

Across the water in Marigot Bay, a telescope jutted out from a large pleasure yacht called *Alcazabar*. It had no sails, instead holding two powerful diesels within its sleek lines. Matarife looked carefully at the scene on deck and then turned to a two-way radio. "They've found something," he barked.

"Time to move before we lose them," replied the disembodied voice of Salboa. "The trap has been set; do you know what you are doing?"

"I've spiked their drinks, so it should be safe to move over there in a little while and check the scene out," replied Matarife smugly. "Never did believe in taking chances."

"Very well," replied Salboa. "No mistakes.

CHAPTER 4

Bermuda
March 1895

It was a bright, clear morning after a very stormy night as James Silver stared contentedly ahead to the island of Bermuda. A self-proclaimed pirate, though never deliberately resorting to violence, he relaxed, letting the early sun dry his sodden clothes. His long yellow-grey hair flowed over his shoulders, blowing manically in the fresh wind. In his late fifties, he cut an incongruous figure in his red turtleneck jumper at the wheel of *Calypso*, a fifty-two foot sailing schooner. The waves increased in tempo and size as they approached the notorious Bermudian reefs, which had accounted for the demise of many ships over the last four hundred years. Silver, or 'Quick', to his colleagues was not concerned, as he knew these waters like the back of his hand.

Calypso was his whole life; a life he had spent touring the oceans always looking for the next cargo. His entire livelihood was here, on the boat, there was nothing else. Like many pirates, Silver had made and lost a fortune over the years. Only now, as he aged and felt the cold wind in his bones, did he yearn for a little extra capital to retire with when his sailing days were done. Three wives had come and gone; each taking most of the money he had accrued. Behind them were numerous offspring, now adults, of whose existence he had little idea. He needed money desperately, now, *Calypso* needed a refit because she was getting old, like him. Even his beloved compass and housing looked a little weather beaten and needed resetting.

The desperate need for cash was the reason he was undertaking this long journey from South Brazil to Bermuda with a new South American crew. In the hull, they carried fabrics from Uruguay and bales of cotton from Wilmington, North Carolina, which was his last stopping point. Silver had made his name running cotton for the Confederates in the American Civil War, helping them pay for armaments from their supporters in Bermuda. That is when the name 'Quick Silver' had stuck.

Nowadays he preferred just Silver; it fitted his appearance and suited him fine. Rumour had it that he had been involved back in

1812 in the British expedition from Bermuda to burn the White House. The tale was untrue, but Silver knew the power of legend and did nothing to dispel the myth. The Civil War work had been risky but very profitable, and he had maintained the trade after the war from grateful Carolinian's and Bermudian's. Now, he and *Calypso* were an anachronism, competing against bright young upstarts with their steam ships who could outrun him, unless the winds were favourable. He had no interest in this new technology and subsequently found himself fighting for trade others didn't want or relying on old relationships. It just about made him a living, not helped by an old and bitter rivalry that he was sharply reminded of as he neared the Bermudan capital of Hamilton.

Silver watched vigilantly as they made their way through the reef area, it took a skilled sailor to navigate without mishap, and it was essential to strictly adhere to the maritime charts. He remembered seeing an old chart of the island literally ringed with shipwrecks and was determined that *Calypso* would never join them.

The crewmen, shouting at each other on the rigging, broke his concentration. They were all handpicked; mostly from jails in the ports he visited. He found gratitude and the gift of freedom a powerful incentive to gain their loyalty. He trusted them all, with one exception, an elderly taciturn Chinese cook called Zhou Wang whose attitude was a problem, but Silver had to admit the man was a damned good cook. He had taken him on in Venezuela three weeks ago after his previous cook inexplicably deserted the ship. The added attraction of hiring Wang was that he bought five strong Chinese labourers with him to the crew. The downside was that, apart from Wang, Silver could not communicate with any of them. He spoke no Chinese, but sometimes wondered if the men just pretended not to be able to speak English. Either way, if he wanted to talk to any of the new Chinese seaman he had to do so either through Wang or in sign language. His trust in Zhou Wang was not improved when he discovered him conducting impromptu meetings and Silver became convinced that there was more to Wang than he was letting on.

In comparison, his second in command, a Uruguayan called Enrico, offered unswerving loyalty and would follow him to the ends of the earth. Silver had rescued Enrico from languishing in a stinking prison on a trumped up murder charge. "That damned

Spanish ship is there," shouted Enrico, who was on the bow-keeping lookout.

"Damn!" groaned Silver looking ahead. Next to the old naval dockyard on his right, he saw the familiar two-mast Spanish brigantine called *Christobel* at anchor. His nemesis Jose Salazar owned her, a devious and untrustworthy Spaniard, who had sparred with him for years. Like Silver, Salazar had built a business reputation around the Caribbean as a man not to be crossed. Rumour had it that he was connected to Spanish noblemen and Salazar did nothing to dispel the rumour that he had powerful friends. Many times the two sea captains had clashed, and now in his hour of greatest need, Silver needed his rival to be in Bermuda as much as he needed a dose of the clap. "How the hell did he get here so quickly?" Silver snarled and flung down his hat, his flowing grey hair catching in the wind.

At the same moment, over on the brigantine Jose Salazar was cursing as he saw the *Calypso*. "It's him," growled the Spaniard, "John Silver." Salazar's chief goal in life was to dominate the Europe to Latin America trading routes, which meant destroying Silver. Now, also in his late fifties, Salazar was ready to retire and enjoy his plundered treasures. Pleased that he had managed to beat his long-term enemy to Bermuda, he had been eager to depart before Silver arrived. Bermuda was an English island and Salazar was well aware that Silver would endeavour to make life tricky for him there, as indeed he did for Silver on Spanish Islands.

He turned to his crewmen and gestured over towards Silver on *Calypso*. Silver, watching, could easily see Salazar's movements, his long black coat and distinctive gait marking him out from the rest of the Spanish crew. Salazar had lost his leg over thirty years ago, and he blamed it on Silver. The story, now legend amongst sailors, was that both captains had once sailed unknown to each other, with prized cargoes of Argentinean beef to the States, both arriving at the same time. In exasperation, the American importer had told them to resolve it between them, as he only needed one cargo.

The answer had been a duel, alone in the early morning. Salazar had chosen guns and promptly missed Silver. In return, Silver had hit Salazar in the leg and walked away, leaving Salazar alone in an old warehouse. By the time someone found him, gangrene had set in and he lost both his leg and the cargo. What remained was a powerful desire for revenge that after thirty years Salazar believed he was on the verge of achieving.

Back on *Calypso* Silver cursed his rival, furious that he had docked in Bermuda. Salazar had a faster sailing ship and his prior arrival meant that he would have already sold to the best traders at prime prices, leaving him only the poorer trade. He had also heard a rumour that Salazar had pulled off a huge gold bullion robbery in Venezuela, making him even angrier. Silver knew that they were like two old dinosaurs driving the sailing ships into extinction whilst the new-fangled steam ships took over behind their backs, but he could not forgive Salazar for stealing his last wife. That had been some fifteen years ago and had cost Silver dearly. Juanita had been a feisty Brazilian with a love of money and had left him because he would not buy her a house.

The next thing he knew Salazar had taken her, along with all his savings. The only amusing thing was that she had since left Salazar taking all his money too. Still, it was an unforgivable insult that he needed to avenge. "Dammit to hell! Enrico, I've had enough of this, it's time to sort this bugger out!" Silver spat angrily. Enrico, a stocky and rugged looking man in his late forties, nodded dutifully. "It's time boss."

"Get Santos and Jacques on deck."

Silver nodded curtly to his crewmen Jacques, Enrico and Santos as they assembled on deck. Enrico Argent was the senior of the three, his powerfully built muscles betraying his time as a labourer in Uruguay. He was totally bald with a drooping moustache and arms like tree trunks, a great deputy to have in times of crisis as Silver had found on many occasions. The other two were mini versions but younger, all good to have alongside in a fight. "Bastardo," cursed the young Santos at the sight of Salazar and his crew. "This time we gullet him."

"No, not so obvious, the British garrison would make mincemeat of us with those guns. So whatever we do, it's legal, no knife work," replied Silver staring into the telescope.

"What do you propose?" Enrico frowned.

"I'm thinking." Silver rubbed his hand across his face.

"Boss, let me handle it at night," said Jacques Santos, a small wiry Brazilian. He had run away from a bungled bank robbery in Rio de Janeiro and was now the unofficial doctor on board. Supposedly, he had done some medical training, though Silver suspected his knowledge wasn't that great. Recently when Enrico had damaged his knee the cook Zhou Wang had known more than Santos.

Jacques was an itinerant Frenchman who claimed he was of noble descent, but had lived his entire life in Venezuela. He was thirty years old and an expert with the knife. Together they were a formidable team.

"No Santos, we handle this my way. Take her in."

"He's high in the water," grumbled Enrico as they sailed into the protected area of the Dockyard with the fort on the hill staring down malevolently at them on their right.

To their left was the island's prison building. "Judging by his waterline the bastard has already unloaded," stated Silver looking around. "Still there's a chance he hasn't sold the stock yet, Take us into the dock area Enrico I've an idea." They sailed slowly into the dock as the sunset ahead of them. Twenty minutes later they were alongside the quay busy unloading the cargo. Silver left the others and made his way to the garrison commander in the castle on the hill overlooking the dockyard. Naval works sprawled out below as he made his way up the hill to the fort.

Two large menacing guns pointed out towards the ocean. He knew it was a well-defended fort and effectively the British centre of naval operations for the western hemisphere. Only Antigua had a comparable naval base and that was well to the south.

"Jumped bail by God!" spat Captain Melrose a portly officious looking career soldier with long ginger side-whiskers. "Yes," muttered Silver. "Left Rio in a hurry having murdered a British citizen. I was told to look out for him, nasty piece of work by the name of Salazar, one leg."

"You sure?" growled Melrose a dour Scotsman.

"It's your chance to be a hero."

"You'd better be right," replied Melrose summoning his sergeant at arms. "Sergeant, bring four men at the double." He turned back to Silver, "Now, you sir, where do we find him?"

"The brigantine down in the dock. Judging by the waterline of his ship, he's sold his load and will be heading away soon. If he's not on board he'll be at the tavern Lady Anne." Silver inwardly smirked as he betrayed his enemy. "Come with me, I need identification," bellowed the Scot.

Jose Salazar was indeed at the "Lady Anne", his tall wiry frame and long weather beaten face looked as if it had been carved out of stone. He grimaced as he saw the soldiers enter and stood up trying to avoid drawing attention to himself. "There he is!" shouted Silver, pointing at Salazar. "Careful he's dangerous!"

"You!" growled Melrose pointing at Salazar. "A question if you please."

"Me?" replied Salazar looking up, his cold eyes boring into Silver, his goatee beard twitching and his yellow waistcoat a sharp contrast to his black coat in the gloom. "Whatever that man told you Captain, it's a lie."

"Were you wanted for murder in Brazil sir?"

"He's outdone himself this time," growled Salazar.

"Well were you?"

"Of course not."

"Your papers, passport."

"Here," replied Salazar staring stony faced at Silver.

"Your cargo manifest?"

"I've sold the goods but here is my original manifest," replied Salazar calmly handing the document across. "You'll see it's all in order."

"I can vouch for this man," said a small man pushing forwards. "Name is Brampton."

"I know who you are sir," replied Melrose coldly, "a trader. Well these appear to be in order. What have you to say Silver?"

"Means nothing, I tell you he's wanted for murder."

"I have no official notification of such an event," replied Melrose.

"Check his ship, I bet he's carrying guns," replied Silver.

"If you wish," replied Salazar smoothly looking malevolently at Silver, "this way."

Silver waited until Salazar and Melrose had disappeared outside then approached Brampton with Enrico. "Those bales of cotton you bought from Salazar are poor Spanish American quality. I can give you higher American quality at ten percent less."

"I made a deal," replied Brampton, a shrewd looking man. "He's Spanish and a crook," replied Silver. "I am an Englishman and prepared to offer you a better deal, twenty per cent off his price."

"Can I see the stock?"

"Yes, and you won't regret it," smiled Silver.

"I hope not."

"Let's celebrate with a drink to seal the bargain," smiled Silver.

An hour later, they emerged from the inn and approached the dockside warehouse where Jacques and Santos had been unloading from *Calypso*'s hull. Strange, thought Silver as he opened the warehouse door, there was no light and no one there. He lit the lamp and stared aghast. Santos and Jacques were on the floor tied up. Untying his men first, he ran back to *Calypso*. There was no sign of his cargo there either. Silver ran up on deck, staring around wildly and looking across to where he saw Salazar's brigantine slowly pulling away from the quayside. "What happened?" Silver demanded of the dazed crew as they staggered up behind him. "Attacked from behind," growled Santos groggily, "We'd just finished unloading into the warehouse."

"Damn Salazar. Where the hell was Captain Melrose?" Silver ran to the quayside. "Salazar! You bastard! What have you done with my stock?" he yelled across the water at the departing brigantine.

"Adios Silver! Hasta la vista! Until next time!" Salazar's triumphant voice echoed across the harbour.

"Sorry sir, but he has the deal, all paid for," said Brampton from the safety of the quay.

"You were in on this." Silver spun round, furious.

"I don't know what you mean." Brampton opened his eyes wide feigning innocence.

"I'll get you Salazar for this, if it's the last thing I ever do." Shaking his fist in the air, Silver yelled across to his enemy, who saluted him from the bridge of his boat. "All square, Englishman." Salazar called out and bowed in the Spanish fashion, then contemptuously turned his back on Silver.

"Bloody Captain Melrose, where is he?" shouted Silver turning angrily to see Captain Melrose walking up the gangplank. "He gave me the slip," growled Melrose. "He told me his papers were in the warehouse. Next thing I know they've locked me and my sergeant in there."

"He's taken my stock Captain. What the hell are you going to do, turn the damned guns on him?"

"They're not loaded," growled the Captain.

"And I suppose our gallant navy are not here?" Silver said in exasperation.

"They are on manoeuvres."

"Dammit man, he's ruined me."

"He must have planned the whole thing as we came in," growled Enrico. "Left his men to do the damage whilst we headed straight into their trap."

"We have to catch him," shouted Santos. "Quick, where's he heading?"

"Spain," growled Silver, "with my damned cargo. Where the hell were you Zhou Wang?" He turned on the Chef who had just arrived. "They locked me and my men in the galley, threatened us. Very interesting," continued the Cook joining them on the bridge.

"What's very bloody interesting?" yelled Silver.

"Heard his men talk about landing a valuable treasure on Bermuda."

"What? When?"

"Few days ago, many apologies Captain Silver, I overhear his crewmen talk of the treasure in whispers, they have deposited many valuables." Wang supplied, confidentially.

"Is that all?"

"We overheard them say it was well hidden in a place no one would ever find it, guarded by a strange man, a devil man."

"Then why sail away from Bermuda, doesn't make sense." growled Silver. "It does if the treasure was too hot to handle," said Enrico. "The Spanish gold stolen in Venezuela! It was him!"

Suddenly Silver was sure that the rumours he had heard were true, "Now he's got the perfect alibi, no-one would ever suspect he would leave treasure here in Bermuda."

"Do we go back to look?" asked Enrico.

"Needle in a haystack," growled Silver.

"So what do we do?"

"Catch the bastard and beat the living daylights out of him. He is taking my cargo to the European markets to sell. We should catch him, he's heavily laden, and we are not."

"One other thing Mr Silver," said Zhou Wang.

"Yes."

"I heard them talking about the Canary Islands. There's a new big job there, something that Salazar wouldn't even tell the crew about. They were speculating what it was."

"Interesting," replied Silver, looking again at the Chinaman.

"It's called the Columbus Cross and it is very special."

"What's special about it?" challenged Silver.

"I don't know, only that it has just come to light in the Canaries and is very valuable."

"How do you know all this Zhou," asked Silver suspiciously. "Salazar's men would not have discussed this with you or Salazar himself."

"I have my ways," replied the inscrutable Chinese man. "I suggest very strongly that you head there also. Ask no more questions Captain," Zhou Wang advised him quietly. "Just trust me."

An hour out of Bermuda, on low rations, it was clear that Salazar was maintaining a lead on them and heading southeast. "Can't gain on him, damn it," growled Silver, "We aren't provisioned to cross the Ocean. We can't go back to Bermuda, so we will have to go to Miami for cargo to fund the crossing and provisions. No doubt, the bugger is onto something big. Are you up for this, men?"

"Why will he stay over there?" asked Enrico. "To keep away from me and to look for this new conquest, whatever it is. Plus he will want to keep out of the Spanish Main for a while until the fuss in Venezuela dies down." Silver was thinking hard as they turned west to Florida. The one thing the men did not know was the likely location where Salazar would have hidden the doubloons on Bermuda. His old enemy had forgotten that Silver knew the island inside out.

Salazar smiled as he saw Silver turn away to the west. The man deserved what he got after the trick he had tried to pull in Bermuda. He was pretty confident Silver would not suspect he had left his treasure there. All he had to do now was wait until the furore died down and then return. Meantime he had something much bigger to concern him, something special, and something that would make his newly acquired treasure pale into insignificance. Salazar had picked up a rumour in Dominica of a fabulous treasure, the like of which had never been seen.

A Chinese man he had met at his local bar in Venezuela, before the gold robbery, had told him about something called the

Columbus Cross, the fabled lost treasure of Christopher Columbus. He was pretty sure that the rumour was genuine, after all none dare lie to the great Salazar, scourge of the Spanish Main. Records from a Spanish wreck recently discovered on Bermuda's reefs had contained information about the treasure, which survived Columbus's voyage back to the Old World. The records also stated that Columbus intended to leave the treasure in the Canaries, though no one knew why.

Salazar thought of his rapidly increasing wealth, the fortune in gold doubloons he had left in Bermuda and now the opportunity of finding this. With the Columbus Cross, he would be secure for life; they would be more than enough for a healthy retirement. In addition, he had Silver's cargo. His rival would not have any money left and would probably have to pawn his ship. He began to plan the treasure hunt for when they made landfall in the Canaries. It would need very careful planning indeed, as he still had a number of enemies in the Spanish homelands.

CHAPTER 5

The old tramp steamer made its way slowly up to the dock ramparts. Lady Victoria Skelton smiled condescendingly at the Captain as she made her way delicately forwards. A stately woman in her mid-forties she exuded the grace and confidence that came naturally to her English upper class upbringing. She had a trim figure and was dressed smartly in a light blue matching skirt and jacket. Her recently departed husband, Lord Harry Skelton, had been a British Diplomat serving in Buenos Aires. Unfortunately, he met with a sudden, violent death nearly a year ago during a hunting expedition in the jungle. They had been hunting for crocodiles when a small party of Argentinean natives had surprised and slaughtered them. It had been a tremendous shock to Victoria, not because of any feelings she had for the man, who was rather a remote figure, but because of the sudden loss of financial support.

Harry's father, Lord Skelton, had made his fortune in the railways, but Harry had preferred the Foreign Office, leaving his younger brother, George, to take charge of the family business. This meant that on the death of his father Harry inherited the title, but little money. Now, since Harry's demise, Victoria was forced to rely on handouts to support her daughter and herself from George Skelton, a dissolute and stingy man, who clearly felt that he was due something in return for his generosity. Fortunately, there was a small trust fund for her daughter, Veronique, but it still left Victoria in an invidious position.

Although Harry had managed to waste most of his money, leaving her virtually penniless, Victoria was armed with one secret, which she hoped, would change her fortune. It was, she was sure, related to her husband's sudden death, although she could not prove it. One of his contacts in the British Embassy in Buenos Aires was a lecherous old British officer called Francis Drampton. He was a drinking partner of her husband's and fancied Victoria, making it plain he would do anything to get her to marry him after Harry's death. He had told them both of a fabled treasure that had come to the attention of the Embassy, a jew-elled Cross that could destroy the Spanish empire. He then ap-peared to regret his indiscretion and swore them to secrecy, claiming that it would upset their Spanish colleagues. Harry had ignored this request and been blasé about it all, talking openly about the demise of the Spanish.

When his battered body, stripped of all his belongings, was re-turned, she became convinced there was a link between the secret and his death. The natives were blamed for the atrocity, but Victoria was very suspicious. Francis admitted that Harry had talked indiscreetly to the Spanish embassy, and that he was seen in the company of strange Chinese men the week before his death.

Francis was so besotted with Victoria that he said he was happy to help her find the treasure and claimed to have a map. The problem was he repulsed her, but that did not stop her accepting his offer of marriage or the sealed brass ornate box he entrusted to her. He told her that the secret location of the treasure, the Cross, was in the Canaries. The box had an inscription, in Spanish, showing it dated back to the sixteen-hundreds. Francis confided that there was a mystery surrounding how the British Embassy came to possess it. Desperate to see what was inside the box, Victoria finally managed to get a local locksmith to open it, revealing a small, sealed metal canister with an inscription. Unfortunately, so far she had been unable to open the canister but could read an inscription showing the name, 'Contessa de Bombadilla Las Canarias'.

Excited by what she had found so far, Victoria became concerned when Francis became the victim of mystery food poisoning, at one point hanging between life and death in an army hospital. Deciding it was time that she and her daughter escaped Buenos Aires she made plans to make her way to back to Europe and her family in England. Taking the brass box with her, Victoria hoped that Francis would understand her decision to go and find the treasure alone if and when he recovered. Francis did recover and reacted very badly to the loss of both his intended wife and the key to the treasure. He quickly made it known to everyone in Buenos Aires that she had stolen the item. Consequently, she was now on the run from the embassy staff, desperate to find an inconspicuous way home.

Miami docks stood before her and her daughter Veronique as they searched for a passage to Europe. Her insurance policy was a powerfully built hunk of a man called Norbert. He was her servant, an ex prize-fighter of limited intelligence, but loyal beyond question. He prided himself on his tough appearance and exhibited three teeth in his mouth, all pointing in different directions, which gave him a fearsome expression. He was very devoted to Victoria and Veronique, even though he had not received payment for months. Norbert's presence was the main reason that Victoria felt far more confident arriving in Miami than when she had left Argentina.

By lucky coincidence, though he later believed it was fate, Jack Silver pulled into the same Miami quay that day. He'd had a trouble free but sombre journey back from Bermuda, still seething over the latest debacle with Salazar. He desperately needed to find a cargo or some passengers to pay for the trip to Europe. He saw Victoria in the distance with Veronique both dressed in very fetching white linens. Tall with auburn hair, the latter was attracting attention from the stevedores at the docks. She strutted along smiling to herself oblivious of her mother's disapproving glare. "Good day ma'am." Silver swept off his hat in a low bow.

Victoria looked down at him imperiously and saw a grey haired, bearded man with a weather beaten face and worn clothing. Behind him, she saw the *Calypso* riding high in the water. "Good day sir," she replied making sure that Norbert was within range. "Would you be looking for transport, ma'am?" Silver questioned ingratiatingly. "Where are you going?" Victoria feigned little interest.

"Europe."

"I might be for the right deal."

"I'm sure we can find accommodation," smiled Silver. "Are there three of you?"

"Yes, I'm looking to go to some islands."

"Islands?"

"The Canaries."

"Why are you going there?" Silver did a double take; it was too much of a coincidence. "Personal business," her voice made it clear she wasn't intending to give more information. "I'll pay you a fair rate and I need to be discreet."

"Why?" he found it difficult to keep his voice level.

"As I told you, personal business, I can take my trade else-where."

"No, no, I'm sure we can come to an agreement."

"Well we are in luck," replied Victoria. "We may have a deal."

"Two hundred dollars for the two of you." Silver began, back on familiar bartering territory. "One hundred and fifty and you include my servant here." Victoria snapped back quickly. "One hundred and seventy." Silver calculated he would need at least half that for provisions. "That's more than I was prepared to pay," replied Victoria. "One hundred and sixty plus the servant works his passage. You'll be the only three passengers aside from the crew, cash now. We leave in two days," said Silver. Agreed," replied Victoria.

"Capital ma'am," replied Silver.

He turned to Enrico who was standing behind him now and smiled. "We'll be seeing Salazar sooner than you thought. Get the crew ready including the Chinese!" "Good," replied Enrico eyeing Norbert up and down. "What do you want me to do with the elephant?"

"Work him hard." Silver chuckled; pleased with the deal he had just struck.

"Wouldn't trust him as far as I could throw him," replied Norbert scowling. "I think you're being a little unfair," replied Veronique, eyeing up Silver's crew, particularly the handsome Jacques. She had become bored on the long voyage from Argentina and was looking forward to a change of scenery in Europe. There had to be more to life than the ridiculous 'wet behind the ears' suitors presented to her at the Embassy. Strikingly attractive with lustrous red hair and freckles that stood out when she became angry, Veronique's calm exterior belied a sharp mind and a spirit for adventure. At nearly six foot tall she was accustomed to dominating whomever she met, which amused her. Norbert grumbled to himself, he did not like the look of Silver and his crew. He had spent his life labouring on railroads and had won Victoria's trust to the level where he saw himself as her personal assistant. He turned to pick up the large trunk belonging to Victoria and Veronique.

Silver watched closely as Norbert carried the luggage towards the exit sweating profusely in the Miami humidity. Silently he nodded to Enrico who moved alongside, pretended to stumble, and then fell straight into Norbert, bringing the trunk and the man crashing down. The trunk broke open and a collection of clothes and books fell out. Silver strode forward to help.

"Let me." Norbert angrily picking things up growled angrily. "I can manage fine."

"I insist," said Silver, his eyes narrowing as they fell on the brass casket. "Looks expensive." He commented with studied care. "None of your damned business," replied Norbert trying to push the casket back into the trunk, before closing the lid. "Let me help you," grinned Enrico. "You deliberately pushed me," roared Norbert springing forward and grabbing at Enrico. "It was an accident," shouted Enrico, taking the opportunity to swing a punch and groaning as it connected with Norbert's head. It felt like he was hitting steel. "Put me down." Enrico screeched, suddenly realising he had been lifted off the ground. A second later, he was flying through the air before hitting a puddle of dirty water. "It appears your servant has a bad attitude," said Silver to Victoria. "He threw Enrico in the water."

"Self-defence ma'am," replied Norbert. "He tripped me."

"Do you have a problem Mr Silver?" asked Victoria.

"No,"

"Then we'll say no more of it. I think we now all understand each other."

"Very well, ma'am." replied Silver, bowing whilst watching Norbert disappear into the distance with the box. "Enrico follow them," he whispered to his dripping wet and scowling assistant. "You need to guard it with your life Norbert," said Victoria a safe distance away, remembering the way Silver had looked at the box. "Yes ma'am."

"Think you can handle him?"

"No problem ma'am."

"Good, then we will go to a small hotel I know of and have a look at the canister." An hour later, they sat in the Imperial Hotel, which had seen better days. "Leave it to me," said Norbert hammering the metal capsule carefully, "I think it's made of copper."

"Be careful." Victoria advised, whilst Veronique watched with interest.

"Ah ha," Norbert suddenly exclaimed as the tube suddenly split open. "Done it!" he shouted. "Is that it?" exclaimed Victoria in disappointment as a scrap of leather fell out. She opened the aged parchment; it was a single sheet written in Old Spanish. She delicately unwound the parchment and started to translate carefully. 'It talks of a gift for Columbus," she said slowly unsure of some of the words. "It says that the treasure was kept illegally by Columbus and hidden on an island."

"Which island?" asked Veronique, interested.

"One of the Canaries," replied Victoria. "It says a copy of this document has been sent to the King and Queen of Spain asking for the traitor Columbus to be arrested. The Spanish Governor in Buenos Aires wrote it. There is a separate note here from the head of the Catholic Church in Argentina saying that it is critical that it is found for the good of the Spanish Church and nation."

"Is there anything else?" asked Veronique.

"Just a small sketch of a land mass, an island and a well with some numbers," said Victoria disappointed. "It must be one of the Canary Islands."

Victoria brought out an old atlas from her trunk and looked at the drawing. She found the islands of the Canaries and looked at the outline on the letter. "It's there all right but which one?" she puzzled.

"Good day ma'am," smiled Silver the following morning, striding forward off the main deck. He was fully provisioned and ready. "Welcome to my humble ship, *Calypso*, your home for the next few weeks." Victoria, reluctantly taking his proffered hand and climbing aboard said a cool "Thank you". The man had indeed done a good job of tidying up the *Calypso*. Silver was anxious to please. "Is she to your satisfaction ma'am?"

"It will be adequate." Victoria replied haughtily. "Good, then there's only one last piece of business to discuss then we can be on our way."

"What's that?" asked Victoria carefully. "The casket ma'am, it has to be guarded. My men saw it and I cannot vouch for its security if you don't store it in the ships safe." "What is it you want of me Mr Silver?"

"James, please. To help you ma'am and a suitable reward at the end is all I ask." Silver was eager to appear helpful, Enrico had heard enough through their hotel room door for Silver to know he was onto something. "Perhaps I do have something valuable." Victoria faltered, unsure whether to trust the man before her, "I'm sure you will protect me, but I will personally look after my valuables and hold you accountable for their safety."

"It would help if I knew more," replied Silver showing the way to his own cabin. "Norbert is downstairs with the crew; you two have my own cabin."

"Thank you, but I will decide if and when I need your help." Victoria responded haughtily, before swiftly changing the subject, "Where do we sail for?"

"Tenerife, I have an appointment there with an old friend. It's the largest of the Canary Islands."

"Very well."

Silver watched her; this was going to be a very interesting trip as she was clearly hiding something.

What he did not notice was the silent shadow of Zhou Wang, smiling serenely to himself in the corner of the passageway. The Chinese cook was a great believer in fate; it was his fate to be here, part of his destiny already mapped out. He walked slowly to the stern of *Calypso* and summoned his Chinese colleagues, his followers. There would be more soon, of that he was sure. He bent down and whispered carefully to them all. After about five minutes of whispered conversation, he straightened up. "Now go forward all of you and make sure you are ready. The destiny of our homeland is in your hands." They all nodded with solemn eyes. "We meet here every two days. I expect you all to observe what you have been told to observe and be ready with your allotted tasks." Zhou Wang smiled coldly to himself. He was at last coming to the nadir of his travels. He had spent years waiting for this moment.

Silver's final preparations had been more stringent than normal, ensuring that *Calypso* was sound and urging Zhou Wang to ensure there was sufficient food. He believed that this was his final voyage, his last chance to raise some money before *Calypso* became a relic of a bygone age. She needed major refurbishment and he could see that this life was over; he even had a nice home earmarked in Bermuda. They cast off on the evening tide with the two females ensconced in his cabin. Victoria and her daughter needed taking down a peg or two, but mused Silver, time, and some rough sailing would soon sort them out.

━━━━━━━━

69

Victoria and Veronique slowly gained their bearings as *Calypso* caught the evening swell. The ship was smaller than they were used to, but it was with a degree of excitement that they watched the Americas slip away and Miami docks recede into the distance. For Victoria it was the chance to put America behind her after twenty years, for Veronique it was a new start. She was an extrovert character whose life so far had been unutterably boring, filled with rounds of dances and insufferable men in fancy clothes talking of banks and business. She was shrewd enough to know that these men only wanted her as a trophy wife, not for who she was. What Veronique really longed for was adventure, the chance to do something different and come into some real money. Like her mother, she had no time for her uncle, George Skelton, and had once caught him looking in the window when she had been changing. She had seen the lascivious look on his face as he gazed at her unpinned red hair and pale skin.

On the first full day on board there was a clear blue sky so Veronique found a small sun deck outside the cabin and lay out in the early morning sun, taking care to adjust her blouse to let the sun's rays warm her. She stared up at the billowing sails and smiled to herself as out of the corner of her eye she caught Jacques staring hard. Although life at the embassy had been sheltered, she was old enough to know how to use her body to her advantage. She smiled over at Jacques, "I don't bite." She assured him. "Yes ma'am." He formally answered, avoiding looking at her directly. "Where are you from, Jacques?"

"Brazil ma'am."

"You can call me Veronique," she smiled.

"Yes, ma'am, I mean Veronique." Jacques stuttered, clearly embarrassed.

"I'd like us to become friends," she smiled at the boy. She had him hooked.

"Cable for you sir," said Enrico handing over a flimsy piece of paper. "Thanks," said Silver looking at the darkening horizon. The barometer was dropping slowly. "We're in for a blow, slacken the main sails and tell the others." He glanced at the paper and grunted. It was from his first wife in England. He had cabled her a week ago to let her know he was heading for Europe. Jane had been an English girl just out of college and living with her parents in Miami when she had fallen for Silver's rakish charms and eloped. It had not been long before she tired of his wandering lifestyle and left him, but not before she was pregnant with a son called Vincent whom he had never met. Jane had gone on to marry a barrister in English society who had given their son, who would now be in his twenties, a privileged upbringing. As he had no contact with his son Silver was surprised and pleased to read the curt note from Jane. "Vincent will meet you in Santa Cruz Tenerife." The wind was blowing strongly now as he set a course south of Bermuda, taking care to sail well south of the treacherous reefs around the island. He was in a good and expansive mood, on the seas, on his ship, in his own world that he understood. At this pace, Silver reckoned that they would be in Santa Cruz within the week, though it may be a journey devoid of comfort for the ladies.

Cambridge University, England
April 1895

Vincent Silver sat in his room relaxing after a ten-mile early morning run. Twenty-three years old, tall, blonde and smart, he was the total opposite of his father. Well ahead of his time in understanding the need to look after his body with the right food and frequent exercise, he avoided alcohol and smoking, instead pursuing a rigid fitness regime every day. He had just that week finished his exams and was moving to the City to study Law. He had contemplated a year out first but was persuaded by his mother to go straight to a job his stepfather had arranged for him in his own Law firm. His future was laid out for him, yet he had an urge to do something different. When his mother had shown him the cable from his father, he had reacted. "I need to see him mother."

"He's a waster, you will be very disappointed." Jane was not impressed by Silver's lifestyle, making her disapproval clear. "Perhaps, but I need to see him. You must understand that." Jane trying to avoid painful memories said stoically. "He won't help you," Everything had seemed so straightforward until the damned cable. She should not have shown Vincent but it was too late now. "It's only natural for you to see him, but he will be a grave disappointment to you Vincent."

"Why's that?"

"He's a rogue and a drunken halfwit."

"You married him."

"I was young." Jane responded, trying to forget the excitement leading up to their wedding.

"He's my father."

"I can't stop you, but don't let your stepfather Stanley down. Why don't you go to Europe with your friends?" Jane suggested in desperation. "I'll take them to Spain instead," grinned Vincent. "You're impossible." his mother said with an indulgent smile.

This was what he wanted, adventure with a father he had never met. He had a Cambridge blue at University for rowing and played for the rugby and emerging football teams as well as consistently winning the hundred yards sprint. His first class degree in law ensured that he would have the pick of whatever career he sought. "There's a group of colleagues I play football with, we were thinking of touring Europe to show the foreigners how to play the English game."

"Then you are indeed fortunate," replied Jane, "just don't expect much from your father he has a habit of letting people down."

What he didn't tell his mother was the amount of football he played. The fledgling football club, the Cambridge Cubs, had instigated association football at the University, much to the disgust of the authorities. The game was new, but did not have the social status of rugby. Unable to find eleven players they made do with five and become part of an inaugural local league. They had beaten all-comers and most important of all had beaten Oxford University. They had even started charging a penny for people to see them play, particularly when they played the semi-professional and tough northern teams. His best friend, Jack Darkson, was the team captain, Reggie Pline, a devoted theology student, was goalkeeper and the key striker was George Akinbus. George was a South African who had the most amazing pace and was the first black man to study at Cambridge.

Victoria groaned as the *Calypso* rode heavily in the waves. The weather had worsened considerably and both Veronique and she had been seasick. She had forgotten how small and uncomfortable it was riding in these small ships. "Having problems?" smiled Silver as he met her and Veronique in the communal area. "You expect us to sail across the Atlantic in this tub, it's horrible," growled Veronique her face drained of all colour. "Miss, she's more than adequate. And just make sure if you are sick that the wind is behind you." Silver doffed his hat.

"Despicable man," snapped Veronique fed up with the daily shipboard routine and wishing she could get her feet on terra firma. Trying to keep looking decent was impossible and she was tiring of the look of adulation in Jacques eyes. Worst of all was the constant nausea; she could not keep her food down. "Our cabin is too small," she groaned to Silver as he retreated.

"Not as small as mine ma'am. Don't worry, when you've found your treasure you can afford to live in real luxury."

"Makes me remember why I don't want to get married again," he whispered privately to Enrico. He turned to Norbert who had been hovering, "If you have nothing better to do help Zhou Wang in the galley."

"I don't work for you," growled Norbert staring at Silver. "You do for now," said Silver walking away. "He can't speak to me like that," complained Norbert, turning to Victoria. for support. "Humour him," replied Victoria quickly.

"They'll just disappear when we arrive, unless we have something they want," muttered Silver to Enrico. "We need to find a hook to dangle them from; they have all the aces at the moment." He looked at the dark sky. The weather was easing and he was beginning to have his doubts about what he would find in Tenerife. He watched proudly as more sails were unleashed; no one could find a wind like he could. There was a shout and Jacques came over waving a piece of paper. Silver clenched the grubby telegram; it was confirmation from Jane that Vincent was on his way to Tenerife with some colleagues. "Enrico, my son, Vincent, is meeting us in Tenerife with some friends from college."

"Fantastic Captain. Now we have a chance, an army."

"Fight Salazar on his own ground you mean," said Silver pointing the *Calypso* further into the wind. The sails tightened and she plunged into the surf.

"This is no job for a man like me," grumbled Norbert staring at Zhou Wang as he lifted the bucket of potato peelings. "Things will change. "The old man told him quietly. "What do you mean?" asked Norbert glaring him. "It's just a Chinese saying; things will always improve when they look their darkest."

The weather improved and Veronique decided it was time to toy with Jacques again; she needed all the men wrapped around her finger. She called to Jacques and then reclined in her chair facing the sun. "I wonder if you could get me a cold drink, please." The sun was fierce in the sky and she was feeling hot and mischievous. She saw Santos staring at her in the distance. "Jacques, I wonder if you could help me with my dress." She let the top slip and smiled as Jacques eyes widened. They were like putty in her hands she thought; she tightened her blouse as Silver approached. "Cover yourself, woman. We've just sighted land and it's time for a talk with you and your mother."

CHAPTER 6

Santa Cruz, Tenerife,
early May 1895.

The island's capital town, Santa Cruz, looked much as it did a hundred years earlier when a young Captain Horatio Nelson had attacked it and promptly lost his left arm in the battle. The twenty-pound El Tigre Cannon that stood looking over the castle rampart proudly claimed to be the same one that nearly finished the young British Captain. The current Governor of this island paradise was a fat, bald and corpulent man called Escobar. Extremely ambitious and ruthless, Escobar enjoyed exercising his power over the people of Tenerife in this backwater posting. He modelled himself on Napoleon Bonaparte, even walking around the island's capital emulating his hero with his hat square across his face the French way. Most of the time he surveyed the bustling port from his palatial villa near the main government building at Palacio Carta.

In truth he was an ordinary man, with an ordinary career in the Spanish navy, the younger son of a previously wealthy Andalusia family who had made their fortune at the expense of the Moors hundreds of years ago. Unfortunately for Escobar he had two elder brothers who, on their parent's early death, 'looked after' the fortune leaving little for him but a career in the armed forces or priesthood. Choosing the former, little action had come his way and he had finished service as a clerk in a Madrid army quartermaster store. His big break came when he found Marietta, the domineering and very plain daughter of a well-connected and wealthy diplomat. Things improved following their marriage, thanks to her father's patronage, and he transferred to the diplomatic service, eventually resulting in his appointment as Governor of Tenerife.

As soon as his wife, Marietta, had outlived her usefulness in furthering his career, Escobar took to having affairs with subordinate's wives. In addition, he now used his position to line his pockets with protection money. This lucrative extortion led him to a gambling addiction, and he ran up huge debts, successfully managing to lose most of his wife's fortune along the way. Marietta threatened to leave him and return to her father many times, but on balance had decided that the social status she enjoyed as the wife of the Governor was too good to throw away. Therefore, she stayed, dutiful but resentful, bitter and angry.

As Escobar's methods of extortion became more and more unpopular, he realised that he would have find new ways to raise money. So, he became subtler in his collections, using his power and status as the Kings trusted emissary to exhort money with menaces. This raised cash, but it was never enough, as he was still liable to throw good money after bad in a moment of gambling madness. Much worse was the news from Spain where his hapless brothers declared bankruptcy, the family fortune lost in less than one generation. Escobar believed it was down to him to recover not just the money but also the honour of his family name.

What his finances really needed was a big break, something that would give him sufficient independence from his wife and her family. He brooded long and hard, relying heavily on increased taxes on the burgeoning export business of wine and cactus plants, knowing that their trade was dependent on his patronage and quickly making himself vastly unpopular. The winegrowers and cactus plant farmers reluctantly paid their taxes, convinced that the governance of Tenerife would soon be changing, as the surrounding islands agitated for independence.

As Governor of Tenerife, Escobar had a small militia of thirty men at his command, to keep order across the islands. One in particular was proving a headache. La Gomera was by far the richest island, after Tenerife, principally due to a very large cactus and wine export trade. The hillsides of the island, though more rocky and hilly than Tenerife, had been perfectly landscaped for vineyards and cactus plantations. It was to this hilly island that Escobar had sent twenty of his militiamen the previous month to repel a tax revolt that occupied the capital town, San Sebastian. Surrounded by steep hills, the insurgent peasants had withdrawn there, closed down the water supply, and put large rocks across the roads effectively blocking the routes into and out of the town. Whenever a soldier headed up the hill, he was shot at from hidden recesses.

It was guerrilla warfare of the type invented by Wellington and the Spanish in the Peninsular War of Napoleonic times.

More puzzling, the locals appeared to have support from a mysterious monastery high up in the Garajonay Mountains. Escobar knew of the place only because his men spoke fearfully of its mystical qualities. He heard that they called it '*Fortaleza Hidalgo*', literally the noble fortress, and he could not understand their reaction to the monks. They refused to go anywhere near the place, even disobeying direct orders, after two soldiers had ventured high up in the mountains and never returned. Escobar cursed their superstitious nature and swore to one-day get even with the monastery.

However, for now he was going to have to put aside his animosity towards the monastery and negotiate a truce with the peasants, particularly having lost six more men. A brute of a man called Raul Servas met him on board his own yacht off the southern Tenerife fishing village of Los Christianos. Servas was a hardbitten local with few words of Spanish, not a man to be trifled with. Following extensive talks, and a considerable amount of money and drink, Escobar convinced the man to conclude peace on certain terms, rather than continue the fight. Escobar agreed that the tax that islanders paid would be set in San Sebastian, and in return, Servas agreed to an alliance where they could both siphon off tax profits from the local businesses.

The lands around San Sebastian were historic and owned by local families, but the hills were relatively cheap and strategic. Escobar realised that if he could get control of those then he effectively controlled the economy of the island, and thanks to Servas support, the islanders were prepared to sell their land. All Escobar needed now was cash for the purchases and a front man who could take control of La Gomera under his guidance. It was with considerable relief therefore when a greasy haired, one-legged adventurer called Salazar appeared in town with plenty of money.

Salazar had arrived the week before from Bermuda and was immediately befriended by the Governor. A good judge of character, Salazar saw in Escobar a fellow adventurer and crook, exactly what he was looking for in his greatest venture. Having left a trail of havoc through most of the Spanish colonies in South America, he was on the trail of the greatest treasure ever. He needed a good ally, someone who could ensure he found the Columbus treasure sooner rather than later, and decided that

Escobar was exactly what he was looking for. The quest to find the treasure had started well as he had soon realized that the likely place for the Columbus treasure was La Gomera. With Escobar's help, he had quickly disposed of Silver's cargo for a good price and happened to mention his interest in La Gomera from an investment point of view. Escobar nearly bit his hand off, offering prime estate outside the capital, San Sebastian. The only problem was that Escobar was selling the mountainous parts, which Salazar thought was probably not where the treasure was hidden. Still, as Salazar had no intention of actually paying for the land he confidently handed over a large promissory note. As far as he was concerned, he would be long gone by the time the stupid Governor realised it was worthless. In the meantime, the bogus sale gave him a good reason to search San Sebastian with a fine-tooth comb.

Cursing to himself, he manoeuvred his false leg painfully; the long sea voyage had not done him much good and all being well he was hoping to retire after this. Frustratingly, he was stuck for a week in Tenerife as the Governor arranged for the interminable paperwork for the land purchase. Trying to relieve the boredom productively, he bought an old book on Columbus and read up on the explorer. The more he read, the more he realised that this search was for far more than treasure, once found it could have devastating implications. Such thoughts kept him humoured as the rest of the crew of the *Christobel* sailed over to the island to meet him. He resided in a rented villa in Santa Cruz, telling the Governor he wanted to settle on the island after his wanderings. In return, he was introduced into Tenerife society and Escobar's inner circle, his tales of piracy impressing everyone, even Marietta.

Following yet another night of drinking and gambling with Escobar, Salazar was ensconced with some of Escobar's cronies playing poker when Felipe his second in command burst in. *"The Calypso,"* he shouted. "Impossible! How the hell did they get here so quickly?" Shouted Salazar dropping the cards and cursing Felipe before shouting for transport. He rushed down to the docks to see the dreaded *Calypso* manoeuvring past the outer buoys. "I'm going to the Paso Alto Castle." he shouted to his men. "I will make them get the damn cannons out!"

"You have no authority," replied the Captain of the fort an old and grizzled veteran.

"The Governor will have your head if you don't fire on that ship," roared Salazar staring past the El Tigre cannon. "I need official orders."

"Get to the ship and get the cannons out," Salazar roared in frustration to the long-suffering Felipe, who immediately ran back to the *Christobel*. Salazar grabbed a telescope and cursed the Captain as he watched the scene unfold. If Felipe could be quick, they might be able to sink the damned *Calypso* yet. After a frustrating wait, there was a satisfying roar and Salazar smirked as he heard the main cannons firing, "Now let's see what you are made of Silver."

Onboard *Calypso* Silver looked grim as water spouted near to his port side. "I can't believe he just did that," he growled to Enrico, "Tighten the sail, and let's pray this wind holds." The next shot missed entirely as Silver deftly spun her hard to port. "We'll get the better of them yet, that was poor shooting!" he crowed. "What do you want me to do boss?" asked Enrico. "Take the wheel and head straight for him, we'll get under the range of his guns that way. He's too busy firing to notice the wind," replied Silver thoughtfully.

Salazar saw what was happening from his post at the castle. "Dammit the bugger is going to ram us," he roared. "Captain you've got to do something, my ship will be ruined." He was impotent with rage but there was nothing he could do but watch.

"Way I see it, he's acting in self-defence," replied the Captain who had taken a huge dislike to Salazar. "You can't let this happen," roared Salazar, going red in the face. The *Calypso* was getting closer and closer. "I'll have you stripped of your rank."

"Well done Enrico!" grinned Silver, as the bow approached the older brigantine. He was under their guns now. "Brace yourselves everyone!" He shouted. With a satisfying crash, he felt the bow of the *Calypso* rip into the side of the brigantine. He heard the timbers crunch and hoped the *Calypso* would hold firm. To his satisfaction, the prow broke straight through the side of the Spanish ship and he saw Spaniards jumping to safety overboard. "Well done Enrico, hard to starboard and get the wind behind us to pull away, don't want to get entangled."

Turning back Silver looked thoughtfully at the abandoned Brigantine; he thought the collision had broken her moorings. He ignored the shouts from behind him as the women tried to move forward to see what was happening. "Come on, come on," he pleaded with the *Calypso*. Slowly he heard the groaning of broken timbers and then the tell-tale movement of the ship. She was pulling free. Slowly *Calypso* pulled away and Silver checked the prow but could see only superficial damage. "Well done Enrico, that made the journey worthwhile."

"Surely you're going to help them, they're sinking," said a shocked voice beside him. Victoria. "Just teaching the bastard a lesson ma'am, that's all. He got my cargo, I got his ship. He'll be stuck now for a while." Silver could not keep the glee out of his voice. "Surely you can't do this," said Victoria. "He stole my cargo ma'am. Ruined me. Now, out of my way," he grabbed the wheel and steered tighter into the wind gaining speed. "We're going in to see how the old bastard feels about being on the receiving end."

An hour later, they drifted into the harbour and Silver ordered the men to dock. "Be ready to repel borders," he yelled. "I guess the grease ball won't like what we did." He smiled as he saw a furious Salazar and five of his men storming down to the jetty. "Looks like we've got company; Enrico, Santos, Jacques get the guns and be ready to repel boarders!"

"You will die for this Silver," yelled an apoplectic Salazar.

"Self-defence Salazar, you shouldn't have fired."

"You've ruined my ship, you'll pay for this."

"An accident at sea, these things happen." smiled Silver. "My crewman is still learning the art of seamanship. Damn clumsy of him, but what can you do?" he replied shrugging his shoulders. "Captain! I want this man arrested," shouted Salazar turning to a man behind in uniform. Silver groaned, he had not noticed the army. "Not until I understand what is going on here," replied the soldier. He moved six men forward with rifles raised. "You two Captains I want you both down here with me now or we will come and get you."

Escobar hammered on his desk for silence as Salazar started to launch into yet another frenzied explanation of why they must arrest Silver. They were in the small courthouse building where Silver and Salazar stood in front of the seated Escobar. Salazar red in the face bristled with indignation as he pointed to the harbour and the damaged *Christobel*, now starting to tilt at an alarming angle. "Arrest him for criminal damage." Escobar would not be rushed in his own courthouse. "I give the orders here." He said coldly, "Now, Captain Silver, perhaps you would care to explain how this 'accident', as you call, it happened?"

"It was no damned accident," shouted Salazar.

"The man was firing his guns at me," replied Silver quietly. "What else could I do but fire back in self-defence? Incidentally, Salazar, I suggest your men start seeing to her or she'll go down in the harbour and block my way out."

"We can't have the port blocked for trade," agreed Escobar, "see to it Salazar." The Spaniard swore under his breath as he turned to Felipe. The small man sped away. "Let me know if I can help," smiled Silver.

"I'll see you in hell for this Silver," snarled Salazar.

"Perhaps, but you'll be there first," replied Silver.

"Enough!" shouted Escobar, determined to maintain his authority and be seen to dispense justice. Salazar had opened fire that was unforgivable.

There was a commotion at the door, Escobar raised his eyebrows as Victoria, and Veronique walked in. "I can vouch for what Mr Silver says," said Victoria in her most imperious voice. "That man fired at us for no reason. It was very dangerous, though I don't condone what happened next. Incidentally, I am Lady Victoria Skelton."

"Why did you fire Salazar?" asked Escobar, clearly impressed by the presence of a peer of the British realm. "He is a criminal, arrested in Bermuda, who escaped. I was doing my duty." Yelled Salazar, seeing the effect the women were having on Escobar. "If I was 'escaping the law' as you say, why would I travel here with this lady as a passenger? It is you who is the criminal, Salazar for stealing my cargo."

"Madam, can you vouch for Mr Silver?" asked Escobar his eyes staring hard at Victoria wondering whether she could become another of his conquests. "I've no idea what he did before I met him and don't want to know," replied Victoria. "However, I will say that he has behaved as a gentleman coming over here. I doubt what Salazar says is true."

"Monstrous!" snarled Salazar. "Are you going to take the word of a woman who is in league with this criminal in front of a Spanish gentleman?"

"A gentleman wouldn't fire at unarmed ships," replied Silver, "leaving me no alternative but to take the action I did." Escobar stood up. "Enough," he said angrily. "My judgement is that this was an unlawful exchange. Any further breaches of the peace and you will both be flung into prison. Do I make myself clear?"

"A word in private please," snapped Salazar.

"Approach the bench," growled Escobar revelling in his power.

"I have purchased the lands in La Gomera. You believe the words of a stranger over my own. I demand that you lock him up."

"I'm afraid not senor. Tell me, Mr Silver, why have you come to these islands? You must have known Senor Salazar was here and it's plain you two have a history."

"That is private business. Last time I checked I believe Spain was a free country. I do not have to declare my plans," replied Silver grandly.

"You do when there is a breach of the peace or would you rather tell me from prison, senor?"

"I am here to transport two ladies from Miami back to England. We stopped here to take on water and refreshments."

"You are well off the routes from Miami to England. Tell me madam why you and your daughter are here?"

"Private business." Victoria responded haughtily.

"Which would be?" Escobar was clearly losing patience.

"Oh, please tell the man mother," said Veronique in exasperation.

"Veronique!"

"Tell me what?" the bullish Governor was quick to notice the tensions between the two women.

"We are here on a private quest to retrieve something that used to belong to our family," said Victoria glancing hard at Veronique.

"Could you enlighten me further?"

"No we could not," replied Victoria.

"Why don't you ask Salazar why he is here," demanded Silver moving forwards. "Or is it a different law for the locals? Never mind I'll tell you. He has come here because he's heard of a vast treasure waiting to be discovered. He thinks he has the inside track on where this treasure is located and doesn't want the rest of us to stop him. Am I right, senor?"

"Don't know what you are talking about," replied Salazar quickly.

"Resolve your petty quarrels without involving myself or my officials," snarled Escobar. "Senor Salazar perhaps you'd reply to this accusation. Have you found a treasure here?"

"Of course not, the man is delusional."

"Has this anything to do with buying land on La Gomera?"

"Ah ha!" exclaimed Silver. "That's where the Columbus treasure lies." He looked across at Victoria. "It is common knowledge that Columbus spent time at La Gomera," shrugged Salazar. "So you don't know exactly where it is and now I've ruined your transport. Gives you a problem if others know the location?" taunted Silver.

"What do you mean?"

"Perhaps the lady knows where it is."

"You lie," growled Salazar looking across at Victoria.

"Tell me more," asked Escobar intrigued. "May I remind you all that no-one can look for treasure in these islands without my permission?"

"A gentleman keeps secrets," sneered Victoria looking at Silver. "Very well I'll tell you what I know." This was not going the way she wanted. "The treasure is reputed to have been stolen by Columbus from the Spanish crown and left here in the Canaries."

"I heard of it in Bermuda, it was common gossip along the waterfront. Even this thug probably knows of it," snarled Salazar.

"What is so significant about this so called treasure," asked Escobar slowly. "Perhaps someone can enlighten me."

"It's just a treasure," said Victoria puzzled, "and I struggle to see how Mr. Salazar can claim any rights."

"What do you say to that Salazar?"

"I have my own information," replied Salazar slowly.

"So two of you claim ownership and rights to something as yet unfound," said Escobar.

"It's been rumoured to exist for many years but no proof exists. Unless the good lady here knows more," snarled Salazar.

"Do you really think I would tell you?" Victoria said tartly.

"I cannot allow people to look for treasure without the government being aware," replied Escobar carefully. "I will not allow either of you to enter the island unless you tell me more."

"In private," replied Victoria stiffly.

"Very well," said Escobar beckoning her forwards. He smelled her perfume and thought again about how he could manoeuvre her into his confidence.

"As Salazar said it lies on the island of La Gomera," whispered Victoria stiffly "but I have a detailed map of the exact location."

"Where is this map?"

"Hidden and will stay that way until we get there, but the location is on the island. I believe that gives me certain rights."

"Should you find it then of course you have rights, providing you pay government tax and it is not deemed to be of intrinsic value to the Spanish government."

"Fair enough."

"If you have anything else you wish to confide I will be only too happy to oblige," he replied obsequiously.

"I own two thirds of the surrounding land," stated Salazar as Escobar lifted his head.

"Technically yes, but irrelevant as it would be government property."

"Don't you think we should wait until we have found this treasure?" said Silver injecting a tone of realism into the conversation. "It may be that it's not here after all and then we will all have wasted a great deal of time."

"We have to establish up front the legal rights should it become reality," said Escobar pompously.

"So we have a standoff," replied Salazar. "You sir, claim the legal position, madam claims to have knowledge of the location and I have ownership of the land. Meanwhile," he said with distaste looking at Silver, "you sir, have no role whatsoever and should be asked to leave."

"Not while I am here he doesn't" replied Victoria forcibly.

"As you say it's a standoff," said Escobar, "and one that calls for more thought. The big problem is that you will all end up fighting and people will get hurt. That I cannot allow. If there is any bloodshed then I will act severely. Do I make myself clear?"

"Could I ask for five minutes recess," asked Silver. "I wish to confer with the good lady."

"Very well," replied Escobar looking across at the scowling Salazar.

"We have a problem," whispered Silver. "It's clear that whatever you do they will follow and claim ownership."

"So what do you suggest?"

"Subterfuge is the only way ultimately but in the meantime we need to get them believing we are playing by the rules. Get everything on the table so to speak. I believe a competition would achieve that, where we can beat them fairly and squarely, whilst making sure the odds are in our favour. Even then, Escobar and Salazar will try every trick in the book, so we need to get a clear statement on the winner's rights. Incidentally, the Governor has his eyes set on you, he's after you ma'am."

"You think I don't know that? I can handle him, believe me!"

"Good."

"So what do you suggest we do?"

"Leave it to me." Silver turned as he noticed a movement to his right and frowned in puzzlement as he saw his cook Zhou Wang enter the room. What the hell was he doing here? "I have a suggestion to take this forward without bloodshed," he said putting the Chinaman out of his mind.

"And what would that be?" asked Escobar.

"A competition, a trial without bloodshed and the winner gets the right to find and take the treasure unmolested. Recognising, of course, that the Governor here will receive an appropriate tax, the winner gets whatever treasure there is."

"And why should I trust you?" asked Salazar.

"Because the forfeit, if anyone cheats, will be to stay on the island working for the government for one year." Silver said thoughtfully.

"Two years," said Escobar liking the idea.

"One year is enough; besides if there's no treasure you can wash your hands of the whole thing."

"Perhaps," replied Escobar grudgingly.

"I'm not taking part in any competition with him until he pays for my boat," snarled Salazar.

"Use my stolen cargo to pay for it," replied Silver calmly.

"I agree to the idea," announced Escobar. "We need to agree on a suitable competition."

"A game of poker," prompted Silver.

"You will cheat like a dog," snarled Salazar.

"Enough," shouted Escobar. "I like the idea of a competition, but it should be a physical challenge that is won by skill and prowess."

"A race," suggested Victoria.

"Sailing race," replied Silver thinking of the state of Salazar's ship.

"Physical contact, I said." replied Escobar.

"I wonder if I may speak?" asked Zhou Wang stepping forward.

"What the hell are you doing here Zhou?" growled Silver.

"As of now I no longer work for you or take your orders," replied Zhou. "You have fulfilled your usefulness to me."

"Why you," Silver stepped forwards angrily but something in the Chinese man's eyes stopped him from going further.

"In my land, the only way to resolve these things is by honourable combat."

"Which would be?" asked Escobar.

"Unarmed combat; martial arts, as taught by my countrymen, with each of you fighting against the other. I also register the right of the Chinese here to take part."

"What rights have you got?" snarled Silver.

"The right of knowing everything you do, and more," replied Zhou Wang enigmatically. "In fact none of you would be here in the first place or indeed will leave these islands alive without my say so."

"I could have you arrested for such statements," snarled Escobar beckoning to the guard.

"But you won't because I have knowledge you need. It is I who spread the news to all of you that this Columbus Cross existed; it is I who made sure you all came to this place."

"What are you talking about?" shouted Salazar.

"I don't believe it," shouted Silver forgetting the others. "All this time I looked after you and you've being scheming behind my back. My men…"

"Your men will do nothing Silver. As we speak, they are under the control of my Chinese colleagues and will remain so until I leave here unharmed. I alone know the challenges that are faced and the real value of this treasure. You are my pawns and will do as I say."

"I can't believe it," growled Salazar eyeing the man suspiciously.

"Perhaps not," replied Escobar coldly, "but you are on dangerous ground, Wang. What's to stop me arresting you now?"

"You will never find the treasure for your debts, or learn the secret of the noble monastery."

"The what?" asked Salazar.

"You intrigue me," replied Escobar to Wang, waving his hand to silence Salazar. How could this man know about the monastery and his debts?

"I know most things." Wang responded as though hearing Escobar's unspoken thoughts.

"If you have the powers you say then you can be part of the competition, but it will not be martial arts as that will involve bloodletting."

"Very well," agreed Zhou looking around.

"There is a new team game that I have heard about. I believe they call it football," continued Escobar. "I've seen the locals playing it."

"Football?" queried Silver not sure he had heard correctly.

"What is football?" asked Salazar puzzled.

"It's a new game of skill using contact and determination by testing your physical strength and ability. It is all the rage in South America," said Victoria. "I've seen it played. It's British in origin."

"Of course Salazar, you may not feel up to it," chided Silver.

"I don't trust any of this," grunted Salazar. "Just lock the bastards up, including the Chinese, and then we can coerce the Lady to cooperate."

"We don't do things that way in my country senor," replied Escobar coldly turning to the others. "Football it is, we will need to get equipment and rules."

"We have the rules," replied Zhou.

"Good, that's a start," said Escobar, getting the feeling that Zhou was always one-step ahead of him.

From what he understood, the game was sufficiently physical to occupy and distract them all whilst he got on with the real job.

He saw the chance to make a lot of money betting on the outcome whilst also ensuring that there was only one winner. They could beat the hell out of each other and then he would walk away with the prize.

"There's not much to understand," continued Victoria. "I witnessed the game played in Argentina by English railway workers. There are two goals and the idea is to kick a ball into them before the other team puts the ball into your own goal. There is nothing more to it than that."

"This is ridiculous," replied Salazar angrily. "I must protest."

"Only because you can't think of a way to cheat," taunted Silver.

"So the two of you play to decide the right to find and own the treasure," continued Escobar.

"Not so fast," replied Zhou Wang. "I demand the right to fight for this treasure also."

"We're not playing against a bunch of Chinese," snarled Salazar.

"I said when I arrived that without us there is no treasure as I control the island," replied Zhou Wang tartly.

"Explain yourself?" said Escobar coldly looking around for his guards. The man was coming close to challenging the Governor's authority.

"It's simple really, no-one can survive on the island without my say so."

"I could have you thrown in prison for such remarks," replied Escobar coldly. "You are using inflammatory words."

"They are not said lightly."

"You'd better be able to back your words up," replied Escobar. "Very well gentlemen and ladies a three-way tournament. The winner will be given one week to find the treasure unfettered by any of us and once the appropriate tax is paid will be allowed to leave the island unhindered." He frowned, at a loud commotion at the door. "A moment," roared a loud voice its owner, a large burly Captain of the German navy.

"What do you mean by this interruption?" shouted Escobar. "This is a private meeting."

"My name is Captain Von Blomburg. I demand to be heard."

"What is your business?"

"I have come to claim this treasure as mine by right."

"What the hell do you mean?" groaned Escobar inwardly. Silver, Victoria and Salazar looked on in dismay.

"I have come here to claim the prize promised to me."

"Who promised you?"

"Perhaps I can help here," smiled Zhou stepping forwards. "A good colleague of mine made your acquaintance sir, after all this treasure belongs to all the nations of the world until it is found."

"I doubt that Zhou. You want it for yourself," said Silver sharply.

"I can speak for myself," growled Blomburg angrily. "I claim the right as I was told to come here to find a treasure before others less worthy take it. I shall not be deterred."

"There are other claimants well ahead of you," said Escobar looking hard at the inscrutable face of Zhou. He would have to watch that man carefully; he was clearly behind the whole thing.

"I have my battleship Dresden in the port," replied Blomburg. "The men would appreciate a little gunnery practice."

"How dare you threaten me sir," growled Escobar wearily staring out of the window at a large Iron clad Dreadnought towering above all the other ships. "Four teams it is."

CHAPTER 7

La Gomera,
De Garajonay Mountain Range,
late May 1895

Standing proud against the high skyline, the old buildings looked haunting to the untrained eye. To Zhou Wang and his small party of disciples it spelled the end of their ultimate quest. They had set off before sun break from their small-tented encampment at the harbour in San Sebastian. Silver had promptly kicked them off the *Calypso* on arrival after grudgingly giving them passage for owed wages. He wanted nothing more to do with them and had avoided Zhou on the short crossing.

Zhou had expected this and had made a point of seeing the Captain before leaving their home of many weeks. "Thank you for your hospitality Captain." Zhou bowed, "you beat the others for me, then you and I will settle our differences later. "My team are taking part as representatives of the Asian continent. You will understand that we shall play to win," smiled Zhou.

"I don't know your game Zhou, but believe me I will see through you before this is done," scowled Silver staring hard at the Chinaman.

Zhou Wang and his five disciples had been walking now for nearly six hours through dense undergrowth, following a barely recognisable path towards the extinct volcano's summit. The men were sweating heavily in the noonday sun, whilst Zhou Wang appeared to be immune to such problems. It was further proof to his followers that he was their leader and above their meagre limitations, a true leader. They walked on climbing ever higher as the path gave way to no more than a difficult rocky track.

The climbing became steeper to the point where even Zhou Wang was starting to struggle when finally they reached the summit and gasped. The sight was dramatic and awe inspiring even for the hardened Zhou Wang. Sheer stone walls rose majestically from the plateau, the sun shining through the higher walls giving it an almost mystical appearance. Ingeniously the monastery was not visible from below the plateau and no one would realise it was there without specific prior knowledge. Zhou Wang marvelled; it was indeed a masterpiece and ideal for his purposes. He could see now why superstitious locals called it '*Fortaleza Hidalgo*', meaning the noble fortress. He could not begin to imagine how they had managed to build the imposing edifice, was full of admiration as they walked faster on the lightly sloping ground, and approached the twelve feet high walls. Zhou Wang looked around for signs of life, saw nothing, and approached the main gates. "Hello!" he shouted at the large wooden door. "We have business here! It has been a long walk."

"Who are you, and why are you here?" replied a voice in heavily accented Spanish that Zhou Wang struggled to understand. "I have come on a mission to see your leader, who I am is of no importance to you."

"What mission?"

"That is for your Leader's ears only," replied Zhou getting agitated with the delay. "Mention the name Zheng He to him and let me in." he stood against the wall cursing as he waited until finally with a clanking noise the door opened. "Follow me," gestured a monk. "Your men stay here."

"They have come far, at least give them water," grated Zhou. The monk nodded his agreement. "Very well, they shall have water where they stand. Follow me, this way," Zhou Wang walked inside adjusting his eyes to the gloom, hearing a loud bang as the door behind him slammed shut.

He was taken down long dark corridors and finally into a small room. At the far end sat an older monk watching him. "You talk of Zheng He, what do you know of such a man?"

"That he discovered the World in 1421, including here," replied Zhou looking around and trying to see through the large dark cowl. "We don't have visitors," said the monk. "Why are you here?"

"I come to help you."

"We don't need any help," replied the monk. "Why would we?"

"Everyone needs help at some time; only a foolish man turns it down."

"We have been here for centuries. We have never had any problems and never needed any 'help' as you put it."

"You've been here since 1421 to be precise," replied Zhou meaningfully, "and you need my help whether you like it or not."

"Why?"

"There are dangerous men on the island, men who would think nothing of attacking and killing your men if they knew what was here."

"What do you think is here?" replied the monk coldly.

"Many secrets," replied Zhou carefully. "I know of them."

"What is your name and where do you come from?" replied the monk raising his voice, its tenor shaking a little to Zhou's infinite satisfaction. "My name is Zhou Wang and I come as your saviour, not as an enemy," replied Zhou.

"We are a simple monastery, I am called Francisco. you must be mistaken,"

"There is no mistake," replied Zhou Wang coldly. "One of your people brought us a message many years ago, a man called Zarco."

"We talk to no-one and abide by our own company," replied Francisco coldly but now visibly shaken.

"Zheng He and Zarco were missionaries, men of vision and I came as the same."

"What do you wish to achieve by coming here?" asked Francisco looking at Zhou for a long time. "An alliance," replied Zhou Wang without hesitation. "I have been searching for you for many years."

"We work in decades and centuries whilst others work in years. Man's greatest failing is he is always in a rush. We are not bound by any known religion," continued Francisco. "We have our own beliefs."

"I want to contribute to those beliefs."

"You want to join us?"

"As a partnership of equals; I have much to offer you, it has been planned a long time. Together we can build a dynasty."

"You would have to sacrifice everything for this."

"I understand."

"Very well," replied Francisco. "I will confer with my colleagues; you will have an answer when we are ready. I knew you were coming," continued Francisco without looking at him.

"Since this morning?"

Francisco shook his head, "No, for many months."

"How?" it was Zhou's turn to look surprised.

"You will learn our ways of knowing. However, there is a more prosaic way that we knew you were physically coming here this morning; by using whistles." replied Francisco. "As do many islanders; it's called 'Silbo' and means communication by whistles. My men are positioned all the way down the slope and have observed your progress; your men are not fit."

"They will have to be in a day's time," said Zhou Wang. He explained to Francisco the tournament.

"What is the purpose of all these people competing in the tournament?"

"I think you know that," replied Zhou Wang. "The significance of the Columbus Treasure is known throughout these islands and the New World. Many suspect that the Cross itself is here on this island."

"They are mistaken." Francisco stated firmly, meeting Zhou's eyes.

"If we are to be brothers we must learn to trust each other."

"Why did you bring your men?" Francisco challenged.

"Support in case you were hostile."

"I am hostile to anything which disturbs the equilibrium."

"It is disturbed anyway." Zhou shrugged, "I know that you see the future and your mission to control human affairs on the earth, a very apt location here at the World's end."

"You are a brave or foolish man. I could have you killed now."

"But you won't." replied Zhou Wang, "You need me."

"Send you men away, Zhou Wang. You stay the night."

"Very well," replied Zhou Wang smiling. He quickly scribbled a few lines on a piece of paper in Chinese.

Twenty minutes later, he was led alone into the inner sanctum. "This is our heart," Francisco told with reverence in his voice.

"I am one of you."

"Once you have heard all, there is no going back, do you understand that?"

"Absolutely," replied Zhou Wang following Francisco down a dark alleyway and into a room. As the door swung open, he gazed in amazement at what he saw; it was beyond even his comprehension. That night he slept fitfully in his cell. He laid for many hours thinking things over in his mind and awoke at dawn feeling as if he had not slept at all.

"We have decided you will join us after a suitable demonstration of your capability," announced Francisco reaching for a piece of paper. "This is how you shall enter our kingdom."

The five Chinese milled around at the edge of the forest. Their instruction from Zhou Wang had being to go to the tree line and wait there. Each had concealed weapons, long swords, underneath their clothes. The tallest, a giant of a man called Johnny Tang looked worriedly across at the others. "He's in trouble, our instructions are clear."

"But what do we do when we reach the monastery?" asked a smaller man called Xian Tie.

"We rescue our leader," replied Johnny. "Come on."

They started for the tree line and then stopped dead. Ahead of them, an apparition emerged slowly out of the forest, Zhou Wang. "We thought you were dead!" shouted Johnny.

"The opposite," replied Zhou Wang. "We have much work to do."

"What sort of work?"

"You will see, come on, we have important work to do."

———————————

Captain Kurt Von Blomburg smiled grimly to himself as he trained his binoculars on La Gomera. In the distance, people were scurrying around like ants converting a small meadow into a playing field. He saw crude looking stands. From a distance, *Dresden* was an impressive sight with three large funnels belching steam, not quite in the new dreadnought class but impressive enough to go where it liked in Africa. From a grand Prussian family, Blomburg had been overjoyed to get his first real command. The new German empire was barely 10 years old and Otto von Bismarck, a close neighbour of Blomburg's family, was Chancellor of the First Reich. He was intent on building an empire to match the British Empire as Germany emerged out of the dark ages. Blomburg's first mission had been to supply the German colony of Zanzibar in East Africa, and he had set off from the port of Hamburg with great pride and excitement. The only dampener was the fact that his passengers were the Von Steppenhoffs, the obstreperous replacement Governor for

Zanzibar and his awful wife. Nouveau riche traders from the Rhineland, Blomburg looked down on them, but not their money, which he envied.

The jumped up Steppenhoff had made his life a misery from the start of the voyage; treating him as a subservient minion and not the Captain. Unfortunately, as they had steamed around Spain and headed down towards Africa they had incurred problems with the steam engines boiler. The breakdown, when it happened, had been spectacular as the boiler exploded. They were lucky they had not sunk, though that was small consolation to Blomburg as he diverted into the African state off the Ivory Coast. It was there that a Chinese engineer, a mysterious man called Lang, had told him about the Columbus treasure. Blomburg, in his darker moments, suspected that Lang had something to do with the boiler breaking down. The Chinese man had told him to head for Santa Cruz and find the Governor of Tenerife before others beat him to it. Seeing the chance to find the fortune that had always evaded him, he ignored the protests of the irate Steppenhoffs and done just that, limping northwards to the Canary Islands under very low steam pressure. He believed that fortune had continued to smile on him as he overheard the heated conversation between Salazar, Silver, Zhou Wang and Escobar from the anteroom where he was waiting to see the Governor, and acted. No longer was he going to be the poor Junker from the north, he would find his fortune and make the Kaiser proud.

"I don't like it Enrico, Salazar is too smug," said Silver onboard *Calypso* as he surveyed his men. "He's in cahoots with the bloody Governor, and as for my bloody cook...." He tailed off thoughtfully.

"Why don't we just steal the map from Victoria?" suggested Enrico. "Then we could just go and find the treasure."

"She's on our side, or hadn't you noticed? Besides you think it's that easy?" said Silver. "There's no choice but to go along with the challenge and await our opportunity. Bloody Vincent is cutting it fine," he muttered knowing that his son held the key to success and he'd never even met him.

"Senorita," smiled Escobar as Victoria entered his temporary residence. "This is indeed a pleasure. I trust you had a good voyage across?"

"As well as can be expected." Victoria responded haughtily.

"You are very welcome to stay here, humble though it may be. I believe it was originally the residence of Columbus's good friend the Countess de Bombadilla?" Escobar smirked.

"What about my reputation?"

"I have servants here and will arrange for a suitable female companion to stay with you." He said, full of reassurances.

"My daughter?"

"Of course."

"Very well then, I accept your hospitality. Thank you" Victoria conceded.

"How can I help you?"

"My husband often spoke highly of the Spanish people Senor," replied Victoria, "he always said they were honourable."

"Of course." Escobar gestured to her to sit.

"He did leave me a little money, as well as the Treasure map."

"How exactly do you need my help?" said Escobar.

"I would like to buy some land in La Gomera," replied Victoria carefully.

"This wouldn't have anything to do with the treasure?"

"Of course it would!" Victoria explained honestly, "I need your help to expedite this as I am a foreigner in your land."

"Senor Salazar has purchased most of the land surrounding San Sebastian."

"I have in mind a smaller plot."

"Where?"

"A small piece of land on the edge of town, a humble building called the Red House. It's on the outskirts, nothing special, but I like it."

"Not easy at such short notice but I guess it could be arranged, for a certain price," replied Escobar greedily looking at her. Victoria shuddered inwardly. "What would that price be?"

"I'm sure there are a number of areas we can cooperate in," smiled the Governor.

———————————

Escobar hammered on the desk for silence, glaring malevolently down at Silver, Salazar, Blomburg and Zhou Wang. "Before we start finalising the details for this tournament, I want to make sure there are no underhand activities. Therefore, in the spirit of transparency, I will make it clear who has purchased land here. As you know, Senor Salazar has bought the uplands from one kilometre outside of San Sebastian. In addition," he paused grandly, "Victoria has today purchased an acre of land to the north west of the town."

"You didn't tell me," accused Silver, staring darkly at Victoria. "How the hell did you have the money for that when you haggled with me over pennies?" he exclaimed. "That's my business," she replied, turning to Escobar who drew himself up and announced. "There will be three games; two matches to determine who plays each other in the final and then the final," said Escobar handing out some leaflets. "There will be five players each, including a goalkeeper. We will play half an hour each way and if there is no score, we will determine the winner by taking penalties, which are a free kick at the goal. I shall be the referee. Now, I have studied the rules, basically there are thirteen Football Association Rules, as formulated twenty years ago in England."

"You can't pick the ball up?" asked Salazar suspiciously.

"That's called Rugby, an entirely different game," replied Escobar patiently.

"So who plays who?" asked Silver wondering where the hell his son was. This would be extremely embarrassing if he didn't turn up.

"Lady Victoria will decide," said Escobar writing the four countries on pieces of paper and then folding them before passing to Victoria who selected the first two passing them to Escobar. "First game will be Britain against Germany in three days' time," announced the Governor.

"Thank god," said Silver from the deck of *Calypso* staring past the flotilla of boats rocking at anchor at San Sebastian, La Gomera. A small steamer was on the horizon. "Vincent!" shouted Silver, as a recognisable form came down to the small jetty, so like him at that age. Vincent smiled back; it had been a frustrating long trip from Cadiz, frequently delayed by the unseasonable weather. "I wouldn't have missed this for the world," shouted Vincent as they stepped down. "Good to see you at last Dad." It felt strange using that name for the first time and he tried to take in the flamboyant sight of his father's flowing locks.

"Welcome, son." Silver looked round at the sturdy men coming down the plank. "Football, Vincent, that's the challenge," he said as they made their way over to the *Calypso*, explaining what had happened at the same time.

"Wow! A great ship," said Vincent taking in the lines of the *Calypso*.

"Are you any good at football," asked Silver anxiously. "I hear it's big in England."

"It's the new game, father, and is taking hold across Europe, very popular with the working classes."

"The stakes are high," continued Silver as they went aboard.

"What are the stakes?"

"I'll tell you in private."

"Hello." Vincent's attention was grabbed by a vision of love-liness.

"Ah, Veronique, my partner's daughter," said Silver turning to see what had diverted his son's attention, and frowning. "She came over with us from America."

"Pleased to meet you ma'am," said Vincent admiringly.

"And I you," Veronique smiled back, her eyes lighting up and locking with Vincent's.

"Keep away from her" whispered Silver to Vincent as they headed below deck. "She's a flirt and spent the entire voyage getting the crew wound up. A spoilt brat and there's no mistaking."

"I'm not surprised," said Vincent whistling at the beguiling creature that was a step above the daughters of Lord's and Judge's he had met so far.

Captain Blomburg was in a foul mood; bloody Steppenhoff was again making his life a misery. He had refused to play saying he was going to report him to Berlin for using the *"The Dresden"* for personal gain. If Bismarck found out that he had been ne-glecting his duty for a football match, he would be ruined. He had one more try with Steppenhoff.

"This is for the greater honour of Germany, think of the glory for the new German Empire."

"It's more to do with your ambition Captain, though perhaps I might relent if you make it worth my while. As you know we industrialists have our price for everything, that's why we succeed in the World against the old dinosaurs."

"Very well Steppenhoff, we will come to a deal and then we win."

CHAPTER 8

La Gomera,
late May 1895

The football 'pitch' had been newly trampled and the coarse grass flattened. Escobar had arranged for a rope to be erected around it, which now measured some fifty metres long by twenty metres wide. Unfortunately, it was very uneven and in many places and Vincent suspected some of the bulkier pieces of grass hid more potent dangers. He looked sardonically at the two stout posts at each end with a rope strung between them and the large leather ball that Escobar had proudly presented. Vincent looked around his team resplendent in white shirts. They had a good understanding as a group and he felt sure that they would acquit themselves well. Aside from himself, the team comprised of Reggie Pline in goal, Darkson as captain, a tough taciturn Scot called Mackay in defence and the flying South African George Akinbus up front. He looked over the field to the far side where resplendent German uniforms hid the German team from sight.

Blomburg supervised last minute instructions. He had no illusions; the British were definitely a fitter team, so they would have to resort to roughhouse tactics if necessary. His men were dressed in Prussian blue with the German eagle resplendent on the shirtfronts. Bismarck would have been proud he was sure, though Steppenhoff was the only German member of the team. The rest were two Norwegian sailors, Oleson and his chunky son Ralph, and a Danish mid-shipman called Backer. The final player was Norbert who had been co-opted as goalkeeper owing to his somewhat diluted Germanic origins and his undiminished hatred of Vincent Silver. What Blomburg had not realised was that Norbert's real loyalty was to Victoria.

"Time to give the Anglos a bloody nose," yelled Ralph. "We play for the Empire."

"For the Empire," repeated Norbert, especially angry because Vincent was enjoying the besotted attentions of Veronique. His sole aim was to make sure that pretty boy was not too attractive after this game.

There were over five hundred locals standing on the sidelines or sitting in the makeshift stands, the more enterprising doing a roaring trade in drink and food. Many were betting furiously, though few had any idea of the game's rules. "Gentleman," shouted Escobar grandly striding to the centre. "I will dismiss anyone caught persistently fouling and free kicks will be given for unfair tackles. I want to see no blood. Do I make myself clear?"

"Yes," replied Vincent and Ralph shaking hands and looking hard at each other. Both knew what was at stake.

"Wait until I get seated," yelled Blomburg striding down the pitch to his seat next to Escobar. On the other side sat Silver. Higher up in the make shift stand sat Salazar with a quizzical frown on his face.

"Go for it Vincent!" yelled Silver as Escobar blew the whistle.

Immediately the Germans were on the defensive as the English launched a quick attack showing their superior technical and fitness levels. Vincent saw the ball coming towards him, twisted and fired a hard shot, which flew straight at Norbert. The big man saw it coming late as it hit him hard in the stomach. He gasped. The ball was heavier than he expected, the leather having absorbed moisture, and he wheezed as he kicked it back up field. From there the match quickly degenerated into a scrappy affair as the Germans ran at men rather than the ball. "There's no skill in this," yelled Salazar limping up and down on the sideline.

After about fifteen minutes, the running slowed down, with only Klaus Steppenhoff and the flying Akinbus seemingly unaffected. From the sidelines, Escobar stared with concern as the game degenerated into a stamina contest with the Germans determined to cancel out any skill by the British. What was more concerning was that it seemed unlikely to reach any sort of conclusion, which meant bloodshed. He signalled to his Captain to remain vigilant. A small group of his most loyal soldiers were positioned strategically around the ground. He frowned as he noted out of the corner of his eye a new group of people joining the crowd. Monks!

"Glad you could make it," Zhou Wang smiled heartily as he saw the monks approach. "Human physical challenge is important to our long term well-being."

"Spiritual health is more important," replied one of the monks.

"Both have their place," replied Zhou Wang gesturing to them to sit. "You are being watched by the Governor gentlemen. Take care for he has many suspicions about you."

"Who the hell are they?" growled Silver to no one in particular as he saw the Monks, "I didn't know there was a religious establishment here."

"They've upset Escobar judging by his facial expression," added Victoria joining Silver. "Zhou Wang is behind this, see, he is sitting with them."

"Interesting," mused Silver, "He's trying to get God on to his side." He turned back to the pitch. "No substitute for skill though, these bastards should be sent off," he said groaning as the German Steppenhoff got the ball and went wide to the left with Backer yelling at him to pass. Reggie Pline advanced to meet them and had his Christian beliefs severely tested as Steppenhoff ran full tilt into him. "Foul!" yelled Vincent to no avail as the ball ran loose. Again, Steppenhoff surprised Darkson with his sheer pace and got ahead of him. Oleson the other half back came over to him. "Nonsense," replied Oleson yelling for the ball as Steppenhoff finally passed it across. Pline made a flying effort to stop Oleson but only succeeded in grasping thin air, missing the ball and hammering into the Norwegian who collapsed unconscious as the ball bobbled over the line.

"Goal!" shouted Blomburg in delight.

"Our keeper was fouled," yelled Silver roaring in disgust

"The goal stands," judged Escobar with finality.

"Cheat!" yelled Silver towards Blomburg who spun around in anger.

"Who are you calling a cheat?"

"You and your damned team of thugs, this is more like war."

"Why you ..." roared Blomburg turning and clambering after Silver.

"Gentlemen," yelled Escobar as he saw Blomburg reach for something at his waist. "Any bloodshed and the whole competition is over. May I remind you that you will all then pay the forfeit of two years labour?"

"I have to defend myself," shouted Silver, reacting quickly at the sight of Blomburg's sword by pulling out his own dagger. They squared up to each other, clashing blades.

"I said stop, or you will both pay the forfeit," yelled Escobar as his Captain of the guard advanced on the men and separated them. "We start again in ten minutes."

The players were grateful for the arrival of half time. Blomburg saw that his team were too tired to respond as they sat slumped in a circle. Oleson was still unconscious so they were down to four men. "We need to get wider and use our pace," said Vincent to Darkson. "They have too much muscle in the centre so George Akinbus take it wide." The South African nodded as the second half kicked off with him doing just that. His speed easily beat the labouring Backer and Steppenhoff and he looked up to see Oleson's son coming towards him. /"You die English," spluttered the big man as George sidestepped him, to see Norbert staring malevolently. At the last moment, he passed to Vincent who slammed the ball past Norbert's despairing arms.

It was one goal each. Vincent felt they had the Germans on the run now. The ball came to him and he cleverly passed it through to George already running to meet it. This time however, Blomburg flung himself towards George and managed to connect. George fell flat to the ground unconscious. "Foul!" yelled Vincent. "An accident," yelled Escobar, "get on with the game." Backer made a run forward and squared a pass to Steppenhoff who hit the ball hard. He was enjoying the game for someone who had objected so vigorously about taking part. Vincent groaned as he saw the ball heading for the low left hand corner, but at the last second Pline somehow managed to stretch across the goal and stop the ball. Quickly, he sprang up and flung the ball towards Vincent. As the Germans lumbered to get back, Vincent had a clear run on goal and concentrated on keeping control of the bobbing ball on the hard pitch. Out of nowhere Steppenhoff appeared, tearing in on his right hand side. Vincent sidestepped and managed to jink past him but showed a little too much of the ball to Norbert. It was fifty-fifty and Vincent's world went black as the bulk of Norbert slammed into him. James Silver looked on aghast. "That bloody gorilla nearly killed him!" he yelled to Escobar. "Play on," said Escobar as Vincent got dazedly to his feet looking grimly at the smiling Norbert.

Play continued with each side trying to outmanoeuvre the other whilst Silver argued profusely with Escobar to the point where they were nearly at blows. The ball bobbed back and forth, as the minutes ticked away. On the pitch, Vincent looked nervously at his watch; "It's now or never," he muttered to himself. Out of the corner of his eye, he saw George move forward. Seeing the chance to avoid a long drawn out game he struck a long pass that landed expertly at George's feet, who looked warily around. He was on his own, except for Steppenhoff who was desperately trying to catch up with him. Norbert gave a bull like roar sensing the danger and moving forward. George evaded Norbert's despairing lunge and Steppenhoff collided heavily with the big keeper. George delightedly realised he was through and ran the ball to the goal line, then sat on it grinning.

"Scheisse," yelled Blomburg angrily from the touchline, this was all going badly wrong, "We need more players." The last few minutes got increasingly manic as boots flew with no relationship to the location of the ball and Escobar threw his hands up in horror. Finally, with one minute to go Vincent shouted for the ball. It came towards him and he started to run forwards. He saw Steppenhoff bearing down on him but knew he had a couple of metres on the German. Suddenly he spun around clutching his neck and fell to the ground. "Someone shot me," he gasped feeling his bruised neck and looking around. He staggered back to his feet. Steppenhoff had the ball and took advantage of the British team's confusion. Looking up he saw Pline advancing too fast. They collided and the ball squirmed under Pline's arm. He desperately groped for it and missed, the ball rolled slowly towards the goal. At the last moment, Darkson launched himself across to steer it wide of the goal.

Salazar had been extremely busy behind the scenes during the match. He did not for one minute think that there was anything fair about the game and intended to gain every advantage he could, putting the word around the island, that he needed the best and fittest young men. It was one of his crewmembers who had fired the slingshot that nearly crippled Vincent. The British had won the first game, which served to sharpen his determination as he looked at his own men. Victoria had more important things to do than watch a crazy football match. She set out to explore the town unobserved. She conducted a thorough exploration of the old town area of San Sebastian before entering her new property.

The Spanish and Asian teams came out onto the pitch, the Asian team in black the Spanish in red and yellow. Salazar sat in the main stand smiling as the locals made their feelings of support for the Spanish team known. "A great unifying force for your island Escobar, you should be thanking me for doing your job for you and making sure we succeed."

"They need to win fair and square," replied Escobar standing next to him at the sideline. "I must admit however that it has opened my eyes to the power of such events, most interesting."

"We will win; the only issue for debate is whether you let me leave the country when I get the treasure?"

"Why wouldn't I?"

"The shame of losing the Columbus treasures would ruin you."

"Your point Salazar?"

"We need to come to an arrangement," whispered the Spaniard carefully.

"Time to start the game," replied Escobar raising his whistle. The match started much like the first one as Escobar listened intently to the Spaniard, his mind working out all the options. He was again puzzled and annoyed to see the monks high up in the stand. What were they doing here and where were they from? Zhou Wang stared down to the line impassively seeing Escobar look up frowning. He turned to Francisco with amusement. "We have him concerned and that is good," he smiled. "The rabbit is in the spotlight. Are you enjoying the meaning of what you see?"

"We only see a game," replied one of the monks. "Where is the meaning in that?"

"The significance of these events will become clear to you all soon. In the meantime enjoy yourselves," said Zhou standing up and making his way down to the front.

San Sebastian had never seen anything like it as the hordes of farmers from the inner island roared their team on. This was their match and betting had been huge, with whole month's salaries at stake on the right result. The quiet life of the island was gone as enterprising locals set up stalls to sell wine and fruit. Salazar's team was full of brawny looking young men wearing heavy boots. Zhou Wang for his part appeared not to notice the antagonism of the crowd, impassively watching his men as they tackled harder and harder. Apart from Johnny in the goal, they were far smaller than the opposition in size but made up for this with their energy and commitment. The predictable melee took place after a badly mistimed tackle and fists flew until Escobar halted the game. Salazar called his son over; a lanky, long nosed twenty-year-old called Gaizka. The match restarted with Gaizka making a long run forwards into the other half, much to the delight of the crowd, before he was unceremoniously deposited on the floor by a tough round looking Chinese player called Tie.

Watching from the side Escobar was pleased with events; his popularity was soaring on the island. They would forgive him the planned further rise in taxes if there were a local victory. The grass was starting to cut up badly after overnight rain and again the match was degenerating into an exercise in who was the fittest. Only Zhou Wang appeared unperturbed as Salazar hobbled along the touchline screaming obscenities to his men. A local man called Perez finally ran free on the wing with a quick turn of pace that left everyone standing. He then proceeded to drift inside with the ball as if it was tied to his feet and finally let rip with a thundering shot, which flew past the Chinese keeper Johnny Tang. Tempers became frayed towards half time as tired legs missed the ball and often hit the man.

The Chinese team ran out of ideas and Zhou Wang made his way down to the front, glancing back at the monks. The Spanish locals, Hortense and Marcella in goal, were stamping their authority on the game not giving the smaller and lighter Chinese players a chance. Hortense, the local shepherd, was cheered on by his supporters in the crowd and responded by getting ever more violent. The man had no idea how to play football, but a very clear idea how to get people out of his way. Barging through the middle, removing Chinese bodies physically with his hands, he had a clear shot at goal and with a great roar lifted his foot and hammered the ball at the goalkeeper Johnny Tang who looked on in horror as the ball hit him full in the stomach and carried him over the line. The game was over and the Chinese players watched Zhou Wang walk across to them poker faced. He bent down and whispered to a couple of them and they gathered around in a group. Minutes later, they walked to the side and Zhou Wang went over to the monks. Escobar watched with interest. Something was going on and he wanted to know what it was. He had a feeling that the monks were trouble; he had an instinct for these sorts of things.

"You have no chance Englishman," smiled Salazar staring at Silver as he hobbled past. "Your scheming will come to nothing when the Spanish win."

"We will see," replied Silver turning away.

"Horrible man," grimaced Victoria joining Silver

"We are going to win, that is if you are still with me?"

"What do you mean?" asked Victoria.

"You're hooked up with the Governor."

"How dare you? I am staying as his guest, no more! It's a welcome change from your smelly ship!" Victoria smarted with outrage. "My apologies ma'am, but we have to get off the island fast when we find the treasure, you will need my help."

"I understand that Silver, there's something you can do to help me," replied Victoria.

"What?"

"I'll tell you later, too many people here."

"I hope you know what you are doing mother. He's a rogue," said Veronique approaching her mother as Silver headed in the other direction to find Vincent. "Of course I know what I'm doing, the question is, do you?"

"What do you mean? Vincent is different to that old rake! Plus, I'm only following orders."

"Like father like son!" Victoria tutted.

"Why are you so keen that I get friendly with Vincent?"

"Insurance Veronique, we need all the help we can get here and need to use then only thing we have in advantage to these men, our brains and bodies." Victoria advised her daughter.

"So you're suggesting I sleep with him if necessary?"

"You are old enough to decide yourself what is necessary Veronique, I do not need to spell it out."

"You're assuming the British will win the game?"

"It doesn't matter, whoever wins there will be cheating and plotting that's why you and I need to be ready. I have other contingency plans."

"Perhaps the others also have contingency plans," replied Veronique thoughtfully walking alongside her mother. "I'm sure they do but ours will be better and will ensure we succeed. This is our chance, Veronique, to put the past behind us and become independent. That is what we need and I will do anything to achieve it."

"Anything?" Veronique looked at her mother incredulously.

"Anything." Repeated Victoria, reinforcing her meaning to her daughter, "By the way keep your eye on the Chinese man, he is the one who will decide the outcome of this venture, providing we are ahead of him we will succeed. There's something very sinister about him, something which is far more concerning than these petty men and their greed."

"I agree, he looks right through me mother, as if I am not there."

"I have great plans Veronique, and they must be allowed to happen. So don't be surprised if I do some slightly unusual things over the next few days. There is too much at stake for us to let things wash over us without controlling them."

"I understand."

"Incidentally I found what I was looking for earlier."

"Brilliant," replied Veronique as they turned towards Escobar's house and walked through a narrow street. Neither of them noticed a shadowy figure quietly move away from their rear where he had heard the entire conversation.

CHAPTER 9

La Gomera,
late May 1895

The day before the football final Silver was in good spirits, finally seeing the treasure within his grasp and convinced his team could outplay the local Spaniards, providing Salazar did not cheat. On board *Calypso* a meal, cooked by Veronique and Victoria, was held for the British team. Silver watched Vincent and Veronique carefully; at least their developing friendship cemented his relationship with Victoria, but he wondered what would happen when the treasure was found. Too many unanswered questions and not enough certainty troubled him, particularly with the scoundrels Salazar and Escobar to say nothing of Zhou Wang and the Germans. He beckoned to his son. "Well done Vincent, proud of you not reacting when the buggers fired that slingshot. Guess you're wishing you were back in Cambridge?" He clapped his son on the shoulder. "On the contrary," Vincent grinned at his father, "I'm starting to enjoy this life; it's helped me come to a decision."

"What decision?" asked Silver hesitantly.

"I want to stay here, learn to sail *Calypso*."

"Your mother will not approve."

"It's my life."

"She'll blame me." Silver said with great certainty.

"I shouldn't think that would bother you." Vincent retorted.

"Quite right," Silver agreed, "But I'm thinking of retiring."

Vincent looked at his father to check he was being serious before saying in a measured tone, "*Calypso*, I'll buy her off you."

"And how will you do that?" Silver was intrigued.

"My share of the treasure, the lads will chip in too."

"Getting ahead of ourselves a little."

"I can keep the Silver name alive in this world."

"The ship is an anachronism Vincent, you need steam to keep up with the others and that means real money." Silver's scepticism was clear.

"I'll think of something."

"Does all this involve Veronique?"

"Don't underestimate me, and try to understand."

"Understand what?"

"Whatever it is you need to understand," replied Vincent enigmatically.

"The game, can you win?" Silver said, eager to move on.

"If it's down to sheer skill we will, but they are younger and fitter."

"Watch that bastard Salazar; he will try anything to make sure he gets his filthy hands on the treasure."

"Did you say he had left a hoard in the West Indies?"

"In Bermuda and that shall be my legacy to you no matter what happens tomorrow," smiled Silver conspiratorially. "What will?" it was Vincent's turn to look intrigued.

"I know Bermuda inside out, if for whatever reason I don't make it take the compass with you."

"The compass?"

"Just remember it, promise me."

Escobar sat alone in the old house of Beatrice de Bombadilla wishing she were here now to tell him where the treasure was. He had heard that not only had she been a great favourite with Columbus but also with Queen Isabella. All of his conscious life he had been aware of the Columbus treasure and now, here he was, possibly on top of the damned thing, yet it still remained elusive. His men had stripped the house to its frame and found nothing, so his best bet remained an alliance with Lady Victoria. Whoever won tomorrow would try to find the treasure and then make a dash for it, so he had taken precautions. He intended to become famous for this, the man who returned the Columbus treasure to Spain. He would first spirit it away somewhere to allow him time to negotiate fame and recognition and maybe even a senior government post in Spain. Escobar was adamant that he would not be content with some paltry reward and a lot of well meaning words. He wrung his hands in anticipation and took a long drink of Madeira wine.

On the dawn of match day Victoria made her way across to *Calypso* having spent a sleepless night at the Governor's house listening to the Spaniard's constant snoring in the other room. "During the match I will get the treasure," she whispered to Silver as they stood on *Calypso*'s bridge watching the sun climb slowly into the sky.

"How?" he replied, intrigued.

"It's in the grounds of the Red House. Why do you think I bought the property?" she continued quietly. "I thought it was too obvious."

"So, I assume, did the others, though Escobar has been snooping around. That's why Norbert slept at the Red House last night on the floor. We've padlocked the doors and gate so it's safe."

"They will be watching you." Silver warned, convinced that it could not be this easy.

"Escobar and Salazar will be at the match, that's guaranteed. I need your men to help Norbert unearth the treasure."

"And then what?" Silver asked.

"To *Calypso*." Victoria said confidently.

"Fifty percent?"

"Thirty, after I've paid Escobar ten percent." Victoria reasoned, "After all it's my treasure."

"It's nothing without me, and nothing goes to Escobar." Silver laid his terms down, making it clear that he wasn't into bargaining.

"But…" Victoria started, and was instantly interrupted by Silver, "Escobar will try and take it all anyway, so speed is of the essence. You need to be onboard *Calypso* so we sail straight after the match."

"I don't know if that is possible." Victoria tried.

"Fifty percent." Silver repeated flatly.

"Very well." She sighed.

"Now tell me where it is."

"Here." Victoria unrolled the small map. "The well in the garden, it's down there. If you look at the measurements, it fits and the signature on the map is Zarco's so it is genuine. Norbert has had a look and says we can get down."

"Of course," murmured Silver, "but surely such an obvious location would have been discovered before? It's over three hundred years ago."

"That's the clever bit; the map shows they dug a side tunnel inside the well about six feet down. It fits the dimensions and location on the map exactly. It makes sense; we'll have to enter it from the well."

"Enrico and Jacques will help you," said Silver. "Just control Norbert."

"They will have guards posted everywhere."

"We need another distraction," replied Silver deep in thought, "leave it with me." Neither of them noticed the shadow below as they left the bridge.

The interest on the island was intense as the final match time approached and extra seating was arranged to enclose the pitch. A little after four in the afternoon the British team took to the field clad in their white strips with long trousers, the Spanish all in red and yellow. Enterprising islanders had set up stalls selling food and drink to refresh the hundreds of people who had come down from the hills for the match as word got around.

Escobar blew the opening whistle and the British team surged into the attack. It was evident from the first few minutes that this was going to be a far more skilful match. Not only had both teams learnt from their first matches but it also became evident that skill not brawn would win. All the players were conscious of the high stakes; none more so than Salazar and Silvers whose respective offspring clashed heartily in the middle of the pitch. They both fell to the floor as the ball squirmed free and Gaizka stared daggers at Vincent. Both sides were evenly matched in pace and skill with the speed of Gonzalez for Spain and Akinbus for Britain cancelling each other out. The Spanish had a new player, a darker skinned youth called Nasrid, of Arabic parents but born in Spain. He played as a defender effectively cancelling out the benefits of George Akinbus's speed.

The ball bounced around the central area for a while before Pline was forced into an early save by a speculative shot from Gaizka. Attack and counter attack followed as each tried to get the better of the other. Hortense started to slowly take control of the central area. A local, he seemed to have the ability to hold the ball to his feet rather than losing it as did many of his fellow countrymen. Seeing an opening, he passed to Gonzalez who found some space on the wing and tore forwards with the crowd shouting him on. He bore down on the goal but Pline timed his dive to perfection to take the ball off him.

It was racy stuff as each team countered and parried. From the sideline, Silver was trying to concentrate on the match whilst wondering how Victoria was faring. She had pleaded a headache to Escobar earlier and left the stand to suspicious looks from Salazar. Silver had no doubt she would be followed, that was where Jacques came in. He was told to take care of any followers thereby allowing Enrico, Norbert and Victoria time to get to the well site.

At that very moment, Norbert was busy lowering a rope down the ancient well and wondering what he was going to find down there. Enrico helped him as the two barely tolerated each other. The Venezuelan was familiar with ropes from sailing, but he was not happy at the dark enclosed space, grimacing at what awaited him. He had seen Jacques take care of two guards hanging around the house. Both were now trussed up inside. Victoria leaned over the side grateful that Norbert's strength held the rope. Enrico tied the end around his foot and Victoria signalled to lower away. Grunting the large man played the rope out as Enrico swung himself over the side.

"Don't let go for God's sake," he shouted to Norbert.

"Stop moaning, the sooner you are down the sooner we can get away."

———————————

Back at the game Silver began to think the British team would never get a break when at last Vincent got free of Hortense. He saw Gaizka heading for him and feinted to pass the ball to George. George shot immediately on the run and Marcella only just managed to palm the ball away. Vincent paused to get his breath back. The locals were far fitter than the Germans and more skilful; it was quite a contest. Of particular danger was Gonzales who apparently had played the game before in South America. He was grateful when half time arose without any loss of a goal and they sat breathless as Vincent looked around and tried to ignore the locals shouting.

"We're trying to beat the crowd as well."

"That's not the only problem," replied Pline. "They are trying to distract me from behind and I keep seeing that bastard Salazar in the stands looking at me."

"He's just trying to put you off," replied Darkson. "Just concentrate on the game; I reckon we have the legs of them and more skill. George, you need to move further forwards so you can use your speed towards the goal, Gaizka is slow. We'll beat them lads."

The second half started the same way as the first with many tackles in the middle of the pitch. Vincent noticed that some of the Spanish players were tiring but conceded that so were his team. Darkson, a tower in defence, was struggling to contain Gonzales who looked like he could run forever. The tackling started to get more and more frantic by both sides as the minutes ticked by. Vincent made some good running but Hortense had the measure of him each time. Salazar and Silver, now seated each side of Escobar, became more and more frantic as the minutes ticked by. With fifteen minutes left, George Akinbus got away on the left wing. He bore down on the Spanish goal where Marcella was waiting the crowd was silent. At the last moment just as Marcella went for him, George released the ball sideways to Vincent who gratefully tapped it home. Silver jumped up delightedly, ten minutes left and they were in front.

Salazar scowled and roared at his son to go further up field. The locals started to shout as Hortense got the ball and ran forwards. Darkson tried to tackle him but was shrugged off by Perez from the side, allowing Hortense a clean run on goal. Reaching the final third of the pitch, he shot it hard towards goal. It struck Pline on the leg and ballooned into the air. There was a scramble as it came down, Pline missed it and it bounced off Gaizka over the line, one goal each.

The pressure became ever more intense and the final five minutes were frantic as boots flew everywhere and the ball remained obstinately in the middle of the pitch. Energy was draining out of all the players, half of whom stood gasping for breath. Salazar nodded his head almost unnoticed and Pline walking forwards with the ball suddenly fell to his knees in agony. The crowd roared as the ball rolled free. "No one was near him," replied the Governor to Silver's outraged yell, as Gonzalez and Akinbus tore down on the ball. Both were neck and neck when suddenly Akinbus stumbled. Gonzalez surged ahead with the crowd roaring him on. Just as he reached the ball looking certain to score Darkson slid across and managed to toe poke the ball away from his despairing feet. Escobar blew reluctantly for full time.

"You cheated," roared Silver, glaring at Salazar. "Someone took a bloody shot at my man again."

"The man is mental," replied the Spaniard ignoring the Englishman. "Besides that was clearly an illegal tackle by the British."

"Says nothing in the rules about that," said Silver. "Your man was too slow."

The crowds were quiet and tense knowing it would now come down to a penalty shootout and the betting became even more frenetic. "Three shots each," said Escobar. "Choose your men." Vincent, George and Darkson strode forwards to be met by Gaizka, Gonzalez and Hortense. Gaizka strode forward to take the first Spanish kick. The entire crowd moved around behind the left hand goal and Pline took up his position. Gaizka ran forward and hammered the ball at Pline who got a despairing hand to it before it bobbed over the line. Vincent ran up calmly and slotted his shot into the corner of the net, as did Gonzalez who comfortably hit the ball to Pline's left.

The pressure was now on George, but he calmly strode up, shooting the ball beyond the despairing dive of Marcella. It was all down to the last two shots, Hortense and Darkson. The crowd stood silently staring intently at the scene unfolding below them. It was if they all held their collective breath as Hortense strode forwards toward Pline holding the leather ball. He set the ball down and walked backwards two paces and then stared at Pline. He smiled coldly and ran forwards as Pline tensed himself to dive.

There was an almighty bang and the ground shook. People screamed and dived for cover as pieces of turf flew around their heads. Silver picked himself up first and looked around at the confusion. As far as he could see no one was hurt, the explosion seemed to have come from the next field. He looked in the direction of where he thought it had come from, the harbour, and then saw another light streak into the sky. "Get down" he roared as the ground again shook. "It's the bloody Germans shooting at us! They're trying to stop anyone winning." He looked around at the total confusion, as one of the makeshift stands started to sway and then collapse. This was quickly turning into a rout and he saw Escobar's startled face trying to stop people from running.

He should have expected this. He ran across to Vincent. "Forget the game, we need to move fast son, Victoria is over at Red House. Come on."

"Just a minute dad, you go ahead, I have to make sure the others are all right."

"Don't you understand we have to go?"

"I'll be a couple of minutes, go ahead," replied Vincent grabbing his jacket to put over his sweaty shirt. Vincent gestured to Darkson and the three men made their way across the field. The crowd had fallen silent, uncertain what to do and fearful of another explosion. It would not be long before the scene started to turn nasty.

Norbert cursed as they heard the shots and nearly let go of the rope as resulting debris narrowly missed his head. He swore and started pulling. "You have to come up," he yelled, hauling away, his muscles glistening in the afternoon heat. "Just a minute," yelled Enrico, "I'm nearly there. I can see it in the recess, one minute."

"Quickly, damn you," yelled Norbert in puzzlement as he felt something sharp hit him. He stumbled and a stone was dislodged as something else hit him, there was no explosion and he realised he had been shot by a bullet in the leg.

"Someone is shooting at me, you have to come now," he yelled pulling away. "Who is shooting?" shouted Victoria crouching down and looking wildly around.

The light was fading slightly making it hard to see into the shadows alongside the wall. She looked down anxiously as Enrico was pulled to the top. Norbert was sweating profusely and bleeding in both legs as they staggered back towards the house. Sensing that Enrico had something in his hand, Victoria turned back to look at a long metal casket. "You've got it," she breathed. "Norbert," she screamed in terror as another shot hit her faithful servant, the big man grunting and falling as blood poured from a chest wound. Leaving Norbert where he fell, Enrico and Victoria scrambled into the house met by a breathless Jacques. "We need to go now!" yelled Jacques, "There is someone at the back shooting at us and there are people out the front."

"Look!" gasped Enrico; motioning to the casket, he was carrying before collapsing on the floor. "It was inside the brickwork but a long way in. Surprised how easy it came out."

"Give it to me," said Victoria taking the casket. "Come on!" repeated Jacques. "There's a small back alley this way," shouted Victoria. They ran down the alleyway, it was still empty. "Follow me," shouted Victoria. "I've memorised the route." She turned left and headed for the waterfront, leading the men through a narrow opening.

"Well, well, what do we have here?" Salazar stepped forward out of the shadows blocking the way and grinning broadly whilst pointing at the casket. "A metre long? Just about the size of the Cross? I am disappointed in you ma'am, so deceitful." He raised his sword. "Now, hand it over. "

"This is my property," replied Victoria coldly. "Keep it Enrico."

"There are three of us, armed" said Salazar, "against two sailors and a woman," he sneered.

"Three sailors actually," came a voice from the gloom. "Drop the weapons," Silver stepped forwards holding a small gun. "Well done Silver," gasped Victoria. "You won't get away with this Silver," snarled the Spaniard as his sword clattered to the floor. "Tie up the Spanish bastard Enrico, and take off his wooden leg, that should slow him down," he grinned. "Then we can get to *Calypso* as fast as possible," he shouted heading forwards. "Well done Silver, we lost Norbert but your man Enrico did excellently to get the box."

"We're not there yet and where the hell is my son?" growled Silver looking around. Something did not feel right. "I haven't seen him," replied Enrico, "or his men for that matter."

"Come on."

They ran down another small alleyway with Silver helping to carry the casket. Struggling, he was surprised at just how heavy the damned thing was and wondered what it was made of. Finally, they were out into the open area before the dock. Silver hesitated; this was where they would be at their most vulnerable. "Be careful Enrico, we just need to get across this square and we're home and dry on *Calypso*. Costa should be watching us now with a gun trained on the area. come on lets…" The sentence was unfinished as Silver twisted and fell as there was another huge explosion and the ground shook around them. "Bloody hell?" growled Silver picking himself painfully up.

"*Dresden*"again," shouted Victoria breathlessly. "I saw smoke from the German battleship. "

"Far enough Englishman," shouted Blomburg coming out from behind a small building with three men beside him. Silver recognised Steppenhoff. "Bloody hell," growled Silver again as the heavily armed German sailors made their way over.

"The casket, hand it over" said Blomburg.

"You're breaking the agreement Captain," sneered Silver.

"There is no agreement as no one won," boomed the German. "The guns are loaded so don't do anything stupid. Thank you so much," said Blomburg smiling as his men lifted the casket. Two German sailors had their guns trained on the party as they headed back to their boat struggling with the heavy casket.

"Damn the Germans to hell," groaned Silver looking at Enrico. "There's no way we can get it back from *"The Dresden"*," he broke off, "Where the hell has Victoria gone now?"

"Don't know," replied Enrico puzzled.

"To the Governor's house," bellowed Silver a horrible realisation dawning on him.

"A brilliant ruse of yours my dear," said Escobar as Victoria entered his main reception room, "to get Silver to take the fake casket. Switching them over was brilliant!"

"We did it together," conceded Victoria. "The match gave us time to divert their attention while we redistributed the wealth."

"Well done Victoria." Escobar said.

"I just hope that Blomburg doesn't realise too soon that he's taken a box of rocks."

"It should take a lot of force to break the locks I put on." Escobar smirked, adding, "How is your man?"

"Badly hurt, your men weren't supposed to shoot him. Suppose it had to look realistic. Anyway, all that hard work last night was worth it. When do we leave Governor?"

"All in good time," replied Escobar smiling. "Where's Veronique?"

"With the British football team I would think, she's besotted with Vincent Silver." Victoria said a distasteful look on her face.

"Well, let's have a look shall we," smiled Escobar lifting the real casket and lovingly opening the lid. "Only had a brief look last night, I kept it until you were back here with me. No-one will disturb us now."

"Don't forget our deal Escobar, the jewellery to me, the Cross for you." Victoria reminded him gently.

"Of course my dear and how fitting that it is here in the Contessa's house that her jewels are returned to their rightful owner. Zarco stole these from this very house, taking the Cross as well to make it look like a robbery." He glanced down as a tablet fell at his feet.

Picking it up, he looked hard at the faded surface. It had text inscribed on it in Old Spanish, which he could read. As he started to read the words, his face froze. "My god the implications for my country are huge," he murmured.

"What's the matter?"

"Why don't you just leave me to read the text, it has historical importance. Here are the jewels," he passed over the bracelets and diamonds. Victoria walked next door to the kitchen admiring the antique jewellery; it was exquisitely beautiful and certainly worth a lot of money, her financial worries were over. She turned as the kitchen door swung open and blinked in terror as a man with a gun bundled Escobar's trusted guards roughly inside.

"Very deceitful mother," came a familiar feline voice.

"Veronique, what are you doing here?"

"I could ask the same of you mother," Veronique smiled thinly, lifting a small revolver. Behind her Vincent told the guards to lie face down on the ground.

"What's the meaning of this?" she continued. The door slammed open and a surprised Escobar stood there looking at the guns.

"You didn't think I was going to let you get away with all this? Vincent and I made our own plans. I've watched you carefully mother, your scheming with Silver on the bridge, you've been very devious."

"Veronique, I told you it would require guile."

"If you try and leave here I will have you both shot down," growled Escobar. "I have men behind you. Drop the guns."

"What." Vincent swung around realising too late that it was a trick. Escobar raised his gun and fired. The sound in the small room was deafening as the shot narrowly missed Vincent's head and he fired back instinctively.

"My God, you've shot me! Get a doctor quickly!" yelled Escobar falling to the floor, holding his leg. "Quickly, Veronique," Vincent grabbed the casket, jamming the Cross back into it and heading for the front door just as Silver and Enrico barged in through the back door. Silver took in the scene quickly as he saw

Victoria trying to help Escobar. "You deceived me lady," he growled. "All the time you were conniving behind my back."

"Later!" screamed Victoria, "Your son and my daughter, we have to get after them! They must not get away, our own flesh and blood."

"You should have thought of that when you sent that harlot after my son," roared Silver. He turned as there was a commotion behind him and Salazar fired his gun as he limped in.

"Arrest this man," he roared at Silver his eyes taking in the prostrate form of Escobar. "What happened?"

"We need to stop them getting away," yelled Victoria ignoring the malevolent glances Silver and Salazar gave each other. "There's still time," she said opening the door to the waterfront and a great deal of excitement and movement.

"No there isn't, he's taking *Calypso*," groaned Silver. "He must have had the damned team ready, it's leaving without me." *Calypso* was steadily leaving the quay, already ten metres away. "Got to stop them," growled Silver running forwards as he saw Vincent and Veronique aboard. "My own dammed son."

CHAPTER 10

La Gomera,
late May 1895

"Well done Vincent," smiled Veronique as they left the quayside behind them a mass of seething people, Salazar prominent in the middle shaking his stick in anger. "It was you who discovered your mother's little scheme."

"And your idea to spy on her," replied Veronique hugging Vincent. "I do love you! You out thought them all, my little shark."

"And I love you darling porpoise, but it's not over yet."

"Why?" Veronique looked momentarily confused.

"The Germans will soon see through your mother's deception, they are much faster than us and unfortunately the Governor's ship is close behind us too," he replied grimly. "I don't understand how that has happened. Escobar is injured so it can't be him, he must have got a message to his men."

"What about our rendezvous?"

"Half an hour around the west coast, I hope Darkson has his wits about him." He climbed onto the bridge thinking how much he enjoyed ocean life and reflecting that it must be in his blood before shouting, "How are you managing Pline?"

"Similar to my father's yacht; basic principles are the same!" Pline yelled back. "The problem is that we only have sails and the others have engines, the Spanish ship is shadowing us already! Still, we have a start and there is a good wind," He veered *Calypso* to the west, heading as directly into the wind as the sails of the ship would allow. "There's no way they can keep up with us if the wind holds, must be a force five," yelled Pline bracing himself as they felt the ship spring to life.

Vincent spun around and watched the two pursuing ships struggle in the swell as they came out into the main Atlantic Ocean away from the islands natural protection. "Nature's elements are stronger than man made," he yelled across to Pline, who grinned confidently back. "Darkson won't let me down, he never has done," Vincent continued, gripping the wheel harder and revelling in the sheer power of the wind. Twenty exhilarating minutes later, he spotted a small beach area on the west coast of the island. "We won't have long in there, we need to be quick." Vincent shouted as he saw the planned rendezvous, a narrow inlet. It had looked easy on the map, now he was not so sure, they would have to take a boat in.

"Darkson should be here," he scanned the shoreline, seeing the small landing area, as he dropped the anchor at Punta de la Nariz headland. Vincent lowered the small boat as Pline watched nervously behind, the rest of the group holding the semi reefed sails in irons and watching the coastline. Costa and Jacques made ready to go ashore. "There they are!" yelled Vincent excitedly. "Get going." Costa started rowing hard against the swell and soon disappeared from sight. They waited onboard for what seemed like an eternity to Vincent before the small craft finally reappeared.

"I don't mind saying I was cursing you son," roared Silver beaming as he scrambled aboard *Calypso*. "I can't say that I hold with you taking my boat and crew like that, it was bloody mutiny."

"Salazar was watching you like a hawk. This was the only way of avoiding him and his men," said Vincent turning hard back into the wind and yelling to his men to lift the sails. "They were posted everywhere and listening to everything you said. The other reason was that Veronique realised what her mother was doing; it was the only way to get the treasure out…Subterfuge."

"Well it worked!" said Silver turning to Veronique. "You my dear are a real dark horse."

"Your son did most of it." Veronique responded modestly.

"Veronique," came a voice; it was Victoria struggling to climb onboard. "How could you do that to me?"

"You owe your daughter a vote of thanks considering the deceit you practised," glowered Silver.

"The Cross, where is it?"

"Here mother," replied Veronique pointing to the casket lying inside the bridge.

"Let me see." She opened the lid and gazed again at the treasure inside, struggling to keep her balance as *Calypso* bit into the wind. "It's so beautiful." She lifted it out for everyone to see. "Look, pure gold and diamond encrusted."

"Must be about eighteen inches high," said Vincent glancing at it. "Worth a bloody fortune."

"What do we do about Victoria?" glowered Silver. "She betrayed us. It was all I could do not to throw her in the sea back there! She let us all down."

"Not true," replied Veronique looking at her mother and smiling. "You see she knew Escobar would have it all planned so she did a deal with him. She planned the whole thing to ensure your safe getaway."

"Is this true?" asked Vincent amazed by this latest revelation.

"Yes," replied Victoria. "I know it was subterfuge, but it was necessary. There was too much at stake; it was the only way to neutralise Escobar and get away myself. Apologies for my seemingly bad behaviour, but it was necessary."

"Well, I'm damned!" said Silver, if what you say is true then I have to say I apologise ma'am."

"We have succeeded Captain Silver, at least so far. Now, what is there to learn from the Cross?"

"There's no inscription on it," said Silver.

"No, there was a separate carved tablet that seemed to upset Escobar when he read it," replied Victoria gazing at the Cross. "He must have hidden the tablet, it's not here! Still we have the more valuable item."

"We're not out of the fire yet," said Vincent looking behind them. "Salazar is as mad as hell and god knows who is sailing Escobar's yacht."

"We've got company," shouted Enrico pointing towards to headland. There at speed and belching smoke came *'The Dresden'*. "Thought it was too good to be true, she must have overtaken the Spanish ship, bigger engines." Vincent groaned. "All hands to deck," bellowed Silver, taking charge. "Sails tight as you can get. Vincent get your men ready, we'll out-run that bugger yet."

The wind was still strengthening and *Calypso* literally jumped, as the sails caught even tighter and she surged into the waves. "Stop where you are or we will shoot," boomed a distorted amplified voice. "Go to hell Blomburg, these are international waters," shouted Silver knowing the German would not be able to hear him. Then to Vincent he yelled "Tighter into the wind!" looking desperately around to see where the wind was. If he could get her positioned right, he could outrun *'Dresden'* yet.

"Ladies down below please, this could get nasty!" He commanded, pulling *Calypso* tighter and praying that she could outrun the lumbering battleship. In the distance, there was a puff of smoke from *"Dresden"*. Silver knew what that meant. "Get down!" he bellowed as a thunderous bang was followed by a whistling noise and a tremendous splash in the water on their port side. "About fifty metres off target, that will take little correcting," he noted grimly to Vincent before yelling, "Ready about, we're taking her around! We need to keep tacking to confuse him." There was another puff of smoke and again Silver judged it landed about fifty metres away. He would need to keep the tacks irregular or the German would work it out.

"Ready about," he yelled. His sole armament was one antiquated cannon that he had previously fired at Salazar. He looked over at *"The Dresden"* as an idea struck him. "Vincent did you say that Blomburg was having boiler problems?"

"Yes, but I heard one of his men complaining that Blomburg had engineered it all in order to come for the treasure," shouted Vincent holding the wheel grimly.

"There's a lot of steam coming from the side and little out of the chimney itself, as if he hasn't enough steam. Get the small cannon out," roared Silver running over to the loaded cannon and quickly training it on the approaching cruiser. If he could hit the funnel, it may create enough of a pressure problem. "Keep down everyone," he yelled as he sighted the small gun and fired.

The recoil nearly knocked him over. He peered through the smoke to see that his shot had fallen well short but he had the range. Quickly he loaded and gasped as *"Dresden's"* next shot came within ten metres soaking him in spray. They were getting closer and it would not be long before they were hit. He fired again and saw the funnel on *"Dresden"* sway alarmingly before righting itself as the great ship steamed on. "Captain you've got to stop," yelled Steppenhoff on the steamship. "The boiler is losing pressure."

"No way," growled the Captain. "This is personal."

"Blast it," yelled Silver, the cannon was damaged and he couldn't load it. Believing all was lost he cursed, and then heard a distant rumble. He looked across at *"Dresden"* and saw its funnel shake and then slowly collapse in on itself. There was a big bang and the cruiser slowed to a halt.

"Vincent head north! I think we've got them!" he shouted gleefully. Within minutes they had put at least one hundred metres between the two ships and he could see the Germans on deck angrily waving their arms. "We have a problem," yelled Vincent from the bridge. "Off bow starboard fifteen degrees."

"I wondered when he would show up," groaned Silver. Escobar's yacht was sailing directly towards them from the north. "Must have come around the top of the island, how on earth did he know to do that?" grumbled Silver. "What are you going to do?" shouted Victoria nervously, her earlier elation forgotten as the wind whistled in the shrouds. On their current course they were heading straight for the beach. There was a sudden crack and *Calypso* shuddered. Silver ducked instinctively then realised it was not a cannonball.

"Vincent, what the hell has happened?"

"The steering, I have no control," yelled his son. "Something must have damaged the rudder mechanism we need to drop the sails."

"Damn!" Silver swore, seeing that the Spanish cruiser was even closer. "Take us onto the beach," he yelled. "The tide will take her in; the dammed rudder must have given way with pressure."

"But we'll lose her," yelled back Vincent.

"Well, it's too deep for the anchor yet so we will need to guide her. Brace yourselves there's a sandbank which should hold us for a while." With a sickening crunch, they hit the sand bank ahead of the beach and *Calypso* leaned alarmingly. "Quick into the water, we need to get ashore in case she rolls," yelled Silver, looking grimly around.

They staggered onto the sand bank, noticing that there was only a short shallow channel across from the bank to the mainland. Silver wondered whether the tide was coming in, if so she would not be stuck for long. He noticed that the Spanish cruiser held steady just off the swell, watching as a boat was lowered before beginning to make its way to shore. Silver saw that Vincent was the last to leave *Calypso* carrying the Cross and the casket. Who the hell was sailing the Spanish ship, he puzzled, it couldn't be Escobar or Salazar. Zhou Wang and his Chinese men!

Silver looked around angrily trying to get his bearings. By his calculations, he reckoned they were near or at Valle Gran Rey, meaning that the town of Vuettas was not far inland.

"That bloody cook," he growled to Enrico. "He must have stolen Escobar's ship!"

"What can we do?" asked Vincent as Victoria and Veronique stared at the approaching Chinese. "We can out fight them," replied Silver grimly. "Then we head back to *Calypso*, she's still seaworthy, and I reckon the tides coming in so she'll float soon." He watched as the Chinese made their way to the shoreline some twenty metres away.

"Zhou Wang! What the hell do you think you are doing?" he yelled as the familiar figure stepped ashore. "I believe you have something that belongs to these men of the cloth," replied Zhou, as enigmatic as ever.

"What do you mean?"

"I told you all that I control the island, and want to avoid unnecessary bloodshed. You have something that belongs to us, hand it over and we will leave you in peace."

"I don't believe that for a moment," replied Silver, staring at two of the monks who held guns fixed on the *Calypso* group.

"Do as I say or they will not hesitate to use their guns."

"Strange behaviour for men of the cloth. Who are these people?"

"You no longer make demands on me," replied Zhou Wang coldly. "Now pass the Cross over before we start shooting you one by one…starting with the ladies."

On the stricken *Dresden*, Klaus Von Steppenhof looked ahead pensively as they came to a halt. They may have lost the Columbus Cross but he knew of something far more important, something that he instinctively knew would change the course of events. He wasn't about to let anyone know, least of all the idiot and bombastic Captain Blomberg. He smiled to himself, let them play their silly games, they would return to East Africa and hunt down the real treasure. Even better, he knew a fantastic remote island from which he could build his own empire well away from the strutting idiots who characterised the German military machine.

"Men of the cloth?" shouted Silver as a monk stepped forward and grabbed Veronique. She screamed as a long wicked looking knife sliced at the top of her blouse.

"The Cross," growled Zhou Wang coldly.

"Do as he says before someone gets hurt," said Silver, gesturing to Vincent to place the casket on the floor and watching Zhou Wang's face lighting up.

"Everything has turned out as it should. I'm afraid I cannot let you leave the island." Zhou Wang straightened up as he spoke to survey the small group.

"You lying bastard," growled Silver springing forwards and getting no further than three feet before a knife buried its shaft deep in his thigh.

"Father," yelled Vincent starting forwards as Silver fell groaning.

"Stay where you are, he'll live," said Zhou Wang. "I will not kill you but none of you will ever leave this island; none of the football tournament contestants will. That is what it was all about, getting you all here. It has taught us much about the different tribes and how to take forward our great mission. You are privileged to be at the founding of a great movement." He lifted the Cross, as if in prayer, then suddenly his whole body jerked as a shot reverberated in the air. Zhou Wang stared puzzled at his hand as the Cross fell away, his fingers dripping blood. His other hand dropped the casket onto the ground as one of the monks sprang forwards to help him.

"Salazar will be beaten by no one," yelled a familiar voice as the Spaniard limped forwards holding a rifle. "You are lucky I am a good shot, Silver," he growled looking at his fallen enemy. "I could finish you off now, but better that you die slowly in your own blood." He lifted the Cross and stared at it as his men, including Gaizka, filed in behind him. "Very nice, makes up for all the inconvenience."

"How did you get here?" asked Vincent.

"Jacques is a lover spurned, he helped me out by telling me that you would stop at this beach, he is a genuine friend of the Spanish," smiled Salazar as Jacques looked guiltily around before edging closer to the Spaniard. "My family… They threatened them.…" he said, as if by way of an apology. "The steering, that was you?" asked Enrico stonily.

"Enough! Move next to the others," growled Salazar gesturing with his Winchester rifle. "Horses brought us here but we'll go back by the cruiser." He walked over to the beach with three of his men behind him. "First of all we have some unfinished business. I don't like monks, never did and my good friend Escobar would be pleased if I cleansed them from the island." Saying that he raised the Winchester and shot the nearest monk. "No," screamed Victoria, "you can't do this to men of the cloth."

"They are not men of the cloth; there are no religious orders here on the island. They're just a bunch of damned fanatics," replied Salazar coldly. He raised his rifle again, smiling coldly, and then spun around towards a blur of movement before falling to the ground clutching his shoulder. "Asian martial arts. He should have known about such things," said Zhou signalling to Johnny Tang who withdrew from the fallen Salazar. "Bloody hell," exclaimed Silver. "Never seen anyone move so fast."

"On the ground," yelled Zhou Wang to Salazar's men, "or Salazar dies." Struggling to speak but prevented from doing clearly so by Johnny Tang's arm in a vice like grip around his neck, Salazar croaked. "You won't get away with this."

"You're lucky to be alive after what you've done to the monks," growled Zhou, "Where's the Cross?"

"Over here," replied Vincent lifting the icon in one hand and a small pistol in the other. He gestured to the others. "Come on; Darkson and Enrico carry my father, Pline you see to the ladies. Thanks for the loan of the little pistol Veronique." Zhou remained calm "You don't realise what you are doing, you cannot defeat us," he said confidently. Vincent was unmoved. "Perhaps not, but I do what I believe in. Now sit down all of you or I'll use this thing." He walked backwards carefully to the shoreline. "Where are we going?" asked Victoria. "To *Calypso*, it's seaworthy and starting to lift on the tide. Now has disabled it. Bring our dear French friend Jacque with us, I am sure he wants to make amends and fix the chains and we can sail away from here. Darkson, before I forget, smash their landing boat we don't want any followers," he said scrambling behind them.

Zhou Wang stood and now watched them with growing anger. "That was a bad mistake Salazar shooting one of our people. You will repay that debt with your own life."

"Give me a weapon and I'll fight for it," spat the Spaniard, "or are you going to kill me in cold blood?"

"I'm not going to kill you. No, there's something you and your son can do which is far more valuable to me and my friends than your miserable life."

"What do you mean?"

"You will see soon enough. It will take more than a few foolhardy people to stop our movement. The Cross is only part of the treasure, and we have the other significant item."

Rudder fixed and *Calypso* re-floated by raising the sails and pulling her off the sand bank, the survivors looked at each other with relief as they set sail for the north of the island. Vincent had assumed command as his father lay on deck groaning. "Your father's leg is bleeding badly, it must be a main artery," said Victoria.

"We can't put into land at the moment. Escobar will have mobilised the local militia, we'd be arrested on the spot."

"He needs a doctor," replied Victoria. Vincent went across to his father. "Let me see, how bad is it?"

"Bad enough," growled Silver. "You have to go on without me and get away from here, drop me off and I'll take my chances with Escobar."

"You can't survive on your own father, we stay together."

"Your father's right, you need to get away with the Cross," replied Victoria quietly. "I will look after your father. I owe him that and perhaps Escobar will show leniency."

"Mother."

"I'm tired of running Veronique. This world is my world not America. Besides I have unfinished business with Zhou Wang."

"What do you mean?"

"It's for the best; the Cross will give you and your man a good start. It's your legacy. Besides, I've rather got to like this island and its people. I can even put up with Mr Silver here in small doses." Silver overheard the remark. "Is that a proposal?" he asked grimacing. "No! It's an offer of help. We have the Red House I purchased."

"It makes sense," agreed Silver. "I can't handle the crossing and there's nowhere else for you to go. If you stay in Europe, they will hunt you down. In America they won't find you."

"I'm not leaving you for a Cross."

"Remember what I said about the Salazar treasure," he whispered to Vincent. "Find that and your future is settled."

"According to this map there's a small village in the north of the island called Chiquere, put us off there," said Victoria. "They will have a doctor."

"Do it son and *Calypso* is yours."

"I'll come back for you."

"If there's anything to come back to," whispered Silver to himself.

Chiquere
Next day

Escobar shifted his weight carefully off his damaged leg and looked across the room. He had been up all night writing a suitable explanation of events for Madrid but he knew deep inside that he was ruined once the story got out. He looked across at Victoria, Silver, Salazar and Blomburg. They had all been brought to him at the town in various stages of despair. Blomburg had survived the rocks but *"Dresden"* was in a parlous state. Salazar had no ship and was a ruined man whilst Silver and Victoria just stared benignly at him. Escobar shifted his weight on the chair and grunted in agony from the bullet wound that had been quickly patched.

It had been an agonizing journey across the mountains but he had good reason to be here. "You realise that you will all now pay the forfeit we agreed," he snapped. "The Silver's got the treasure so I don't see why," replied Silver looking at Victoria. "That damned Chinaman and your son outsmarted us all. I should have you all locked up for that alone!! Is there one good reason why I shouldn't? It wasn't just trinkets in that casket," said Escobar, turning in alarm as there was a disturbance at the door. He heard shouting and then grunts before the door was wrenched open. "What the hell is going on out there Captain," he yelled.

"I told you all I was in control, that is your future." A familiar voice came from the doorway and Zhou Wang strode in. "You've got a nerve," stormed Escobar, "Guards arrest him." Zhou Wang gave a thin smile "Your guards are trussed up," he said coldly. "You have all been privileged to witness a great event here and will now work with us on the next stage."

"What the hell are you talking about?" growled Escobar. "Talk sense man."

"We have forces on this island well beyond your very limited abilities," Zhou Wang told him coldly. "You will find that this entire town is surrounded."

"This is preposterous," growled Escobar.

Fernandez joined the Chinaman as he continued. "You are all going to accompany me on a journey," Escobar tried again to stop his flow of words. "I cannot allow…" he started, realising with a feeling of dread that he was ruined. "You allow nothing," replied Zhou Wang. "Your lives are forfeit. You do whatever I desire." He gestured to the monks and they filed in. "As your leader I decree that all men here will be disciples, that you will be dedicated to the promulgation of our faith and beliefs across the world. Our quest has begun, a quest that will never cease until the world is returned to its correct order, however long that takes. Your lives as you know them no longer exist; time in the world of the eastern peoples has a different dimension to the West, do not think that way anymore but think of yourselves at the vanguard of a great astonishing movement that will be talked about for centuries."

CHAPTER 11

Marigot Bay,
St Lucia,
present day

Guy groaned as he awoke, his head felt as if a herd of elephants had trampled on it. He got up shakily and stumbled through into the main cabin area, rubbing his eyes and looking around. That had been the strangest dream, he thought, almost as if it had actually happened. He saw Rose lying inert on the port side bench. "Wake up," he said gently. "What time is it?" she asked, rubbing her eyes. "Eleven in the morning; I've never slept as deeply as that, it's as if we were..." Rose finished his sentence, her face aghast "Drugged!" she whispered. "I wonder." Guy stumbled to the galley and looked for the glasses they had used. "That bottle of wine we drank, where's the bottle?" Rose looked around quickly the said, "Gone, totally gone, and the two glasses also."

"Someone has been onboard." Guy gasped.

"How can you tell?"

"I can feel it, sixth sense." He went over to his lockable chart tabletop where he kept all his papers and opened it, putting on his glasses as he did so. The papers had been moved. "Who would want to search the yacht?" he asked. "The same person who is behind all this," replied Rose. "Someone who thinks they can manipulate us."

"What makes you so sure?"

"Someone is following us, expecting us to lead them to the Cross."

"The compass," they exclaimed in unison looking at each other. Guy picked it up and looked underneath. The note was still there exactly where he had replaced it. "I had the strangest dream," said Guy shaking his head.

"Tell me."

"I saw into the past; everything was vague and faces were blurred, it was as if I was above it all looking down at the action. It must have been a combination of the alcohol, drugs and what we read in the diary."

"Who was in it?"

"My grandfather; I dreamt of the football match."

"So what do we do now?" asked Rose.

"Firstly we need to contact Blackie and Beatrice, they'll be concerned."

"The radio," Rose reached out but Guy got there first. "It is broken," he said, picking up the handset to show her. "I got it fixed before we left and now the thing is dead."

"Or deliberately damaged." Rose said thoughtfully. "My mobile," said Guy looking around, "that's gone too."

"Stolen," replied Rose slowly. "Fortunately I keep mine in an unusual place." She lifted it out of the inside of her waistband, "it has a small holster which has served me well in the past," she said activating it. "Beatrice?" She heard the distorted but familiar voice reply. "Rose, where are you,"

"In Marigot Bay."

"What's happening, have you made progress?"

"None yet."

"Blackie is useless." Rose heard a grunt in the background. "Are you sure you have nothing?"

"Just one thing," replied Rose carefully.

"What's that?"

"Stop, don't say anymore," hissed Guy fiercely. "If they are as thorough as we think they'll be listening in."

"What is it?" shouted Beatrice.

"I'll call you when I can but be careful, very careful," said Rose. "It's more dangerous than you think."

Guy explained his fears; "Anyone can listen in these days using tracking or bugging devices." Breaking off, he pointed to prove his point, "Look, see that large yacht across the bay. They've been there since yesterday." She followed his pointing finger. "Grunt and Viper," she whispered.

"What?"

"You're Grunt, as that's all you do," smiled Rose.

"And you bite, is that it?"

"When aggravated yes," replied Rose. "Useful to have code names, don't you think?"

"Could be, but not sure on your choice, prefer Bear."

"Ok, they're here to stay; we need to recap where we are."

"One; we have two diaries that may or may not contain hidden references. Two; we have the compass clue and, three; we possibly have someone who is using us. Four; we think that there is this valuable Cross that our respective families believe is worth all this trouble."

"It is," said Rose hotly.

"And that yacht is definitely following us and we definitely had an intruder onboard last night"

"Are you sure?"

"Look at the decking; there's a small sliver of glass. Whoever it was removed the two glasses we drank from and then dropped one of them. It gives them away," concluded Guy.

"So what options do we have?"

"We have to find the Cross first."

"What's made you suddenly interested?"

"I dreamt about the damned thing, but more importantly that bugger over there has convinced me. This is getting personal, I'm sick of being messed about after my experiences in Hong Kong. My father told me to *"Remember what I taught you."* Rose struggled to see a link. "Why?" she asked. "Because he taught me about the explorers; the sea explorers going back centuries, he even had a pet theory that the Chinese discovered most of the world before the Europeans. He was going to write a book on it. It was one of the reasons that he was in Hong Kong doing research, as well as lecturing on psychology." Rose smiled. "Welcome to the world of probabilities," she said "I'm glad you are with me on this now."

"If our ancestors did bring the Columbus Cross back across the Atlantic where would they have put it?"

"Perhaps it was broken up," Rose suggested.

"Doubt it. It has to be in the diaries."

"I'll get them," said Rose bringing the books.

"Wonder why our guests didn't take them," mused Guy.

"They want us to lead them to the treasure, do the hard work," replied Rose opening the diary and reading the pages slowly.

"Give me the French one," said Guy.

"Ah, here it is," she said, "your grandfather talks about coming back to St Lucia and getting married on the island, setting up a banana plantation and purchasing the house. He mentions that those who search for them need to always be vigilant. He then talks about their sheer joy at the birth of their daughter Claire in the year 1895. Interesting, wasn't she the one who died on the *Lusitania* in 1915?"

"I believe so. Look, they must have had funding to buy a plantation," said Guy.

"It talks here about restoring *Calypso* as well, and sailing to the devils fish hook."

"What?"

"The devils fish hook, it says. He never saw his father again after leaving La Gomera. He talks of restoring *Calypso* to its past glory and taking a long voyage. The rest is insignificant events, no mention of the Cross."

"Better than nothing," replied Guy. "Your Veronique talks mostly of domestic arrangements as far as I can see."

"Ah, here's a little more about the Canary Islands; he uses bolder handwriting, something about a Challenge in La Gomera," continued Rose, absorbed. "Some sort of match with four teams including a team of Chinese."

"Really?"

"It says that the Chinese team entered at the last moment, led by a man called Zhou Wang."

"What was the challenge?"

"Football."

"Must have been one of the first ever games played," said Guy in wonder. "It was just starting to be taken seriously in England in the late nineteenth century." Rose had a serious look on her face. "It has to have more significance because he talks so much about it. Incidentally," she said standing up, "the other yacht is moving."

"Devils fish hook, I wonder," replied Guy looking across the bay and then grabbing his atlas and leafing through the pages. "It may fit with the note on the compass about Rodney and Cockburn and Devil's isle. Yes here it is, got it."

"What?"

He lowered his voice "Nothing yet, I won't say in case those bastards have a microphone trained on us. Come on we're going to get supplies for a long trip."

"What about Blackie and Beatrice?"

"Too dangerous, let them enjoy each other's company. After all, they share the same grandmother, Claire Silver, so they should have plenty in common! Come on we have to think of a way of getting away from our pursuers, I'm putting classical music on the speakers just in case of bugs."

"Oh no! Can't we have some modern music for a change, some Rap for instance?"

"Not on this boat Viper, not whilst I still have my hearing intact."

<hr>

Salboa carefully preened himself in front of the mirror. Extremely vain, he combed his moustache many times a day. He'd arrived the night before from Cadiz and boarded his yacht called *Alcazabar* in secrecy. He was a man used to command and barked orders to the crew in a long practised fashion. He stared out of the telescope. "You bloody well dropped the glass didn't you Matarife?" he scowled. "It was an accident." Matarife's response was hesitant, fearing his boss's unpredictable temper.

"Of course it was a bloody accident! I didn't think you did it on purpose! Only I don't like accidents, they spell incompetence." Matarife was contrite. "Yes boss," he replied, head bent. "Just like the accident you had in England. I ask you to do a simple job and now they suspect us. For now, follow the boat so they can't see us."

"Where do you think they are heading?"

"I know exactly where they are heading. It's the precise location we need to know. The bugging device is working?"

"Yes, but we're only picking up garbled stuff."

"They're probably on their guard now after what you did."

"How far do we stay behind?"

"Use your judgement. I don't want any confrontations yet despite your ham fisted efforts on the boat last night. We cannot afford accidents Matarife. I have waited all my life for this chance to avenge my father." Salboa looked around the ostentatious cabin as he headed below. Unlike *Hidalgo*, *Alcazabar* was a motor yacht, a rich man's plaything. Salboa portrayed a wealthy and ostentatious life aboard his luxurious yachts in the Caribbean and Mediterranean but in reality, his empire was teetering on the brink of financial ruin. This treasure hunt was his opportunity to change his fortunes.

"What are we waiting for?" growled Blackie. "We have to do something." Beatrice, heartily sick of the old man snapped. "What exactly?"

"What did Rose say?"

"She said nothing and it would be nice if you made yourself useful for once."

"I'm trying my best."

"Then stop drinking," growled Beatrice.

"Look we need to work together on this," replied Blackie standing up in the main lounge at Soufriere. "There must be a lead here somewhere, just the simple fact that you were told to come here." She stared at him coldly. "So what do you suggest?" she said. "I'm thinking," said Blackie eyeing the nearly empty Brandy bottle. "Well think fast."

"What's the history of the house?"

"It's all in this old brochure here," replied Beatrice. "God but the place needs some serious decorating, it's a mess." Blackie had no interest in the standard of decoration.

"Just tell me what the brochure says about the house," he demanded impatiently. "It's over two hundred and fifty years old and over a thousand feet above sea level which accounts for the cold. The original French owners built the botanical gardens. There are lots of French families around here who inherited land, from the days when France ruled this whole area."

"Who lived here previously?"

"My mother, Marie lived here all her life; she was the granddaughter of Veronique Silver. Her husband was a sailor; he retired and was responsible for looking after Pigeon Island that's an island off the north west coast."

"That picture, is that him?" Blackie asked, pointing to a large painting on the main wall. "Yes." She said. "There's an inscription at the bottom; *'Guardian of the Island'*," he read. "There's something else there," continued Blackie looking hard. "*The Battle of All Saints*" Why does it say that when there is no battle? My God I've got it," he shouted exuberantly.

Leaving the bay had been ridiculously simple after the motor cruiser had suddenly vanished. They were clearly playing a cat and mouse game so Guy decided to take the advantage and head as fast as possible in what he hoped would be the least expected direction. He considered that moving south would confuse their pursuers before turning north. The wind had dropped to no more than a slight breeze, so he started the diesel engine to give steerage as it was getting dark.

"Rose, we have to stop for the night whilst I plot a course. I don't want to be on the open sea for any longer than necessary," he told her several hours later, and anchored in a small unlit bay that slowly disappeared into a ghostly ridge as the light faded. Guy cursed as he saw a light to the south. "Two lights; green port and red starboard; it means something is heading this way. I'm going to go ashore and take a walk when it's completely dark."

"Where?" Rose asked concerned.

"Up onto the headland to find out who is following. I was always taught that the best form of defence is attack so it's time to strike back and try to slow them down. I don't want them behind us as we cross the sea. I noticed the bay over there has some paths so with a bit of luck I should be able to snoop on them."

"Could be dangerous," Rose said carefully.

"I'll take the flare gun; it gives me a couple of shots. If you see it fired then start the engine and head north," he instructed.

"To where? You have no phone remember?"

"My house higher up the coast near a place called Denning. Stop there and go to the old house on the far end of the street. I'll cut across land and meet you there; the keys are above the shed window."

"Watch where you put your feet, there's poisonous spiders and snakes on the hillside in the Rain Forest." Rose warned.

"What sort of snakes?" Guy grimaced.

"Very poisonous, small snakes, only about a foot long. You need to be careful, Bear, I read about them last week."

Guy casting aside the snake concerns and lowering his binoculars said. "Just as I hoped, they've anchored down in the bay. I need to get going Viper. Perhaps I'll meet your namesake!" he smiled, heading for *Hidalgo*'s stern and one of two small inflatable craft he kept stowed on the stern deck. He rowed carefully ashore not at all certain of what he was going to do but hoping he could turn the tables. He grabbed the torch, noting that the hills were eerily silent, and tried not to think about snakes as he reached the summit and looked down.

Faint moonlight revealed a bay and he thought he could see a light. The other boat was down there, he was sure of it. He quickened his pace taking care to keep the torch low to avoid being seen. The boat was moored at the other side of the high rock promontory. By his calculation, he was near the '*des Cartier*' trail, now used mainly by tourists. He vaguely recalled a local guide saying that whole families used to walk the trail to Soufriere market carrying their wares for sale. As he rounded the corner, he saw smoke and lights ahead. His quarry had stopped for the night. He noticed a cave and sat down to watch the bay below as he had to be sure it was the *Alcazabar*.

After a short while, he saw a slight movement and stiffly stood up. They were on the move. Smiling grimly to himself, he saw the large motor cruiser. He stretched, his foot slipped caus-ing a rock to rattle down the sharp bank He quickly lay flat again, cursing his luck, as something glinted and he heard a sharp noise above him like a whip striking. The bastards were firing at him! He scrambled backward out of range as another shot cracked through the air. He deduced that it must be the mystery Spaniard firing and moved downhill fast to the waterside taking great care to stay in the shadows. Finding a large rock, he sat behind it look-ing through his binoculars trying to see what was happening.

Nothing; the night was deathly quiet, eerie. He presumed they had assumed the noise was an animal, and settled down for a long wait. An idea formed in his mind. He must have nodded off as he woke later to a light splashing noise. He shook himself awake and saw a small inflatable heading slowly for his cove. They were coming over, either to investigate or to get water. He shrank back into the shadows, taking care to make no noise and watched. The inflatable was making hard work of it. He watched carefully as a small stocky man climbed out cursing as he slipped, carrying two large plastic containers. Guy moved slowly, watching the man start to climb rocks, presumably looking for fresh water.

He watched a little longer until the man disappeared from view then quietly made his way forwards. Silently he pushed the craft out and started paddling slowly towards the *Alcazabar* whose white hull gleamed in the moonlight about twenty metres away. As he drew nearer he let himself drift quietly rather than use the oars. He listened intently, becoming increasingly nervous as he approached the side of the craft. He could hear several voices as he paddled slowly to the stern and looked for the engine hatch and tanks. Carefully, he pulled himself up onto the stern gunnels and padded across to the main fuel tank. The voices were at the bow of the vessel and he whoever was talking was speaking in Spanish.

Carefully he opened the door to the galley and looked around shaking, unsure if this was from fear or just cold. He found what he was looking for immediately. It looked as if everyone had retired for the night except the man sent to get the water. Quietly he opened the fuel tanks and poured a bag of sugar in. That should stop them for a while.

Suddenly a light flashed in the distance followed by a shout. He cursed silently; the man must have returned and found his boat gone. Guy dropped overboard and jumped into his own dingy. He began paddling furiously as lights flooded the water from two men on deck *"Alcazabar"* with powerful torches. One of them suddenly shouted and the beam blinded him as they searched. Cursing under his breath as a shot rang out, followed by two more, Guy heard the bullets whistle perilously close. He rolled out of the dingy seconds before machine gun fire spattered the dark sea, water erupting all around him and the inflatable starting to hiss.

Guy dived down deep, hoping he had not been hit. He swam underwater towards the north end of the bay. Gasping for breath, he broke the surface and looked around, adrenaline still pumping, calculating his position to be about twenty metres away to the north of his last surface. They were still firing into the water clearly expecting him to head back to the shore. He took a deep gulp of air and went down again just before a large light arched across the water where he had been. He swam until he felt his lungs bursting and came to the surface again. In the distance he could just see them still swivelling the arc lamp across the water in large sweeps and preparing another inflatable. He had to keep swimming.

Fortunately, their attention appeared diverted to the return of the water gathering man. Swimming hard he finally reached the northern bay and looked around. Making sure there was no one there, he pulled himself shivering out of the water and made his way over the rocks. He was frozen and still over an hour away from Rose, which meant that his pursuers would be there before him. He had to protect her, so reluctantly he reached for the waterproof bag at his waist that contained the flare gun. Scrambling, he climbed quickly up the bank and extracted the bulky snub-nosed flare gun. Carefully he fired two flares in quick succession, flung the gun down and made his way rapidly up the hill before they pinpointed his position. He headed as high as he could, hoping that Rose would carry out his instructions immediately. If she did not they would go for her; though he hoped his earlier sabotage of their fuel would slow them down. He had at least fifteen miles to cover as quickly as possible wet and frozen.

"Where are we going?" asked Beatrice as they drove to Pigeon Island the next morning. "The Battle of All Saints, it's the clue." Replied Blackie. *"All Saints to Devils Isle and Vice Admirals Rodney to Cockburn"* are written on the inside cover of the diaries, it means that your dear ancestor Veronique, left us a clear clue," Blackie bubbled away excitedly as he parked and they walked across the narrow land area to the peninsular called Pigeon Island. "Here we are!" he shouted as they reached a sign and then read out the inscription, "Listen, *'The Battle of All Saints 1782 - Vice Admiral Rodney set sail to intercept the French fleet seen from this hill at Martinique'* There were over one hundred ships at sail," continued Blackie. "Now all we have to do is track down an island where the British fleet also headed for a great battle."

"I'm lost Blackie."

"Rodney's fleet sailed to defeat the French at the Battle of All Saints from here and it changed the history and balance of power in the Americas in the favour of the English over the French," explained Blackie patiently.

"So?"

"My God I've got it!" shouted Blackie, ignoring Beatrice's puzzled frown and grabbing a tattered old book he carried. "Devils Isle, the sailors used to call Bermuda Devils Isle. What's more, Vice Admiral Cockburn sailed from Bermuda to set fire to the White House in Washington. A double clue! It has to be the answer," he said excitedly hugging a still confused Beatrice.

It was after midnight as Guy now nearly exhausted, made his way down through the tightly packed trees onto the familiar pathway.

It was the route he took on his Suzuki only a few short days ago, but it already felt like another lifetime. He walked on by moonlight, instinct telling him to head in a north-easterly direction. He estimated that he had walked about ten miles; his feet were blistering from the seawater and he was still shivering with cold. He hoped Rose had followed his instructions; she was experienced enough to understand the electronics and workings of the boat, providing she had not panicked. He could see nothing out to sea and assumed that if *Hidalgo* was there Rose had turned all the lights out. He finally saw the familiar village of Denning in the distance and made his way along the pathway to the house. He approached the old house from the back and entered the old shack to get the key. He lifted his hands up and felt along the ledge for it. Nothing!!

"Rose," he whispered as loud as he dared, "are you there?" His fears started to mount she should have arrived by now. Where was the dammed key? He felt around again but there was nothing; Blackie must have removed it when he left with Beatrice.

He was shivering now, exhausted and needing warm clothes. He reckoned it was about three in the morning. Deciding he had no choice, he went to the back window behind the kitchen and found a piece of wood. Taking great care, he pushed hard on the old window frame that gave way with a crash, making him grimace at the noise. Looking around he saw lights come on a hundred metres away and quickly unlocked the small window before climbing painfully inside. He looked around. There was nothing out of the ordinary, but where the hell was Rose?

He quickly changed into dry clothes, including a large woollen sweater and warmed himself by the gas stove grateful as the heat permeated his frozen body. He began to feel dreadfully tired and drifted off to sleep, before waking suddenly to a noise. There was an intruder in the house; was it the Spaniard? Tensing, he stood up and walked carefully into the kitchen; someone was there he could sense it. Grabbing the fire poker, he tensed and switched on the main light. "It's me!" shouted Rose dazzled by the sudden brightness. "My God, you gave me a shock," replied Guy dropping the poker. "You didn't exactly help my nerves either," she replied dropping onto a chair. "What happened?"

"Thank god you made it," said Guy with relief as he related the story as quickly as possible.

"When I saw your flares go up I started the engine and headed north. It was very dark and I struggled to see where I was. Thank god for the satellite navigation system. It showed me a boat approaching behind me and gaining fast."

"The Spaniard?"

"Yes, I think so. Strangely, just as they were nearly on me they suddenly stopped about two miles away. I was worried I can tell you."

"Sugar." Guy stated smugly.

"What?"

"I put sugar in their tank! They will be stuck there for a while unless a wind gets up," smiled Guy. "Come on, we need to make a move."

"Where to?"

"Bermuda of course, that's where the treasure is."

"You sure?"

"As sure as I'll ever be, I also know now that these people are dangerous. If they get near us we are in big trouble."

"How can you be so sure it's Bermuda?"

"The notes on the compass," smiled Guy. "The island used to be called Devil's Isle and if you look at it on a map it looks like a fish hook. Admirals Rodney and Cockburn both launched major campaigns. Rodney launched from St. Lucia against the French, and Cockburn from Bermuda to burn the White House."

"Well done Bear."

"And you Viper, you did well with *Hidalgo*, she's complicated and temperamental."

"They taught us more than how to shoot in the Army Cadets, Bear," replied Rose smiling.

"We only have a few hours before they'll have the engine cleaned out. By that time I want to be outside their range."

"Do you think we can beat them there?"

"Hopefully they don't realise yet where we are heading but it will depend on the weather. If there is a strong wind we can get up to thirty knots out of her, they wouldn't be able to match that."

"We should inform the police." Rose said doubtfully.

"Grasshopper and Cricket would probably arrest me first and ask questions later. Besides we will soon be outside their jurisdiction."

They used the spare small inflatable with an outboard motor to get back to *Hidalgo* and then set off on full sail in the dark. The wind was veering to twelve knots and Guy relaxed as their speed increased to eight knots. "Look!" shouted Rose pointing at the screen. "Damn," he saw the blip and realised their pursuers were moving again. "I'll start the engine."

"We seem to be losing them," shouted Rose excitedly ten minutes later. "Good," replied Guy staring at the screen. "They appear to be deliberately slowing down, unless the choppy seas are too much for them."

"Perhaps they just wanted to scare us."

"Possibly," said Guy thoughtfully. "Alternatively he knows where we are going and is playing with us."

"Cat and mouse."

"I'll think of something to lose them as we get nearer Bermuda. In the meantime, I suggest you get some rest whilst I cope with this wind. I am going to have to reef the mainsail slightly; we're at our limit on twelve knots of wind with full rig. Get some rest and if you cannot sleep, read the diaries. I'm going to put Mozart on the speaker system, just what I need to relax. We need to find any clues we can to help us find what we are looking for. I've a feeling that the answer to all this lies within those pages."

CHAPTER 12

Bermuda

The small jet came into land at Bermuda International Airport not a moment too soon for Beatrice and Blackie. They walked through customs and checked transport arrangements. Blackie was back in his disguise as a minister and had breathed a sigh of relief when he had left St Lucia. Guy's warnings about the local police being on to him were irrelevant now. All he had to contend with was the Bermudians who he recalled ruefully had much closer ties to the British administration systems; he decided to stay in his disguise. "So where do we go now?" asked Beatrice looking around the small airport and staring disdainfully at the steel band who were welcoming visitors. "To the only hotel I know," replied Blackie. "I booked it last night; hire cars aren't available on the island so it's a taxi."

They headed down the small winding roads very reminiscent to Blackie of roads in England and for a fleeting moment he felt homesick; they reached the Fairmont Southampton Princess hotel in the Southampton district of the island. He had thought a lot on the flight and was sure that Constance's son, Joe, had been attacked here in Bermuda. All he had to work out now was where the Cross was located. "Did you try Rose again?"

"I've been trying for the last two days. Either she has turned her mobile off or it's out of signal range," replied Beatrice as they arrived at the hotel and drove up the long circular driveway to the grand entrance. "This looks luxurious, just look at the views," she squealed. "It stands on the highest point in the island so you can see both the south and north Atlantic," read Blackie from the brochure in his hands.

Three days later, tired but exhilarated, Guy and Rose sailed into Bermuda Great Sound harbour past the old British fort on their right. The satellite GPS navigation system had proved its worth plotting them through the many treacherous reefs. They had also discovered that they worked well together as a team, sleeping for no more than four hours at a time and sharing tasks. At times during the sail, they had had to jump out of their bunks to reef sails, particularly when the wind reached twenty knots, well in excess of a force six. Even Guy had been worried at the howling wind and rough seas one evening, but with Rose's help, they had taken the sails down and used diesel power. Amazingly, rather than feeling tired they both felt refreshed and ready for anything that the island could throw at them.

On the last day of the crossing, Rose had a breakthrough when she found a small Bermudian travelogue amongst Guys books and a small hidden notation in Beatrice's great grandmother's diary to one Leila Martinez, Waterlot Inn, Bermuda. She had done well to spot it as it was written in very small pencil on the inside cover at the back. Excitedly they realised that Leila was the first name of the daughter of one Jacqui Oleson, who in turn was the daughter of Marie Silver, one of the twins whose mother had died on the *Lusitania*. According to Rose's research Beatrice was the real aunt of Leila and the fact that Leila lived in Bermuda was too much of a coincidence. She was their best hope. Feeling pleased with her work Rose and Guy stood in front of the Waterlot Inn as they entered the bay at the foot of the dominant Fairmont Southampton Hotel. They anchored on a buoy, endured a short customs inspection and went for a swim off the back of *Hidalgo*. "We should wait until the evening before risking upsetting the snakes nest," said Guy as they sat in the cockpit. "Who's the snake?"

"The mysterious Spaniard, I think we can assume that he will be here soon and it could get nasty."

"Maybe we should have involved Beatrice and my Uncle." Rose suggested doubtfully. Guy was adamant, "They would have been a hindrance not a help."

"They will be as mad as hell when they find out."

"They will thank us if we find what we are looking for."

"So what's the plan of attack Bear?"

"First stop we go to the Inn here and ask about this Leila lady."

Guy winched down the small inflatable, attached the small outboard motor and they headed to land. Together they walked the short steep incline towards the Waterlot Inn, part of the Fairmont Southampton Hotel group. They reached it at six pm just as it was starting to open for the evening's trade. A small jetty behind it was home to the ferry that plied its complimentary trade between the two Fairmont hotels in Bermuda and at Hamilton across the bay. They could also see a Jet Ski school next door. They made their way to the front door and went inside. Guy noted the visitor's plaque on the wall stating that Winston Churchill and President Eisenhower had visited the Inn during a Trans-Atlantic conference. "Can I help you sir?" asked the waiter, a dark skinned Bermudian resplendent in the obligatory Bermudian shorts and smart jacket.

"I'm looking for a Leila Martinez," said Guy.

"Never heard of her." The waiter responded quickly.

"Is there anyone else here to ask? It is important that I find her."

"Who is it asking for her," asked the waiter.

"A relative," said Guy smoothly, "we have something for her."

"Wait here a minute."

Four minutes later a taller man came back. "You're asking for a Leila Martinez."

"Yes."

"Fair hair, about six feet tall, green-blue eyes?"

"Could be," improvised Guy.

"She works next door at the Jet Ski and diving centre but she's away at present."

"Do you know when she will be back?"

"Sorry, no."

"Look, here's my mobile number, please ask her to call me when you see her, it is important and will be to her advantage." Guy said firmly.

"You should have pushed harder," said Rose as they walked away. "He was hiding something, I'll stake whatever possessions I have on it."

"And what would that have achieved?" replied Guy as they walked back to the inflatable. "She will call me."

"How do you know?"

"Who can resist a message like that?"

"Hope you're right," grumbled Rose.

"Come on let's go and eat, I fancy some sea food, and the brochure says it's great down the other side at the Whalers Inn."

"But that's down the other side of the hill," complained Rose.

"We can get the complimentary hotel bus," replied Guy. "Come on Viper."

Within an hour, they were eating lobster overlooking a crystal blue sea with white sand. "Lovely location," said Guy appreciatively looking at the views from the Whalers Inn.

"We might afford to come here on holiday if we find this Cross, otherwise we'll probably end up as a waiter here!" grumbled Rose. "It's over two hundred dollars a night for goodness sake." Guy looked up at Rose as his mobile rang. "Just relax Viper," he said and confidently answered. "Hello." A woman's voice greeted him. "Mr Silver?" she asked. "Yes." He replied. "It's Leila Martinez, you are looking for me." The woman said it as a statement rather than a question.

"Yes."

"Why?"

"I have some news for you."

"Which is?" Leila responded guardedly.

"I have to see you face to face. It is too complicated to explain over the phone"

"Try me."

"I have information relating to Veronique and Vincent Silver." Guy relented, convinced that she would hang up if he did not interest her soon. "The Cross," whispered Leila quietly. "Who are you?"

"I'm directly related to Vincent Silver, he was my great-grandfather."

"Why should I trust you? There are a lot of bad people interested in Veronique Silver, what makes you different?" Leila sounded aggressive.

"I have come a long way to help you."

"Do I need your help, or do you need mine?"

"I have nowhere else to turn, please can we meet." Guy almost pleaded.

"I'll need more than this to convince me."

Guy set about trying to convince her. "Your great grandmother Veronique Silver came from England originally, her mother was called Victoria. She married Vincent Silver and they left the Canaries with the Columbus Cross at the end of the nineteenth century," said Guy. "We know there are a number of people also after the Cross. I need your help." Leila relented. "The naval dockyard tomorrow morning at ten, come alone. I'll see you, don't bring anyone else or there's no meeting."

"Where in the dockyard, it's a big place?"

"The dolphin park in the old castle grounds," the line went dead.

Next morning they took *Hidalgo* across to the main dockyard. There were few people around and Guy wondered whether Leila was waiting for the regular ferry to arrive. If so, they would surprise her. Rose expertly tied up and they walked together up the slight incline to the castle area. "Well done Rose, we'll make a sailor of you yet." Rose bristled. "Don't patronise me Bear."

"It was a genuine compliment."

"Well see you don't do it again," she smiled.

"Leila said come alone; you stay here whilst I go through to the dolphin park."

"If I must." Rose looked unhappy at being left behind. "I'll signal you by raising my hand." Guy left her and made his way to the dolphin park.

According to the map, it was part of the museum and actually lay inside the castle walls. He wondered how Rose would be able to see him once he was there, mistake number one. He made his way up the steep path to the park and then through the pay area to the Dolphin Sanctuary. No one was around so he sat down on the bench, watching the shadowy shapes in the water whilst wondering if Rose would be able to gain a vantage point.

"There are two males and three females all bred in captivity."

"Pardon," he said and spun round.

"You came alone?" asked a female voice.

"Yes," replied Guy. He turned slightly to his left and saw a tall slim figure with a hood. A strand of fair hair that looked to have an auburn tinge peeked out and as he watched the hood was thrown back. He gulped, transfixed by the pale translucent skin, well-defined nose and pretty face that shone out from underneath the sheath of hair. Her eyes were a mixture of green and blue and were bewitching. "Was I what you were expecting?" Leila asked mockingly. "Er," the question caught him unawares. "I don't know what I was expecting." He looked closely and saw her eyes were actually green and azure. Just like his great grandfather, Vincent had described Veronique's eyes in the diary; this had to be the right person. "So Mr Silver, why should I believe a word you say?" looking directly into his eyes. "Because I know the Columbus Cross is here and I believe that between us, we can find it." Guy said assuredly. "What makes you any different?" Leila continued to gaze at him suspiciously. "From whom?" he asked quickly. "There are others."

"Who?"

"A Spanish man, he is evil and threatened my mother and I, he believes we know the whereabouts of the Cross." Guy had to ask. "And do you?" he said. Her response was deliberately evasive. "Possibly."

"Where is your mother?"

Ignoring Guy's question, Leila continued, "You surprised me by coming early; did you drive around the coast road?" Guy shook his head. "No, we sailed," He said. "We?" suspicion was still evident in her voice. "Yes, a sailing colleague, she's at the boat." Guy bent the truth a little. Leila's eyes narrowed. "Where?" she asked. "Down at the harbour," he assured her. "Look can we start trusting each other?"

"I trust no one Mr Silver."

"It's Tresanton actually, my mother's maiden name is Silver, and can we start by you calling me Guy." Leila's face softened slightly. "Perhaps," she said. Guy tried again "A Spaniard has chased me across the Atlantic and is probably only hours away from coming through that entry to the harbour over there." Guy pointed to the harbour entrance.

"He's an animal." She said vehemently. "You know him?" Guy's shock was evident.

"I know of him, that's enough. My mother Jacqui knows him, or should I say knew him." Leila's face clouded over again.

"What do you mean, knew?"

"She disappeared two weeks ago whilst diving here. We run a diving school. He was threatening my mother. She went down without me and I never saw her again." Leila's sadness and worry was in her voice.

Guy was astonished. "The police? She can't just disappear, can she?" he said. "Can't find her, it's as if she disappeared from the world. Divers went down and couldn't find a trace. Since then I have been in hiding. Now do you understand my caution?" Leila met his eyes and he could see courage there as well as grief. He pressed what he thought may be an advantage. "I have to confess I was sceptical about the whole idea of the Cross but having been on the receiving end of an attack by the mystery Spaniard, I'm getting more convinced by the day." Guy confided.

"What makes you think there is a Cross? What if it's all a myth?"

"Why would this Spaniard take such an interest if he wasn't sure it was more than a myth?"

"Maybe there is something else, something of value that he wants a great deal."

"Could be," conceded Guy, "however my Uncle's convinced his stepson was attacked in the process of finding The Cross."

"Here? What happened?"

"He was attacked whilst diving." Leila gasped. "We saw him! Well, my mother did actually, she saw a lone diver go down and come back injured, that's why she dived in the same place to have a look. It intrigued her."

"Where?" Leila shook her head. "Sorry, I don't trust you enough for that." She said firmly.

"At this stage I'm willing to take on board all theories. We can help each other."

"Possibly, who's that?" Leila looked over Guy's shoulder to a figure appearing in the distance. He looked before answering, "Ah, that's Rose, she was supposed to stay at the yacht."

"Then why is she here?" Leila's face closed again.

"Disobeying my orders, pretty typical I'm afraid."

"I told you no."

"Very well, let me stop her coming further." Guy ran down the hill cursing. "Why the hell couldn't you wait?" he hissed at Rose. She held her hands out as if to ward off Guy's irritation. "I was concerned, it's been a while."

"Rose, I said I would contact you, please go back to the yacht, this is difficult, she's very jumpy." Where is she?" Rose continued undeterred.

"Over at the park."

"I don't see anyone."

"What? Now see what you have done, she has gone. For God's sake Viper if only you could learn to do as you're told!" Guy exploded.

"Don't treat me like a child; you could have been in trouble." Rose refused to apologise. "Well I wasn't, and now we've lost her dammit." Guy ran forwards angrily scanning the Dolphin Park without success. There was no one around. Leila had simply vanished off the face of the earth. "I'm sorry," said Rose.

"We've lost the only lead we had." Guy looked crestfallen, running his hands through his hair. "So what do we do now?" Rose said in a small voice, regretful now that she had not remained hidden. "We wait," replied Guy. "And I, for one, am going for a lie down in *Hidalgo*," he went down to the main cabin and slammed the door shut putting Mozart on the speakers.

It was afternoon when he re-emerged to see Rose sitting on deck eating a bacon roll. "Do you want one?" she offered in a conciliatory tone. "Thanks." He picked up the spare roll, with a small smile, and ate hungrily. "What time is it?"

"About three pm, you've been out for a few hours. There's a lot of activity over at the diving school but not much else to report. Am I forgiven?"

"Yes, what sort of activity?"

"They seem to be going out for a dive; there are fifteen of them getting into that boat over there." Guy looked to where Rose pointed and took out his binoculars. "She's amongst them!" he shouted. "The one with the blonde hair, come on."

"Where are we going?" Rose was confused now. "We're going to follow them out to the reef; it's the only way to get near Leila again." He started the diesel engine and they circled around ready to follow the large diving ship as it headed out to sea. They followed at a hundred metres and Guy slowed down as the diving ship slowed then anchored. They sat watching as one by one the divers went down. "Wonder how long they go down for?" queried Rose.

"No idea, but we will soon find out," replied Guy watching attentively.

He saw Leila's familiar fair hair as she went to the side and put her goggles on. He sat wondering what had spooked her so much about Rose. It was odd. Twenty minutes later the divers started to emerge, but no Leila. He tried to count them in and realised one was missing, it had to be Leila. "I'm going to go over to find out what's happening," he said to Rose. He started the engine and released the throttle. Just as he did, there was an almighty explosion from beneath the sea and a huge jet of water erupted into the sky. Rose and Guy instinctively braced themselves as a tidal wave hit *Hidalgo*.

Recovering quickly, Guy motored over to the diving boat where everyone was milling around. "What happened?" he asked, sensing the panic and fear. "Explosion," replied one of the divers, an Australian who introduced himself as the dive leader. "Did a girl come back up? Name of Leila." shouted Guy.

"There was only one girl down there," replied a bearded man, "don't know her name poor soul. They told us there was a danger of unexploded ordinance. It is one of the reasons we chose to go down as they are going to close the area off to divers soon. Now look what has happened, someone has been killed. Oh my God," he wailed. "They'll have our licence for this." The Australian dive leader said grimly. "Can't someone go back down? She might still be alive. I can't dive but surely someone has to at least try to find her," snarled Guy looking around. Could the mysterious Spaniard be behind this? He looked around for the familiar motor cruiser in frustration. Now he really was up a blind alley; without Leila, his only lead had gone. What could possibly be worth so much pain and misery, surely not just an old Cross?

The Australian, cut across his thoughts, "Too dangerous," he said. "If it is old munitions down there then there may be more. The police are on their way." Guy saw the police launch thundering across the bay and turned to Rose. "We'll head back to our mooring," "Don't want to get caught up in any police investigation. I just can't believe she was down there."

Chief Inspector of Police Brian Montcalm, colloquially known to all as Monty, was a tall dominant man. Of French Bermudan origin, he wore his badge with pride and liked to think that the island was a leading example of good police practice. At five feet eleven inches tall and heavily built, Monty was a dark haired slightly balding man in his late fifties. He had a slightly bizarre habit of keeping a pipe in his mouth, even though he rarely lit it. Tipped for the job of island Commissioner in a few years, he had developed a fearsome reputation for solving islands crimes, whether it be drugs or casual violence. A chess fanatic, Monty ascribed his crime solving success partially to his methodical approach to crime.

He had a particular dislike of the rich 'yachties', as he called them, who came on their floating gin palaces and thought they were above the law. He had an even greater dislike of murder on his patch and was scowling deeply as he sped across to the scene of the explosion. There had been too many disturbing incidents recently, particularly the strange tourist diving accident a few weeks ago and now the disappearance of Jacqui Oleson. It was a police officer's nightmare, a well-known, good-looking female who had simply disappeared without trace. He had had his divers scouring the area for weeks with no luck. He had a feeling in his bones that something big was about to happen on his patch. There were various scraps of evidence to support his premonition; including the unexplained disappearances and wild rumours of hidden treasure.

With Monty was his Sergeant, Paul Linbar, a smaller unprepossessing man in his early forties. "Radio for police divers, immediately," he shouted above the roar of the engine to Linbar as they arrived. "A Miss Martinez has apparently not surfaced with the other divers before the reported explosion. That is a Miss Martinez …" he repeated trying to place the name. Then it dawned on him; Miss Martinez was Leila Oleson. She had been using her mother's maiden name since Jacqui disappeared, convinced she was being followed and in danger. He cursed to himself. If he was not careful, this affair could affect his unblemished police record and ruin his career. "You sure that was her name?" he asked the dive leader who introduced himself as Dirk. "That's what she called herself," Dirk told him "She joined us at the last moment, said she wanted to have a look before she left the island. We were only checking out the old warship down there."

"Which is forbidden. I'll speak to you later about that. In the meantime, describe Miss Martinez," growled Monty looking around as he did so at the usual collection of diving fanatics.

Dirk gave a quick assessment. "Tall, good looking with long fair hair. Good diver too, experienced."

"That's the Oleson girl," muttered Monty to Linbar. "You sure she was still down there when the explosion happened? You couldn't have missed her?" he asked the trembling Dirk. "She was down there, though it was pretty murky, this harbour's not the cleanest you know."

"Stick to the facts," said Monty. "You're in enough trouble already." Dirk looked bemused. "Why?" he stuttered. "Diving in a dangerous site for one thing and possibly a manslaughter charge, so I suggest you cooperate." Dirk looked frightened now. "Manslaughter?" he said. "I didn't tell her to go down."

"No, but as their leader you are responsible for health and safety. Now I'll try again, was she down there?" growled Monty putting the ubiquitous pipe in his mouth and chewing.

"I saw her go down, no question," remarked Dirk thoughtfully.

"Did you see anyone else down there?"

"No just us, oh, except that yacht over there he came over."

"Which one?"

"The big one heading over to the bay seemed keen to leave when you arrived. He was pretty upset and wanted to see if someone would go down to look for her."

"Was he indeed, so he knew it was this Miss Martinez?"

"Look, I meant no harm," said Dirk.

"Don't leave the island."

"What I don't understand is why she ran from me," said Guy for the umpteenth time. "It's not as if she had anything to fear."

"Perhaps she was spooked by something else we couldn't see," replied Rose. "She sounds very nervous."

"She had a right to be, particularly if this wasn't an accident."

"But who could have arranged this?"

"The Spaniard?"

"But Guy, there's no sign of his yacht."

"Means nothing, maybe he flew here and the yacht will follow," said Guy taking a long drink of beer. "If that's the case then we had better watch out, it might be us next."

"Perhaps we should tell the police," said Rose.

"Tell them what? That we think a Spaniard who we've never met murdered a woman we don't really know!" Guy was struck by the absurdity of it all.

"Where are we going?"

"Back to last night's anchorage. It was safe enough last night, so it should be again tonight."

He wondered what to do next. The answer was supplied for him. "We've got visitors Rose," he grunted as the police launch headed over. "Police!" shouted Monty as they drew alongside. "I have some questions for you."

"Come aboard," said Guy helping the Inspector. He seemed to be making a habit of this, he thought wryly to himself. Inspector Montcalm, you saw the explosion?" asked Monty showing his badge to Guy and Rose. "Everyone saw it," replied Guy. "Man over there says you were very upset by it." Monty pointed back to the dive boat. "I thought I knew the girl down there." Guy murmured in a non-committal tone. "And do you?"

"Not sure now," he hesitated, "if indeed there was anyone down there."

"Why are you here?" asked Monty abruptly changing the subject. "Travelling around and wanted to see Bermuda," replied Guy carefully. He hoped this was not another Grasshopper. He had been feeling more positive recently with something tangible to work towards and the constant spark of Rose. In fact, for the first time in ages he was looking at a girl as a friend not a potential lover. What he did not need was police harassment. "I need your details," said Monty scanning the decks of the yacht. "Is she yours?"

"All mine, little else in the world. I do yacht charters from St Lucia."

"Really," said Monty looking at *Hidalgo* with distaste. "You're here on holiday?"

"Yes."

"Who was the girl?"

"I'm not sure, I may know her, and it may be a mistake. Can you find out what happened to her?"

"We have divers down so will soon know."

"I take it you're here on leave too?" said Monty turning to Rose.

"Yes"

"No other reasons?"

"No."

"Passports please."

"British and American. Rose Ling," said Monty scanning the pages and reading aloud. "Strange second name."

"American by adoption," replied Rose. "I was born in China."

"I need you to stay in the area," Monty said firmly.

"Are we under suspicion?" asked Guy.

"I may need more questions answered," said Monty turning back to the launch and putting his pipe in place, a sign that he was thinking hard. "He's hiding something," he whispered to Linbar, "and I intend to find out what."

"Do you think they're linked to the Oleson woman's disappearance? Linbar whispered back. "Possibly, my instinct says that the Columbus Cross has something to do with him."

"You mean the Tucker Cross?" asked Linbar.

"No, the Columbus Cross is a bigger one than that. It cost my father his career," replied Monty. "My father was a police officer in Bermuda too, responsible for showing the cross to the Queen on a state visit. It was he who realised it was a plastic fake, but instead of being treated as a hero for uncovering a crime, he never recovered from the embarrassment of being the policeman who ruined the island's Head of State visit. The real Columbus Cross has become the stuff of gossip and legend; no one knows what happened to it. But I've heard about it from a few people recently, which is very suspicious," said Monty sucking hard. "They say that it's much bigger than the Tucker Cross and obviously worth much more and therefore a big headache to you and me. I'm taking this case full time now."

"God I hate the police," said Guy angrily as he watched the police launch draw away. "He doesn't trust us."

"You're probably right," replied Rose thoughtfully.

"Come on let's get a meal on shore that will help restore my good spirits," replied Guy. "I'm beginning to wonder whether events are starting to spiral out of control, and we're getting nowhere."

"I hate to say this but I think they just got even more out of control. Take a look at what I see," muttered Rose pointing to the shoreline at Waterlot.

CHAPTER 13

Bermuda

"How the hell did they find their way here?" groaned Guy looking across at the ungainly sight of his Uncle and Beatrice on the waterline. They had spotted *Hidalgo* and were making their way down to the boatshed. "Don't know, but I've just had an idea how to find out what eventually happened to Vincent and Veronique. I can trace them through the records office and data files we have in Chicago! Keep the relatives busy whilst I have a look." Rose sped off below deck, clearly excited. "Why didn't you tell us you were coming here?" shouted Blackie fifteen minutes later as Guy rowed them across to the *Hidalgo* in his inflatable.

"I've had enough of the old bat," he whispered loudly, pointing to Beatrice. "She's trying to domesticate me."

"That will be good for you! Anyway, this treasure hunting is very dangerous," replied Guy.

"Meaning you want the treasure for yourselves, I knew I shouldn't have trusted you," grated Beatrice, "So what have you found?"

"Nothing yet, nothing at all," said Guy quickly, "Rodney and All Saints, the clues, you two figured it out too?"

"We did," replied Beatrice as Blackie looked at her quizzically. "Have you figured out where the Cross is?"

"We only arrived yesterday," replied Guy. "We have had company, a Spaniard."

"Where is he now?" asked Beatrice boarding the boat and sitting uncomfortably on the cabin seat, "and where is Rose, more to the point? I thought she would have come with you to get us!"

"Coming up in a minute Aunt," shouted Rose from below decks.

"We managed to lose our Spanish pursuer," said Guy explaining the details of what had happened, omitting the Leila link.

"You know, the man who told me about the house in St. Lucia was Spanish," pondered Beatrice, shifting her bulk in the narrow seat. "If that's the case, then he's using us," said Guy, "anyone for coffee?"

"And the diaries?" Beatrice asked, refusing to leave the subject alone. "Nothing much of any use," replied Rose, appearing smug and smiling to Beatrice. "Nothing!" complained Blackie. "I would have thought you would have found a clue by now, unless you're hiding something?"

"I'm not interested in what you think Uncle, only in finding the Cross."

"Come on boy, in private, tell me what you've found," whispered Blackie joining Guy in the galley as he made coffee. "Nothing, except that this Spanish man seems very interested in the same thing, and has been threatening us."

"It's a week since we saw you, the diaries must say more."

"You forget we had a long voyage to get here. We weren't just sitting in an aeroplane seat," replied Guy, joining the others with hot drinks.

"I've been reading the history of Bermuda," said Beatrice taking a drink. "We are probably looking for something that would have been here at the turn of the last century when our great grandparents were here."

"Is there any more?" asked Guy. "We need to know more about Vincent and Veronique; Rose have you found anything? You look like the cat that caught the canary!"

"There is more, much more, it's a real life tragedy," replied Rose reappearing melodramatically with her laptop. "I've just found a reference on the internet. I've managed to find out what happened to your grandparents and it hangs together, though it's a very sad tale. It was all there, we just needed to know where to look and the Chicago police were most helpful."

"What happened?" they all chorused.

"Veronique and Vincent came back to St Lucia from the Canaries and made their own life on the island for the first fifteen years of the twentieth century sharing their time between the two houses. In 1900, they had a daughter, Claire, who they adored. The tragedy was that Vincent and Veronique sailed with Claire on the Liner *Lusitania* when it left New York bound for Liverpool in May 1915. I can only assume that Vincent wanted his mother to meet Claire, despite the fact that Britain and Germany were at war. They must have been assured that *Lusitania* was the fastest ship afloat, her nickname was 'the greyhound of the seas', and that the U Boats couldn't catch her. Unfortunately they did, and

158

she was sunk off the coast of Ireland with the loss of over one thousand one hundred passengers, including Vincent and Veronique.

Miraculously, Claire was one of the few hundred that survived. She went back home to St Lucia got married, and in time gave birth to twin daughters, Janice and Marie. She must have found the diaries and decided to leave them hidden, along with the clues left by her parents. Apparently, she served as a volunteer nurse for the American army during the Second World War and was killed on duty. A sad tale, don't you think?" Rose concluded to her spellbound audience. "Well that explains why Vincent and Veronique didn't have time to retrieve the Columbus Cross, if indeed, that was their intention," continued Guy thoughtfully. "Yes. This left her twin daughters, Janice, your grandmother Guy, and Marie, Beatrice's mother, to grow up with an aunt. Perhaps they knew about the Cross but wanted it to remain a secret? We shall never know as they are both dead, but somehow other people, including the Spanish man, got hold of the story too. So here we all are, searching for the Cross."

"A sad story," agreed Guy looking across at Beatrice and Blackie. "There's a little more," replied Rose. "One of the twins, Marie, also had another child, called Jacqui Oleson, whose daughter is reportedly living somewhere here in Bermuda."

"Really, where?" asked Blackie becoming interested, "Did you know about this Beatrice? Have you found her yet Guy?"

"Can't find her yet," lied Guy, pleased Rose had not mentioned Jacqui's daughter Leila yet. "We can start searching tomorrow either at the Royal Dockyard, Hamilton, or St George's."

"Too late to do anything tonight," replied Blackie. "Sun is on its way over the yard arm, time for a real drink."

"Much as I hate to say it, he's right," Guy said to Beatrice and Rose. "So where do we start?" asked Beatrice eyeing him distrustfully. "We have to find the Cross before the Spaniard arrives. I suggest we split up and cover Hamilton and St. George's, check out old places; museums etc., there have to be clues. We've done the dockyard, so I suggest Rose and I check out Hamilton whilst you check St George's."

"I've got a leaflet here for the Bermuda Underwater Exploration Institute in Hamilton," replied Rose. Beatrice looked smugly satisfied. "Good, then I suggest we start there as so far the clues have been nautical." She said.

The following morning was bright and clear as Guy and Rose motored *Hidalgo* across to Hamilton and moored. Blackie and Beatrice had taken an early taxi to St George's. "Thanks for not saying anymore to Beatrice last night," said Guy as they tied up on the nearest available buoy and a small service boat took them ashore. "Nothing more to say," replied Rose. "It's complicated enough and Beatrice is not discreet. I don't think it is right to tell her she has a living relative on the island, not yet."

"The Underwater Exploration Institute it is then," said Guy as they walked south from the harbour.

It took about half an hour's walk to the sign posted museum, which fortunately was quiet. Guy relaxed as they wandered off separately, each looking at the various exhibits. He was enthralled at the various depictions of seafaring life around the island and the sheer number of wrecks that littered the reefs, ringing the mainland. The Bermuda reef had managed to ensnare ships around its entire circumference. His attention was drawn to a set of newspaper cuttings on the wall in a glass frame, "The Tucker Cross." He gave a start as he saw a whole display devoted to the fabled Cross.

With rising excitement he started to read. Tucker had been a renowned diver and had discovered the wreck of a Spanish galleon called the *San Pedro*. The galleon was sailing from Cartagena in Spain to Havana, Cuba but was wrecked off the Bermudan reef in 1595. Amongst the lost artefacts was a spectacular twenty-two carat gold and emerald cross. A picture of the cross, closely resembled Guy's visualisation of the Columbus Cross, except that it was only six inches high and not the twenty or so inches the Columbus Cross was reputed to be. He read on; a diver called Teddy Tucker found it in 1955, apparently, it was made of gold and had seven emeralds, still in their settings. It was considered the most valuable artefact ever found in the Western hemisphere. "Rose, come here!" he shouted. "I've found something, listen to this," he read aloud, "Like a Chinese puzzle the cross opened in four parts and is thought to once have held a religious relic. Just prior to a visit from the British Queen Elizabeth II in 1975 the Cross was taken out of the museum for cleaning and discovered to be a plastic replica. It has never been found and is the perfect crime as no one has any idea when it was swapped!”

“There has to be a link here,” exclaimed Rose excitedly. Guy agreed. “You’re right, but this all happened long after the Columbus Cross was bought here.”

“Yes, but they have to be linked, it’s too much of a coincidence. We were led to this island and to a Cross. I am convinced that wherever the Tucker Cross is we’ll find the Columbus Cross,” exclaimed Rose.

“Possibly.” Guy conceded, “However, we could be going off in totally the wrong direction.”

“I don’t think so Bear, but whoever found the Tucker Cross may have just broken it down.”

“I doubt it. The components are only worth a fraction of the complete Cross; together they are invaluable. They have to be linked; someone has brought the two together so let’s focus on the Tucker Cross,” Guy said, thinking furiously. He bent down and re-read the inscription. “It was found to the south east of the island. Hey! Isn’t that where Leila said her mother went missing? There could be a link, what do you think?”

“It mentions a cave,” said Rose reading the smaller words and smiling. “Well spotted,” replied Guy following Rose’s eyes. “Tucker’s Cave was where he used to live as a hermit. It seems Tucker made a name for himself as a diver but once the Cross went missing he disassociated himself from the rest of the community.”

“A slightly unconventional life; living next to the sea and spending most of his time under it,” continued Rose. “My God, I do believe we are on to something here.”

“So do I, we should head over there and find out,” replied Guy, “we must be able to find the cave, what’s its real name?”

“The Faustian Cave,” said Rose reading the notation.

An hour later a taxi dropped them off at the end of a deserted road, clearly puzzled that they had not wanted to go to the Crystal Caves, a major tourist attraction on the island. They made their way down to the waterfront across rugged rocks. “Careful, there’s a small path down here,” said Guy catching Rose as she stumbled. “The place is overgrown and not for tourists.”

“Thanks,” replied Rose, grimacing with pain in her ankle as she slipped again. “That was stupid,” she muttered to herself, limping on until they finally reached the bottom of the cliff. Looking around, they could see they were in a small cove hidden from the rest of the island and only visible from the sea. To their right lay the Atlantic Ocean with the surf pounding on rocks five feet below. To their left was a small grassy flat area. "Look, there are signs that someone was here recently," said Guy stirring the ashes from a small fire with his feet. Rose looked around carefully. "Wonder where they are now?" she said.

"I see a small entrance to a cave up ahead, but that looks fit for animals only. Wait, I can see tracks leading up the rocks it. God, that's a sheer cliff face climb," said Guy walking across. "Wonder if I can get up there? I can see a larger cave entrance."

"I can't climb there," said Rose pointing to her ankle. "I'll go on my own," said Guy. "You wait here and check out the small cave over there." Rose gave him a worried look. "Be careful Guy, it could be dangerous." Guy grinned at her. "I'll shout for your martial arts Viper, if I need you," he said.

He grabbed a handhold and carefully started to pull himself up, his feet kept slipping. Concentrating hard, he followed the path as it veered right. He saw a narrow resting place about two metres away in front of the cave mouth. Straining, he clambered on, pulling himself up and around the ledge into the front of the cave. Too late he sensed something coming at him and instinctively ducked before the world went black

Groggily Guy regained consciousness, struggling to look around and wondering how long he had been out. Slowly sitting up he could see he was inside a cave. Hopefully Rose would have gone for help by now. Instinctively reaching for his pocket, he realised that his mobile phone had gone. Sensing movement, he tensed, aware that someone was approaching the cave. "You!" he said, in total surprise. "Sorry I hit you so hard, but you shouldn't have come here," replied Leila Oleson quietly. "This is my private area and now you've ruined it." Guy rubbed the back of his head absently. "You didn't have to hit me!"

"I couldn't see who it was and couldn't take any chances."

"You've been here since the explosion?" Leila nodded, her voice not betraying any emotion. "Yes." She said simply. "How did you arrange that?" asked Guy, suddenly certain that she had organised the so-called 'accident', "it was certainly dramatic."

"We have a store of explosives at the diving school. I just put them on a timer, made sure that no one else was near and then swam like hell. It deafened me for about five hours. I had a boat hidden around the other side of the pier. But enough, how did you find this place?"

"The Tucker Cross display at the marine museum, it talked about a cave here."

"Same way we found it," replied Leila shivering.

"You're cold."

"You shouldn't have come here; I don't need your sympathy. Yours, or that girl's. You do know that she's with them?"

"What do you mean 'with them'?" Guy was truly confused. "I saw her with the Spaniard on his boat weeks ago." Leila insisted. "You must be mistaken." Said Guy shaking his head, this could not be true. "I know what I saw," replied Leila coldly.

"All right, even if you're right, she's not here now. Nearly killed myself getting here and then you hit me," he said feeling his bruised scalp.

"There's an easier way to get here," Leila told him staring hard at him, then shrugging. "You shouldn't have come, you've ruined everything. Everyone wants to hurt me," she continued, her face dropping and her eyes watering. She started to cry and turned away, furiously rubbing the tears away so that so he would not see. Seconds later, she swirled around and flew at him. Guy held his arms up to defend himself. "Hey, come on Leila, I want to help you."

"No one who wants the Cross wants to help me. They're all too greedy."

"Well, I'm not," he said, carefully grabbing her raised arm. She twisted away and sat down hard. "My mother's disappeared; people want to kill me and you tell me not to worry!" she replied, crying openly now. "Look, I'm serious; I do want to help you."

"No one wants to help me." She shivered again. Guy put his arm around her. "Here, let me warm you up."

"I'm so tired," she whispered, "it's hard sleeping up here. There's a big man who has been tramping around making a lot of noise and cursing. I thought you were him." "Well I'm not," replied Guy quietly. "Lie down in the corner if you like. I'll stand guard."

The sun was now shining into one corner of the cave and she huddled there, trembling and lifting an old blanket. "How can I trust you?" she asked. "Because we share a common ancestry, I told you that. Your grandmother and my grandfather were married," he replied, feeling a sudden, intense longing for the defenceless girl. "Guess I have no choice then," she replied turning over. "Half an hour, then wake me." Guy moved to the cave's edge. "I'll be fully alert," he smiled.

The sun was starting to wane and her light breathing was making him feel tired; he lay down next to her. The next thing he knew, Leila stirred, opened her beautiful blue green eyes and looked across at him. To his surprise she put her arm around him. Reaching up, he stroked her face tenderly and as she moved closer, he could not resist leaning forward and kissing her on the lips. Sensing her respond, he pulled her closer, cradling her in one arm, whilst his other hand moved tentatively downwards to her breast. He felt her hands on him hungry and intense; the stress of the last few days fell away as they frantically discarded their clothes. Leila was very sensuous and he was very gentle, until the final frenzied moments, after which they both fell back blissfully sated. "If that's the price for getting hit on the head, please hit me again," he smiled. "Perhaps," replied Leila, smiling back before becoming businesslike again. "Do you mean what you say about helping me?"

"Of course; I am convinced the Tucker Cross leads to the Columbus Cross and that they are both here in this area," replied Guy, wondering at the girl's sudden change in emotions.

"My mother was convinced too," said Leila as she began dressing, "and obviously a few other people are pretty sure as well."

"Your name isn't Leila Martinez is it?"

"Leila Oleson actually; I changed it for my own safety."

"Please feel safe with me. I have read Veronique Silver's diary it is in French. I know a great deal about her life and her thinking. Her other relative, Beatrice, is with me on the island. She is your aunt. This Spaniard you talk about fired at me in St Lucia."

"Can I read the diary?"

"Of course you can, did Veronique leave you anything?"

"I have private letters from her," replied Leila. "I guess you can see them as we are related," she added slowly. "Only distantly," Guy was keen to point out, "too distant for it to matter."

"She was a remarkable woman," continued Leila. "They tell me a great deal about her and Vincent. They had a happy life together on the island of St Lucia until the tragedy."

"What tragedy?" asked Guy, pretending not to know to check the story he had heard from Rose. "Their daughter drowning on the *Lusitania*, with her twins left in America."

"What did they do when they heard?" asked Guy.

"So you don't know?"

"Know what?" Guy looked at her innocently.

"Vincent and Veronique were on the *Lusitania* too; they all died together, a terrible tragedy and the reason that their estate was left in disrepair. The twins Marie and Janice were brought up by an aunt in America and then Janice came to England,"

"My grandmother," said Guy, his brain registering that this was not quite the same story Rose had recounted. "And Marie met a Frenchman Bernard de Roque and went to St Lucia to Soufriere. It was there that she gave birth to my mother in 1955." "So the clues we followed were fortuitously in place before that happened."

"Perhaps they knew they were taking a huge risk, after all the German U-boats were starting to fire at any shipping in the Atlantic. They wanted to make a pilgrimage to Vincent's home and never made it. Still, by all accounts they had a happy life."

"The diary says that the Columbus Cross was brought here by Veronique and Vincent. We found clues they left." Guy shared.

"I believe they left it here in return for a gift of some sort; that's what we are trying to find. Back to Tucker, he lived here in this cave," continued Leila. "My mother believes that someone managed to get hold of both Crosses and hid them. I think that the same person is responsible for her disappearance."

"This Spaniard wants the Crosses as much as we do, so it can't be him." Guy theorised.

"He's called Salboa, and he has something to do with my mother's disappearance, I am sure of it." Leila responded adamantly.

"The Columbus Cross has been talked of in our family for years; we have to stop this Spaniard from getting it first and in the process destroying us."

"You are the first to understand the link to Tucker, after my mother and me. It was all going so well until Salboa found us and got nasty when we wouldn't tell him more."

"Do you sleep here?" asked Guy, looking around at the sparse cave.

Leila shook her head, "No, I move every other night to keep ahead of Salboa and his men. He thinks I have what he is looking for."

"And do you?"

"No, I'm still looking. I will trust you - but not the girl."

Guy nodded thinking again about Rose; did the Viper have poison in her veins after all?

Guy changed the subject. "How long has your mother been missing?" he asked her. "Three weeks now."

"Have you other family?"

"A twin sister called Lorna who, when she's not at University, is with our father. She's the splitting image of me but we're very different."

"Your father?"

"Man called Oleson, we don't talk. I chose my mother she chose our father after they split up."

"I'm sorry."

"You don't need to be, I'm not."

"Does he know about your mother?"

"Don't know and don't care; he's had no interest in us ever since he left my mum for another woman." Leila looked as though she was about to get upset again.

"So where do we go now?" asked Guy.

"The Crystal Caves further on down the cliff. Many of them have still not been discovered; my mother and I are convinced that this is where the answers lie."

"Have you found anything in this cave?"

"Yes, a small carving under a rock," said Leila hesitating then making up her mind.

"What does it show?" She lifted up a rock revealing a crude drawing. "Two Crosses and a picture of Jesus. My mother was convinced that there must be a way from Tucker's Cave into the main Crystal Cave complex; she believes they are linked through the sea. I think she may have found it and that's why she disappeared."

"So we should go to the Crystal Caves?"

"That's the problem; they are guarded by a strange man. He disturbs me and I need help to manage him, I've been trying to figure out a way to get past him."

"I'll come with you," said Guy rising. "We need to go back the way I came first and find Rose,"

They clambered back to where Guy and Rose had parted, what seemed like hours before. "Rose, are you there?" Guy called out, frantically looking around. "She's gone," said Leila. "Probably saw me and ran."

"I told her to stay here until I returned. She must have gone back up the road to get help or something." They walked back up to the main road. Still nothing, "I don't understand," said Guy in puzzlement. "She couldn't have just gone."

"She's gone with her colleagues, I did tell you she was not on our side," said Leila stonily, "Means they are also around here somewhere."

"She's not one of them Leila, I've told you that." Guy struggled to believe that Rose could be so treacherous. "Then where is she and why did I see her with the Spaniard?" Guy looked grim. "I don't know, I want to ask her," he said. She smiled.

"Come on, my car is broken so I have no transport, we have a little walk to make, I hope you are fit." She said.

"How far?"

"About five miles over the hills; it's safer to go across country and avoid the roads," she said striding out, her long brown legs providing a welcome sight to Guy as he hurried to keep up with her. They climbed about three hundred feet before reaching the summit and walking along the skyline.

An hour later Leila pointed and took a right turn into a developed area. "The Crystal Caves," she said as they reached the main road back into civilisation. "So I see," said Guy, feeling strangely disappointed as his private time with Leila ended and civilisation encroached on his world. As if to emphasise the loss of his idyll his mobile rang. "Blackie," said Guy groaning inwardly. The last thing he wanted now. "Have you seen Rose?"

"She's with you, isn't she?"

"Lost her, actually," said Guy. "Have you found anything?"

"Nothing of note," replied Blackie. "We're heading back to the hotel. Where are you?" Guy thought swiftly. "Looking for Rose in Hamilton," he lied. "Come to the *Hidalgo* later tonight. I'll pick you up at the shoreline at eight."

"I hope you know what you are doing. There is one other thing, my boy; Rose bothers me."

"What?" Guy was aghast, wondering what his uncle had picked up.

"She may be linked to a Spaniard called Salboa; he runs a freighting company here."

"Why do you say that?" asked Guy being careful that Leila did not hear. "I can't hear you Uncle," he shouted, then realised that his battery was going flat.

"I saw her heading to a yacht, so I asked around as I didn't think she knew anyone apart from us here. I'm told it belongs to one Senor Salboa, by all accounts a big shot in these parts. Lots of rumours about him; could be dangerous. If she's in league with these buggers then you will be out of your depth." Blackie gave a quick resume of what he had discovered, before the phone went dead. "Battery has gone!" exclaimed Guy to himself. "How far did you say this place was Leila?"

"Another mile," replied the girl, as they turned left off the road and onto a well-worn pathway.

"Another mile," repeated Guy moving after her, again mesmerised by the back of her brown legs. For the first time in months, he felt a real interest in a female outside the purely carnal. Perhaps it was her vulnerability after the loss of her mother, or perhaps it was love? It was too early to tell, and certainly terrible timing, yet he felt a fiercely protective urge to look after her. He pushed the thoughts with difficulty to the back of his mind. He had a job to do first and there was no giving up until he found what they were looking for. He was sure that the link to Columbus and the Old Spanish treasure was the link his father had sent to him in his dream. The thing he could not work out was the connection between that and Rose's relationship to Salboa.

"We're here," said Leila, as she came to a halt in front of the Crystal Caves sign. "I've trusted no one since my mother disappeared, please don't let me down." "Of course I won't," replied

Guy. "Police Inspector Monty would no doubt want to talk to you about the explosion though, if he was here."

"I'm sure he would," replied Leila. "I'll contact him when I am ready and on my terms before my Aussie diver friend, Dirk, gets into trouble."

"No more trouble than I will be in if Monty thinks I am part of all this," replied Guy. "I get the impression that the police here are not keen on rich yachters like me, even though that boat is all I own in the world."

"He's a policeman," replied Leila as if that statement answered the question. "It looks pretty quiet down there at the cave entrance. It's after visiting time here, which is both good and bad. Good, because we won't get interrupted, bad because the caretaker will be there on his own. We are depending on him to let us in."

"I'm in good capable hands," replied Guy looking around also. "Why didn't you come here before if you are so convinced that the Crosses are here?"

"I only recently discovered the carving and as I said I need support going in here. The caretaker is called Steve, and I don't trust him. Call it feminine instinct, but he'd have his hands all over me if he had the chance."

"Okay, just whistle when you need me." Leila smiled showing Guy another side to her sombre looking face. "I will…" She stopped talking as she saw the look that he gave her. She started again, "Look, what happened back there meant nothing. This is a professional relationship only, let's keep it that way."

"If that's what you want then its fine by me," replied Guy, inwardly confused. "Until we have found the Crosses, then I will try my hardest."

"Your hardest to do what?"

"To seduce you of course," he smiled as they entered the visitor complex.

The place looked a little run down and gave him the creeps; the hairs on the back of his neck stood up, he felt that he was being watched. He looked around the barren landscape but saw nothing. The dreams would come again tonight he was sure; this place was the sort of landscape to start them.

The hunched man on the far hillside watched them without expression, as he had done many times before. He was known, by the very few that did know him, as the Searcher. His was a silent world where no one ever saw him, but that was what he was hired and paid well for. Of Asian appearance and dressed sparsely he carried essentials only; he had no need or desire for life's luxuries. His was a parallel universe in which society did not exist, only his own interpretation. He lived off the land; merging with animals and foliage, shunning contact with other humans unless it was absolutely essential. He talked to no one; expected nothing from anyone and gave nothing that was not paid for. An expert in martial arts, he was also a crack shot with the small gun he kept well hidden in his old clothes.

He grimaced to himself as he saw Guy and Leila head down the path towards the Crystal Caves, pulling out his old notebook. He shook his head as he saw them enter the complex, momentarily off balance. The one thing he could not do was go underground as he suffered from claustrophobia. Still the consequences of losing his quarry would be fatal for him. He knew he was now a very valuable tool to those that employed him, something he would make the most of when he eventually returned to the homeland.

Bermuda

The gleaming financial headquarters of Z Technologies Worldwide, shone brightly in the afternoon sunlight. No one, except the mysterious owner, knew what the 'Z' meant. Bermuda was deliberately chosen by ZTW to keep its assets hidden from the prying world of tax inspectors. The company had grown rapidly from simple electronics assembly into a major enterprise spanning all the major continents. It kept its operations very secret; so secret in fact that none of the forty thousand employees who worked for it knew what they were a part of. Each business was compartmentalised, whether it was electrical motors in Asia or high technology design work in America and Europe. It boasted low employee turnover record and high staff morale. Its other headquarters were in Zurich, Switzerland and Denver, Colorado with its centre of operations in Vietnam.

Occasionally the reclusive owner would come to Bermuda to inspect the financial accounts, arriving late at night by private jet and leaving early the next day.

Invariably a visit by him would instigate a silent, efficient major financial movement of cash. In the regions where ZTW manufactured it would only deal with heavily vetted customers and suppliers. Queries as to the structure of the company provided a standard response; it was confidential information. What people could see were the stunning operating profits, often in excess of fifty percent margins, with twenty percent growth year on year. Enquiries as to where sales came from always elicited the response that they were involved in high level and confidential government contracts. Local authorities trying to understand the businesses hit a similar dead end. The standard response was that they were a local employer who paid above the industry average, paid their taxes on time and had an excellent employee record. The threat was implicit.

The monthly board meeting of ZTW was about to begin. It was evenly balanced with two females from China and Denver and two males from Zurich and Bermuda. The head of the Chinese arm of ZTW, Elsie Tan, looked at the video screen and then smiled at her fellow representatives. She was not an unattractive woman, but her tight mouth gave away the ruthlessness required to get her to her current elevated position. Her work at the Shanghai Conference had been risky but deemed appropriate by their leader. It had achieved its goal and further cemented her reputation as someone who got things done. "Good Morning," she smiled, looking to Kristina the American leader of the Denver site as she did so. A tall woman in her late thirties, Kristina, walked with a slight limp, the result of a horse riding accident. "I was asked to talk at this monthly meeting about our biggest growth country, China."

"You may have the biggest growth Elsie, but do not forget we are a team here," came a disembodied voice from the wall. He was their leader, known to them all as the Teacher. "Of course I don't forget that, not for one moment. All growth targets have been met for this month," she continued, slightly unnerved by the disembodied voice. It was rare that the Teacher intervened in their debates, to the point where they tended to forget he was there. Hence, when he did it was particularly alarming. "You did well with the Shanghai assignment; it had the desired effect,"

"Thank you Teacher, he lost his job immediately."

"This is a pertinent point for you all," continued the disembodied voice. "From time to time our mission demands tasks such as our colleague, Elsie, has just completed. They must be done without question and will be appropriately rewarded. However they will not distract you from our main task."

"Whilst we are together I think it is time to start coordinating our efforts more; we are successful individually but not as a group," said Jacques Saviour, the Swiss Head of Operations, who had decided to take the plunge as the Teacher was being far more forthcoming than normal

"Why?"

"I am concerned that we do not leverage our various companies well enough. If we had common sales targets, access to each other's products and even combined operations and procurement it would improve performance."

"You do not need such things." The Teacher's voice brooked no argument.

"We are losing some customers who get global deals from our competitors," replied Jacques heatedly.

"I said 'No!' Mr Saviour. This company is about challenging each other not working together. That is how I built this company, and that is how it will stay. You will all compete with each other. That is how people succeed; your competitors will grow fat and happy and their customers will return to us because they see us for what we are, the most efficient and effective. Do I make myself clear?"

"Perhaps I can add a point here," interjected the voice of the Bermudian representative.

"You may Mr Salboa, but I hope it is more successful than the state of your company at present," replied the Teacher.

"We should not lose customers at all," said Salboa. "There are other ways of keeping them."

"Such as?" asked Saviour, sounding thoroughly annoyed.

"Subtle intimidation," replied Salboa quietly. "Everyone has their weak spot, their Achilles heel. It is only a matter of finding it."

"We cannot afford adverse publicity if such things become uncontrolled," said Kristina the Denver representative hotly. "We must be seen as responsible and accommodating."

"You're absolutely correct," replied the Teacher. "However, a mixture of the two is ideal, so for our first major assignment you will work together."

"What?" Salboa exploded, horrified at the news, "I work alone!" He hated the American woman; she was an opinionated loud mouth, although he had to concede that she was attractive. However, as a lesbian, she was immune to his charms and he just knew it would be intolerable to have her around at the moment of his greatest venture and triumph. He angrily fidgeted with his long grey hair and wispy beard, as he tended to do when agitated.

"Do as I say, Salboa." The Teacher made it clear that the topic was closed before moving on, "Now, you will continue with your meeting. I do not expect to see any reductions to the financial results over the coming time and I want more growth stimulated by my investments. You will be called upon to perform additional tasks for me as required. Let me remind you that we are entering an interesting and critical time. You will all be at the forefront of major developments around the world and will be exhilarated by your role within them. Secrecy remains our number one mantra and no one will be excused for failing in that regard. If you continue to follow me, as well as you have 'til now, then all the rewards and success you have ever dreamt of will be yours. We are going to change the world but not always in ways that you will be able to comprehend."

CHAPTER 14

The Crystal Caves Bermuda

"Leave the talking to me," said Leila. "Steve can be a little funny at times." "Fine by me," replied Guy looking around. There was an eerie menace about the old outbuildings as the wind whistled through them like a cheap B movie western. "When were the caves discovered?"

"In the early twentieth century by two boys playing with a ball; Veronique refers to coming here in her letters soon after the discovery. The funny thing is that she implies that she knew of the caves before they were discovered."

"Interesting, so she was here at the caves?"

"Yes, and your great grandfather," replied Leila entering the cave complex. "Which cave, Leila?" Guy asked, noticing that there were signs to two caves. "The main one is called the Fantasy Cave, so we start there," replied Leila. "Ah, there he is, that's Steve. Let me talk to him first," she said pointing to a heavy-set man with curly hair. As the man turned, Guy noticed that he was older than he had first thought with a slight stoop, grey beard and a weather beaten face.

"The caves are closed. You shouldn't be here, it's strictly against regulations," Steve said glowering at Guy. "Does anyone else know you are here?"

"No," replied Leila. "Can we go down now?"

"I've turned the systems off. What is it you want to see?" the man was as unfriendly as possible. "The Fantasy Cave," replied Leila carefully. "I am doing an article on the caves for my diving magazine. Guy here is helping me. Please Steve."

"I will have to come with you," said the man moving forwards and walking heavily down the steep steps. "That's the regulations, I could lose my job."

"Any specific area we're looking for?" whispered Guy.

"Not really, the inscription said Jesus, but it could have just been prophetic, that's all I have."

"Impressive," said Guy as they headed down the steep steps. It was like entering a different world as artificial light played strange patterns on the illuminated stalagmites and stalactites. In places, they joined to form a single column from floor to ceiling. "The stalactites are the one going downwards the mites go upwards," said Steve by way of explanation as they reached the bottom. "How old are they?" asked Guy fascinated. "Millions of years old, it takes a hundred years to grow one inch. It's to do with the chemistry of the rain as it permeates the limestone."

"How deep is the water," asked Leila as they reached the main cave, with crystal clear water across its entire area. "About fifty feet in parts; there's a whole network of caves down here that you would need diving equipment for," replied Steve as Guy started to feel claustrophobic. "The water?" asked Guy, starting to feel the cold. "Fresh not sea water, even though we are close to the sea," said Steve switching more lights on. "Ideal place to hide something," whispered Guy to Leila. "A place where things age slowly, a natural freezer."

"Are you the only key holder, Steve?" asked Leila. "Yes, there's a strict policy on security here. You've no idea what it's like these days, regulations for everything! I can't do anything without getting a permit." Steve grumbled. "It could be anywhere, where do we begin?" whispered Guy turning to Leila. "This article for the diving school, what do you want to cover?" asked Steve suddenly. "I get lots of requests to come down here; I need to protect the place and its image."

"Some tourist shots of the cave," replied Leila quickly. "I've got a mobile phone to take preliminary pictures, but we will need to come back for good ones. It should mean more business for the caves. Incidentally, are divers allowed into this water?" "They are, but only with a special permit and under strict guidance," replied Steve. "Look, I can only give you a few minutes more, it's time to lock up."

"I understand," replied Leila, desperately looking around for signs.

"We need to shake him off or use him," said Guy.

"I know I'm trying to think of a way. If only we can find the link to Jesus."

"Someone told me Jesus is down here?" wondered Guy aloud. "Jesus?" echoed Steve quietly. "Yes," replied Leila carefully. "He's over there," said Steve pointing to a stone on the far side of the water. "Where?" Leila and Guy asked simultaneously. "Look closely and use your imagination. If I drop the lights you can just make it out." Steve pointed. "Ah yes, I see," replied Leila excitedly, seeing where a rock profile in the corner looked uncannily like the head of Jesus. "How long has it been like that?" "Over two hundred years at least, it is formed by the movement of the water and ice, much like the stalactites." Steve replied, taking the opportunity to show off his vast knowledge of the caves. "Amazing," replied Guy making out the broad profile of Jesus head. "I can see what you mean."

"Can we get across there?" asked Leila. "What for?" Steve clearly thought he had misheard. "It's ideal! The article has a Christian theme, this will bring them in their droves," she improvised quickly. "Is it possible to get over there to that wall? It's surrounded by water," asked Leila carefully. "It is with a series of planks that I use," replied Steve suspiciously. "Why would you want to go over there?"

"I would like to see it closer," replied Leila, "we need to take a photograph with the mobile"

"The rock face is very delicate," Steve faltered, "I'm not sure I should let you."

"Please." Leila flashed him one of her winning smiles. "I will get the planks," he replied slowly, seeming to reach a decision. "Thanks," replied Leila looking at Guy.

She watched as Steve extracted two very long planks from a platform underneath the rock. "I have to go over there once a month and clean my babies," replied Steve lifting the planks. "He's a bit odd," whispered Guy carefully to Leila, "he's acting like we are in his private domain."

"Exactly why I wouldn't come here without you," said Leila. "I never liked the way he looked at me when we came here once before."

"You stay here, I'll go over with him and have a look," said Guy following Steve as the man went across the planks.

Guy looked down and wondered what would happen if he fell in there, it looked very cold. He reached the other side and stood on a narrow ledge. The floodlights were pointing directly at the two of them making it very difficult to see properly. "So what exactly are you looking for?" asked Steve his tone harsher. "Don't honestly know," replied Guy carefully kneeling down and looking under the ridge. He let his fingers run along the rock. "I can't feel anything," he shouted across to Leila. "Keep trying," shouted Leila from across the water.

Guy felt along under the water line wincing at the cold; it was absolutely freezing. He had to admire the ingenuity of using it as a hiding place, if indeed that was what it was. He tried again, this time sweeping with his hands reaching much further down until he was nearly in the bitterly cold water. His hands suddenly touched something unnaturally smooth, like metal. "There's something here," he gasped, withdrawing his hands and getting their circulation back. He felt around again, working the flat surface until it moved slightly, sure that there was something metallic. He tried to keep calm as he worked it loose until he felt a handle. Finally, with a great tug, he pulled out a metre long metal box up, over the rock, and on to the ridge, gasping at the effort. "Be careful with the rocks, you'll damage them," growled Steve looking at what Guy had found. "Well done," shouted Leila, "well done." "Certainly interesting," replied Guy as he manhandled the box across the planks to the other side and showed it to Leila.

She tried to open it but it was stuck fast. "There seems to be some sort of lock here," replied Guy giving the case a bang with a loose stone. It looked old, very old, and he felt awed that this could be the first time it had seen the light of day since their grandparents had deposited it there. With a mighty strike he managed to dislodge the lid and it fell to the side. Inside the container lay two Crosses wrapped in cloth, one about three feet long and the other six inches. What was most striking, aside from the dull glint of the gold, was the inlay of diamonds and emeralds across them both. "They are so beautiful," breathed Guy, "We've found them both, well done Leila."

"I can't quite believe we've finally done it," said Leila her eyes glistening. "They are beautiful aren't they? I just wish my mother was here to see them too"

Guy started to smile, and then tensed as they were suddenly plunged into darkness and a cold voice boomed across the cave. "You should not have come," intoned Steve's disembodied voice. "I didn't want you to come, you have ruined it all, you know too much."

"I don't understand," said Leila gripping hold of Guy's hand. "Why did you help us, Steve, if you didn't want us here?"

"No one else can know about this place, that's why you two have to die just like all the others." He continued, ignoring her. "What others?" asked Leila, feeling scared. "You have forfeited your lives; I really liked you Leila, such a shame. I don't like your companion though, he will go first."

"You or your associates stole the Tucker Cross 1975," replied Leila quietly. "You stole everything, didn't you?"

"They belong here; together. The big man has tried many times to get me to tell him, but he and his men will never find them. There have been too many visitors to my kingdom. The Crosses are mine and have to stay in my kingdom, they are my possessions," continued the ghostly voice. "I don't understand how you found them," said Guy trying desperately to locate Steve in the dark.

As his pupils dilated he could vaguely see a faint outline above and to his right, but he could not be sure. "I am rich in my own kingdom, but no one else must be allowed to see these things. They are mine and only mine," replied Steve. "He's moving," whispered Guy, realising the man was making his way to a different position. Instinctively Guy also moved slightly, feeling his way carefully along the cold, wet rocks. One slip into the icy water would be fatal in the dark. He sensed that Leila had moved also. "Tell me what is so special about the caves Steve," he said, conscious that he needed to keep the man talking whilst he moved around. He had no idea whether the man was armed. "Our kingdom existed long before their discovery at the turn of the last century," replied Steve in a monotone voice. "They say it was two small boys looking for a ball, but my family has been down here for centuries longer. It's my kingdom given to me by my father. We have been the guardians since then and will be for the future. My ancestors were entrusted with great treasures, deposited here over a hundred years ago, a service we provided to those beyond the law."

"The Tucker Cross?"

"It was brought here by my father," replied Steve.

"The bigger Cross has been here for a hundred years, Steve," said Guy.

"Brought to my grandfather by a couple, a long time ago," said Steve, his voice moving again. "They trusted my grandfather and my father, but we always had our own special hiding places we shared with no one, not even our own flesh and blood. They don't know about my special hiding places."

"But why, Steve?" continued Guy, still moving. "Why did people leave them here?"

"Because they knew this place didn't exist to anyone else. If it hadn't been for those stupid boys, it would have remained so for many more centuries. My people left in peace."

"I still don't understand why they hid the Columbus Cross here," continued Guy still moving closer to where Steve's voice was coming from, wishing he could just find the light switch. "This has been a trusted hiding place for many centuries, known only to a select few," replied the disembodied voice, "and my dear family."

"It was our great grandparents who deposited the Columbus Cross here," said Leila her voice coming from higher up.

"So you are related?"

"Only distantly," replied Leila.

"I knew you were lying to me about the magazine," Steve snapped coldly. "Everyone lies to me but it does them no good. So, you've come to collect what you think is yours,"

"Yes."

"There are many others after these Crosses but they will never leave here, never."

"Let me understand this," said Guy anxious to keep the dialogue going. "Our great grandparents brought the Crosses here because they knew it was a safe hiding place and presumably because there were a lot of people looking for them. What would they get as security for leaving them here?"

"They would have taken treasure away as a payment, but I prefer to keep everything here in the kingdom," replied Steve.

"That's it," said Guy remembering. "The dairies talked about Vincent's father James Silver knowing of a secret hiding place where Salazar left his fortune, Vincent obviously came to collect it. That's where their money came from, although maybe he meant to return later. So how do you ensure you have security for all these valuables?" he asked.

"They go to my special place, the Holy Cave," replied the voice, which Guy noticed, had moved again.

"And where is that?"

"The Holy Cave is where no one enters," replied the voice harshly. "It is my home."

"So you live down here?"

"This is my kingdom; you may only enter and leave with my permission."

"Are you telling me that your family has lived here for generations?" asked Guy incredulously, "a subterranean family".

"There's only me left, I live with humans when it suits me. They trust me, as they have all my family, with the guardianship of the caves. We protect the world from intruders," continued the voice moving again. "It is the law of the kingdom and has been so for hundreds of years."

"He's bloody mad," whispered Guy urgently to Leila. "I need to try and make a move before he gets on top of us. Keep him talking, if you can." Leila, did as Guy suggested. "Tell me more about your life, Steve," she asked as Guy made his way slowly down to the water's edge as quietly as possible. "No one survives who comes here uninvited," said Steve, "for they will seek to destroy my world and so have to be sacrificed."

"What do you mean?" asked Leila with mounting horror. "I cast them into the water for they are impure," replied Steve, "so they are despatched from the Holy Room."

"The Holy Room?" Leila's voice cracked in fear.

"The room where I prepare them for their journey to the other side."

"Where is this Holy Room?" asked Guy. The man was talking in a monotone as if reciting from a well-worn script. "You will be shown the Holy Room in preparation for your departure," said Steve in the same toneless voice.

"We have the Crosses, Steve," said Leila. "You want them back?"

"They are my property, the big man also wants them, but he won't get them either."

"You will have to come and get them," replied Leila coldly. "But you won't get them as I will cast them into the water and then the big man will be angry." There was a sudden flash and the lights came back on. Both Leila and Guy gasped and shielded their eyes. Guy cursed as he inadvertently dropped his mobile into the water. He squinted desperately into the glare and could make out Steve's moving shape slightly higher and to the right of where he had thought. He also saw the glimmer of a reflection from a small handgun. "Pass the box over," said Steve pointing the gun at Leila. "This is a German Walther PPK and I don't want to hurt such a beautiful face."

"You will have to come and get it," replied Leila bravely. "I'll shoot you." warned Steve and pointed the gun directly at her. "You're going to kill me anyway, so I don't care," said Leila coldly. "You are mistaken," said Steve. "You will not die yet; I want to spend time with you first just like I did with your…."

"My what?" asked Leila horrified, "Did you mean my mother?"

"No."

"She's here isn't she? You took her when she dived down," trembled Leila.

"You are mistaken; now pass the box or the man gets it."

"Tell me about my mother or the box goes into the water now."

"I will be able to retrieve it."

"No you won't, because the water goes into the sea doesn't it? It's not a closed fresh water lake at all. That's your secret, access to the outside world."

"I warned you, now the man has to die," shouted Steve swinging the gun around. As he did so Guy flung the small rock he had just grabbed with all his strength and anger. It struck Steve on the side of the head, who staggered and dropped the gun. Guy watched as he tried to steady himself, groaning and scrambling to stay upright and then ran across the rocks and punched Steve hard in the stomach. The large man cursed loudly, before toppling backwards with a scream, and falling down into the water.

"Are you alright?" shouted Leila to Guy.

"Yes, I need to check where he is, can you find the gun?"

"I'll try," said Leila. "I need to find out about my mother."

"You will," replied Guy stepping carefully down to the lakeside.

For a moment he thought he saw Steve floating on the surface, but then realised he was actually swimming away in a different direction. "He's heading away from us, I need to follow him or he will get away."

"I've found the gun," said Leila, brandishing it in the air.

"Keep it trained on the water whilst I go to look for him. At least we have the Crosses," he continued, noticing that Leila was pale and shivering.

"My mother, she's in here, I can sense it. What has the bastard done to her?"

"I'll find out," said Guy looking around. "This must be one of a complex of interlinked caves. It will be like looking for a needle in a haystack in there, but I need to track him down."

"He'll be waiting for you, Guy," replied Leila. "Let me think a moment. There has to be something we can do." She sat down on the cold rock. "I can't believe he's actually lived down here, him and his wretched family all these years. There must be many people who have gone missing down here."

"Probably," replied Guy looking around and examining the ancient Walther.

He checked he knew how to use it and stood up. "We need police help down here, this is way beyond my ability."

"I'll get them."

"He's injured and probably confused at the moment but he has to be stopped before anyone else gets hurt. Fortunately there's a torch here in the light box that I can take with me."

"Are you sure you want to go alone?"

"You owe me a dinner after this"

"Just make sure you go above ground, you're shivering." He tried to tuck the Walther into his trouser waistband.

"Here, put it in this plastic bag," said Leila.

"Thanks," smiled Guy as he made his way slowly into the water, gasping at the cold and not looking forward to the dark forbidding depths ahead of him. He started to swim slowly in the same direction as Steve had gone, shivering as he entered the next cave. The small flashlight gave off an eerie glow and the water got even colder as he swam down about five feet, gasping as he did so. He was swimming in water and entombed in rock. Slowly he became aware of a different taste to the water, salty. Seawater!

So, Leila had been right there was a link through the cave system to the sea. He swam on under a rock ledge, convinced that this is where Steve had gone, before seeing that the water rose to the roof of the cave structure. There was nowhere to go, and he realised with dread that he would have to go underwater, deducing that there must be an outlet back into air and eventually the sea. He trod water taking great lungfulls of air before diving into the murky depths, feeling his sodden clothes drag. He swam on and on in the gloom and was starting to panic over his ability to hold his breath much longer when he saw a small light ahead.

Striking out, he made a last effort and rose with relief into a different cave with air. In the distance, he could see Steve sitting on the other side, holding his arm, as he made his way to a small enclosure. This must be the Holy Cave. Gasping for air Guy slowed his breathing down to a normal rate, hoping that Steve had not seen him. He was in luck, Steve did not turn around. He made his way forward slowly towards the water edge as Steve disappeared out of sight. He could feel the water moving underneath him and realised it was the natural current of the seawater. This place must have lain undiscovered for centuries; he pulled himself on to the rock face and cautiously made his way forward. There was a small shed structure built onto the side of the rock face. He looked cautiously ahead and thought he saw a movement. He peered in and saw nothing, where was Steve?

Suddenly there was a blur and something flew past his head. Instinctively he ducked and felt something hit him on the side of the head. He dropped and felt blood on his temple. He thought for a moment that he had been shot, but then realised that something had glanced off him. Then he saw the catapult; the man was firing rocks at him. Cursing he rolled to the side as another shot flew past. Desperately he tried to get the Walther out of the bag. Another rock narrowly missed him and he ducked instinctively back into the water. He scrambled into a recess in the rock face and as he pulled himself in tightly his hands closed around something long and narrow. He looked down; it was a long harpoon pole, he grabbed it. At that moment, Steve came out into the open brandishing the catapult.

"This is the Holy Cave defiler, where you come only when invited or are dead," he spat.

"Give yourself up Steve, I have your gun," replied Guy.

"You wouldn't dare," he sneered, "your sort haven't the guts for that."

"I warned you," shouted Guy and pulled the trigger. Nothing happened. The gun must be waterlogged, he thought desperately before reaching for the harpoon.

"You will die slowly," snarled Steve raising the catapult.

"I warned you," shouted Guy trying to keep the man in sight in the poor light. Waiting until the last possible minute, he thrust forward with the harpoon. It struck hard into Steve's side and Guy gasped as it jarred his shoulder. Steve gave a great bellow and twisted as he did so driving the weapon from Guy's grip. It fell to the floor and Steve stared down at his side and the blood.

"You bastard," he roared.

"Stay where you are," yelled Guy grabbing the Walther PPK and shaking it to get it to fire. "One step further and I will shoot you."

"You can't kill me, human," growled Steve looking down again at the blood. "I am indestructible in my kingdom. No one can kill me." He smiled coldly and stared malevolently at Guy. "You are going to die a slow agonising death. Not so much fun as the females but it will be slow I promise you that. You will plead with me for mercy in the end but the Holy Cave will have its sacrifice."

"Stand back," shouted Guy brandishing the Walther. "I mean it I will shoot you if you don't sit down now."

"I will come back for you later and you'll plead with me to kill you," Steve turned and disappeared into a hidden recess in the cliff face trailing blood after him.

Guy rushed forwards firing blindly and dropping the Walther with shock at the power of the recoil. He could not remember the last time he had fired a gun. With a sickening feeling he realised that Steve could well be heading back to the Fantasy Cave and Leila. He made to jump back in the water then had a second thought. He opened the door of the small shack and looked in. What he saw made him want to retch; the remains of a human body lay there. Remains were a euphemism for what he could make out was a torso and a leg. He turned and retched violently then swearing he ran for the water, if he was not quick, Leila would go the same way.

Leila sat looking into the water in the Fantasy Cave as if expecting her mother to appear at any moment and instead only seeing the face of Jesus. She cradled the Crosses and rocked back and forth. Her mind started to play tricks on her, she thought she saw her mother coming out of the face but it was only an illusion. She saw patterns on the water but they made no sense. The Crosses were not worth all this suffering and she started to think again about throwing them into the water. However, in a strange way that would be giving in to the lunatic.

She gasped at a sudden movement in the water followed by a blood-splattered apparition rising out of the depths. Steve lumbered towards her, blood dripping from his side and mingling with the water. "I always wanted you, did you know that? I wanted to make this a special place for you to carry our bloodline on. That's why I agreed to bring you down here; I was going to tell you eventually but not this way," he told her. "Where's Guy?" she screamed, holding the Crosses in front of her as if to ward off the devil. "Dead, it's just you and me now my darling," smiled Steve.

"Keep away from me or the Crosses go in the water," she screamed as Steve walked steadily towards her saying. "Give them to me and we can be together forever. You must not fight me, we are meant to be together in this life and the next,"

"No!" screamed Leila,

"Just you and me forever," he repeated, grabbing her shoulder roughly, she dropped the Crosses onto the rocks.

"Leave me alone," she screamed in despair.

"Turn around Steve, very slowly," said a harsh voice.

"Guy!" shouted Leila in relief.

"You are really starting to annoy me, man," said Steve turning and raising his catapult. "Time to dispose of you for good!"

"I don't think so," replied Guy trying to get his breath back.

"Leila and I are together, a partnership," growled Steve.

"He killed your mother," said Guy coldly walking out to the side and trying to dry himself. "You killed her in cold blood."

"Is that right," shouted Leila hysterically.

"He lies," said Steve smoothly advancing back to within arm's length of Leila. "Is it true?" she screamed. "She became a nuisance," said Steve coldly suddenly firing the catapult and narrowly missing Guy. "Put the catapult down," he shouted, ducking and freeing the Walther from the bag and bracing it against his shoulder. "You don't know how to use that properly," smiled Steve advancing down the rocks. "Try me," grimaced Guy trying to get a foothold and stop his arms shivering with cold. "This is my Kingdom, it's time for you to die," Steve raised the catapult.

"I warned you," shouted Guy sighting the Walther. He fired but to his dismay, the kick of the gun sent the bullet high above the man.

"Idiot," smiled Steve getting ready to fire. Suddenly he groaned and staggered. The blow from Leila had caught him unawares as the large Columbus Cross hit him on the back of the head. He stumbled and fell down into the water blood streaming from his head wound and his side. Guy angrily fired at him again in the water, not sure if his bullets had hit the man, showing no remorse after what he had seen. Blood started to spread in the water and the shape drifted away.

"Well done Leila," shouted Guy picking up the Columbus Cross.

"My mother, where is she?"

"I can't take you through there Leila, please understand."

"I have to see her."

"Please no. I brought you this," said Guy producing a chain and locket he had found in the shed. "Come on we have to get out of here, he's still alive and dangerous."

"My mother," screamed Leila.

"Please Leila, do as I say, come on." He dragged her furiously to the steps. "There's still a great danger that he may come after us." They staggered up the steep pathway to the entrance, Guy carrying the box with the Crosses, Leila following numbly behind. With relief, they reached the heavy wooden door at the top of the stairs and Guy closed it, making sure that the bolts slid home hard. It was wonderful to see daylight again, after what felt like an eternity below ground. He took a deep breath and relaxed then heard a noise.

"Glad to see you've made it out of there," said a familiar voice. Guy turned to be confronted by Blackie and Beatrice. "I thought you were at the hotel."

"Came to help you dear boy, looks like you need it," said Blackie

"Help me with Leila then, she's had a bad shock," said Guy gesturing to the girl. "Of course," replied Blackie, grabbing Leila's arm with Guy on the other side. "There's a small café over there, just had a word with the owner he's opened up especially, even though it's out of hours. Nice bloke, come on."

"Thanks," said Guy as they finally sat down at one of the tables. "How did you know I was here?"

"Intuition," said Blackie sitting down heavily and gesturing to the man at the bar. "Two coffees "he ordered and then turning to Guy said. "You've got the Cross in there my boy?"

"Yes we've got them," said Guy wearily. "I need to call the police."

"Well done, let's see then."

"In a minute Uncle, we've been through an ordeal down there."

"What have you done with Rose?" said Beatrice coldly.

"She left of her own accord," replied Guy. "I'd like to talk to her myself."

"Pass the box over," gestured Blackie importantly.

"I want to know about Rose," said Beatrice.

"For God's sake woman there's a madman down there and we barely escaped with our lives. We need to call the police and all you can do is talk about Rose. Are you all right Leila?"

"Better with the hot coffee," said Leila quietly.

"The Cross," said Blackie impatiently.

"Very well," said Guy opening the box.

"Very impressive, very impressive indeed," said Blackie staring at the Columbus Cross. "It's worth a bloody fortune, what about the other smaller one?"

"It's called the Tucker Cross," said Guy.

"Well done," said Blackie. "Wow, to think after all these years of family rumours and it was actually true. We'll be worth a fortune."

"We?"

"The team," replied Blackie, quickly summoning the barman called Rod to provide more drinks. "The girl needs more coffee and perhaps something a bit stronger."

"I'm going to call the police," said Guy. "That madman has to be stopped."

"Who is he?" asked Blackie

"It's a long story but he is the lunatic who was responsible for the death of your stepson," said Guy going over the events quickly and watching Leila slowly recover.

He started to feel unbearably hot after the cold of the caves. "This is a police matter now."

"Exactly my boy, but let's just savour them first, eh?" He gestured to Rod at the bar. "More drinks all round, we have something to celebrate! In fact, make it one of your specials, these two have earned it."

"Where is the man who took you down?" asked Rod as he brought more coffee over.

"Down there," replied Guy." Do you know him?"

"He would sit here for hours talking to no one but himself, a real queer fish," said Rod, turning back to his bar.

"I can't believe we have got the Crosses," repeated Blackie incredulously, "after all this time."

"You're right," conceded Beatrice staring down at the two Crosses. "I'm very worried about Rose."

"Oh, she'll be alright," said Blackie standing up. "Told you I saw her in the harbour, she's probably gone for a bit of peace and quiet."

"You told me you saw her going to the Spaniard's boat, when was this?" Guy asked, suddenly remembering.

"About three hours ago, she'll be ok."

"I want to call the police; she could be in big trouble."

"Shame we have to bring the police into it, the finder's fees won't be a fraction of what they're worth on the open market."

"Forget it Uncle, this is a police case, I'm through with going it alone," replied Guy angrily. "I'm more concerned with that madman down there. We have to get the police here before he gets loose and kills someone else. Get me a phone please, I've lost mine."

"How do you know he has killed anyone?" asked Beatrice.

"My god, I'm not getting through to you people am I? You are totally blinded by this dammed Cross! Now listen to me whilst I tell you about this madman's Holy Cave."

"My God, it is bad," said Blackie when Guy had finished. "You're right we do need to get the police here as soon as possible. "

"Good, now again, please get me a phone, I've lost my mobile," said Guy his head starting to feel very heavy and drowsy. He saw the area begin to swim in front of his eyes as he lost focus. Now what was happening? It felt like Shanghai all over again. He held his head, trying to stop things swaying and then saw Leila fall to the floor. "What the hell is going on Uncle? The damned drinks were spiked." He fell to the floor seeing an elongated version of his Uncle's cleric's collar before blackness enveloped him.

189

CHAPTER 15

Bermuda

"Cerveza, beer Matarife, this dammed weather is hot," growled Salboa, staring around the harbour and gesturing. They had arrived an hour ago in the *Alcazabar*, averaging over twenty knots an hour. It had taken nearly half a day to properly clean the engines, making the whole trip an ordeal for Salboa. He would never get used to the sea and hated being confined to the boat for days on end. He had judged it necessary, however, as Tresanton was more than capable of taking a different direction at sea without direct surveillance. He was still angry at Guy's audacity in damaging their engines with sugar right under their noses.

He was grudgingly impressed that it had not taken Guy and the other pawns long to work out that Bermuda was the location of the Cross. He resented having to follow them, but even though he had always known that the Crosses were hidden in Bermuda, without access to Veronique and Vincent Silver's diaries he had no way of knowing the exact location. Still, he consoled himself, they could do all the work and he would collect the prize when the time was right. "Another beer," he growled.

"We have good news senor," said Matarife excitedly.

"What?"

"They've found the Crosses! I just got a call."

"Fantastic, where they are?" Salboa could hardly contain his glee.

"The caves."

"I always thought it would be there, but they've actually found them, are they secure?"

"Yes."

"Then go and meet them, I trust no one with this, we can't take any other risks. Now, I have other business to see to."

"You will be on your own."

"I can take care of myself," glared Salboa as Matarife hurried to the side and gestured to the two Leon brothers Raul and Alfonse to un-sling the inflatable. "Raul will protect me if the girl suddenly attacks me," he commented sarcastically. He headed down to the main master bedroom. The last ZTW board meeting had annoyed him, despite successfully outmanoeuvring Saviour. He saw himself as the Teacher's natural successor and did not appreciate references to the parlous state of his own company. Worse, he now had that interfering lesbian Kristina watching him like a hawk. Well to hell with her, she would not approve of what he was about to do but he never could resist a pretty girl.

"So how is my little girl?"

"Don't patronise me," snarled Rose angrily even though she was tied to the bed by her wrists and ankles. "I came in good faith and this is how you treat me!"

"You applied for a job with me a month ago young lady, I did not ask you to come back."

"I came back as a gesture to warn you to leave the country. The police are well aware of the Cross, so you have no chance of succeeding. And you treat me like this?"

"I will treat you as I see fit."

"Enough people have been hurt. Incidentally, I didn't appreciate Matarife drugging me in St Lucia."

"We do what is necessary."

"Why is the Cross so important?"

"Do you really think for a moment that I will tell you?"

"I suppose not."

For the umpteenth time Rose regretted her decision to go and find Salboa. Two months ago she had applied for the role of private security agent with Alhambra Lines and been interviewed by Salboa on a smaller yacht than the *Alcazabar*. She had been uncomfortable with the way he looked at her, so had gone home and forgotten the incident until Leila's overheard words reminded her. It had all then come flooding back and she realised that Salboa and the mystery Spaniard were the same person. She had struggled for days whether to tell Guy but decided against it for the time being and events had overtaken her.

"I don't need you to warn me of anything. How naive do you think I am?" Salboa sneered.

"I came in good faith."

"Well it's all in vain; we have what we want now so you are dispensable. Ordinarily I would be disposing of you, but others I respect want you alive; however, there are no stipulations as to how I treat you."

"Untie me, please," begged Rose.

"I don't think so," said Salboa, reaching for a handkerchief and some tape. "In fact I'm tired of hearing your whining voice." He bent down and fastened the industrial tape over Rose's mouth. "My dear girl you are only on the periphery, an amateur amongst professionals just like sailor boy, Guy. You have been a nuisance, but also helped me inadvertently. Sailor boy has been neutralised, so I think a little humility is in order." He smiled nastily and drew a knife. "Know what this is?" Rose shook her head. "It's a Bowie knife; useful for what I'm about to do." Rose's eyes widened in horror as he leaned forward, expecting pain but instead seeing her blouse ripped. She twisted and struggled as hard as she could but the ropes held firm. The bastard was going to rape her. She tried to turn to one side as she saw the gleam in Salboa's eyes and felt her shorts sliced apart. She groaned inwardly feeling totally exposed, despite retaining her bra and pants. Salboa slapped her face hard and stood back smiling as her cheek burnt red.

"Now my dear, what else shall we do to humiliate you? I could have my wicked way with you, which would be fun, or I could carve you up a little as a constant reminder of me. Which would you prefer?" he smiled, "Oh, I forgot, you cannot speak. Well, I must admit for an aggressive little runt you are quite attractive so I think we will have a little of both." He leant forwards and sliced her bra away touching the knife to her left breast. A primeval scream rose in her throat as the knife pressure increased.

Guy was lost in a long dark tunnel with no end in sight, a dream without the usual haunting, when finally he saw a small light and opened his eyes. He looked around; he was lying in a small wooden hut with someone else beside him. His head throbbed badly and he tried to sit up but could not. It all came flooding back; he had been drugged again. He looked closer at the other person as his focus returned. "Beatrice, wake up." He whispered hoarsely. "Where am I?" she grunted.

"We've been left here trussed up like pigs." He looked around. "Where the hell are Leila and Blackie?"

"Oh my head, I feel so ill," groaned Beatrice trying to move.

"Here, let me help." Guy sat up and reached across, gasping. Beatrice was covered in blood. "You've got a nasty cut on your head; you must have fallen badly when you passed out."

"I feel sick and so weak," she moaned.

"I'll see if I can get help," said Guy lifting her and staggering to the side of the hut. He tried the door; it was locked. Looking around he saw an old chair lying in the corner. Picking it up, he launched it at the door. He fell back from the impact but felt the door move slightly. He launched himself again and this time it shifted on the hinges. Finally, after five more strikes, he felt the door give way and he stumbled through into the café area.

"We're in the back of the dammed café!" he shouted. "That bastard Rod! I didn't trust him from the start; he must have spiked our drinks then locked us here and taken the other two away." He turned to Beatrice. She was looking very weak and he realised he needed to get help quickly. He felt in his pockets and then remembered that his mobile was gone. Looking around he saw a telephone and grabbed the antiquated handset, wanting to scream with frustration when he realised that it was dead. He cast his mind back and recalled seeing a roadside phone at the gateway to the caves. "Beatrice, I'm going for help, hang in there, I'll be as quick as possible."

He pulled her up on to the chair and then ran as well as he could up to the roadside. Judging by the light it must be well into the evening; he noticed that his watch was gone too. What the hell was going on and where were Blackie and Leila?

"There he is," Monty, gestured to Linbar as they screeched to a halt in front of the Crystal Cave café, the police car kicking up a storm of dust. "You seem to attract trouble," he said to Guy as they ran through into the café area, "what has happened?"

"We must get the lady to hospital; she has concussion and is still bleeding."

"We've called for an ambulance. Linbar, make her as comfortable as possible and chase the ambulance, they should be here by now." As if hearing him, a loud siren punctuated the night air and an ambulance screeched to a halt. "Tell me how this happened," asked the senior ambulance man, an officious looking individual called Spence. "It's a long story," said Guy but quickly explained what had happened in the cafe. "She's got bad concussion, she keeps asking about someone called Rose," replied Spence. "Tell her I'll take care of it. The drug may still be affecting her," said Guy grimly. "Quite possibly," said Spence shutting the door. "We'll get her to hospital."

"This man, Steve, is he still down there?" asked Monty watching as the ambulance drove out of the cave area. "I assume so," replied Guy, explaining what had happened and leaving nothing out. He noted the police officer's eyebrows rose at the mention of the Crosses, but told it as he had seen it, realising that this was far beyond his capability now. He was still shaking at the thought of what he had seen down there. "We locked the door but he may have gone out to the sea cave, though he was badly hurt."

"And very dangerous," added Monty. "I've known of him for some time, he was under surveillance but events have moved faster than I expected."

"There may be other bodies down there," continued Guy.

"And Miss Oleson, she was here with you?"

"Yes."

"She's a resourceful girl staging her own disappearance like that. I'm going down into the caves with a couple of men but I'll want to talk to you later."

"My Uncle and Miss Oleson have disappeared, I'm sure the café owner had something to do with it. Can't you find them first?"

"Linbar will put out an alert," replied Monty. "Incidentally you can call me Monty, most do and it looks like we shall be spending some time together. Now, I want you to stay here whilst I go down, I also want you to draw me a diagram of the tunnels, I've got police divers coming over."

Guy watched them go to the cave entrance and looked around. Salboa was behind this he was sure of it. He had to find him fast before it was too late. He had no intention of just hanging around doing nothing until Monty returned. He noticed an old motorbike in the corner; probably Steve's but he wouldn't need it. Even better, the keys were in the ignition. Without another thought, he jumped on and revved the old engine, glancing around as he did so to be sure no one was watching.

Rose screamed, but no sound came out as Salboa towered over her, a trickle of blood dripped from her left breast where he had nicked her. She glanced desperately around looking for a way to escape. She saw with disgust Salboa grinning as he removed the last of his clothes, a repulsive man, old enough to be her grandfather with long, grey hair hanging loose. Desperately using her tongue, she managed to move the gag slightly at the side of her mouth and screamed as hard as she could.

"You can shout all you like my dear, there's only Raul here," he laughed. "No one else will hear you," he grinned lifting the Bowie Knife again. "Perhaps I should give you a little more to scream about," he smirked moving the knife to her right breast. "Matching marks I think." Rose jerked forward with all her strength as Salboa bent forwards, intent on his task. Screaming at the pain in her wrists, she smashed her forehead hard against his nose. Satisfyingly she thought she heard the cracking of bone as Salboa cursed and fell back, dropping the knife and clutching at his bloodied nose.

She looked around desperately and saw the knife next to her left wrist. She grabbed it with her fingers and sliced at the rope on her wrists. Salboa sat on the floor holding his bleeding nose and cursing. Quickly she sawed the rope free, grimacing in agony at the pain, until with relief she felt the rope give way. "You're going to pay for that, bitch," roared Salboa looking up in anger. He hesitated as he saw Rose using the Bowie knife on her right wrist. "Come any closer and it's you who will be dead," she said through gritted teeth.

"Drop the knife, bitch." Salboa commanded.

"Go to hell," she snarled, quickly freeing her right wrist with the blade, before transferring the knife over to her other hand. Watching him carefully she cut the ropes on her legs. "Get back against the door," she shouted, "before I castrate you, old man"

Salboa backed off scrambling for his clothes. Another noise interrupted them. "Boss, we have visitors," shouted Raul from outside the room.

"I'll see to you later," growled Salboa opening the door. "We have unfinished business. Raul, come and subdue this bitch, be careful she has a knife." He turned and slammed the door.

Rose looked wildly around as she freed herself from straggles of rope. What remained of her ruined clothes were scattered on the floor. She searched desperately for something to wear as the door opened and Raul put his head cautiously inside. She grimaced as the pain from the small cuts on each breast reminded her what had happened. Salboa was going to pay heavily for this.

Raul looked at her cautiously and raised his Mauser pistol. Quickly, she turned and opened the door to the en suite bathroom, locking the door behind her. It would give her a few more minutes. She stared desperately around the small room trying to slow down her breathing. There was nothing to help her except a small porthole. She grabbed a chair, climbed up and managed to open the small window, gasping as the cool night air flooded in. The hole was about fourteen inches diameter; it would be tight but the fact that she was nearly naked was a bonus. There was no way she would get through with clothes on. Inspired, she jumped down and rubbed some Vaseline from the bathroom cabinet over her body, wincing as it touched her breasts. She reasoned that the petroleum jelly should also offer some protection from the cold water, as well as aiding her escape.

Back at the window, she noticed an inflatable boat approaching the bow of the cruiser. She thought she recognised Blackie and Leila; were they captured and where were Guy and Beatrice? Suddenly, there was a loud bang behind her; Raul was breaking the door down. Frantic and feeling extremely vulnerable, she forced her whole body through the narrow gap, grateful for her slim figure and screaming as her breasts caught the sides. The bathroom door flew open with an almighty crash and Raul stormed in, but with a final desperate push, she was through, diving straight into the water. She dived as deep as she dared and then started swimming in the darkness towards Fairmont, shivering at the cold shock to her body.

Guy abandoned the ancient motorbike in the main street of Hamilton and walked down to the waterfront where, to his relief, he saw *Hidalgo* moored as he had left her that morning. He looked across the bay and thought he could see the lights of Salboa's yacht and an inflatable approaching it. Could that be his Uncle and Leila? He ran to the edge of the pier and looked harder. The yacht was at the other side of the bay nearer the Fairmont Southampton than Hamilton. Boarding *Hidalgo*, he grabbed his powerful binoculars and watched remote figures climb aboard the other yacht. Then, looking harder, he was sure he could see someone waving wildly in the water. He checked *Hidalgo* over as quickly as he could, but everything seemed normal.

In minutes, he was motoring across the bay on the diesel engine. It was pitch black and he had to motor for nearly an hour before he saw the steep bank to the Waterlot Inn and moored at the same place as before. He went below, making himself a hot drink and revelling in the peace and quiet for a few minutes whilst trying to figure out what to do next. Suddenly he heard a noise, a scrabbling noise; someone was trying to get on the boat. Angrily, he grabbed the long pole he used for catching buoy lines and stormed to the stern of *Hidalgo*, making a mental note to restock the flare guns. "Come out into the open," he shouted. "It's me," whispered Rose. "I can't get aboard." "Rose, I can't see you?"

"Down at the hull line, idiot," she gasped. "Grab this," shouted Guy, unrolling the rope ladder. He watched mesmerised as a dripping, naked, Rose emerged shivering from the sea. "Bear, stop staring at me, you've seen a naked woman before! Now be a gentleman and get me a blanket."

"You've cut yourself," he said, eyeing her bloodied breasts.

"A long story," she gasped rubbing herself hard to get the circulation going before sitting down with the blanket around her shoulders.

"Where the hell have you been?"

"That bastard Salboa kidnapped me," said Rose. "God was I glad to see you! I couldn't see where to swim and I couldn't exactly turn up at the waterfront like this. I was beginning to despair when I saw the good old *Hidalgo* coming across like a shining knight, didn't have any energy left to shout," she gasped.

"Where have you come from?"

"The *Alcazabar* brigantine over there," she pointed, "The Spaniards name is Salboa, he's behind all this."

"Leila told me you knew him." Guy said, searching her face for truth. "I can explain that," replied Rose, struggling to pull on a jumper and shorts and wincing at the pain from her cuts. She felt much better as the warmth started to spread around her whole body. "Please stop staring at me, Bear; you've obviously not been with a woman for some time."

"As a matter of fact I have, I was just comparing shapes actually, Viper. Here take my hot coffee. So you have met Salboa before?"

"He interviewed me for a job a month or so ago, but Guy, he wants this Cross really badly."

"He tortured you?" Guy motioned to her bloodied body. "He's going to pay for that," replied Rose with feeling. "Beatrice! Where is she?"

"Hurt and in hospital, I'm afraid," said Guy, explaining recent events. "She will live and the even better news is that we found the Crosses."

"Well done, fantastic."

"Not really, Salboa probably has them now."

"It is all such a mess. I was trying to do things my own way and was taught a lesson, a painful one,"

"I was concerned Viper, why did you disappear at the cave?"

"I overheard you and Leila talking at the main cave and couldn't climb up. I knew she would run off again if I did, so I thought I could solve the problem by telling Salboa to back off. Crazy, I know. He recognised me immediately. I've been stupid and paid the price," concluded Rose ruefully. "Just promise me one thing; I want ten minutes with the bastard first when we catch him."

"Got to catch him first and he has all the aces. He set all this up using us as pawns to get what he wanted. Now he has the Crosses plus Leila and Blackie, things couldn't be much worse," said Guy, grabbing a bottle of water. "We could both be dead," said Rose coldly. "Funny thing is Salboa doesn't want that."

"Why?"

"A guardian angel, perhaps? He said it was alright to knock me about a bit, but not to kill me."

"Viper, it's good to have you back, it really is," smiled Guy hugging her. "God you're shivering still, get a hot shower too and let me know if you want help with bandages."

"I'm sure you'd love the chance to fondle my breasts, Bear, but you will have to come up with a better excuse than that!"

"You're a like a sister, Viper," shrugged Guy, his face reddening. "So tell your sister what happened in the caves," smiled Rose, sorry now to have embarrassed him. "I've thought of what we can do," said Guy after telling her everything and reflecting how good it was to have the feisty American Chinese girl back with him. "It's the only thing I can think of."

"What's that?"

"Well, we know where he is, but I doubt he knows where I am, so we have the advantage of surprise. He's in his floating palace with the Crosses, all we have to do is go, take them back and rescue Blackie and Leila at the same time," continued Guy. "All pretty easy."

"We have to do something, but it's not easy," replied Rose coldly. "None of this has been easy, particularly being tied to a bed naked in front of a maniac with a knife and then swimming here."

"Sorry, Viper."

"You're forgiven."

"We need to get Monty involved once he's got over me leaving him at the caves. We'll need help, as I'm sure Salboa is a law abiding citizen with influence."

"Monty?"

"The Police Inspector who was here earlier."

"First name terms with the police!" Rose crowed, teasing him.

"At his suggestion."

"Salboa lives here, "said Rose, "and knew all along that the Crosses were here, so why the subterfuge?"

"Because he couldn't find them," replied Guy, "And I'm not surprised thinking of that maniac we met in the caves. He needed us to steer him because we have access to our ancestors diaries and he must have realised that was where the secret lay. To him, it's a big Chess game and we are the pawns. Well, it's time the pawns started showing they have a mind of their own and can check mate kings."

"He has a company operating here and probably has political clout of some sort, he's greasy enough to have thought of that," said Rose. "I wouldn't be surprised if the police were under his thumb."

"Doubtful, having met Monty, but possible. So you agree with my plan. We're on our own and don't have much time."

"When do we go?" asked Rose.

"After midnight, when they are least expecting it."

"And what do we do when we reach the cruiser? It's well guarded," said Rose. "I have a plan of sorts," replied Guy quietly looking across at the Spanish cruiser, "there's probably little chance of success, but I'm not letting him walk out of here with everything I hold dear."

Across the bay in Hamilton, in the gleaming Caribbean headquarters of ZTW, only one office light still shone through the darkness. The Teacher sat there absorbed with a number of files in front of him. He shuffled the folders, as if playing cards, every so often looking up and across the bay of Bermuda. He spent a great deal of time here, ensuring that his riches were correctly managed. Looking down, he saw the familiar *Alcazabar* where he knew Salboa would be slavering over the Crosses. The man was a concern for him; one of his inner disciples, yet a man who could not even run his own shipping company the right way. Very like his father and grandfather before him, the Teacher mused.

That was the problem with the Salazar men, or whatever name they chose to call themselves. They were headstrong, overly ambitious and even worse, too set on their own goals to play a team game. Well, the stakes were too high for that, so he would have to learn the hard way. The Teacher would have to help him, for his task was too important to allow failure and he was the key to the first stage. An operation that no one would realise the significance of until it was too late. Step one had been achieved with finding the Crosses; now it was time to activate the second, grander stage of the three-stage plan. The Crosses were merely a conduit too much larger and more significant goals.

He lifted the phone and called the Shanghai office, where it was early morning. Hotlines to the metal exchanges of both London and the emerging Shanghai exchanges were all part of his network. He listened carefully to Elsie as she explained where they were on the day's work and then came rapidly to a decision. "Buy on nickel and zinc as both are suitably unstable, driven by unscrupulous mine owner producers in China, Russia and South America."

"Are you sure? It's a lot of money," replied Elsie cautiously. "It is time Elsie. Don't question what I do, just carry out my orders," said the Teacher coldly, "The Chinese demand for these metals is extreme." Composing himself, the Teacher explained that the zinc buys were merely a smokescreen to hide the real intent on Nickel, which drove stainless steel, and in turn the Chinese Car industry. Without it, the automotive industry would go into panic mode, as they had no substitutes. He, the Teacher, would then control how they received supplies.

He would be in control of not just one of the world's largest automotive market, but eventually all of them. Next, he would move to silicon and other precious metals, which would bring the electronics industries to their knees. He would then sell heavily, causing confusion and ultimately panic as prices fell. Panic would beget panic and in no time he would be effectively controlling the world's rare metals, and by default the economics. That was all a long way in the future, but the tools were slowly moving into place. He had specialists carefully monitoring the world stock positions and all other factors that went into the world pricing of metals. The markets were like children, which was appropriate because he was the Teacher.

"The secret is never to become too greedy." He concluded, "Always leave them wondering where these movements are coming from, so they feel vulnerable and out of control. That brings the sharks like speculators in for a feeding frenzy. Providing all our companies do as I say we will be calling the tune."

"Ingenious, Teacher," replied Elsie carefully.

"It's only one small cog in the wheel, Elsie. Other events in the next few days will put this activity in the shade."

"Please share more of your plans with me, Teacher, so I am prepared."

"You know my golden rule; all operate as separate cells with none knowing what the other does. You will all get your tasks allocated all in good time. There is only one problem," continued the Teacher, slowly staring across Hamilton harbour.

"What's that?"

"Go to the camp in Vietnam and take care of a few errands for me. The red-haired girl, Sabine, is ready for her first full assignment, her first trial she is ready."

"What of Yen Lie?"

"I will take care of Yen Lie. Sabine is to bring the prophet with her, our first disciple."

"The one especially trained for this assignment."

"Of course; remember Elsie our movement is like a snake, many different cells that can survive if the tail or body is cut, but strike off the head and we all die. I take it you get my meaning."

CHAPTER 16

"Where are we?" muttered Leila weakly as she was bundled roughly from the powerboat onto an island, her hands tied behind her back. "Our private island," replied a tall woman with long brown hair, reaching over to grab her with a vice like grip. "Where's the others?" gasped Leila, struggling to break free and looking desperately around as she was dragged into the entrance hall of a mansion house. She could see the Southampton Fairmont Hotel across the water; but the island she was on was a rocky outcrop with trees in the centre and about two acres in size. "Who are you?" she demanded of her captor. "A friend of Salboa's, that's all you need to know," replied the woman, a cruel smile marring her classically handsome face. "I was drugged," gasped Leila, feeling groggy and unsteady as she was thrown into a chair.

She vaguely recalled collapsing in the Café. She looked up as a man entered the room. "You drugged us," she shouted angrily. "Be quiet," replied Rod coldly, turning to the woman. "Kristina, the others are over at the yacht, this one is to join them immediately."

"When I'm ready," replied Kristina, angry that the man, a mere servant, used her first name. "The man wants her on the boat, I know you want a little fun first but there's no time."

"Listen, I do not report to Salboa, remember that. I will take her over when I am ready. I want to find out a few things first, now run away and play."

"Very well," growled Rod turning away. "They plan to sail soon; it makes no difference to me."

"What are you going to do?" gasped Leila as the woman approached her.

"That depends on you, my darling. There are a few things I need to find out before we join the others. You can make it easy or difficult, the choice is yours."

"My mother has been murdered by a madman, I don't know anything more," replied Leila angrily.

"Difficult then; firstly I'm going to fasten those pretty legs of yours," said Kristina bending down. "The madman has caused a lot of trouble over the years, hiding the Cross from its rightful owners for a century, but the police will take care of him. What was in the diaries?"

"I don't know." Leila screamed as Kristina hit her hard in the face. She could feel blood trickling down her cheek.

"Believe me; it can get a lot worse, my girl. Don't think just because I'm a woman that I can't hurt you. I know better than a man does the areas that will cause you the most pain. They just get carried away with a pretty girl and lose sight of what they are trying to achieve. Me, I know how to hurt and I enjoy doing it, so it will give me the utmost pleasure to torture you. Now, tell me about the private letters your ancestor left you at La Gomera."

"Where?" gasped Leila screaming again as she felt the woman's hand on her crotch.

"Try harder my dear."

"My great-great-grandmother Veronique escaped from La Gomera with the Cross and her husband Vincent. The others have the diaries not me."

"You've had access to Veronique's private papers for some time though, haven't you? That's why you and your mother were confident of finding the Cross."

"There were a few letters that we burnt long ago."

"Dear me," said Kristina lifting a long needle, "I do so hate to see such a beautiful body damaged, particularly when I could give you so much pleasure." She moved closer with the needle, staring dispassionately at Leila's legs. "Where would you like me to start, my dear?"

"All I know is that there is a tablet and some Treaty document."

"Go on." Kristina encouraged, seeing Leila about to give in.

"Kristina, for god's sake Salboa is making a fuss," yelled Rod, "he's in a bad mood so I would make a move."

"I don't know any more," screamed Leila as Kristina slipped her hand roughly into Leila's waistband and lifted the needle.

"Oh yes you do, and can do much better than that," said Kristina bending down and making to push the needle into Leila's groin. She raised her head level with Leila and smiled as the girl whispered something. "Well done my darling, you and I shall get to know each other better later, now that you have seen sense." She freed Leila and pushed her stumbling forwards. "Well done, now we can be friends. You'll find you need all the friends you can get where you're going, so you were wise to cooperate."

"Go to hell," snapped Leila feeling groggy and disgusted with herself for saying too much.

"Probably," replied Kristina smiling coldly and shrugging philosophically as they walked towards the boat. It always made sense to have a contingency plan, now she had one and a suitable victim. The Teacher had asked her to watch Salboa and make sure it went as planned and the Teacher was always right.

Monty gestured wearily to the divers and climbed into the police car feeling disgusted and tired. What he had seen down in the caves was sickening, a nightmare unsurpassed in all his police experiences. The man, Steve, was an animal and should be put down in his opinion. Well, he would make sure the bastard was locked away for life. Steve was currently babbling away in the back of the police van about his kingdom. He had lost a lot of blood but it had still taken three men to restrain him, whilst he threatened them all with eternal damnation.

They had found an enormous store of bones, which from their size looked mostly human and currently had his assistant checking the missing people's registers hoping it would close off a number of unsolved cases. What he could not figure out was how the man had done it; surely, he must have had an accomplice? He signalled to Linbar to drive him back to Hamilton, winding down the windows to breathe mouthfuls of wonderful, fresh air. He was annoyed that Guy had disobeyed him, but not surprised, he expected to find him on his yacht. Tresanton intrigued him as he attracted trouble like honey to a bee. Twice he had been in the middle of a major incident and twice was too much for Monty who by nature did not like coincidences. As for the girl, Leila, he was still of a mind to charge her with wasting police time for the harbour explosion.

He chewed heavily on his pipe and looked out of the window as they drove towards Hamilton. He had known about Steve for some time but had never been able to prove anything. This was now the big time, the Tucker Cross had been the cause of many ruined careers in the Bermudan police and now he nearly had it within his grasp. Well, he would find it, he owed past generations of Bermudan police that and besides his policeman's instinct told him that there was much more to this case, much more.

Lifting the radio handset, he made a call then settled back. Something the madman had babbled about was odd and fitted with a recent enquiry from a colleague in Andalusia, Spain. A Police Inspector called Jorge Cabbalas had told him about rumours of a Spanish icon, the Columbus Cross, which was of great value and believed to be hidden somewhere on the island of Bermuda. At the time, he had been following another fruitless lead on the disappearance of the Tucker Cross and thought it an odd coincidence but nothing more. This was personal as the Tucker Cross loss had destroyed his father's career in the police. The madman had babbled about two Crosses. The radio beeped. "It's five in the morning Monty, you have something important?"

"We've just arrested a man who claims to have had the Columbus Cross you mentioned to me. He says that he also had the Tucker Cross, both were hidden by him in a cave complex but were recently stolen."

"You mean he had them but lost them," replied Jorge. He was just past sixty, tall for a Spaniard at over six feet, with short grey hair and a moustache that set off his unusual bright blue eyes. Like Monty, he lived alone and was dedicated to his work. At the mention of the Cross, he was wide awake. "You have seen these Crosses?" he asked eagerly.

"No, the man claims that someone has stolen them from him."

"It's linked to something large over here to do with a prophet I'm told, its essential you find them," replied Jorge his voice rising. "We have some interesting developments that I need to share with you, confidentially."

"What's so big Jorge?"

"I can't tell you over the radio, please find the Crosses urgently. All I can say is that it's a matter of life or death and certainly my career."

"What can be so important Jorge? I need to know more than that," replied Monty, puzzled. "Be careful, very careful." His colleague warned him. "Careful? I've just arrested the madman and he's practically already confessed!" Monty scoffed. "Tip of the iceberg," replied Jorge. "Does anyone know what you have found?"

"No."

"Please keep it that way." Jorge advised.

"Actually there is someone, a person called Tresanton and a couple of girls."

"Find them and get them quarantined quickly."

"For god's sake Jorge, you have to tell me more."

"Soon senor."

<hr>

The dark outline of the *Alcazabar* towered high above them in the water. It was nearly two o'clock in the morning and both Guy and Rose were clad in diving suits that kept the worst of the cold at bay. Guy was rowing the inflatable slowly; anxious not to make any noise he had muffled the oars with rags. They were within ten metres of the Spanish cruiser when he stopped rowing. "Time to part," he whispered, pulling on his mask. "Remember what I said, forty minutes and then call the police, you have Monty's number."

"I wish I was coming with you."

"You know that makes no sense, if Salboa gets hold of you again who knows what he will do, and I need you for a quick getaway."

"Take care."

"Thanks Viper, and for what it's worth I'm delighted you weren't working for Salboa, I trust you."

"Thanks," replied Rose grabbing the oars as he disappeared into the water.

Guy gasped as he felt the bitter cold, despite the wet suit, and feeling very vulnerable as he swam below the water line using a snorkel. After ten minutes, he saw the familiar dark hull of *Alcazabar*. It looked enormous from water level. He pulled himself carefully around to the stern of the cruiser, memories of the recent night in St Lucia flooding back. He recalled that there was a stern ladder near the rear fuel tanks and he could make out their shape without needing to use his small flashlight. There was no one around. He looked for the ladder and was relieved to see a small indent in the hull where the ladder reached down and began climbing. Satisfied that there was definitely no one around he pulled himself up on deck and got his bearings.

Carefully he made his way forwards on the deck until he saw a small light glowing ahead, a cigarette. He heard the low murmur of voices as he made his way to the aft stern door. Opening it silently, he stepped inside, noting that to his left lay cabins. Slowly he made his way along, looking for one that might hold Leila or his Uncle. He was assuming they were both on board and was tortured imagining what the Spaniard might be doing to Leila after hearing Rose's experiences. He tried the second door on the left towards the stern, empty. It was the same with the next one as he stepped to the starboard side. The next one had a key in the outside lock. With trepidation he opened it and looked inside; this time there was someone there, a woman.

Cautiously he entered and walked silently across to a familiar inert form. He was overjoyed to see that it was Leila, and slowly put his hand over her mouth and shook her; she jerked awake trying to scream. He held his hand firmly in place until she recognised him and stopped struggling. "Guy, how did you get here?" she gasped. "By water, are you alright?"

"I think so."

"Have they hurt you?"

"An American woman, real bitch, I'll tell you later."

"Where's Uncle?"

"I thought he was with you," she said, puzzled.

"No, he's here somewhere. I need to try to find him, but we have a boat waiting. Can you move?"

"I need to get dressed."

"Do it whilst I find Uncle. Where are the Crosses?"

"No idea, I've only met the American woman and a small Spaniard called Matarife. He keeps ogling me all the time."

"We'll get you out of here; get dressed and I'll come back as soon as I find Uncle."

Guy headed down the corridor of half a mind to leave his Uncle and get Leila out. Where should he look next? He stopped as he heard a voice talking. He was outside what looked like the main bedroom. He knelt closer to the door keyhole and held his breath as he heard a low voice. It was heavily accented Spanish but he could make out the words *"Teacher and Prophet."*

He cursed as a door suddenly opened behind him. He turned quickly and headed for the other side of the cruiser. At the bow was a larger cabin, he quickly opened the only door and saw to his relief the familiar sleeping face of his Uncle. He shook the man. "Uncle, wake up."

"Guy, what are you doing here?" mumbled the older man coughing.

"That's not much of a welcome."

"But of course I'm pleased to see you. How did you get here?"

"Later, Uncle we need to get out of here, I've already got Leila."

"What about the Crosses? We can't just leave them after all this!"

"No way can I get the Crosses; I just want to save our lives."

"I have to have them."

"Don't be stupid, Uncle, these people will kill you as soon as look at you."

"You head to the boat, I will get them."

"No, please come with me."

"Just give me a minute; I think I know where they are."

"You bloody stupid old man," growled Guy as Blackie headed off in the other direction. "Well sod you, I'll get Leila and we'll get out alive at least." He made his way stealthily to the stern. "You won't be going anywhere," boomed a voice as the main lights flooded the decks. "Stand absolutely still, unless you want this bullet inside you," growled Salboa, looking grim and pointing a small gun. "Ah, it is sailor boy; did you really think you could just waltz in here and help yourself?"

"Perhaps," replied Guy, seeing Blackie behind the Spaniard. "I suggest you drop the gun, you're surrounded."

"I'm afraid not my boy, I've cast in my lot with the other side so to speak."

"What?"

"I drugged you back at the caves; it was for your own good."

"I can't believe this," rasped Guy.

"There comes a time at my age, with my problems in England, where priorities have to change. Blood is no longer thicker than water. I need a pension fund and this is it. My colleagues here helped me get out of England in the first place; I don't think I could have done that on my own."

"And the Cross?"

"Needed your help, just like Salboa here."

"You bastard," shouted Guy incandescent with rage. "My own family! My mother was right after all!"

"Enough," hissed Salboa, gesturing with the gun for Guy to walk into the main cabin where an angry looking Matarife waited. Salboa's nose was red and still throbbing, which made him feel angry, despite getting the Crosses and now Guy. "Rose, go!" shouted Guy at the top of his voice, before Salboa's gun knocked him reeling to the floor. "You shouldn't have done that," warned Salboa, "very stupid behaviour."

"She'll have the police here in minutes," spat Guy, trying to pick himself up off the floor, "and as for you Uncle."

"Matarife, get the twins, find the Chinese girl, if she's out there, and get the engines started; it's time to go out to sea. Make sure the girl is back in her room," he shouted gesturing with the gun for Guy to sit on the chair. "You've caused me quite a few problems, Tresanton, but you are now disposable since you kindly took care of the madman. You saved me a lot of time and trouble but I've tolerated you long enough."

"I didn't do anything to help you," rasped Guy, rubbing his head as he felt the cruisers powerful engines start up. His relief was palpable when he heard Raul shout that he could see no one out there. At least Rose had escaped certain death and hopefully she could get help. His anger at his Uncle threatened to boil over again as he contemplated how much trouble he was in. All he could hope was that Rose would do as he had instructed. "That pretty little friend of yours, Rose, will be found. She and I have some unfinished business to take care of." scowled Salboa, staring out of the window at the sea spray battering the glass. "And don't think quaintly that the police can help you; firstly we will be outside national waters in minutes and secondly I own them."

"She's well away from you pervert," growled Guy as Salboa knocked him back to the ground. His skull ached and it was with great difficulty that he managed to stay conscious. He looked around in anger at his Uncle, "To think I trusted you", he said bitterly. "Trust doesn't pay the bills my boy."

"You're dealing with the devil."

"Be quiet," growled Salboa turning to Blackie. "Bring the Crosses out, let the sailor boy see them before he dies, and bring the girl here too"

"You said nothing about killing him," replied Blackie, looking shocked.

"Well I am now."

"He is my own flesh and blood."

"You should have thought of that earlier old man, just do as you're told."

"He's protected," said Blackie desperately.

"Not anymore he isn't," replied Salboa distracted by Kristina and Leila coming into the room. "What's the rush?" demanded Kristina angrily. "There's every rush," snapped Salboa feeling his nose.

"So this is Guy Tresanton, the sailor boy," said Kristina crossing to Guy and staring hard.

"Leila - are you alright?" asked Guy, ignoring the American woman.

"I'm ok," replied Leila quietly.

"Has she hurt you?"

"Enough questions sailor boy," replied Kristina pulling Leila roughly away. "Take her below Raul, I'll see to her later. You've led Salboa a merry dance sailor boy."

"I haven't finished yet; the police will soon be here."

"And I will give them a drink, then send them away with a donation to their benevolent fund," snapped Salboa.

"Not internationally, your case is now with Interpol and they'll track you wherever you go. They know you have the Crosses." Guy warned. "We will see," said Salboa before shouting instructions to the Captain.

Guy shivered in the night air as the yacht's powerful twin diesel engines picked up speed. He reckoned they soon would be doing thirty knots out to sea. He looked across at his Uncle with disdain as Salboa returned from the bridge. "You're related to Salazar?" he ventured. "His grandson I would guess." Blackie regarded him blankly. "Don't know what you're talking about?" he said. "Yes you do," Guy insisted. "Salazar was your grandfather and you are the son of Gaizka Salazar," he hazarded. The man who just entered the room said grandly.

"I'm Salboa, and this man is Matarife, which translates into Spanish as slaughter-man. Your Uncle may have explained who he is."

"No," said Guy puzzled. "He hasn't."

"He's the man your Uncle tried to kill, before murdering his wife," replied Salboa. "He followed him all the way from England."

"The snitch who told the police in St Lucia about my Uncle; it all fits now." Suddenly a number of loose ends fitted together in Guy's mind.

Salazar continued. "My grandfather lived to a grand old age and my father Gaizka Salazar also reached ninety years old before leaving my legacy to hunt down the thieves who stole the Cross. I modified my name because it suited me. Now are there any more questions from the condemned man?"

"The diaries say the Cross was won fair and square in a football match."

"Stolen," repeated Salboa. "The match wasn't finished, as you know if you read those diaries, so they are now returned to their rightful owner, where they will stay. Incidentally, the diaries are not worth the paper they are written on now we have the Cross, so don't think you can bargain with them."

"Salazar came here to find his treasure all gone didn't he?" guessed Guy.

"Of course he did and the Cross was also gone. He found your ancestors, the Silver's," snapped Salboa with distaste. "They of course denied any knowledge of what had happened, said they had sold it to a madman family in the caves for a few gem stones," Salboa said angrily. "They would never reveal where it was hidden and we came to suspect that no one knew, except the madmen in the caves."

"They didn't sell the Cross," said Guy. "They hid it there with no private gain at all. What money they had was made honestly." Salboa waved his hand contemptuously. "They were stupid," he said. "Your grandfather hid other gems in those caves didn't he?" asked Guy. Salboa looked at him with venom in his eyes and said. "And your great grandfather somehow managed to escape the madman with our money."

"Explains why they hid the diaries," replied Guy quietly. "So you acted once my Uncle's stepson Joe stumbled on the Cross."

"By accident yes, but I've long suspected links to the Tucker Cross so don't applaud yourselves."

"So why didn't you collect the Crosses?"

"Didn't know the exact location, that's where your Uncle and that stupid woman came in."

"Why didn't you torture Steve like you've done to everyone else?"

"We did and the stupid bugger wouldn't say a word. Hence your role and you've done your job well, I will grant you that."

"And I am now expendable?" Guy added sarcastically.

"Exactly," replied Salboa.

"How did the stepson find something you couldn't?"

"Probably because we were dealing with the irrational mind of a madman. Somehow, he his trust working at the caves and I assume must have gone down there and found something. Next thing we knew, he appeared on the island ranting and raving about being attacked."

"So you looked after him?" said Guy sarcastically.

"He died of his wounds, we did our best."

"What happened to Vincent and Veronique?" asked Guy knowing the answer but intrigued by Salboa's view, "did Salazar kill them also?"

"Don't care, as far as I know they died paupers on some godforsaken island; no more than they deserved."

"So after the stepson told you nothing you went for Leila's mother."

"We followed her and realised that she had disappeared down into the caves with the madman. She never returned and I lost two good men."

"I saw their bones."

"How divine," said Kristina coming over, "A real life cannibal, I should love to meet him!"

"You're as sick as he is," replied Guy.

"Well, you have spirit; I'll say that for you. I like men who fight, makes what I have planned for you more fun." She mocked.

"The police are going to be very interested to hear that the Tucker Cross is being spirited out of the country."

"Do you believe in reincarnation sailor boy?" asked Salboa

"No."

"No, I didn't think you would. Kristina take him away, he's heard enough and is starting to bore me."

"Reincarnation of who?" asked Guy trying desperately to play for time. "Time's up for you sailor boy, you will annoy me no more," turning to Matarife, he said "Take his diving gear off."

"It will be a pleasure," the smaller man grinned. "Leave me alone," shouted Guy, struggling as Raul held him while Matarife yanked at his diving suit. He felt helpless in his underwear as his hands were roughly tied behind his back.

"Don't worry sailor boy, you're not my type, I prefer girls," said Kristina drawing a knife. "However, we must make sure you'll appeal to the sharks." Guy groaned in agony as she scored the knife across his chest, cutting the skin lightly so that blood trickled from the wound. "Throw him overboard," yelled Salboa as the yacht pounded the higher waves outside the confines of Bermudan waters. "Wait until we're across the reef." Guy looked around desperately as he stood on the deck of the speeding cruiser starting to shiver as the cold, fast moving air hit him. "At least it will be quick sailor boy," smirked Matarife. "Unlike your Uncle who will die much slower when the time is right."

"You won't get away with this," replied Guy grimly.

He looked into the yacht and saw his Uncle sitting morosely at the chart table. He could not believe it was going to end like this after all that he had been through. There had to be a way. "I'll help you with the police, say you were led," he shouted. "Dream on sailor boy," smiled Matarife. "Time to show us whether you can swim with the fishes, I reckon it's about three miles now to the shoreline. Should be easy for you as you'll have a bunch of sharks chasing behind, have fun."

"At least untie my hands," pleaded Guy.

"I'm a sporting man, I guess, I'd like to see you have a chance," he laughed as he lifted Guy, slashed the rope free, and threw him overboard in a single movement.

Guy gasped as the cold water rose to meet him and he felt himself go under. He knew he would not have too many minutes before hypothermia took over, providing the sharks didn't get there first. His mind whirled in despair, there was no way out of this one; no one would find him here. Struggling to breathe, he came to the surface and looked around feeling his lower body already starting to go numb. In the distance, he saw the lights of the harbour and behind him the departing wake of the *Alcazabar*. As the engine noise faded the silence was deafening. He tried to breathe slowly and kicked his legs to keep the circulation going. Why did it have to end like this? He started to swim towards Bermuda cursing and shouting aloud as he swam, knowing he had to keep active and not give up.

After ten minutes he felt his body temperature was dropping and his jaw aching. Angrily, he focussed on the task of keeping alive, but his mind started to wander. Was this what it was like to die? A strange peaceful feeling started to sweep over him as if in the early euphoric stages of getting drunk. Then he started to shiver uncontrollably. Darkness started to enter his mind, he wanted desperately to let go and fall into the comforting void.

Leila screamed silently in despair as she saw Guy go over the side, trying to break free from the small bedroom. She started hammering on the door until Matarife came along and opened it angrily. "If you don't shut up you will join him," he growled pushing her back to the bed. "You killed him, you bastard." She screamed at him. "He fell overboard, an unfortunate accident," replied Matarife grinning. "Murderer!" she yelled.

"You might get lucky if you shut up and I'll keep you as a housekeeper, providing you look after me in the bedroom. Would have already tried you out but the boss wants first go. You've got that delight to come."

"Beast."

"No, Slaughter-man," laughed Matarife, shutting the door and going up on deck seeing Blackie slumped at the chart table. "You've got it coming old man!" he told him. "I'm not scared of you," growled Blackie. "I've waited a long time," said Matarife. "I had to put up with cold, miserable England to find you and your stupid wife. You did me a favour killing her."

"You bastard," roared Blackie jumping up. "I've had enough of your lies."

"Come on then, I'd love to shoot you, like you did me. The boss will let me when he's finished with you."

"Enough," roared Salboa. "Blackie is my guest Matarife, so remember that. He has work to do and friends in Spain who will not take kindly to your attitude."

"Yes boss, what about the girl? She's making a racket."

"Leave her. I want them both kept healthy for now, I don't want any trouble on the trip."

"Are they both coming with us?" asked Matarife privately.

"Yes."

"When do we leave?"

"Just got a few loose ends to tie up then we go," replied Salboa. "Back to the homeland?" asked Matarife. "To unleash the tiger," smiled Salboa, looking at Kristina. "I've waited years for this, now we have the Columbus Cross it is time to proceed. Wait until the old guard see what we are about to do." Kristina asked if she could see the Cross. "Here," replied Salboa opening the box."

"What about the rest of your grandfather's treasures?"

"We have the two Crosses so it's a good trade off. Grandfather's ill-gotten gains can rot away with him. We are playing for much larger stakes."

"I'm here on our leaders order Salboa."

"My burden."

"Your problem, Salboa, just think of me as a guardian angel and don't try telling me what to do."

"This is my show and you're here on sufferance only."

"I won't follow you like a puppy dog, but I'll always be there in the background in case you get careless and I have to clean up after you." Kristina warned.

"That won't happen."

"This is bigger than the two of us Salboa, remember that," replied Kristina turning away.

"There's nothing here," cried Rose as they did another sweep of the area outside the harbour. She was with Monty on the police launch. "He's got to be here somewhere."

"Why are you so sure?"

"I told you I got a text message from his Uncle saying they had thrown him overboard."

"Can he be relied upon?"

"It's all we have."

"He may be working for them and trying to mislead us," suggested Monty looking at the dark water.

After two hours in the caves, he was not in the best of moods. Steve was safely behind bars, but totally incoherent and would probably end up in a psychiatric hospital. The bugger should be strung up, and would have been if Monty had his way. These days, he would probably get some liberal do-gooder talking about his violated rights and end up in some comfortable cell while the poor buggers he had murdered were left to rot. Monty admitted to himself that he was in a foul mood, not improved by a near hysterical girl ranting. "There!" shouted Rose excitedly, "I saw something, over there to the right," she was certain she had seen something moving in the water and pointed to where she had seen it last. "I can't see anything," said Monty scowling at the girl. "If Tresanton has been kidnapped by Salboa we have a problem anyway as he is one of the most influential people on the island."

"So, does that mean he can do what he likes, including trying to rape me?"

"No, of course not but it makes things very difficult," groaned Monty wishing he was in bed, and angrier than ever with Guy. If only the headstrong idiot had taken his advice.

He had gone to *Hidalgo* to find Guy and now found himself on a wild goose chase. His passion in life was chess and he was starting to see patterns emerging the more he got into this case. The last thing he needed was a fruitless search. "It's a dead sea-gull," he growled looking across at white feathers. "I'm sorry but we're going back, I'm frozen and there is no one out there. We will come back in the morning"

"Just another half an hour," wailed Rose.

"You need to rest."

"He will die if you leave him here all night. Please."

"If he's in the water he won't be alive now my girl, it's below freezing, no one would survive long, you may have to accept that he is dead."

CHAPTER 17

Guy opened his eyes and saw nothing but darkness broken by pinpoints of light from distant stars. His chest was throbbing from the knife wound and he realised that he must have passed out for a few minutes. Under his left arm, he felt a tree branch that he must have subconsciously grabbed, effectively holding him above water. The silence was deafening and his body was very numb. He knew that he would not be able to hold on for much longer, his brain was sluggish and he felt overwhelmingly tired.

With great effort, he spun three hundred and sixty degrees in the water scanning the horizon, a last pirouette before death. Then he saw it, a weak light, slowly growing brighter. He shook his head feebly, was it his imagination or a hallucination? He started to shout but had to stop as the motion submerged him. The light was slowly coming closer and he prayed that it was not Salboa coming back to watch him die. He breathed a sigh of relief as it became evident the boat was a lot smaller than *Alcazabar*. Finally, it was nearly upon him and in danger of running him down in the water. Using the last of his strength he splashed the water furiously and to his incalculable relief the fishing boat slowed down and an arm appeared over the side. He filled his lungs and yelled as hard as he could. An old fisherman put his head down over the side. "Thought I saw something in the water," the old man grunted in amazement. "Incredible you are alive," he grunted in English. "I thought you were an old tyre; I was going to take it as a fender for my boat."

"Please get me out," replied Guy weakly, almost hysterical at the thought of the old man tying him to the front of his boat. He grunted as his bare chest caught the side of the boat and started to bleed again, but he was so cold he could not feel any pain. Then he started shaking as blood started to spread around his torso, stumbling to lie down in the boat, unable to hold the cup of hot liquid the old man offered him. "Lie still, I've seen this before," the stranger responded kindly. "I'll pour the liquid down for you." Guy felt the warmth spread through his body and the shaking cease. The fisherman covered him in an old blanket and within minutes, he felt himself fall into a deep sleep of pure exhaustion.

"You were very lucky," exclaimed Monty, looking down at Guy in the hospital room. "Few have survived so long in the water."

"Guess so," whispered Guy through clenched teeth, smiling weakly at Rose who he had just seen at the corner of the bed. "What happened to you?" asked Monty. "They tried to drown me," replied Guy relating the events. He had recovered slightly, though still felt like he had been walked over by a herd of elephants. "I can't believe I've been unconscious for twenty hours."

"Your body's way of coping with it," said Rose.

"You should have stayed at the Caves," said Monty chewing on his pipe and frowning at the news that Salboa definitely was involved.

The fact that Salboa was a respected local businessman did not make his job any easier, but he resolved to see this one through to its bitter conclusion, after all murder was murder. "I had to stop Salboa leaving!" Guy protested. "He's a very powerful man here." Monty started.

"And very dangerous, you have to stop him." Guy interjected, "He has the crosses and Leila!" He also had Blackie, mused Guy, but as he had chosen Salboa over his own family, he should take the consequences. "Where was he heading, do you know?" Monty cut through his thoughts.

"No idea," replied Guy. "I thought I heard the words *'Teacher and Prophet'*. Not sure what it means but it seemed important to Salboa."

"Are you sure?"

"Those were the words, why?"

"I've heard them before," said Monty replaying in his mind the conversation with Jorge Cabbalas. "One of my hobbies, chess, most of my cases lend themselves to a suitable analogy with the game."

"So what's the link here?" asked Guy. "Salboa sees himself as the King with you as a pawn. For me, Salboa may have overplayed his hand. Think about it, after playing a defence game he has suddenly gone into attack mode, but worse thinks he has the game under control. That is precisely the point where a chess player is at their most vulnerable! They think the game is won and expose chinks in the armour. Question is where are those chinks?" he continued thoughtfully. "You two are still in great danger, but I guess you already know that."

"I'd like to get some rest now," muttered Guy quietly.

"We'll talk later. I'll be back tomorrow."

"Very well,"

Guy turned on his side and slept deeply, so deeply that the dreams were the most vivid yet. The Chinese man was there, as usual, staring at him wordlessly. Guy's head filled with both male and female voices. He saw a man in the distance, a man of power, standing on castle walls. Below him were crowds of people listening to his every word. Guy was beside the man, who was a messiah, talking of a new era to reclaim what was rightfully his. In the corner was the Chinese man smiling enigmatically, seeming pleased by what was happening. He awoke with a start and looked warily around the room; it was empty, he was still in the hospital. Had he experienced a premonition? He looked down at the bandage on his chest as the door opened and the Inspector came back in. "Feeling better?" Monty enquired. "Another long sleep, I guess."

"We need to talk."

"Have you found Salboa?"

"By the time we got a warrant to search the ship he had flown the nest, taken a helicopter to Miami and from there a scheduled Iberia Airline flight to Madrid. Does that mean anything to you?"

"Not a lot."

"There's someone here interested in seeing you," replied Monty, rising as the door opened.

"Hello, Bear," smiled Rose, "how are you?"

"A lot better for seeing you, Viper."

"Good, but you're not going to like the next visitor," she whispered confidentially as the door opened again. "Hello, Tresanton," boomed a big man walking in. "Trouble and you are good bedfellows."

"Grasshopper," said Guy weakly. "Your Uncle turned on you I hear," replied the large man, sitting with difficulty. "You should have told me where he was back on St Lucia and you'd not have had this trouble," he said, rubbing his hands in his traditional way.

"You seem to know it all," replied Guy weakly.

"Enough to know you're in big trouble."

"I'm not ready for this Grasshopper," said Guy, looking at Monty pleadingly.

"I've asked Inspector Pollard here," said the Inspector, "because he's got some knowledge of Senor Salboa, plus he knew you." Grasshopper, adjusting his huge bulk, said. "Oh, I know them both very well. Salboa has caused problems all over the Caribbean. I'll park any natural hostility towards you, Tresanton, but don't think I've forgotten or forgiven."

"I'm sure you haven't, how do you know Salboa? Your daughter told me of your Spanish roots, is that the link?" Guy asked, nervously mentioning Grasshopper's daughter. "She is mistaken, my roots are in the Caribbean only," replied the big man brusquely. "Anyway we are not here to talk about me; you are the subject. It might amuse you to know that Salboa's behind much of the smuggling I have been investigating in St Lucia. Maybe you even worked for him?" Grasshopper dropped the last comment in craftily. "No idea what you're talking about," replied Guy stiffly. "Very well, perhaps not," said Grasshopper. "Anyway, as the Inspector told you he's now fled to Spain and we want to know why."

"As I told Monty I have no idea why he would go there."

"What about the Canary Islands, does that ring any bells?" continued Monty looking hard at Guy. "Not directly," Guy lied. "Oh, I think it does Tresanton," commented Grasshopper angrily. Monty interrupted stiffly. "Thanks Pollard, we'll take it from here, I'll let you know if we get a lead."

"Watch him carefully, Inspector, he's a slippery customer," Grasshopper advised him, rising from the chair. "You'd be wise to keep me involved in this; after all I have spent a lot of time here on the island. Know my way around."

"Thanks for the offer Pollard, I'll call you if I think you can help,"

"As you wish Inspector," replied the big man, opening the door. "But remember, two heads are always better than one."

"Where did you drag him up from?" groaned Guy.

"There's a strong rumour of a so-called prophet returning to Spain; only problem is, no knows who it is referring to," continued Monty, ignoring the question, before concluding, "You two don't get on."

"You don't say?" Guy shot back sarcastically, "look, can I have a few minutes alone with Rose, please?"

"Guess I had better placate Pollard before he dreams up a charge for you. Just don't forget you need me now, no more heroics. This is far too dangerous for amateurs, even those as gifted at finding trouble as you."

"We won't forget, Inspector," said Rose moving across to the bed.

"Call me Monty," said the Inspector leaving the room.

"I know where they are heading," Guy whispered urgently as Rose sat down.

"La Gomera," replied Rose, smiling.

"We need to go there now, before they do what they intend."

"Are you mad? You nearly died out there! The doctor says you need a week in bed." Rose looked astonished that Guy should even consider it. "I have to stop Salboa and save Leila! Besides, they can only be going for reasons associated with the Crosses. Clearly there is far more to this than we realised."

"Perhaps, but is Leila that special?"

"She has to be rescued from those lunatics," he replied, side-stepping the question deftly, "besides, I owe my Uncle."

"You do owe your Uncle your life; if he hadn't sent that text…." Rose trailed off.

"However, let's not forget he was also responsible for getting me captured, speaking of which, how's Beatrice?"

"She will survive, but has lost her ambition; she wants to go back to St Lucia."

"Don't blame her, and you?"

"I'm coming with you." Rose looked determined.

"Then we need to get out of here, without the police."

"We need them now Guy, you heard Monty, we can't fight these people on our own or we will both end up dead."

"But they work too slowly, there's the bureaucracy. Besides, with Grasshopper here I have a real problem, that man is only interested in his own skin. I don't trust him an inch."

That evening, just prior to midnight, Guy heard a knock and opened the window quietly for Rose to slide inside from the fire escape. Together they made their way back down the metal structure to the taxi that Rose had hired and were soon speeding down Bermuda's narrow roads to the airport. Guy regretted having to leave *Hidalgo* but it was heavily guarded and they needed to move fast. "It has to be La Gomera." He said, thinking over the rationale of La Gomera for the hundredth repeatedly concluding that it made sense. "How can you be so sure?" asked Rose. "I had another dream last night," replied Guy. "I saw a prophet or messiah figure at a castle wall, like an apparition.

"The Chinese man?"

"He was there as always."

"I dreamt of my father," said Rose, "he was trying to warn me, he seemed more agitated than normal."

"La Gomera is where they held the football match, but there is little else about the island in Veronique's diaries," said Guy, looking around the airport as they arrived. It was quiet, with only two flights scheduled to leave before morning. "There's something more than that in Vincent's diary; something evil," said Rose, "I know it sounds dramatic, but I can sense it."

"Reinforces why we need to go there," replied Guy, grimacing as his chest started to ache again. "You got us flights to Spain I take it"?

"Yes. What about the police though? I'm frightened what will happen if they catch us and worse what could happen if Salboa does."

"I told you I don't trust Grasshopper," replied Guy stiffly. "If they are together then they work as a team."

"They didn't sound like a team to me," replied Rose. "I think Monty isn't a great fan either."

"Grasshopper would rather see me in jail than help me," said Guy. "There's one other thing I don't understand. He was lying about his heritage; his daughter was proud of their Spanish links."

"This is the one you eloped with?"

"Nothing of the sort, we were just, shall we say, good friends. She told me that he was always coming over here to Bermuda, and two or three times a year would disappear to Spain."

"Come on Bear, you're seeing conspiracy theories everywhere! He probably had good reasons for his trips, which have nothing to do with his ancestry. In the meantime, we have more important things to worry about. I'm assuming that you can handle the language in Spain?" Guy shook his head. "You know I can't,

Viper! If they don't speak English then I'm dependant on you, that's why I'm paying for you to come along."

"Gracias."

San Sebastian
La Gomera

Salboa strode into a small but smart isolated town-house at the back of San Sebastian, gesturing to Matarife and Kristina to let him do the talking. He strode across to a tall swarthy looking man and nodded to him, gesturing for him to sit down. "Good to meet you El Hajj," he greeted the man in English, their only common language. "Salboa, I have heard much about you. Together we share a heavy burden, but the fates are with us." El Hajj responded. "Have you seen the prophet yet?" Salboa tried hard to keep the excitement out of his voice. "No, he's still being prepared. My friends on the mainland have met him and were most convinced. Amazingly similar to how I imagine the original would have been." Salboa, looking around the room said.

"That's the whole point of it," then added. "Nice house."

"It befits a man of my stature," replied El Hajj, pompously looking hard at Salboa.

He was of Tunisian birth, but Islamic first, Tunisian second. He believed passionately in the resurgence of his faith. In his mid-forties, swarthy with black eyes, his dark black hair was short cut and complemented by a pencil thin moustache. He had a cruel looking face with impassive cold eyes and a hot temper that made acquaintances fearful in his presence. This and an air of superiority, carved out of years of presenting a confident front amongst the tribes of his homeland as they battled for power, rendered him ideal for the role he was about to play.

Unfortunately for him, similar to Salboa, his business was in trouble. Gun-running had suffered badly as Tunisia's role with the PLO had diminished. No longer was it the centre of their operations, and no longer was Arafat alive. El Hajj had turned his attentions to other interests after a fascinating meeting with the man called the Teacher. It had taken place at the historic town of Carthage, once capital to the leading power in Europe, but now just rubble on a hillside overlooking the sea. It had been a deeply significant and religious experience for the Arab and he had become a convert to the Chinese man's vision. So here he was, ready to act, with everything dependent on the next few days, convinced he would not fail.

Working with Salboa in the most crucial phase, El Hajj could not help reflecting that it was unfortunate that they didn't see eye to eye. In fact, he had no respect for Salboa, and it was all they could do to remain civil to each other. "Where is he now?" asked Salboa.

"Hidden; he will be with us tomorrow at the agreed place," replied El Hajj, stiffly. "That is how it was planned."

"Everything has to go like clockwork," reminded Salboa, bristling at El Hajj's attitude. "Starting now, with what we are here for," replied El Hajj meaningfully.

"I will show you the Cross but it's not yours until we get to Spain, that was the deal, remember."

"I stick to our agreements," replied El Hajj coldly.

"I'll call Matarife to bring it in."

"I don't want to be seen by any of your people, Salboa."

"Matarife is my most trusted lieutenant."

"He'd better be," replied the Tunisian coldly. "What are your plans?"

"That is my business," replied Salboa. "We mind our own business; that is how the Teacher works, I for one intend to do that."

"El Hajj is a man of honour," spat the Tunisian lifting his head as Matarife opened the box. The Columbus Cross lay there on its own, Matarife having removed the Tucker Cross earlier as it was of no relevance to El Hajj. "Very impressive, congratulations." He said after a brief examination. Salboa smiled. "It has taken many years, all the time guarded by a madman. Even the best logic cannot defeat the vagaries of the human mind, buried all this time under our noses."

"I take it that you will have all the necessary details to ensure people believe its real message and significance?"

"That El Hajj, is why we are here; we will meet again at the agreed rendezvous."

"Arrogant bastard," growled Salboa, when El Hajj was safely out of earshot. "I sometimes think the Teacher deliberately selects such people to test our resolve."

"Worth it in the end though," said Matarife quietly.

"Perhaps, now we go back to the cruiser and make ready to head up into the mountains."

"Kristina gives me the creeps," said Matarife. "Do you want me to take care of her?"

"No, don't go near her."

"She has no emotion at all, I saw her with the girl. She would have killed her if she hadn't got what she wanted. I question her loyalty, maybe she works for others."

"Of course she's working for others Matarife! She works for the Teacher, and that is my other cross to bear. However, soon you and I will not have to care about such things, providing you don't get carried away with the old man, understand me?"

"As you say," growled Matarife as they made their way onto the large Sunseeker powerboat that dominated the small harbour of San Sebastian, its twin diesels capable of in excess of thirty knots. "We leave at first light," Salboa announced to everyone eating in the main dining area onboard. Kristina joined him, and Matarife sat alongside a very subdued Blackie and Leila. The latter two had little to say. "I would like to come with you tomorrow," said Kristina firmly. "I want no delays or interference," growled Salboa. "The mission is of the highest importance, as well you know."

"And one commissioned by the Teacher himself, so it is advisable that you have me with you," said Kristina meaningfully. "Who'll guard the girl?"

"I will," replied Blackie.

"No, you all come with me, including the girl," said Salboa with finality. "That way we have plenty of support if things go wrong. Why the hell couldn't you arrange a helicopter Matarife?"

"Our instructions were strictly to go by foot if you recall, the location is very difficult to find and they are paranoid over security."

"Foot it is then," replied Salboa irritably. "What is it they call this place?"

"I was asking around in the village about it, the nickname is *Fortaleza Hidalgo*, which translates as Noble Fortress," said Matarife.

As Salboa had predicted the journey to the monastery was long and arduous. It was impossible to drive more than a third of the way, the rest had to be done by packhorse and eventually by foot. Wearily in the morning heat they made their way up the high path, as Zhou had done a century before. Leila made little attempt at conversation as she conserved her energy for an escape attempt. Trouble was she had little idea where she was, and even less of an idea what she would do if she did get away. Her mind was returning to normal after the shock of her mother's death. She despised herself for giving way to Kristina's threats, but consoled herself that Salboa must already know everything she had told the woman. Under duress, she had told Kristina the secret of the monastery that she had found in a hidden letter in Veronique's possessions. The letter had been written by Veronique's mother, Lady Victoria. In it, she had talked about looking after the injured father of Vincent Silver until his death, and mentioned a secret associated with the Cross, a secret that gave the icon its real importance. This was the knowledge she had revealed to Kristina, and Leila was conscious that the American woman was capable of using it to suit her own ends.

Blackie stumbled along behind her wrapped up in his own misery. Despite sending the text message to Rose, he was consumed with guilt for his nephew. It had been El Hajj who had provided him with the means to escape from England. Now the man didn't even acknowledge his existence. He was not even sure why they were keeping him alive. He had realised, when he saw the violence in Bermuda, that he had made a bad mistake. He was especially wary of Matarife, convinced that the man would knife him in the back, given half a chance. Even the realisation that Matarife started the fire that killed his wife didn't help; he knew he was in trouble whichever way he looked at it. He was terrified that he would be handed over to the police, and could not handle the thought of jail. As he saw it, his only hope lay in finding a way to steal the Crosses. Hot and cross, he couldn't understand why they were heading up the mountain, but as he walked the glimmer of a plan slowly started to form in his mind.

They were now high up in the Island's main mountain range, dominated by the peak of Alto de Garajonay. The peak itself was visible to them as they breasted the current rise and saw the breathtaking sight of the monastery laid out before them. After another half hour's hard walking they reached the building itself, standing proud on a rock face and built in dark, forbidding stone.

After a long wait, a monk eventually opened the door and stared at them.

"Who are you?" he demanded. "We are here on the orders of the Teacher," replied Salboa with authority. "Wait here," said the monk. The door closed fast, and they were left in the sweltering heat. Ten minutes later, it swung open. "Follow me, only you," said the monk pointing at Salboa. "They are all with me." The monk pointed to a waiting room "They can wait in there," he said. "Do as he says, but come in for me with the gun if you haven't heard anything in fifteen minutes," whispered Salboa to Matarife.

He followed the monk along the long, winding corridor. They walked for about five minutes, then turned left to enter a wider courtyard area and then into a small-darkened room. "How do I know you are with the Teacher?" The sound came from a small man, almost entirely hidden by a monk's cowl, who sat in the dark recesses of the room. His voice was strangely distorted, giving it a metallic ring. "I am on his executive at ZTW Corporation," replied Salboa, haughtily. "What is it you seek?"

"The tablet of Zarco."

"What tablet?"

"The tablet found with the Columbus Cross," continued Salboa, trying to keep his temper. Who did this jumped up monk think he was? The whole island was only a hundred and forty square miles and the man seemed to think he was its emperor. "Why do you seek this tablet?" the monk intoned.

"It has special meaning to the holder of the Cross."

"Do you have the Cross?"

"I do, but not here."

"I have to see it to release the tablet."

"Look, whoever you are, I have come here on the Teachers instruction. My orders were clear; to go to the monastery and obtain the tablet, nothing more." Salboa was becoming agitated. "I don't work for the Teacher," replied the monk coldly, his metallic voice raising a pitch. "I want to see the tablet." Salboa hissed through gritted teeth. "We shall meet tomorrow at a convenient house on the outskirts of San Sebastian."

"Long way to come for nothing," grated Salboa, thoroughly annoyed.

"Sometimes we have to make much effort for that which is worthwhile. This meeting is over; we meet at the Red House tomorrow at ten in San Sebastian. You'll find it by looking for the colour red," he continued sarcastically. "That's all?" gasped Salboa in astonishment. "Tell me about the Teacher whilst I am here," growled the Spaniard." You know better than to ask that," replied the monk. "However there is something I will give you."

"What's that?"

"A piece of advice. You are dealing with forces beyond your comprehension so tread carefully and do not presume to give your superiors orders."

"My superior is the Teacher."

"I knew your grandfather well Salboa; he was like you, obdurate and full of his own importance."

"My grandfather was here?" Salboa could not hide his surprise.

"As I said, there is much you do not know. You will come to understand that. Go now, you are tiring me. Be grateful that you have been allowed to leave here alive and do not tell others about this place."

"I could demand you tell me more."

"You have been watched ever since you entered this valley; you and your colleagues could have been killed easily. You should pick better people."

"They are not all my people," growled Salboa, turning away. Something about the monk's demeanour told him to back off.

"What a bloody waste of time," he growled to anyone who listened as the small party made its way down the hill, "we should have used the guns." Materife Disagreed. "Good job we didn't," he said. "The monks were heavily armed under their cassocks. I saw what looked like Uzi machine guns under two of them. They were along the hill line all the way here, this place is better guarded than Fort Knox."

"We come heavily armed for the meeting tomorrow," grumbled Salboa as they started to make their way down the steep hillside.

Four and a half hours later, he sat luxuriating in a bath on the Sunseeker when there was a knock at the door. Cursing, he got out of the bath and wrapped his bathrobe around him. "Who are you and where's Matarife?" he snarled though the door. "I dismissed him for the night," purred a feminine voice. "You did what? Who gave you the authority to do that and how did you get here?" Salboa was almost apoplectic with fury as he yanked open the door. "I come from the Teacher," replied the girl walking past him, into the stateroom. "Not another one, has he sent you to spy on me also?"

Sabine, looked around the room with interest. "I've come to help you," she purred. This man lives well, she thought, that would make up for his age and physical appearance, which she likened mentally to a shaggy lama with rhinoceros skin. "I don't need any help, go and find Kristina and compare notes with her on how to please your boss," he said sarcastically, looking at the tall and very slim woman. "She would not appreciate what I have to offer," replied Sabine, knowing that Kristina would if she had the chance. "Besides I'm my own person and I certainly do not work for Kristina, I work alone."

"So what is he looking for this time, another report?" Salboa sighed.

"Nothing at all actually, I have come here to build relationships. After all, that is what makes most organisations succeed don't you think? We all have to trust each other."

"Guess so," replied Salboa As his anger diminished he noticed how attractive Sabine was, with her long hair framing a feline face. She wore a figure-hugging jumper, which accentuated her sizeable breasts and a short skirt showing off long, shapely legs. "What's more I like to show my appreciation for those of you out in the front line," she purred, raising an eyebrow and noting Salboa's eyes travel down her body.

She smiled to herself and bent down to ensure Salboa saw her cleavage; it was so easy with men. "What do you mean by 'appreciation'?" asked Salboa huskily. He thought quickly; he had been planning to get Leila up to his room for some relaxation, but the girl was all skin and bones and had a severe attitude. Whereas this one was something else, she had far more in the curves department; he could feel himself stirring at the thought of what lay underneath the clothes. "I always believe one good favour deserves another, don't you," said Sabina lifting her jumper slightly to show her pierced belly button. "I could show you my other piercing if you are interested."

"What do you want from me?"

"Only trust and support, we all have to know who our friends are and I would like to count you as one. Someone who will think first of me, especially when success occurs."

"So you want to be in on the action," said Salboa hoarsely.

"I wouldn't put it as crudely as that," purred Sabine knowing the man was totally under her control, she so enjoyed the process of bewitching men. She turned to the door and slid the bolt home before spinning around and lifting her jumper over her head. "Now, my Spanish friend would you like to see my nipple piercing?" she smiled, as she undid her bra clasp expertly. "That would be most acceptable," nodded Salboa, his senses reeling.

He had never been in such a situation before and at his age was unlikely to be in the future. He had always had to do the taking and was still aroused over the episode with Rose despite the resultant damage to his nose. Now, here he was with everything he desired offered on a plate. He gulped as Sabine suggestively disposed of the bra, revealing her nipple piercing. He was intrigued, having never seen such things before. "Unique my dear, don't they hurt?" he asked, stroking back his long hair and subconsciously brushing his moustache with his fingers. "On the contrary, they stimulate me and I have more piercings to see if you play your cards right," murmured Sabine suggestively wiggling her hips. "What exactly do you want to know?" asked Salboa, dimly aware that she was so expert at this that she must make a habit of it.

———————

The Red House was on the edge of the 'playing field' on the outskirts of the town, characterised by a well in the garden and red adobe walls. Salboa entered alone carrying the box, as he suspected no one else would be allowed in. He looked around the deserted room, feeling his muscles ache slightly after last night's entertainment. "No one here," he growled, and then jumped as a voice boomed out. "Place the box open on the table," called a disembodied voice, the same one he had heard yesterday.

"I want to see you." Said Salboa truculently.

"That will not be possible. Now open the box. I take it you realise the significance of the house you stand in?"

"Should I?"

"It belonged to a lady over a hundred years ago, one of our most impressive converts to the cause. That Cross you hold was originally discovered here along with the tablet you asked for."

"In this house?"

"In the well, to be precise," replied the voice. "It was the last time the two items were together before today; a momentous occasion."

"Indeed, where is the tablet?"

"Under the chair." Salboa reached down and picked up a cloth bundle. Inside was a flat stone and on it were inscribed words in a strange language. "How do I know this is genuine?"

"Trust the Teacher," replied the metallic voice. "The Cross is real so is the tablet."

"I can't read the words."

"Then give them to someone who can."

"Can I see you now?"

"You are not privileged to do so. Go with the tablet, but take great care as there are those who would seek to destroy it and you." The monk turned off the screen at the monastery, his scanning technology at the Red House confirming the authenticity of the Cross. It was genuine all right but he hoped the Teacher knew what he was doing.

———————————

Guy and Rose arrived on the three o'clock hydrofoil ferry from Tenerife. They had left Bermuda airport without any sign of either Monty or Grasshopper. Guy had slept most of the journey still recovering from his ordeal whilst Rose had spent much of the time reading about the history of the Cross and repeatedly reading Vincent's diaries. With Guy's help, she had made a rough translation of Veronique's diary from the French. Both diaries were secure in a small pouch that Guy had around his waist. As they approached the small island, she handed Guy a drink of orange juice. "What exactly are we looking for?" asked Guy sitting up. "San Sebastian is a start I guess, but I have a hunch."

"Which is?"

"The monastery in the hills; it's referred to reverently in Vincent's diary as a place of significance and a place of retribution and of learning. A hunch, that's all."

"Either way we're going to find them and free Leila," replied Guy firmly.

"She's got under your skin, Bear, hasn't she?"

"It's hard to imagine that she has any relationship to your aunt's family," replied Guy scowling. "Chalk and cheese spring to mind."

"There's more I've wondered about from the diaries," continued Rose ignoring the comments. "Go on."

"The football matches must have more significance, they are mentioned so often."

"There has to be more significance to the diaries," agreed Guy as the hydrofoil slowed down to enter the harbour. "Just a minute," said Rose suddenly. "That Sunseeker yacht over there! I thought I spotted Matarife on deck."

"Where?"

"There," pointed Rose, as they drifted slowly into the harbour.

"Can't see anyone,"

"I'm sure it was him, I'd recognise him anywhere, he gives me the creeps," said Rose with distaste.

"If it is him, we need to be careful as they're bound to be heavily armed," said Guy carefully, wondering how he would react when he saw the Spaniard again. "We'll go ashore and look discretely around."

It was dark at seven o'clock and there was little light around the old harbour. They sat quietly in a small beach café off to the left of the Sunseeker, moored at the end of the pier. "Fascinating to think that over four hundred years ago Columbus himself sailed from this exact spot for the New World," said Rose. "So, what do you suggest we do?"

"We have to get aboard before they leave here," replied Guy his mind elsewhere. "We need to move fast."

"Guy just stop and think for a minute, we don't want a repeat of Bermuda," replied Rose. "There has to be smarter way."

"I can't think of one."

"Have you wondered whether we are being set up? Perhaps Monty let us leave Bermuda deliberately so we could do his dirty work for him. After all, he could have held you under arrest as a required witness against Steve."

"Possibly, but we can't just sit here. Leila is on that boat."

"We need to even the odds, Guy. You can't just walk on there; exactly the same thing will happen as last time, only this time they'll shoot you first before throwing you in the sea."

"For all I know they could be getting ready to leave in the next few minutes."

"Possibly," Rose conceded, "but we still have to get smart."

"What do you suggest?"

"A diversion," replied Rose carefully.

"What sort of diversion?"

"One of us leads them away from the yacht by phoning them to say we are onto them and need to meet. Perhaps we can say we are willing to trade new information we have found in the diaries?" suggested Rose. "Yes, that could possibly work," Guy conceded. "There's a mention in Vincent's diary of this Red House in San Sebastian; I'll say that I need to talk to them urgently, he won't be able to resist."

"Nothing to lose except our lives," replied Guy. "So whilst you're doing that I get aboard?"

"That's the plan."

"You haven't a number to call Salboa."

"I'll call Blackie's mobile."

"It's for you," said Blackie. Salboa frowned as the mobile was handed over and he listened with growing incredulity as Rose talked urgently. He looked around at the others and stood up, walking to the bow of the yacht. He then turned abruptly and summoned Matarife. Blackie watched them talking animatedly before Salboa came back over. "Seems like Sailor Boy and girl are more resourceful than I gave them credit for," he said thoughtfully. "Somehow he survived the sea in Bermuda and apparently is here. Someone must have helped them." He looked closer at the mobile in his hand and then saw something. He looked over at Blackie, and reached a decision.

They made their move in darkness. Rose headed up town as Guy walked down to the dock area, keeping his eyes on the Sunseeker at all times. There was no movement on board and he wondered whether Rose's idea would work. He sat in a small stone building next to the dock watching as light rain started to fall. He was concerned for Rose's safety. He was able to contact her, thanks to two cheap mobile phones they had purchased on their way over, but Salboa was capable of anything. They used a

simple coded text message system to ensure no one would understand, using the Bear and Viper names.

He looked up as a message flashed across the screen telling
him that she had found the Red House. He looked back at the
Sunseeker; there was still no movement so presumably Salboa
had not fallen for it after all. Suddenly, there was a flash of light
and three figures emerged from the yacht making their way down
the pier. He recognised immediately the distinctive bulky figure
of Matarife and the two Leon twins. Therefore, Salboa was playing it safe by sending the foot soldiers out to do the dirty work.
He sighed at least it evened the odds for him. By his calculations,
that should only leave the American woman, his Uncle, Salboa
and Leila aboard the craft.

He quickly let Rose know that they were on their way before
making his own way forwards, taking care to keep the stonework
between himself and the three men. Rose would need to keep on
her toes so the men did not catch her. He walked quickly along
the pier seeing a familiar figure on deck, then cursing as Blackie
turned and headed back inside. He stood, concealed, and waited a
minute before hearing raised voices. "You can't do that!" shouted
Blackie. "She's not for me! I am taking her for Salboa, he wants
her old man, so too bad," replied Kristina's voice as she dragged
a screaming Leila.

Guy couldn't see Leila but could imagine what was about to
happen. He ran to the side of the craft noting that the portholes
were dark, just like the *Alcazabar*. He could not get onto the craft
without a ladder, as it was much higher off the water than the
Alcazabar. He was next to an open porthole and looked in, startled to see another woman, one he had not seen before. He listened carefully and then heard raised voices again. "I said leave
her alone," roared Blackie, followed by a scuffling noise. Guy
cursed silently to himself as he heard the gruff voice of Salboa.
Scrambling, he managed to get a small porthole to open an inch,
but no more. "You!" a strident female voice resounded from
above him. He twisted as there was a metallic noise and he felt air
whistle past him, a gunshot. Instinctively he ducked, but he had
no chance, he was an open target. Above him, he heard Kristina
laugh as she slowly raised her gun. "You've troubled us enough,
even I can't miss from this distance sailor boy, and then you can
join your Uncle in hell."

CHAPTER 18

La Gomera

Guy waited for the bullet to strike and tried to brace himself. Instead, he heard a scuffle above followed by a scream. He dived behind a bollard, grimacing as his foot twisted. "You stupid old man," screamed Kristina, knocking the lunging form of Blackie away. "I should shoot you now."

"You couldn't," scoffed Blackie, scrambling away back inside as she raised the gun and fired. "Sailor boy, how the hell did you get here? Too tough for the sharks?" she yelled down to Guy. He didn't stop to answer as bullets flew around him. He managed to get further behind the bollard, flattening himself against the far side whilst trying to get his breath back. With a twisted ankle, he realised that he was a sitting duck if she came down. There were more shouts and then he heard the unmistakable voice of Salboa. "What the hell is going on?" he growled. "Sailor boy is back," snarled Kristina. "So I was right, it was a diversion," replied Salboa looking around. "Well, Matarife and the twins will see to the girl. Where is he now?"

"Down by the bollard there. He may be armed."

"Get him Kristina." Salboa instructed.

"To hell with that, Salboa! I'm not one of your minions."

"Then we'll handle it my way," snarled Salboa, heading back inside. "I've got some unfinished business and to hell with the consequences."

Guy lay still, his heart beating frantically. Once again, he had failed miserably and now both Leila and Rose were in great danger. He looked around, seeing movement over by the stonework; Matarife must be back. Silently, he made his way around and stopped, bracing himself for a knife in the back at any moment. He saw a shadow and held his breath as it came closer. Tensing he made ready to strike. He had no weapon and would have to rely on surprise to knock his would be assailant into the water. "Hi," said Rose breathlessly, "Managed to give them the slip! Have you had any luck?"

"Rose, I nearly threw you into the water! Sorry, no luck, I couldn't get in before they started shooting at me. Where's Matarife?"

"No idea, I saw them coming and ran for my life. We have to leave Guy; there is nothing more you can do."

"The bastard is going to mess with Leila, she's been through enough."

"There's nothing you can do," repeated Rose. "You're weak."

"You know me better than that."

"Guess I do."

Guy grabbed a large piece of wood and keeping to the shadows made his way carefully back down the pier, expecting to be shot at any moment. Five metres away from the craft he was startled by a sudden roar as the engines started; she was pulling away. Throwing caution to the wind he ran forwards, ducked instinctively as something flew overhead and into the water on the far side of the boat. A body! He watched in agony as the yacht's powerful diesels started to roar, the bow thrusters pushing the craft backwards away from the pier. The yacht was too fast for him to catch it. He looked at the water and saw movement below the surface; whoever had gone in was still alive. Euphoric he ran to help, and then he recognised an all too familiar form.

"Blackie," he shouted, as he saw the old man struggling.

He ran to the side of the pier, ripped off his shoes and jumped into the foaming water. Swimming hard and groaning at the pain in his chest, he grabbed the floundering body of his Uncle and with difficulty managed to manoeuvre him into the lifesaving position. With a great deal of grunting, he managed to get the old man to the shore and dropped him on the sand, shouting to Rose as he did so. "Blackie, can you hear me?"

"Yes." muttered the old man. "The bloody Spaniard stabbed me as I was stealing the Crosses."

"Where is the wound?"

"In my side, reckon I'm done for."

"Rose, quickly go and get help from the town. I will try to stop the bleeding. Keep talking Uncle. Tell me what happened."

"They were abusing Leila. I stopped them and got the box out of his stronghold when Salboa knifed me." Blackie croaked.

"What's happened to Leila?" Guy knew that his uncle needed his full attention, but he had to ask. "Saved her for now, I think,

Salboa took it out on me instead," gasped Blackie. "Bloody boat is full of rapacious women, another one joined the other night. The new one puts Kristina into the shade. God this hurts."

"Why did you betray me?"

"I'm sorry Guy, I needed money, and they offered me plenty. Nasty piece of work called El Hajj. Found out that the bastard Matarife burnt my house down," he gasped, "it's too late now, it's all for nothing."

"I will find them, but first we have to get you treatment."

"You survived, boy?" exclaimed Blackie, for the first time realising the fact.

"So they still have the Crosses?"

"Yes," whispered Blackie, finding it difficult to breathe now. "Plus something else they picked up today, a tablet. Kristina is translating it and I found out her surname is Eltobar, or something like that. They speak in Spanish half the time, hard to understand."

"What I don't understand is where are they going, Uncle?"

"The Spanish mainland. There's a man there who is going to cause mayhem. A prophet, you need to stop them"

"Why did they suddenly leave?"

"You spooked them; Salboa went nuts when he heard you and the girl were still around, left their men behind also. World's getting cold and dark," he murmured falling forward unconscious. "A doctor is on the way and we need to keep an eye out for Matarife," shouted Rose returning. "He'll be more concerned about catching the Sunseeker I should think. They have sailed without him!"

"Did your Uncle say anything?"

"Enough to realise this prophet is a reality. He's in a bad way."

"We need Monty, Guy."

"I'll call him," agreed Guy. "One thing Uncle said surprised me. You and I apparently have Salboa spooked. Now, why would that be?"

"No idea," said Rose bending down to Blackie's unconscious form and feeling for a pulse. "He's alive, but only just."

"There's a larger force at work here, it's worrying."

"Our karma, destiny."

"Perhaps, together we are linked."

"Both of us have lost our fathers in Asia, we get frequent similar nightmares. Perhaps it's a test; perhaps it's a test we can't win."

"We have to see this through, Rose," said Guy feeling a cold chill on his neck. Instinct made him turn suddenly as he sensed movement. A hooded monk stood behind them. "Who are you?" Guy asked him. "You are in great danger." The monk said.

"We are well aware of that fact," replied Guy, looking to Rose and then up into the darkened face. He tried to make out the features. "I can save you."

"And if we don't need saving?"

"The girl called Leila does. She will die in two days from now by ritual sacrifice," replied the monk coldly. "How do you know that, you must be one of them," Guy said angrily, glancing at the fast disappearing Sunseeker. "My Uncle is in a critical condition and Matarife and his thugs will be here any minute, so pardon me if I don't react favourably."

"The ambulance is on its way Guy," said Rose looking down at the ashen faced Blackie. The monk resumed his conversation. "I understand your situation; you need have no fear from Matarife and your Uncle will survive providing he gets care. How did you know about the Red House?"

"It was in the diaries," replied Rose, without thinking.

"Ah, the diaries of Vincent and Veronique. I was wondering how you had progressed so far so soon."

"How do you know about Leila?" asked Guy coldly. "To know that you must be with Salboa and his thugs,"

"I know them well enough. She is in grave danger because of others, you need to follow them." The monk turned slightly at hearing an unfamiliar noise. "Ah, that is the ambulance coming; we do not have much time. I must not be seen by others,"

"Why not?" asked Guy. "Because I do not exist on this island, I am a non-person; I don't pay taxes, have an address, or vote."

"So where are you from?"

"We are from wherever we want to be from," replied the monk enigmatically. "Now in our remaining moments it's more important to talk about you two."

"You know of the Teacher and Prophet?" asked Guy coldly.

"There is no more time for questions; your lives are in grave danger. I have come to help you."

"Why should we trust you?" asked Rose

"You have no one else to trust." The monk said simply. "There are some that may look after you, but do not place reliance on that. The Red House was used over one hundred years ago by Mrs Victoria Silver, the mother of Veronique, to find the Cross," continued the monk, turning as the ambulance came within sight. "Veronique's mother had a map showing where the Columbus Cross was buried didn't she," said Rose quickly. "Correct, and they escaped with the Cross as a result," replied the monk. "Do you still have the diaries?"

"Yes, but why is that of interest to you?"

"Victoria spent the rest of her days here on the island, becoming a great force for the movement. She did many great things, including looking after Vincent's father until his death."

"What movement?" asked Guy angrily, "I wish you'd stop talking in riddles."

"The Elders. They control many things."

"And the Teacher?"

"I cannot tell you about the Teacher," rasped the monk. "Salboa is part of a bigger machine that threatens many, he has to be stopped."

"So that's why you are telling us this! You want us to do your dirty work! Well, I am through with all that, all I want to do is save Leila. So, tell me, how do I do that?"

"I cannot help you there."

"I could force you to," replied Guy angrily as the ambulance rounded the corner. People were coming out of their houses. "At this very moment you are surrounded by my men," replied the monk, "so I would not recommend you doing anything stupid."

"Where has Salboa gone?" asked Rose urgently, seeing the Monk getting ready to leave. "The Sierra Nevada, mainland Spain. Now, listen to the news, read your history and you will find the reason," replied the monk, moving away surprisingly quickly. "How will we find you?" Rose called into the shadows. "I will find you." They heard him say, then he had vanished.

"We are now moving into the critical phase and total discipline is vital," rasped the Teacher. The international ZTW conference call had started late, with a palpable tension in the air. All unit heads were present, including Salboa and Kristina who were communicating via the Sunseeker intercom system. Kristina, who enjoyed the Teacher's confidence more than most, could sense the stress in his voice. "The first phase is successfully completed with the icons in our possession and a degree of panic buying starting in the industrial world."

"You mean the metals buying?" asked Saviour.

"Nearly sixty five percent of nickel has been booked and forty percent of Zinc, which is enough, ladies and gentlemen, to be able to control the markets in steel and therefore the car industry, both in Asia and Mainland Europe. The markets are starting to realise that they don't know who the mysterious buyers are. The west is blaming the Chinese and the Chinese are blaming the Americans. As a result, speculators are now involved and are driving up the prices through the Shanghai and London Metals Exchanges to unrealistic levels. We control the prices because we control the supply and demand."

"So we are ready to move forwards?" said Saviour, learning from his last outburst.

"Salboa and Kristina will lead us in the next stage, ably assisted by Sabine from Vietnam," replied the disembodied voice. "In addition, other disciples from Vietnam are now in place and ready to act. So, Salboa tell us the latest."

"The key meeting is tomorrow," replied Salboa. "We will generate chaos within three days, then we strike."

"What can go wrong?" asked Saviour

"Nothing will go wrong," said Salboa forcefully. "We have the Cross and Tablet, I cannot see how anything can go wrong."

"Have you translated the Tablet?" asked the voice of the Teacher.

"We are working on it. It is in Old Spanish, which is difficult to understand," replied Salboa, cursing the Teacher silently. The bloody thing was undecipherable, but it wouldn't defeat him. "Kristin has taken responsibility for its translation and has been talking to one of the universities," he continued making sure he was covered. "I do not accept failure," said the Teacher coldly. "See to it that you deliver." He replaced the transmitter and looked around the compound with a practised eye, summoning Elsie to him. "We need to strike simultaneously," he growled. "Yes, Teacher," replied Elsie, one of the few ZWT members privileged to know the Teacher personally. "Sabine is already in place and will not let me down, make sure that the prophet is well taken care of."

Almeria
Andalusia Spain

The ancient port of Almeria lay shimmering in the early morning sun as a large station wagon drew up and four people climbed in. The town boasted one of the hottest climates in Spain, and a fabulous history. It was one of the last strongholds of the retreating Moors in the fifteenth century and had been a bustling centre of the Arabic trading world in the centuries before that. Overshadowed by the Costa's for years, it was only now enjoying a revival with a burgeoning tourist industry and renowned garden produce. In the station wagon, Matarife sat at the wheel, with Salboa next to him in the passenger seat. Behind the two men sat Kristina, Sabine, and a subdued Leila. Leaving the port, they made their way along the road E15 turning left towards Granada.

Matarife gripped the wheel, a stony expression on his face. He had joined the others by air from Tenerife, having spent the previous night locked inside the Red House. He had not been amused to find himself stranded and had not yet forgiven Salboa for sending him there. "The drive will be about an hour and a half," shouted Matarife, over the noise of the huge diesel. "We are driving up to the Sierra Nevada just short of Granada itself, I suggest you settle back and rest."

Leila tried to clear her head and think positively, but there was not much to be positive about. Anyone who had tried to help her had died, and now here she was in the enemy's heartland. She sighed again, poor Blackie had given his life for her. The only encouraging thing was that she had overheard Kristina shouting and shooting at Guy, so perhaps he was not dead yet. Looking out of the window for distractions, she noticed the edge of an American Indian encampment and the signs to a Western theme park.

"Spaghetti Westerns," said Matarife, noticing her eyes in the driving mirror. "They filmed them here in the Seventies with Clint Eastwood. It's now a theme park so don't expect Clint or the American 7th Cavalry to come and rescue you." He sniggered nastily, joined by Salboa. Leila turned her head away from the two men's cruel laughter. After another two hours of driving, during which she dozed off, they finally pulled into a small village called Orijiva, just south of the peak of La Veleta in the middle of the Sierra Nevada.

To her surprise, they were surrounded by snow and the darkening sky was full of ominous looking clouds. "Bloody cold here," cursed Salboa, as they got out of the car and he led them to the largest house in the town, conveniently situated on its own. "El Hajj we meet again," he greeted the Arab. Salboa," acknowledged the Tunisian. "I trust you had a successful visit to La Gomera? I see you bring your own harem." His eyes roamed from Kristina to Leila and then finally to Sabine. "Very successful," said Salboa, ignoring the jibe, "are you ready?"

"All ready; you're just in time to see the first demonstration. It is due to start in twenty minutes; we have a video feed for your enjoyment."

"Where is this demonstration?"

"Carthage near Tunis, very apt don't you think? From the ruins of one empire, to the start of another. Carthage challenged Rome, we challenge the Christians. Tomorrow it will be all over Spain, come through to the main room and watch," he said, indicating a large LCD screen in the corner with a sweep of his arm. Leila watched, fascinated, as the grainy picture slowly improved in quality to show a man in Arab dress and of medium height walk onto a small stage amidst cheering fans. He held his hands up in the air for quiet. "This is the bit where the Spanish get a shock," whispered El Hajj, smiling at Kristina and Sabine.

"Ladies and gentlemen, not many of you know me, but I can assure you that if you had lived four hundred years ago my name would have been on all your lips. My name is Mohammed or officially Mohammed I. I come originally from the town of Arjona in central Andalusia seven miles south of Andujar where I was an Emir for the Nasrids. I will henceforth be known as Nasrid, and if you will humour me I will give you a small history lesson," he looked directly at the camera with his intense eyes. In his mid-thirties, he had an open face and compelling, light blue eyes. His hair was unusually light for a man of Arabic and Spanish origin.

"The Moors ruled the Spanish mainland for many years and are responsible for some of its most outstanding architecture. My family and I ruled from the Alhambra Palace in Granada as benign successful leaders in the 1480's, and even sent five hundred men to help the Christian King Ferdinand and his Queen Isabella capture Seville from other tribes. My empire ruled all of Andalusia from Seville and Granada in the West, to Mojacar in the east. Why did it all change? I hear you ask. Well, the Jews betrayed us, along with other religions, so that Queen Isabella and her Spanish armies were able to drive us out and forced us into hiding. The good news is that today, I am back." He was interrupted by a disbelieving voice from outside the camera view. "What trickery and stupidity is this? You cannot possibly be back after nearly six hundred years!" the sound of disbelief in the voice was unmistakable. "I was wondering when that would get asked," smiled Nasrid. "Ask me any facts about the last great and benevolent ruler of the Moor Kingdom, and I will be able to answer. I am Nasrid, and have returned to reclaim what is rightfully mine. There are people all over the Arab World who have their rightful homes in Andalusia. Spain would be nothing without our culture and our architecture. I simply intend to reclaim what is ours in the country that today is known as Andalusia. We will free our country from the Spanish and make it the northern edge of the Islamic empire, symbolically of course."

"You will not be allowed to do such a thing," intoned the same disbelieving voice. "What you are talking of may have worked in the fifteenth century, but not now!"

"Of course you are correct," replied Nasrid, beaming as he lifted his head again to the camera, his real audience. "Force is not my intention; I renounce all use of violence. It is not the correct way. No, my friends, I will use the democratic way, the tried and trusted way. The state of Andalusia has its elections in three weeks and I will be declaring my Mayoral candidacy tomorrow."

"Who will vote for an Arab in Spain?" asked the same voice again.

"All those who wish to avenge past injustices and have had their heritage suppressed." There was a huge roar from the crowd. "Again, this is not a holy war, my friends. We are merely going to return to claim what is rightfully ours. I am calling for the re-establishment of culture and benign rule in a state that has lost its way in corruption and greed. Just look around you at the most corrupt states with land deals and you will see it is Andalusia, where rich men get richer, and the poor, poorer."

"How will you do this?" asked the same voice again, actually one of El Hajji's own men called Kemet. "It will not be easy, but nothing worthwhile ever is. We will go to Spain and ask for our voice to be heard. There are enough of our people here to help us, all legal immigrants who went to work there. I have one other message, and it is to the non-Moor Andalusian people. We mean you no harm; we once ruled your country benevolently and will do so again in harmony with the Christians. We will be elected democratically. You will all have a role to play and there will be no differentiation. I will address the chronic problem of local housing, where we have rich foreigners coming to our lands leaving local people unable to afford to live. I will stamp out corruption, and crush the crooks that take your money. I come with abundant money to make your lives more agreeable, including substantial tax reductions."

"This is all electioneering, nothing more," replied Kemet. "You talk big words, just like all other politicians."

"The difference, my friend, is that I carry through with my promises. Tomorrow in Spain I will unveil incontrovertible proof of our historic mission, which will convince you all of the historic rights of our cause. That is all for now."

"My God, all hell will break loose," said Salboa admiringly, as the screen went blank. Both Kristina and Sabine nodded approvingly. "Where was this broadcast?"

"Over all the Andalusia channels, it will be all across the place by tomorrow," smiled El Hajj. "He did a good job, and will arrive here tomorrow for our march into Granada." Salboa was grudgingly impressed. "This was more than he had expected of the first reincarnation. "To think of the power of what we are doing," he marvelled to El Hajj. "A few more of these and we will have total chaos!"

"Exactly as planned," replied El Hajj quietly. "I have an important election in Tunisia in a few weeks."

"So being associated with a successful Islamic rising in Spain will do you no harm at all, eh?"

"Exactly," replied El Hajj. "Either way we will see a major breakthrough."

"Guess so," replied Salboa, thinking it was clear what El Hajj was really after, then shrugging off his concerns; the Teacher must know what he was doing.

"My God!" said Leila to herself, looking on in disbelief at what she had just witnessed. What had she been brought into? She sat quietly in the corner. "Don't worry, my dear, you will have centre stage yourself soon," said Kristina noticing her astonished face.

"What does that mean?"

"Ah, well, that would be giving it all away," smiled Kristina. "Let's just say that you and I should make the most of our remaining time together as a couple."

"Don't kid yourself; I wouldn't sleep with you for anything." Leila spat contemptuously. "You may reconsider, my dear, the alternative is one of those butchers, or little old me. Even Sabine over there has her eyes on you, and believe me, she is a sadist. So, I would strongly suggest you humour me before I decide to hand you over."

———————————————

The private jet touched down at the small airport at Granada. A tired looking Inspector stumbled down the steps to be met by colleagues. "Good to meet you at last Monty," said Jorge Cabbalas as they shook hands, "don't worry I speak English, so there is no need for an interpreter. You saw the video?"

"In Madrid, when I changed planes," replied Monty wearily chewing on his small pipe as they made their way to a waiting police car, avoiding the small terminal. "I don't mind telling you that my neck is on the line with this one," growled Cabbalas, as they sped away. "It hit the news hours ago and my phone hasn't stopped. It has caused uproar in Granada with people panic buying supplies. It doesn't take much to turn a society into a disorderly rabble." He shook his head as if in disbelief at human stupidity. "Just how serious is this Nasrid? He looks and sounds like a bit of a nutter to me," said Monty before taking a long drink of water. "He's real enough, and I believe is already in the country. Intelligence reports have someone of his description; we believe he's in the Sierra Nevada."

"And all this is linked to the Columbus Cross?" asked Monty.

"The so called 'Prophet', I was hoping you could help me with the rest."

"Let's start by discussing the proof the man claims to have."

"I don't know what he can be talking about," said Cabbalas uncomfortably.

Although of medium height, the Spanish Guardia Civil seemed to have shrunk in stature beside Monty. The Bermudan concluded that Cabbalas was lacking any real evidence and needed as much help as possible. "The Cross and Nasrid have to be linked, so logically wherever Nasrid goes the Cross should not be too far behind. More importantly, whoever is behind this whole thing will be there also. My mission, Cabbalas, is to retrieve the Tucker Cross for my own country. Of course, I will help you where I can."

"We've got to get them first." Cabbalas murmured ruefully.

"There might be a way to sort this mess out without too much bloodshed," replied Monty thoughtfully. He had discreetly let Guy and Rose leave Bermuda, rightly suspecting that they would find the next link better than he could. He had lost them in La Gomera, but was sure that they would find their way to Granada before too long.

———————————————

"So, you say the attack is two pronged?" asked Salboa, staring into the faces of Kristina, Sabine, and El Hajj. They were comfortably ensconced in the luxurious villa, ringed by a group of bodyguards, supplied by El Hajj. "Yes, the speeches in one place, whilst the proclamations are done here. That way it spreads confusion," replied El Hajj. "It's ingenious," said Salboa, looking up from the plans as another person entered the room. "Ah, Nasrid, there you are a very impressive performance. You are conversant with the character that you play."

"I don't play any character Salboa, I am that man. Teacher taught me that."

"As you say," replied Salboa, catching the glint in El Hajj eyes. "Are there any other details we need to cover? It's late now, and I'm tired."

"The girl captive; she will be central to this. A European cosmopolitan, not Islamic, to keep the Europeans happy, is that understood?"

"Yes," replied Salboa.

"I want to see her now in private."

"Don't get too close to her Nasrid, she's a hell cat."

"I'll be the judge of that, senor."

"Get your dirty hands off me," shouted Leila angrily as Matarife dragged her into Nasrid's bedroom. Nasrid, smiled at her and told Matarife to leave them. "You are very pretty," he said to her.

Leila stared at the man they said was going to rule Andalusia. He looked smaller and less prepossessing in real life. "Don't worry, I am not going to touch you tonight, or any other night," replied Nasrid quietly. "I just wanted to see you and let you see me."

"Why?"

"Does there have to be a reason?"

"I guess not," replied Leila quietly, unused to being treated with any form of respect since her kidnap. "Very well, we will have time in the future," he gestured to his assistant who had been standing silently in a corner of the room. "Achmed will look after you for now, until we are together."

"We have to crack this dammed Tablet code, and fast," growled Salboa to Matarife. "I can't do it boss, it is way beyond me."

"I'm stuck, reduced to asking the lesbian for help," groaned Salboa, calling through to the main room where Kristina and Sabine sat deep in discussion. "So, you can't do it without me," smiled Kristina triumphantly. "I thought not! How disappointing for you, but don't worry I'll crack the code; for a price of course."

"There is no price! This is your job, and the first useful thing you will have done! That is, if you can do it." Salboa mocked.

"The girl, Leila, I want her."

"You're mad; it's the Teachers decree that she will belong to Nasrid."

"Leave that to me; just you keep your hands off her."

"I have a far more interesting specimen than her Kristina."

"Oh, you mean dear Sabine, be careful when you spend nights with her Salboa, she is more than capable of stealing your mind as well as your body."

She smiled sweetly and turned away with the tablet. "Oh, and by the way I will have an answer on this tomorrow after a dear friend at Madrid University gives me his findings. He is, of course totally trustworthy, unlike the lovely Sabine."

<hr>

Guy and Rose flew into Almeria airport later the same day, having flown via Madrid from the Canary Islands. After the large international terminals, the local airport was small, and in a strange way, comforting. They went straight from the baggage conveyor to the car hire desk. The monk's prediction had been correct; the news headlines were full of a rogue broadcast from Tunisia. It had caused widespread panic, so they had avoided Granada and flown to the smaller airport of Almeria. This way, they figured, they avoided any possibility of Salboa spotting them at Granada, and could enjoy a leisurely drive to the Andalusia capital. They hired a small BMW car and set off along the same road Salboa had taken earlier.

"Rose, what on earth do you have in your luggage?" asked Guy as he started driving. "It is bloody heavy!"

"I took the monks advice and read every history book of this place I could whilst you were sleeping," said Rose, pointing to a pile of paperback books in her large bag. "What did you discover?" asked Guy, altering the seat height to avoid the seat belt catching his chest scar. "The Moors ruled this part of the world for decades," said Rose quoting from a book on her knees. "It says that they were responsible for many of the democratic laws in place today, and many of the best palaces."

"I still don't understand the link between the Cross and Nasrid," said Guy. "Christopher Columbus," replied Rose, continuing as she noticed Guy's look of surprise, "He hated the Moors and fought to help Isabella get rid of them. When he found the Cross he realised that it had a religious significance to the Moors."

"I thought the Christians had the Cross as an icon?" asked Guy, confused. Rose nodded and said. "The Moors embraced the same sign. In addition, with Columbus on his first voyage was a leading Moor, Zarco. On their return, Zarco publicly announced that the Cross had originally been owned by his people. He claimed that Columbus was complicit in stealing it. This caused mayhem, and the Queen very nearly arrested Columbus, as she was anxious to preserve the fragile empire she had just built. The

248

only reason Columbus survived was that he generated so much money for her, but he lost all his titles."

"So, we have a missing Cross and the Moors desperate to get it back. Pagan stuff really, no one is going to fall for all that clap-trap these days." Guy scoffed. "Listen to the radio, Bear. It is all over the airwaves here. Sorry, I forgot you do not understand Spanish. They are speculating as to whether this man really is the returning leader, it's serious all right."

"I'm more concerned about saving Leila." Guy reminded Rose. "Don't you see what the monk was really telling us?" Rose asked in exasperation. "No." he said shortly. Rose continued. "We have the ability to do something. Don't ask me why or how but that's why he contacted us. They want us to survive for some reason, and the monk knows that. I just don't understand why" Guy thought quietly for a moment then said. "So how do you read this situation? There is no historical precedent for people claiming to return after 600 years," Rose agreed. "Perhaps not, but I'll be dammed if we're not there when this new Messiah returns," said Rose.

"Your dreams."

"I dreamt of a cataclysmic event." Rose agreed.

"And I dreamt of the Castle," said Guy quietly.

"So we need another dream to tell us where," replied Rose. "Except I think I know where. The logical place is the Alhambra Palace, the last great, peaceful stand of the Moors. It has to be where Nasrid will symbolically return! "

"To think, all this came from a football match in La Gomera a hundred years ago," said Guy. "I still can't piece it all together."

"What I do know for certain is that this Teacher is either be-hind it all or a major contributor. Maybe he or she is the master-mind and the one we really need to find."

"He may not be, there may be others, like these Elders," re-plied Guy. "Anyway finding this Teacher will be impossible."

"I am sure he will be somewhere near tomorrow."

"The best thing we can do is ensure that Salboa and this nut-case, Nasrid, fail. That way, the Teacher might be forced to show his face."

Guy was struck by the beauty around him as they drove high-er into the Sierra Nevada on the E15, past the sign for the West-ern theme park. "Ironic." He smirked. "What is?" said Rose.

"That Western Theme Park, that's the place we need really, for a showdown." The mobile phone on Rose's lap jangled into life. She put it to her ear and said. "Hello" She looked over at Guy. "It's Inspector Monty." Guy looked surprised. "How did he get your number?" he asked. "I sent him a text the minute we landed," said Rose sheepishly. "We need his help and I kept his card."

"Talk to him then," said Guy, thinking furiously. After e few minutes she turned to Guy and said. He wants to meet us tomorrow morning at the Alhambra Car Park."

"You were right, all roads do lead to the Alhambra," said Guy. "How does he know for certain that it is the right place?"

"They picked up radio traffic, apparently from Salboa. There's one other thing that I am not sure how to tell you."

"What's that?"

"He has news of Leila; she's joined the opposition. The radio traffic announced that Nasrid will marry Leila at the end of the speeches tomorrow."

CHAPTER 19

Granada

Nasrid looked around with pride as he saw men and women hurrying out of the side streets to join his peaceful march in the town centre of Granada. Months in the training camp in Vietnam had prepared him for this moment; he was the new Nasrid Mohammed. Always the star pupil, he was honoured to be selected from the elite for this mission. All his life he had dreamed of doing something special and this was it. During the rigorous preparation for this first mission, he had fully immersed himself in the persona of Nasrid, to the point that he now believed that he was the dead leader reincarnated and destined to recover his lands.

Nasrid had only just started the march, wary of police interference and pleased that so far there had been none. This was mainly due to his quiet dignity and the respect he had shown for local laws, carefully avoiding flouting any. Seeing ordinary people join the crowds, waving and shouting his name made him feel stronger and stronger. Let the authorities think he was interested in using the democratic process to stand for elected office for the governance of Andalusia; the truth would come out in time as he brought Islamic influence to bear on this outpost. Even if he had not been on a mission from the Teacher, he was convinced that this was the real way to expand the word of Islam, not through bombs and bullets. He would have the rule of law behind him. He had studied Hitler's legitimate rise to power with particular interest and intended to replicate it as far as possible. Soon, he would take the American woman, Leila, as his bride and would tolerate the Teachers disciples Salboa, Kristina, Sabine, and El Hajj. He lifted his arms high and waved to the people. Turning to El Hajj who was struggling to match his strides, he said. "How far to the speaking area?"

El Hajj hastened to reply. "Inside the Alhambra, Nasrid, it's about three miles from here, so we will get there around midday at this speed, unless we take a car," he suggested hopefully. He knew that today his thoughts were of secondary interest to Nasrid; the man had spent years training for this. "The people have to see me first," Nasrid, said firmly, "Are the television crews ready?" El Hajj assured him they were. "They are filming your every move; it's all going out live across the world as we speak."

"How can you be so sure that the authorities will let us use the Alhambra?"

"The Teacher has taken care of it." El Hajj was quick to confirm, "Have no fear, the appropriate bribes have been paid so that we have a couple of hours without disturbance. Money well spent."

"What about the film?"

"We have film footage of you leaving Orijiva in the snowy mountains. It has been digitally enhanced to make it look as though you are coming down from the heavens to reclaim what was lost six hundred years ago. We are also coordinating demonstrations in other major cities in the region so they can see we mean business," smiled El Hajj. "We also have large video screens ready in selected public places."

"Who has the Cross?"

"It's taken care of, Nasrid. We will produce it at the end of your speech; it is all timed to perfection."

They started walking up hill and Nasrid stopped to look in awe at the sight of the Alhambra with the snow-covered mountains in the background. "It is truly awesome. I know now why our ancestors chose it as the capital of the Moors, even though it was mainly built by Christians, there is a certain irony to that."

"Alhambra means red or crimson castle, and you can see why," commented El Hajj looking upwards at the striking building. "The main part was built by the Nasrid family, the Emirs, in the thirteenth century," said Nasrid proudly. "You know your history," replied El Hajj, struggling as they picked up pace. He turned around and called Salboa on his mobile. "Where are you? You should be here with the crusade."

"You know that's not wise, El Hajj," soothed Salboa's voice over the line, "I have too many enemies in the west who would immediately link my appearance with the Cross, better that we appear when the Cross does."

"You have the appointed time." El Hajj agitated.

"You can rely on me," replied Salboa, gesturing to Matarife, Kristina, Sabine, and Leila to follow him. "Kristina, look after the girl, she's a valuable commodity now, and we can't afford to lose her," he said, looking at Kristina. "Have you cracked the tablet code yet?"

"It's imminent," she replied, turning away as Sabine entered the room.

Salboa smiled at the taller woman; another night of sexual gymnastics had revitalised him and he felt ready for anything. His was currently a supporting role, but he knew his time would come. After all, this was his home turf, with his people. "How are we going to the Alhambra? The roads are very crowded," queried Matarife looking at the television. "Don't worry," sniggered Salboa, "it will be dramatic."

That night Guy and Rose stopped at a remote motel near the town of Guadix on the E15. To save money they shared a room with separate beds. Guy thought of Rose as the sibling he had never had, a feeling he knew she reciprocated. With no income of any sort, cash was becoming tight, and after paying for the flights by credit card, he knew next month would be painful, unless they had something to show for all their efforts. Rose comforted him over the news of Leila's supposed betrayal, dismissing the whole idea as ridiculous. Exhausted, they both fell asleep early.

The nightmare, when it came, was the worst yet for Guy. The Chinaman had fire coming from his mouth and stared with sightless accusing eyes at him. In terror, he felt himself falling into a never-ending void, falling down and down until he saw the earth coming inexorably towards him. He could not escape it; the earth had a face of the devil, cold and unwelcoming. This was a strong and powerful message; someone was going to die, someone he knew well. The shrill ringing of Rose's mobile phone broke the nightmare. She turned over sleepily to answer it, listened for a moment, and then turned across to Guy. "It's Monty; he wants us to meet him urgently."

"It's four in the morning, ten in the evening American time, for Christ's sake," growled Guy. "Does he still think he's in Bermuda?"

"I suggest we do as he says," replied Rose, standing up shakily and heading for the shower. "There will be a good reason."

Over three hundred people had joined the march, a rich mixture of ethnicity and cultures. Some had joined because they were genuinely interested and supportive, some because they were inquisitive and others came for the free breakfast offered at the Alhambra. Nasrid was particularly pleased to note that a good third were of European background. This was what he wanted, a cosmopolitan movement. They turned a corner and he saw a gathering ahead. Traffic at the busy intersection had come to a halt. Six young men were shouting anti Islam insults, telling them to 'go home'. Three of the group had skinhead cuts and brandished swastikas on their arms.

Nasrid gestured to two of El Hajj's henchmen, smiled at the men serenely, and walked on. Out of sight of the crowd, the men descended on the youngsters, bundled them out of the way down a slope into a hidden area, and proceeded to beat them senseless. "It's a democratic county," announced Nasrid, smiling at El Hajji's laboured breath as they reached their car." I trust your men listened to their opinions first." El Hajj breathlessly collapsed gratefully into the car.

"Of course," he replied.

They drove up the back way, finally reaching the top to see the Palace spread out dramatically below. "Any problems getting access?" asked Nasrid as they made their way down to the large entrance area, "after all it's Spain's main tourist attraction."

"We advance purchased two hundred tickets nearly three months ago under different names, the rest will have to queue here, so we have control," said El Hajj confidently as they strode through to the booths.

The man waved them through the fast track route. "Turn left Nasrid. We need to go down to the Alcazabar, the oldest area next to the Torre de la Vila with the bell tower. There's a large square there, that is where your people used to make their speeches and that is where the new Nasrid will make his." Nasrid corrected him. "The returned Nasrid," he said and strode confidently down to the complex. He noted the elevation of the chosen site. It was a fitting area indeed to declare his candidacy and to proclaim the start of a new era. He smiled at the odd tourist staring at him with curiosity and beckoned to El Hajj. "I assume we will not be interrupted."

"Tactical use of force may be necessary Nasrid; we have to close the area. My men are doing that whilst the camera crews are coming through. There is a natural podium over there where you will speak in about an hour. Everything has been taken care of;

we have sufficient people in place. Our only opposition is a bunch of old and out of condition guards."

"Keep everything legal, we mustn't give them an excuse to use force, not yet. I will retire to finalise my speech. Please make sure Leila is on the podium at the allotted time." Nasrid said, dismissing El Hajj.

The crowd behaved well as they assembled in, what was to most Spanish people, hallowed ground. El Hajj with meticulous planning had arranged for the free breakfast food and drink. The Tunisian looked around carefully, impressed by the sheer size and grandeur of the palace designed and built by the Moors. As the square filled, he arranged for traditional Spanish music to be played in the background, then just before the appointed hour he rose to the podium himself. In front of him he saw over three hundred people with two banks of television cameras, both doing live feeds. This was his moment and good preparation for his own campaign in Tunisia.

He raised his hands for silence and then addressed the crowd in Spanish. It would ensure the crowd felt comfortable though they had arranged for Nasrid to speak predominantly in English for the wider television audience. "Ladies and Gentleman, the time has nearly arrived that you have waited nearly six hundred years for; time that you will talk about to your own grandchildren in years to come. Nasrid is here in this building, and will shortly speak to you in this most hallowed of Moor places." He turned as the crowd noise rose and saw Nasrid walk across to the stage, smiling broadly and shaking hands like a consummate politician. He could not help but admire the man. At that very moment, a helicopter came into view, landing on a clear area on the far side of the main bell tower. Within minutes Leila, Kristina, Salboa, Sabine and Matarife (who was carrying a large bag), joined Nasrid. He welcomed them publicly holding up his hands, aware that the eyes of Islam and Spain were now upon him. Nasrid rose slowly as if unsure of himself with such an audience.

"Ladies and Gentlemen, my friends, I am pleased to welcome you here to this most revered of places and former capital of the Kingdom of Moors to proclaim the rebirth of a new dynasty." Nasrid paused his speaking in Spanish and then repeated the same words in English. "I will continue in English for the benefits of the wider world," he continued, switching language effortlessly. "It is one that will, like the last one, rule for hundreds of years and bring culture, prosperity, and enlightenment to us all." He paused to let the applause ring out.

Before he went any further, he turned directly to the camera. "Spanish citizens, have no fear of me. I am one of you by birth; I speak your language and respect your culture. This is my home and I have no intention of doing anything other than bringing prosperity to Andalusia." He turned back to the crowds. Those words should keep some of the hot heads quiet for the time being. He knew that there had been an emergency debate in Granada's council last night over what they could do. As he had known, there was nothing they could do; he was breaking no laws. He was also aware of the political climate following the Madrid bombings and the Spanish government's aim to maintain relations with the Islamic population.

His biggest fear was that someone from Al Qaeda would infiltrate his organisation, or the crowd, and give the Spanish people, or indeed the press, an excuse to reject the whole concept. He assumed the Teacher had worked behind the scenes with the authorities, gambling on the slowness of democracies to react. "As I mentioned on the video address, I am the Emir of Nasrid henceforth to be known for short as Nasrid. I am not the devil that they claim I am; I just want to claim back what is rightfully ours. This will be done democratically." A lone voice from the crowd boomed. "Do you actually claim to be a man who lived six hundred years ago, a sort of modern day Rip Van Winkle? Or are you, indeed, a charlatan?" Salboa cursed, that was not the sort of comment they needed at present. "I do not claim to have lived six hundred years ago, if that is what you mean," replied Nasrid carefully. "However I do claim to be the same man and if you believe in reincarnation you would have no problem with that. All of you here will have existed in the past as someone but a few of us are blessed with the knowledge of who we were. That is a belief not inconsistent with my religious faith. I am Nasrid and will repeat what I did once before, returning this wonderful country to peace, harmony, and prosperity. I want to continue the work my predecessors did."

"Do you intend to declare independence for Andalusia if you get elected?" asked the same voice. This was not an implant and El Hajj looked around with concern. He saw the man and pointed him out to his henchmen. They should have spotted him earlier, a journalist out to make a name for himself, or even worse. The man had an inordinately loud voice, either that or a hidden microphone, either way they had to do something. Nasrid seemed unconcerned by the interruption and answered smoothly. "Of course not. As with my previous existence and the good works we did with Ferdinand and Isabella, we will work with the Country's Leaders. If anyone has any worries on that score all they need to do is read the history of my previous existence. I have to tell you, this feels like coming home, this is my home and we will succeed together."

"If what you say is true, why do you think this is the time to return?" Salboa made a slashing motion with his hand to his men who were edging closer to the troublemaker, a persistent Spanish journalist in the third row. "I am glad you have asked that question," continued Nasrid, expertly keeping his tempo and smiling. "I could say it has all being preordained but I have something much more powerful."

"Which is?" asked the journalist seeing a burly man coming closer to him.

"First of all let you introduce you all to my good friend, and I'm pleased to say my future wife, Leila." He bade the girl to stand, which Leila did without saying a word. Kristina had her hand behind Leila's back, holding a knife. "This is to show that we Christians and Muslims are one family. Now, as to the gentleman's question let me show you the proof I mentioned." He turned, reaching down for the bag. He was brilliant, thought Salboa; first, the soft words then the hard reasoning.

"This, my dear friends, is The Cross," said Nasrid slowly holding the spectacular Cross aloft. "But it is no ordinary Cross it's the famous Columbus Cross that has lain undiscovered since the great explorer left it in the New World. A very valuable icon I am sure and only just rediscovered thanks to the hard work of my Spanish colleague here, Senor Salboa. Take a bow my friend." Salboa smiled stiffly and bowed before returning to his chair. "This is not just an icon," continued Nasrid, "no; it's far more than that. It signifies the unification of the Muslims in Spain and just as important, my friends, there is a tablet containing a prophecy that has been reunited with the Cross this week. It has inscribed on it the words:

'When the Columbus Cross is returned to its original owners then the Moors will be united.' Check your history, my friends, and you will see that it is written in the books that it is so. The Cross has returned, and the tablet is quite clear, the Moors are back."

What he did not say was that the translation of the tablet was an approximation and Kristina was still struggling to decipher it. "Isn't the Cross a Christian symbol?" Asked the journalist, beginning to fear for his safety and deciding the best thing to do was keep talking. "But also one of Islam," replied Nasrid, brandishing The Cross above his head. "However, this is far more than just a Cross," he paused dramatically, then with a flick of his fingers he sprang the Cross apart. From inside the main shaft came a long bejewelled sword. "My friends meet the Sword of Islam; the real treasure that is hidden within the Cross. Symbolic as we the Moors rise again to claim what is rightfully ours." A huge roar greeted his last remarks.

"He's a natural!" exclaimed Salboa. He cursed Kristina for letting him down with the tablet and made a mental note to speak to the Teacher about her at the first opportunity. It would have been the icing on the cake to quote the actual words during Nasrid's address, but that could come later and they could claim a genuine mistake with the translation. As for now, they had a network interview planned where Nasrid would declare formally his candidacy. The crowd was in uproar and he could imagine the histrionics of the newscasters. "Well done, Nasrid," congratulated Salboa. "Time to go, always keep them wanting more," he smiled, as he gestured downstairs.

A movement caught his eye in the distance and he frowned as he thought he saw police movement at the edge of the crowd. What if the bribes hadn't worked? He knew he could control things better in a smaller group, which was why they were heading down to a smaller gathering. They walked quickly down into the room set aside off the main square, appropriately called the Court of Lions.

The press were eagerly waiting to see the man of the hour. Salboa looked across at Matarife and smiled, satisfied that things were going broadly to plan. He waited until everyone was seated and raised his hands before speaking, motioning for quiet. "Gentlemen, you have heard what Nasrid has to say, and you can examine The Cross accordingly. I will now ask the man himself to tell you more about his plans. Please feel free to speak to Nasrid in either language."

"I have a question first," asked the same journalist Salboa had sworn to sort out earlier. "Yes," Salboa replied, struggling to hide his displeasure. "How did you come by this Cross and Tablet, if indeed they have been lost for so many centuries?" he asked bravely, aware that he was in some danger. "We found them after a painstaking search," replied Salboa vaguely. "Think of it as destiny."

"Yes, but where, exactly, was this 'destiny' found?" asked the journalist sarcastically, gaining courage. El Hajj growled beside Salboa. The Spaniard drew his finger across his throat whilst staring hard at El Hajj's men. There was a sudden scuffle and the journalist disappeared from sight.

To attack people in a public gathering for expressing their opinions is not very democratic is it?," boomed a different voice in English, a voice that dripped with authority, the voice of a police officer. "We must give Nasrid chance to explain his economic policies," replied Salboa hastily, trying desperately to locate where the voice had come from. It was somewhere at the back of the hall and he gestured desperately for his men to move around. "That is why you are all here; we must look to the future not to the past." The same authoritative voice continued relentlessly. "We'd still all like to know where exactly this Cross came from," it insisted. "I think we should stick to economic issues," replied Salboa firmly.

"Is that because the answer is embarrassing?" the voice refused to be deflected.

"I suggest that we take a short comfort break, then we will resume," said El Hajj hastily cursing as he saw two uniformed police officers, Monty and Cabbalas. How the hell had they got past his men?

For the first time he became worried, it had been essential to keep the police out. He cursed as one of them raised himself on to a chair above the crowd, stealing attention. "I'll tell you all why they can't, or don't want to, answer this question. The Cross was stolen from my own country, Bermuda. What's more, it was stolen by that man in front of you, Senor Salboa," shouted Monty striding forwards, his loud voice booming out much to the consternation of El Hajj who was desperately signalling to his men.

"What nonsense is this?" shouted Salboa, standing up angrily. "It was discovered after a long and expensive hunt and I would remind you that it is now the property of Spain not Bermuda. If anyone has a claim it is the Spanish or indeed my own family."

"A court of law will have to decide that," replied Monty firmly, seeing two burly bouncers heading his way as he tried to shoulder his way to the front. "And perhaps you are right. However, I am also talking about a second Cross in your possession, the Tucker Cross, which is most definitely the property of Bermuda's government and stolen from us. As a result, Senor Salboa, under the authority granted to me by my colleague Cabbalas here, you are under arrest and will be deported to Bermuda to face the appropriate charges. Men arrest that man."

Nasrid, stood protectively in front of Salboa "How dare you?" he growled. "You have no right to come to a private meeting with such charges."

"He has every right Senor," announced Cabbalas, stepping onto the small stage. "The law has been broken not only in Bermuda, but here too, by holding an illegal rally." Nasrid looked at him coldly. "This was authorised by the appropriate authorities," he said "It is obvious to me that this is victimisation." Then turning quickly to the cameras he said. "What you see here, my people, is the reason why we need a change from oppressive corruption."

"Shut down the cameras," bellowed Cabbalas, belatedly realising what Nasrid was doing. "So is this a police state?" asked Nasrid, speaking fast and directly to the cameras. The networks were having a field day and could not believe their luck. "I call upon the Spanish people here, and at home, to allow democratic debate. If there has been an infringement of the law in Bermuda I am sure it can be handled formally later."

Monty climbed onto the stage "You have no legal rights to that property or to this gathering!" he declared. "In fact, we are talking here of attempted murder."

There was an audible gasp from the crowd as the word 'murder' was rapidly translated into Spanish. "Why is that, may I ask?" growled Nasrid realising the whole event was now in great jeopardy. "The Crosses were both found in Bermuda by a Mr Tresanton. Salboa stole them and left Mr Tresanton for dead. Therefore, I am charging you, Senor, with attempted murder," he continued staring at Salboa. "This is madness!" shouted Nasrid seeing his plans disintegrating in front of him. He pulled the frightened Leila to him dramatically. "This is all politically motivated to try and damage my campaign."

"The cameras are off now, by police order, so spare me the rhetoric, you are nothing but a fraud," declared Monty, turning on Nasrid. "All part of a large con. I have a shrewd idea what you are trying to do, but it won't work."

"You know nothing about me." Nasrid responded, haughtily.

"You come from a secretive sect seeking to infiltrate modern society."

"You can't prove a word of this nonsense," snarled Salboa, cutting in, "so I suggest you get off the stage and let us finish what is a democratic gathering under the Spanish freedom of speech act, unless you are trying to deny us that."

"Excuse me, I can offer evidence. I am the one that was attacked and will sign any legal statement you care to name to that effect," intoned a different voice from the back. All heads turned as Guy strode confidentially forwards with Rose besides him. "I have proof to collaborate what the police claim. That man Salboa did try to murder me on two occasions."

"Matarife, here, with me," hissed Salboa, painfully aware that events were heading rapidly out of control. Fortunately, he had had the foresight to plan a quick escape in case of such unforeseen complications. Together they bolted for a side door leading to a secret passage. Matarife and Salboa made it to the door carrying the Crosses and slammed the door shut behind them.

"After them!" bellowed Monty, running for the door. "You, Nasrid, are under arrest," shouted Cabbalas. "And get the dammed cameras out of here."

"Arrested for what?" asked Nasrid. "Incitement to mass disturbance, impersonation, and kidnapping the girl. That will do for starters and I'll think of a few others." Cabbalas ticked off the charges as he spoke to make his point. "This is an outrage," shouted Nasrid, signalling desperately to Kristina and Sabine. "My followers will not let you get away with this."

"Be quiet," growled Cabbalas, looking around. "Where the hell did they go?" Behind him, the door opened and Monty ran back. "They're heading east towards the Generalife buildings," he shouted, "It's a bloody labyrinth down there we will have to go carefully."

Guy and Rose watched the unfolding events grimly. The plan had been for Monty to disrupt the gathering to throw them off guard, and then for Guy to enter at the right moment to declare attempted murder. They had foiled Nasrid's plan to control those that entered the Alhambra by assembling there at six in the morning, long before the first of El Hajj's army had taken up their station at the entrances to prevent unwanted people getting in. They had hidden in the Old Palace itself, half a dozen policemen, Cabbalas, Monty, Guy and Rose. Monty's unplanned interruption had been the only way to stop the rally, but now there were so many people around they could no longer see their quarry.

They scanned the hundreds of faces desperately, without success, trying to spot Salboa or the others. Guy wanted to yell in frustration, he could not recall seeing any of the girls since making his own entrance. Where the hell were they? He had to get to Leila before it was too late. He turned back to the centre of the hall and with anguish noted that both Nasrid and Leila had disappeared. Where the hell had they gone? they had been there a few minutes ago! "Leila and Nasrid, where are they?" he shouted over Rose. "Didn't see them," replied the girl, running towards him. "They must have escaped in the confusion."

"Use the mobile to call Monty," shouted Guy through the milling crowd, looking around again with mounting frustration.

The plan had been Monty's and they had positioned policemen at all the entrances to the hall and courtyard but they hadn't expected that there would be secret escape routes. Out the corner of his eyes, he thought he saw Kristina's distinctive head heading the other way. He heard Rose's mobile and remembered belatedly that he had a mobile police radio in his pocket. "Monty says they're heading for the eastern side, towards the Generalife," shouted Rose. "We have to assume they will stick together, though I have my doubts." He knew from the guidebook that the Generalife was one of the newer buildings, built after the Christians took control, about a hundred metres north of the main Palace set amidst landscaped lawns.

They ran as fast as they could and Guy thought he saw a familiar flicker of movement in one of the higher windows. "Matarife is up there," he shouted down the radio to Monty, "on top of the Generalife, four floors up."

"OK," replied Monty. "We're coming up behind them." Five minutes later Monty's head emerged one floor below Matarife. "There he is," shouted Rose pointing up to where a scowling Matarife stood holding what looked like a gun. "They must all be up there with him."

"Matarife, throw down the gun," bellowed Monty from below, "You are surrounded and the place is sealed off."

"Go to hell," shouted the Spaniard. "Two minutes, then we will come and get you," yelled Monty, signalling to the Spanish police. "Monty, they're going to use the dammed helicopter they arrived in to escape," shouted Guy into the radio. "I'm certain of it; you need to rush them quickly." Where was Cabbalas? Monty wondered; he had not seen him since the initial skirmish. He was now in the building with half a dozen Spanish police who knew very little English. Perhaps Cabbalas had found another way up the tower. He tried to contact him again, with no success. It was no good; he would have to charge the room without him. Accepting Guy's fears that the helicopter was the escape route were correct, he signalled to two of the policemen. "We're going in," he shouted. "Keep down," he called to Rose as they heard the distinctive rattle of machine gun fire.

They instinctively ducked as they saw a vicious gun battle enveloping the top floor. "We've got them trapped in the top room," shouted Monty into the handset as he looked around. "The helicopter is coming closer," yelled Guy, looking upwards into the cloudless sky. "All right men, we need to go in now," yelled Monty, running forwards and firing as he went. Shots ricocheted around them and one of the policemen collapsed to the floor holding his leg. The door gave way under a huge kick from Monty. They ran in and saw Matarife defiant at the far wall. "No further," he yelled, "the floor is booby trapped; I want safe passage out of here." Monty, looked around desperately. "Why should I give you that?" he said.

"He's playing for time," shouted Guy franticly into the radio as he heard the exchange. He could not see any sign of Leila as figures started to appear on the roof above them. "They are on the roof, lifting the Crosses into the chopper," he yelled. He lifted the radio and then heard a flurry of shots. A man staggered across the top, then looked down at his shirtfront, covered with blood, before grinning manically and slowly toppling out of the window onto the courtyard below. "You've hit Matarife, but where's Salboa," yelled Guy into the radio, looking around the tower. "Not here," replied Monty running forwards to the top of the building and looking around.

He saw the rope coming slowly down from the helicopter. "Stop Salboa or I'll shoot!" he yelled as he saw the Spaniard emerge from a hiding place and making a desperate grab for the rope. "Go to hell, policeman," growled the Spaniard, grimacing in pain as two shots hit him in the back. Turning slowly he fell forwards onto the roof and then down. "The Crosses," yelled Guy into the mobile. "They're already in the helicopter, we have to stop them." He looked up as the large machine bucked violently and then headed west across the Palace forecourt towards the Alcazabar.

He realised with a jolt what they were doing as the ladder came slowly down again from the machine. "Leila!" shouted Guy turning and yelling towards Monty, who was now almost back down with him. "Salboa led us on a wild goose chase! Leila was with Nasrid, Kristina and Sabine over there all the time. Matarife and Salboa were just a diversion." Monty reached Guy and tried to get his breath back. "What do you mean?" he gasped desperately. "The helicopter is the getaway vehicle, look," shouted Guy pointing to the Alcazabar and the bell tower.

He saw Leila's blond hair emerge with two men that he thought were Nasrid and El Hajj. How did they get across there? He wondered, a worried frown creasing his forehead. "Cabbalas," yelled Monty into the radio. "Where the hell are you? They are getting away by the bell tower. Damn, the man has just disappeared. Come on, we need to try and get there," he shouted to Guy. They started to run towards the helicopter, followed by Rose who was grumbling about being denied her revenge on Salboa. They raced across the courtyard trying to avoid the milling throng of bemused people still present. As he ran, Guy thought through what was happening. The helicopter had the Crosses already. Salboa and Matarife were obviously expendable to the grand plan, though they must have trusted the pilot enough to pick them up first. Perhaps the Teacher was in the helicopter! Someone was directing operations.

They finally reached the main square where only half an hour ago Nasrid had given his address. Thirty metres ahead were the Alcazabar and the bell tower where Nasrid and the others had now gathered. He saw the first figure starting to climb up the ladder. Taking two stairs at a time Guy raced up the ancient tower, desperate to save Leila. The frightened look on her face had told him Rose had been correct, any so-called alliance or marriage to Nasrid was a sham and nothing more. In his blackest moments he had had his doubts about Leila but now he was sure and he had to get to her.

Emerging from the top of the Alcazabar minutes later, he was hit by a massive down blast of air from the helicopter. He staggered across the roof, gasping for breath, towards the final stairs to the bell tower. He saw the others emerge onto the ladder and ran forwards to the bell tower taking the stairs two at a time, desperation driving him on. The steps in the old tower were circular around the wall and they became steeper as he climbed higher. Gasping for air, his lungs bursting, he staggered on and then stumbled badly as his feet hit something hard. Struggling to keep his balance, he looked down and saw stone bricks laid across the stairs. There was a hole in the adjacent wall and rubble laid everywhere. The hole in the wall, what did that mean? It was clear from the rubble that it had only just been done; they had removed something from the old building but what?

He started at a noise behind and saw Monty and Rose were catching him up. He was determined to make it to the top before the helicopter left but it was going to be touch and go. Finally, with his lungs nearly bursting and feeling physically sick with the effort, he staggered into the fresh air to see the helicopter hovering slightly to his left. The noise was deafening and as he spun around he saw out of the corner of his eye the crowd below, now transfixed by the spectacle above. Level with him, but hanging at least five metres out from the tower, were Nasrid and Leila, both hanging desperately onto the rope ladder in mid-air. He presumed all the others were already in the helicopter. "Leila!" he shouted in desperation, looking across at the widening gulf between them.

A movement caught his eye, and he saw Nasrid motion to Leila to keep climbing above him as the helicopter moved slowly away from the tower. Guy cursed in anger and frustration; he could not possibly reach them. He shouted again, and Leila turned to look at him as he stared, beseeching her to hang on. He smiled encouragingly as she mouthed something he couldn't understand. "Tresanton," yelled a voice from high above. Guy turned to look upward and then felt as if a red-hot iron had been slammed against his shoulder. He gasped as something hit him hard and he felt himself spinning around out of control before hitting the floor with a bang. He tried to focus his eyes, dimly seeing the helicopter still hanging there. "Let them go," he yelled futilely as Rose and Monty arrived on top of the bell tower panting hard.

With horror he saw what was about to happen. "No!" he yelled "No," he yelled again, as Leila's face turned towards him with what was almost a peaceful smile. Reality hit him like a hammer blow; she was going to die. Then it happened and he screamed as in apparent slow motion the ladder came away from the helicopter and the two bodies fell downwards beyond the walls of the Alhambra. "No! No God! Please no," shouted Guy at the top of his voice as Rose grabbed hold of him. She held him tight as Guy looked accusingly upwards at the helicopter and saw the faces of Kristina and El Hajj. Then he saw another face, a face from the past, a face that he recognised as he collapsed in sobs to the floor. It was over, all over and he had loved her dearly. The monk was right she had been sacrificed.

CHAPTER 20

The Alhambra sits like a garland on Granada's brow
On which the stars are entwined

Zamrak 1450

"What happened?" stammered Guy sitting down at the bottom of the bell tower, he felt as if a mule had kicked him. Rose and Monty had helped him down, dazed, from the tower. "A bullet, they shot you; fortunately it just grazed your shoulder. You'll live," replied Rose. "I've put a loose bandage on; police medics are on their way."

"Leila?"

"You know the answer; perhaps it was better that way."

"I saw her face," groaned Guy. "It was as if she wanted her road to peace at last. The killers got away?"

"We will find them," replied Monty grimly replacing his police radio. He was heavily preoccupied with something and twiddled his pipe absently in his fingers. "Cabbalas has tracked down their destination through the registered flight plan. It's in the Nevada's; he's scrambled a helicopter to take us there."

"I'm coming too," replied Guy.

"No, you're too emotionally involved," replied Monty.

"I said I'm coming," growled Guy standing up. "We can take all three of you if you want," indicated Cabbalas coming across and looking worried. "They will pay for this, there could have been many more killed and it was pure luck they missed the crowd when the ladder was released."

"Very well," replied Monty, "we can catch them yet."

"Why did El Hajj sacrifice Nasrid and Leila?" asked Guy, holding his left shoulder with his shirt off. He could see clearly where the bullet had grazed him, leaving a long abrasion over six inches long. An inch closer and he would be dead, but perhaps that would have been better, he thought emptily. "No longer of any use to him. Nasrid was exposed and Salboa dead. Either El Hajj thought they were becoming an inconvenience or an embarrassment, either way it was ruthless and cold hearted," replied Monty. "I killed Leila," said Guy morosely, "I should have kept her out of this."

"Nonsense, it had nothing to do with you," replied Rose, putting a comforting arm around his shoulder. "You did what you had to do. I'm very sorry about Leila, I know she meant a great deal to you." She added quietly. "Our helicopter is two minutes away," shouted Cabbalas. "We have to move fast."

Guy, his head starting to spin again as a police medic brusquely tied a tourniquet around his shoulder and replaced his shirt said numbly to Cabbalas. "There was a face in the helicopter, someone I recognised."

"Later, tell me later…Come on," yelled Cabbalas, motioning to the approaching police helicopter. "What of Salboa?" asked Guy, as they ran together. "In hospital, but he won't recover," replied Cabbalas. "I checked on him, he's unconscious." Monty agreed. "He's done for," he said looking across at Cabbalas. "I checked him myself just to be sure." Guy gestured to the thronging crowd. "What are you going to do with them? They will want to know what is going on," he said. "They know that Nasrid was a charlatan, but he's re-ignited old passions. However, the gunfire subdued them," replied Cabbalas as the helicopter came into land, making a deafening noise.

The Sierra Nevada mountains were pristine white as they flew over them heading southwards. Guy grimaced as his shoulder throbbed with the violent jerking of the machine. He was wedged between Monty and Rose in the back seat, whilst Cabbalas sat up front with the pilot. They all wore earphones to avoid the din from the rotors. "We have a fix," shouted Cabbalas turning around, "a remote house up in the national park."

"Here in the Sierra Nevada?" asked Monty.

"Yes, I plan to land about half a mile from a small village called Orijiva near Le Velete. Police drivers are racing to meet us there. I have also arranged for a trained negotiator to attend, and he should be there before us."

"Good," said Guy, finding that the hectic events were keeping his mind off Leila and the pain in his shoulder.

He looked down at the stunning views and saw two police cars in the distance as they flew closer to the ground. Bitter memories flooded back as he realised his dream had been an accurate premonition. His mind wandered; what was happening to him? How could he see these events in advance? He shook his head in anger; he had long since given up trying to understand.

Better to focus on the present; how did it all link together? For there was a link, of that he was sure. Suddenly a thought hit him like a thunderbolt.

The diaries,
The football match,
A name on a passport,
A face at a window
A hole in the wall.
An incorrect name

It all came flooding in together. "We need to get there before there are more murders," he whispered to Rose, lifting her headset as he did so. "What do you mean?" asked Rose, struggling to hear. "I'll explain later," replied Guy. Rose looked at him quizzically. His head was spinning at the complexity and importance of what he had belatedly realised. Twenty minutes later, they landed and drove manically across to Orijiva in two cars. Guy, Rose and Monty were in one and Cabbalas with his officers in the other, the Mercedes cars shaking at high speed along the narrow roads. "We need to be very careful," said Cabbalas as they entered the village and assembled in front of the two cars. "There are at least two men and two women in there, probably heavily armed."

"One of the women will be Kristina," replied Guy. He desperately needed to talk to Rose privately. Something caught his eye on Cabbalas's wrist, a charm with the letter 'E' on it.

They were now on the outskirts of the village with snow-laden fields all around. "So, we do this my way," Cabbalas told them harshly. "I'm going to go ask them to surrender and I need you three to stay in the background." They walked towards a long driveway. "I would like to come with you," replied Monty. "I will shout for you as soon as it's safe," replied Cabbalas brusquely. "We are trained in this, besides I can't risk foreigners getting hurt."

"If you insist," replied Monty, less than graciously.

The three of them stood by the larger parked police car and watched as Cabbalas and his two colleagues made their way carefully up to the house on foot. They saw movement off to their left and shortly another car, a Fiat, pulled up and two more policemen joined Monty. "Escobar," Guy whispered urgently to Rose. "Does the name mean anything to you?"

"No."

"The history of Andalusia book, have you got it?"

"In my bag in the car."

"Please go and get it and look up the name Escobar and check Vincent's diary; there may be a reference to the name there." Guy hissed. Rose could not understand why Guy wanted her to leave now. "Why?" she asked him. "A hunch that's all, it fits a name I heard mentioned recently."

"I don't understand."

"Please get the book."

Rose disappeared as Guy turned to Monty, "Do you think he will succeed?" he asked. "He seems confident," replied Monty, shrugging and quietly watching. "Looks like they are talking, which is a start," he continued seeing Cabbalas slowly making his way back. "Just remember one thing Guy, if I shout, then do exactly as I say."

"Why?"

"You'll see later, no time to explain now."

———————————

"They have agreed to negotiate the return of the Crosses," announced Cabbalas arriving back. "I've allowed them ten more minutes to discuss."

"I'm uneasy about this, Cabbalas, they might try and get away out the back whilst we wait," replied Monty. "We have them surrounded Inspector."

"But returning the Crosses is only part of this; you can't let them get away with murder," said Guy agitatedly. "Later senor, in the meantime kindly let me do my job," Cabbalas said brusquely. "It's a difficult negotiation and I have to let them think they can get away to ensure we get the Crosses. I have a special negotiation expert still in there working with them."

"How did he get there?" asked Monty quietly." I didn't see him."

"He works alone and came around the back; he doesn't like to have any distractions. Don't worry, he knows what he is doing, he is a specialist."

"How many are in there?" asked Guy. "I want the person who released the rope ladder and shot at me arrested."

"I only saw El Hajj," replied Cabbalas. "Now, no heroics Tresanton let me handle this," he said turning away. "You can both follow but keep ten metres behind me."

They followed carefully leaving Rose at the car. "Keep behind me," said Cabbalas as they saw the large villa for the first time. He opened the door with his gun drawn. "I am coming in," he shouted. "You are not alone; the deal was just you Cabbalas," came the voice of El Hajj. "They are only observing; they will not come any closer."

"Bring them into the entrance hall," replied a familiar female voice. "We talk from there."

"Do we have a deal? The Cross for safe passage, as we discussed," shouted Cabbalas.

"Who is with you? We have guns, so don't do anything stupid," said Kristina.

"Tresanton and Police Inspector Monty," replied Cabbalas.

"We deal with you alone Cabbalas," said El Hajj.

"I agreed that, as did my negotiator."

"Then you have a deal."

"Afraid I have a problem with that. Who killed Nasrid and Leila?" shouted Monty, staring up into the gloom. "That is not part of the discussion," replied Kristina coldly. "It was cold blooded murder," shouted Guy. "It was an accident," snarled Kristina. "Come to the head of the stairs where I can see you."

"I am here," growled Guy. "If we come any further you will shoot us, just like you did before."

"You liked the girl, Tresanton."

"It was you who killed her; I call that cold blooded murder."

"Ah, so that's it! You fancied her! Well I'm afraid she preferred women like me." Kristina sneered. "Careful, she's trying to provoke you," whispered Monty, looking across at the angry face of Cabbalas. "Keep her talking, there's something urgent I have to do," he said turning away quickly. "Okay," replied Guy puzzled and sensing that something was wrong. "Tresanton," continued Kristina, "You are becoming very tiresome, but don't think for one moment you can stop us."

"I understand what you are doing."

"I don't think so," replied Kristina, leaning over the balcony. "The movement is far too clever and resourceful for the likes of you."

"You failed with Nasrid didn't you?" taunted Guy, his temper rising, ignoring Cabbalas urging him to calm down.

"Nasrid was a pawn nothing more; we can replicate him at will."

"What was stolen from the bell tower?"

"Not your concern."

"What's the significance of the Elders?" asked Guy trying to keep his temper, aware that Monty was making his way back up the path. "Enough Tresanton, I only wished to understand you a little more before you and your female friend die," came the voice further away now. "Run," yelled Monty, charging into Guy and flattening him to the floor seconds before an almighty explosion shook the villa to its foundations.

The house filled with dense smoke and Guy felt a blast of air in the gloom. There was total silence and shaking his head he realised his hearing was impaired. Slowly, sound returned and the silence gave way to pain as his ears started to ache and his eyes stung from the acrid smoke. He looked around cautiously, his injured shoulder in agony, realising that he had been saved by a combination of Monty's push and the heavy door lintel. He turned to see both Monty and Cabbalas rising unsteadily to their feet, Monty looking by far the worse for wear of the two. "Stun grenade from the top floor," shouted Cabbalas. "A diversion tactic, wait for me and don't move, there could be more, I need to see what has happened to the negotiator."

He ran up the stairs holding his gun and emerged again after about two minutes at the head of the stairs, shrugging his shoulders. "Stay down there, this is dangerous."

"Nonsense," replied Monty, suddenly gesturing to Guy to join him. They ran up the stairs and past the protesting figure of Cabbalas just in time to hear two high-powered motorbikes roar away at the back door and across a field behind the villa. Astride them were the recognisable features of El Hajj and Kristina with Sabine behind her riding pillion. "Damn the man," growled Monty. "No doubt they have the helicopter waiting on the other side of the hill."

"You mean this was planned," said Guy instinctively turning his head to the corner of the main bedroom and seeing the Columbus Cross in the corner. "Definitely," growled Monty, rushing ahead to the main bedroom. "I'll check the other rooms," replied Guy his eyes drawn almost inexorably to the left and to a man he knew well, very well indeed.

"Grasshopper! My god, I thought it was you in the helicopter," he exclaimed.

"Small world Tresanton, small world indeed," replied the big man rising from behind a large table and lifting the Cross into the original box. "For God's sake Pollard, what are you doing here?" growled Monty turning at the sound of the voice. "There's no one else here so I assume you were the mysterious negotiator."

"I told you that I could help you. Now, thanks to the skills of the good Inspector Cabbalas and I, the Crosses are returned. You can thank me later." Grasshopper said.

"Can I indeed," replied Monty frowning. "I suggest we do that downstairs with your friend."

"How the hell did you get here?" asked Guy coldly as they walked downstairs to join Cabbalas. "Told you I was following Salboa; he was working my patch. I merely extended my services to where they were appreciated," said Grasshopper pointedly, looking across at Monty. "Anyway, we have successfully achieved our objective," he said, putting the large box on the hallway table and looking across at Cabbalas. "In the meantime we need to take care of these two beauties, don't we Cabbalas."

"We certainly got the desired results," replied Cabbalas, reaching inside his jacket. "Drop the gun Cabbalas," shouted Monty lifting his Mauser automatic and shouting across to the astonished policeman.

"What's the meaning of this? Have you gone mad Monty?" blustered the Spaniard. "There's nothing worse in my book than a crooked policeman. You are totally mixed in with them aren't you Cabbalas?"

"How dare you," shouted Cabbalas, looking around frantically for an escape route, his blue eyes blazing mad. "Your men are taken care of Cabbalas; I had the foresight to have three loyal officers come with us. They are outside with your men now, hand over the gun."

"This is an outrage," protested Grasshopper. "The man has done a great service. I demand you put the gun down, don't forget you are under the Inspector's jurisdiction here."

"You too, Grasshopper, move over and join your friend before I shoot you both now. Throwing that stun grenade could easily have killed us and don't think I didn't notice, Cabbalas, how you made sure you were well out of the way. It was one of many things that gave you away."

"How dare you," spluttered the big man, going red in the face. "This is an outrage. Cabbalas call your men over, he's gone mad."

"It's taken two amateurs to uncover your deceit, but make no mistake I've got you," snapped Monty grimly, training his Mauser pistol on the policemen.

"You're stressed out Monty," said Cabbalas slowly raising his hands. "You've being under a lot of pressure, we all have. Let's talk this over like fellow officers."

"I gave you enough rope to hang yourself, Cabbalas, That's why I let you control the situation here, but it's over now. Don't think I was taken in by your disappearing act at the Alhambra, either. As for you Pollard, or shall I call you Grasshopper as I think it's more befitting your status. I've had my suspicions since you joined me in Bermuda."

"This is outrageous Inspector; you should remember that I called you here in the first place." Cabbalas blustered.

"To help you succeed, but thanks to Guy and Rose we've figured you both out."

"An ingenious scheme," acknowledged Guy, stepping forwards and gesturing to Rose to join them. "Rose, perhaps you could educate them, or should I say remind them, of what they seem to have conveniently forgotten."

"It will be a pleasure," replied Rose, entering the house for the first time as Monty slipped a spare Mauser into Guy's hands and three more armed officers entered. "I suggest we start by using your correct common name, Senor Escobar."

"What nonsense is this?" replied Grasshopper angrily. "Your real name. In fact, both your real names, despite what you both choose to call yourselves. Your common family is Escobar, both of you," replied Rose. "I can prove it if you insist, and how you took your current names."

"Nonsense."

"I noticed the pendant on your wrist with the letter E," said Guy.

"Changing names isn't a crime." Cabbalas interjected.

"No, but murder and stealing the Crosses are."

"Monty, for God's sake end this charade," appealed Cabbalas. "El Hajj is getting away from us."

"As indeed you intended him too Cabbalas; besides it's you two I want. There is no point chasing El Hajj when everything we need is here. Now, I suggest the girl continues."

Rose smiled confidently. "First a little history lesson gentlemen," she said. "Spain in the early sixteenth century was still many warring and independent states, even though the King Ferdinand and Queen Isabella had proclaimed unity. Nowhere was this stronger than here in Andalusia where the Escobar's ruled a territory recently freed of the Moors with absolute decree. How did they do that? Simple really, they fermented a Moor revolt by getting a hapless Moor Prince who still lived in the country to reclaim his right to the lands. Sound familiar to today's events?" she stopped to give a wry smile to her now captive audience, "This Prince leads a futile revolt, the Moors are discredited and it culminates with the Escobar's arranging for the Moor Prince to be thrown in public off the bell tower at the Alhambra. *Again familiar?* Because of all this, Escobar takes martial control, with the blessing of Madrid, and under draconian laws builds one of the biggest family dictatorships and fortunes in Spain. He plunders the immense Moor wealth, which was still here, thanks Isabel's policy of coexistence."

"What of it? I fail totally to see the relevance of all this?" scowled Cabbalas. Rose continued. "A hundred years ago a direct descendant of the Escobar dynasty was Governor of Tenerife when a football match occurred between nations; which leads directly or indirectly to the creation or development of a secret sect. This sect is run, or heavily influenced, by a secretive enigma called the Teacher. He is the man who controls people like Salboa and El Hajj. So to the present day; what we have is a pair of rogues, cousins probably, judging by appearances, you aren't brothers, who realised there was a great opportunity to avenge the family name and become rich.

"Both of you were privy to the Nasrid plot because you had both gained the confidence of Salboa. You realised you could make yourselves rich and famous by retrieving the Crosses which is why you dragged us here to this remote place to witness your moment of glory. You were effectively playing both sides off against the other and emerging as the winners. On top of all that you had the family honour to avenge as Governor Escobar died a broken and penniless man after the La Gomera challenge went wrong for him."

"What relevance is all this nonsense," scowled Grasshopper his small eyes staring furtively around. "Kindly hand over that leather scroll from inside your jacket," said Monty coldly.

"I don't know what you mean," replied Grasshopper, scowling as Guy grabbed him and extracted a leather package and showing it to Monty. "So here we have an interesting tale," replied the Inspector, unrolling the leather document, "a treaty document written in Spanish. Rose could you do the honours please?"

"The infamous *'Treaty of Alhambra*," paraphrased Rose. "Its very existence long denied by anyone in authority and here in the light of day for the first time," she read the document as quickly as she could in Spanish and then looked up coldly. "The gist of it is clear to me. This was the reason you helped stage the whole event in the Alhambra. Salboa and El Hajj were concerned with Nasrid, but you two wanted only this. You needed a diversion whilst you dug around in the Bell Tower for it, probably with El Hajj and Salboa. I would guess you even manoeuvred them to have the Nasrid event here to cover you whilst looking."

"Hence your convenient disappearance Cabbalas, when I needed you most," said Monty coldly. "How did you know all this?" asked Cabbalas quietly, realising he was exposed. "The missing tablet Salboa retrieved from La Gomera pointed the way to this treaty. I know that because I read it," said Rose.

"What was the significance of this Treaty?" asked Guy.

"It laid down a formal agreement between Isabella and the original Nasrid that in return for him evacuating Andalusia, Isabella would award him sovereignty of any lands that Columbus discovered. This is why she immediately funded the explorer's expedition after months of procrastination," continued Rose. "Why would she conclude such an agreement when she was winning anyway?" asked Guy realising that Rose was way ahead of him and becoming more impressed by the minute.

He had derived a conclusion with the Escobar name after thinking through Grasshopper's role, but this was impressive. Not for the first time he felt glad he had Rose on his side. "Remember, in 1492 the Queen was absolutely desperate to get the Moors out of Spain but they were entrenched, not just in Granada but the whole of Andalusia across to Almeria and further. Her whole reign had been predicated on the goal to unify the Spanish nation, and one thing stood in her way, the Moors. So she offered the original Nasrid the deal."

"Would that be enough to cause modern Spain problems?" asked Guy. "Yes, it is significant enough for the Spanish nation," replied Rose, quickly scanning the document again. "Specifically it promised the Moors first refusal on ownership of any lands discovered by Columbus, in return for their exit from Andalusia. You can imagine the outcry if all this had come to light."

Monty extracted his pipe and chewed on it. "But what is the real significance for these two?" he asked. Rose resumed her commentary. "Proof that the Moors have rights to Spanish lands is something I am sure these two knew could be auctioned off to unscrupulous individuals. It would be priceless to someone keen to embarrass the authorities, particularly if it had Islamic undertones. I should imagine they would have gone to the Arab nations with it. Imagine the embarrassment, particularly when you think of some of the lands Columbus found in South America, rich in oil and even drugs. Such a treaty has been rumoured for centuries, but now we have the proof," finished Rose. "Not for much longer, set fire to it Guy," commanded Monty. "You can't do that," yelled Cabbalas, jumping forwards desperately. "Light it, Guy," shouted Monty again, and producing his lighter. Guy lit some paper and soon had a blaze going in the fireplace before throwing the leather parchment into it as the others looked on incredulously.

Monty stared impassively at his prisoners. "End of your dreams, Cabbalas, gone up in smoke, and the best thing for such a document in our dangerous world. Incidentally, before Salboa conveniently died, I got a taped confession from him. He confessed that he worked with you two, but that you betrayed him. He would have survived the gun-shots, perhaps, but certainly not the poison you injected just to make sure, which in my book makes it murder. Whilst on that subject, I assume it was you who released the ladder Pollard. After all, Cabbalas was busy getting the Treaty."

"You can't prove a word, Monty," growled Grasshopper. "I always thought you were too bloody liberal; always going by the rule book, you wouldn't shoot us now if we walked out of here! It would be against your pathetic rulebook, Monty, you and your bloody chess games! Well, real life isn't like that."

"But I'm not bound by any rule books or any chess rules," interjected Guy coldly. "You were in with Salboa from the start weren't you Grasshopper? No wonder you always knew where to find me! It would give me great pleasure to kill you now that you have admitted killing Leila."

"What if I did, boy?" snarled Grasshopper, moving forwards with surprising speed.

"Stop!" yelled Guy, trying to raise the Mauser and failing miserably. Too late, he saw the glint of steel in the police officer's hand as they made contact and braced himself for the pain. Instead, there was a deafening explosion and Grasshopper grunted before collapsing to the floor clutching his leg. "You're lucky, I spared you for prison," said Monty coldly, moving his gun to cover Cabbalas. "So where were we? Oh yes, so El Hajj was still one step ahead of you both, wasn't he?" he continued, looking dispassionately down at the groaning man. "The bastard betrayed us," growled Cabbalas. "Nasrid was never expected to succeed was he? For El Hajj it was all merely a distraction to direct attention away from something else."

"I wouldn't know," replied Cabbalas coldly, looking down at the writhing Grasshopper.

"I would," replied Rose. "I was on the Internet on my laptop in the car. There has been a global metals crisis triggered by a massive sale of metal stocks, at exactly the same time today as the Nasrid speech. As a result, the price collapsed, pulling silver and gold down with it. Secondly, El Hajj has been linked directly by Reuters to an emerging liberal wing of a radical Islamic party in Tunisia. I'm guessing that today was planned to destabilise a major western country, which very nearly succeeded. I guess then El Hajj could step forward, claiming to be the reasonable and responsible face of Islam, and be feted by the West for stopping Nasrid. I would even guess that a ritual sacrifice of poor Leila was planned to make it look like Nasrid was the bad guy."

"That's what the monk told us," replied Guy grimly. "Only for you two," said Monty, looking at the two corrupt police officers, "this was all about money and little else,"

"You're quite mad," growled Cabbalas, looking around wildly for an escape route. "I will talk to my boss, this has gone far enough."

"I have already taken the liberty of doing that just a few minutes ago, and he gave me permission to act, why do you think I have police support?" replied Monty coldly. "He told me that he had his suspicions about you for some time."

"As for you Grasshopper," said Guy, "as I told you in Bermuda, I remember your daughter telling me about your Spanish ancestry. She also said that you were practically living in Bermuda at weekends, to the point where your wife and family were convinced you were having an affair. In reality you were working with Salboa."

"Clever little bastards aren't you? But you won't stop me," growled Grasshopper through a pain filled leer. He had managed to drag himself to a chair and was tying a handkerchief around the wound. "You don't know the half of it, boy."

"But I do," replied Monty. "It was no coincidence that the Cross was suddenly found in the Caves by this so called madman, Steve. You looked after the idiot didn't you? You were the 'Big Man', manipulating and controlling his simple mind."

"You've no proof." Grasshopper scoffed.

"He has identified you by photograph."

"The word of a madman against a policeman."

"It's enough. You encouraged him to murder people. He was unstable anyway, and you cynically took advantage. I guess you even led him to the poor man who was attacked before he found the Cross! You are going to do a long time in prison, Pollard." Monty concluded firmly.

"Stupid idiot never told me anything!" roared Grasshopper finally losing his composure. "I lost good people forcing him to reveal where the dammed Crosses were! In the end it was these two bloody amateurs who found them under my nose!"

"I'll take that as a confession," replied Monty, turning to Guy and Rose. "We've lost El Hajj and the women, but the consolation is that they have failed with Nasrid and don't have the Treaty or the Crosses."

"Who is this other woman?" asked Guy.

"She's called Sabine and seems as hard a case as Kristina. Real bitch, according to your Uncle, but Salboa had good things to say about her. She was probably sent directly from this so called Teacher to seduce him, if I have to hazard a guess."

"The tablet has gone," replied Rose.

"Worthless without the Treaty, what drove you to do this, Cabbalas," asked Monty, "aside from the money."

"They ruined our family, as Rose says."

"Ancient history, what of your career?"

"I hate the Muslims," growled Cabbalas, "I lost my brother to them in the Madrid bombings, but you would never understand, it was additionally for his honour, this job pays a pittance and I have debts. Salboa promised me a lot of money if I helped."

"So, you cut a deal with Salboa then betrayed him. You planned to let Nasrid have his moment in the sun, and then cut and run with the Treaty and Crosses, helped by Grasshopper. I wondered why the police presence was so low key at the Alhambra, until I took control. You knew all along that they were going to kill Nasrid. Salboa told you. You then engineered the helicopter escape whilst finding the Treaty. What I don't understand is why you let Kristina, Sabine and El Hajj go?"

"They threatened to expose me," growled Cabbalas. "They got their freedom and I got the Crosses and Treaty," he continued, looking around like a caged animal and staring in disdain at Grasshopper. "The perfect plot until you came along. We would be rich, the honour of the family would be restored, and no one would be any the wiser. Sorry Monty, but the shame is impossible," he muttered, leaping forwards revealing a hidden snubnosed revolver in his hand.

As he aimed the gun there were two quick shots in succession and he collapsed to the floor, blood pouring from his chest. The two policemen brought in by Monty lowered their guns. "Thanks, but such a dammed waste," grated Monty, looking at Cabbalas slumped to the floor, "such a waste of a good policeman." Guy watched the police take Grasshopper away to a waiting car in handcuffs, an ambulance had been called for Cabbalas. "So this enigmatic Teacher still wins, wherever he is," he commented to Monty. "So many are dead, but the puppet master survives."

"Perhaps," replied Monty. "From what you say of this monk, and your dreams, you have a mission. As for me, mine is complete with these two rogues. It is the worst thing in my profession, bent policemen," he replied sighing. "I've a feeling one of the Teacher's team was in league with these two. They were far too effective in the short term without help somewhere, two policemen amongst rogues."

"Perhaps you're right," replied Guy thoughtfully.

"Who could it be" asked Rose?

"I'd rather be certain first."

Monty grinned. "As you wish, "We've captured the Queen but the King remains at large, sorry that's the last chess analogy of mine," he smiled. "I have much work to do here and I thank you for all your help. I also apologise for misleading you in Bermuda, but I knew you would want to head down here whatever I said, so I reasoned it was best to let you get on with it. Also, I had my hands full with Grasshopper and wasn't sure how to handle him, you have both done me a great service. Therefore, I wish you the best of luck with your quest. I've a feeling that your job is only just beginning."

"What of the others?" Guy asked.

"I can only assume they have long since left the country. They will lick their wounds and try to salvage something out of the whole sorry affair. I would not like to be in their shoes if this Teacher exists and confronts them. You really think that there is a larger conspiracy here?"

"Certain of it, far larger than any of us realise," replied Guy grimly.

CHAPTER 21

The Grand Hotel Palermo was showing signs of wear and tear in the late afternoon sun, a testament to better days. However, its grand façade was totally in keeping with the dark windowed limousine that sped along past the afternoon tourists and street vendors. It swung across the oncoming traffic on Via Roma and pulled up in front of the hotel. No one looked twice; it was a common sight in the homeland of the Mafia and their clandestine world. Two men climbed out wearing hats and sunglasses. They were ushered straight into the hotel by uniformed attendants, and through into a private room where a man and two females were waiting in trepidation.

"Sit down," hissed the Teacher, his appearance hidden behind his hat and sunglasses, which he declined to remove. His visible features were stony and expressionless. He looked around the table at the attendees El Hajj, Kristina and Sabine. "At least you are alive," he whispered menacingly.

"We will continue to plan for the mission?" asked El Hajj hopefully.

"The plan is being delayed, thanks to your incompetence in Spain. We will have to move slower," rasped the voice ominously. "I do not like, or accept, failure particularly when it could have been avoided. You failed to keep Nasrid alive long enough to succeed and you have cost me a lot of money."

"But he was meant to fail eventually," replied El Hajj puzzled. "I accept that the plan was for a week of disruption, but the result has been the same."

"The result has not been the same," replied the Teacher coldly. "You cannot hope to succeed in Tunisia with this result. I do not take unnecessary risks and that would be unnecessary. You will have to wait, El Hajj."

"But...."

"And if you wish to have a future with me you will speak only when asked," continued the Teacher witheringly. "Now, to the rest of you and your part in this debacle; Salboa was out of his

depth, had bad judgement and got greedy, a great disappointment. He should never have trusted those two idiotic policemen,
but worst of all a couple of amateurs and a Bermudan cop out
thought you all! Inexcusable, you should have seen that coming,"
he said looking around. "As if that were not bad enough there is
something else, something much worse than incompetence," he
turned deliberately to his male assistant. "Zie Lai, my most trusted lieutenant, assures me that all this could have been avoided,
even with the mistakes, but other things conspired against us," he
continued looking to the smaller man. "That concerns me greatly."

"The two policemen had help from someone other than Salboa," replied the Chinese man, Zie Lai, slowly speaking for the
first time, revelling in the discomfort of the others as his cold
eyes flickered across the room. "So are we going to get a confession," growled the Teacher. "Perhaps it was you, El Hajj? You
have cost me millions, getting the metals markets ready for your
accession to the throne. Perhaps you thought you were above us
all?"

"Never," protested the Arab vehemently. "I am totally loyal to
your cause, Teacher, it was simply that Salboa let me down," he
continued, shaking his head. "My movement is still ready to
move forward, as originally planned."

"You will wait until I judge we are ready. It is most vexing to
me to have to come here in person; it goes against all my principles. However, the situation is serious enough to warrant it."

"It is safe here, Teacher, the Mafia have been paid." Zie Lai
reminded him. "I assume they have, and I would not desire to go
personally to Africa. I have done that once, to Carthage, and have
no desire to go again. However, that is not what I meant, the cells
must remain independent at all times and we have been forced to
break that rule."

"I am ready when you say so Teacher," persisted El Hajj.

"We need the support of a grateful Spain and America, and
we do not have that now. Nor do we have the Crosses or the
Treaty."

"The policemen did seem to know everything," replied El
Hajj warily echoing the words of Zie Lai. "Of course they did,
because they were told," replied the Teacher coldly. "That is what

we are investigating. The one thing that we cannot accept under any guise is disloyalty."

"Told?"

"Not by you, El Hajj. Like many fanatics, you rarely use deviousness as you cling to the foolhardy belief that you are above such things. Still, at least what you see is what you get. Is that the case with you all here, I wonder? No, it's not you El Hajj, so you will take over from Salboa and run the Alhambra lines. Hopefully you can make a better job of it."

"Thank you, Teacher." El Hajj bowed, grateful to have another opportunity.

"Don't thank me until you have succeeded," he said, turning to Kristina. "Now, my dear, how do you explain your failure?"

"Salboa was an idiot; you were right, Teacher, to send me to watch him."

"You were sent to ensure he did not fail, why did you not succeed?"

"We were deceived by the policeman, Cabbalas, as El Hajj says," replied Kristina trying to remain calm under the unremitting glare of the cold eyes. "It was more than that though, wasn't it?" asserted the Teacher. His voice was now brittle like ice. "Tresanton and the girl, they have uncanny powers," said Kristina. "I have not forgotten their role, or your failure to manage them," continued the Teacher staring hard at Kristina. "You, above all, have let me down and will go with Sabine for re-education."

"That is grossly unfair," stammered Kristina, shaking badly. "You failed Kristina; I will personally have to take care of the interfering amateurs."

"We have the treaty document," said Kristina, with a flourish passing across a leather parchment. "You made it clear that this was important."

"A forgery; what do you take me for, an idiot?" snarled the Teacher angrily.

"It can't be true, it's genuine," said Kristina desperately.

"I had an interesting call from this policeman, Cabbalas, a couple of days ago suggesting a suitable payment for the real one. How well do you know him?" asked the Teacher.

"I don't know him," replied Kristina.

"Strange, because he said he knew you well. He admitted that he had switched the Treaties because he wanted the money, but he said that you helped him identify the Bell Tower as the location, and actually helped him dig it out. You have sold us out, girl. You are the main reason we failed; your treachery coupled with Salboa's incompetence, a lethal combination."

He rose abruptly from the table and turned to Zie Lie. "Time for us to go," he said, looking meaningfully at both El Hajj and Sabine. "The vision of Admiral Zheng He, I suggest you study his life carefully. Now, I have an urgent appointment to attend to further advance our great movement." He strode from the room with Zie Lai. "You don't believe what he said," whispered Kristina. "I'm afraid we do," replied Sabine coldly. The tall girl stood up and lifted a wicked looking dagger from her skirt folds. "You forget that I was sent to follow you and observe all your activities. You met with Cabbalas on two occasions and I recorded your words. You helped him find the Treaty and never forgave Salboa for not giving you Leila as your plaything. Perhaps all this treachery was because of your distorted and unnatural desire for the girl? You should have known better than to mix business with pleasure."

"What are you going to do," said Kristina in horror as they tied her hands together with twine. "Bring her," said El Hajj coldly. They walked out to his hired car and Kristina was bundled into the back, Sabine holding the knife close to her skin. El Hajj drove in the busy afternoon traffic for five minutes before arriving at the Coppelia Palatina e Tesoro, a Norman built Chapel, on the main road. He parked the car and they walked into the deserted building. "You'd be interested in the significance of this place," he said conversationally to the trembling Kristina as they walked through the large building. "Built by a Christian in 1130, but decorated with Arab honeycombed ceilings and Byzantine mosaics. A great illustration of the power of unity with our faiths, but no defence against treachery," he gestured to Sabine to go into a small knave area with Kristina, as he knelt down to pray.

"Sabine, you and I can work this out," stammered Kristina in the small room, desperately trying to think of a way out. "You know, Kristina, there was a time when I admired you, trail blazing the way for women in this organisation. Unfortunately, as I grew in experience I saw you for what you were. Incidentally you failed because of one elementary mistake."

"What do you mean?"

"You never used your main asset properly; never used it to manipulate the men, as I do. They will do anything for the chance of sleeping with me. Simple really, Salboa, the Teacher, El Hajj, all of them will tell me anything and do anything for me, in return for my body. Because of that, I knew exactly what Salboa was planning all along. He told me all about you from the start, so I knew to keep well clear. He suspected you were deceiving him behind his back, and I knew all that while you were too busy with your girls."

"Don't assume that I knew nothing," grated Kristina, desperately trying to think of a way out of her predicament. "You and I, we could be an item, and work together, no one need ever know."

"Sorry Kristina, you are in my way, you see I am fiercely ambitious and no one will stand in my way. Perhaps not even the Teacher when the time is right. You are an impediment to that ambition and have to be crushed, and I have the Teachers blessing to do just that."

"Please Sabine, I'll do anything." Kristina begged.

"Oh, there is one other thing I nearly forgot to tell you in your last minutes on earth," said Sabine, smiling for the first time, "and it's kind of important, I guess. You are the reason I joined this great organisation."

"That is not possible. We are all selected independently. You could never have heard of me before you joined; that is not the Teachers way."

"Correct. Except for one simple fact Kristina, you see you do not even remember me, your younger cousin from the wilds of Texas. You and your family were too good for us Texans, living in high and mighty Denver, but I knew about you Kristina. I heard of all your great successes, and then that you just disappeared. My mother always raved about the blonde girl up north, asking me why I couldn't be more like you, even though we'd never met. I tracked you down through your mother who was heartbroken at losing you. You gave it away in a letter to her, postmarked Tay Ninh from Vietnam. The rest was easy, I went there after you had left and advanced in the organisation on field duty. I took it slowly because I wanted to prove to myself that I was better than my lesbian cousin."

"We can still be a great team."

"You are guilty of the most heinous crime against our great leader, Kristina."

"You don't believe all that do you?" Kristina said, appealing to her cousin.

"Unfortunately for you, yes, I do. You see, I also know through our family that your father's name is Escobar, the same family as Cabbalas and Pollard. I knew you were scheming behind our backs, and that is all the proof I need. Little did I realise that I would have the chance to finish you for good."

"My God cousin, please, you cannot kill me. We have to work this out, there has to be a way." Kristina begged desperately. "Too late for that, as I said you are in my way, so I'm afraid there is only one answer," Sabine told her, and in a blur, the knife was thrust viciously into Kristina's chest. She gasped, looking down at the spreading blood, before collapsing. Sabine stood looking remorselessly down at the dying woman. "Thanks for all your help; it's always good to learn from someone before disposing of them. Guess you'd like your body on show as you go," she smiled, as the woman's eyes glazed over. She bent down and expertly slit away Kristina's skirt and blouse to make it look like a crime of passion had been committed in a holy place. The police in Sicily would think the Mafia had been busy again. She walked quietly out, nodding to the kneeling El Hajj. "It is done; we have much work to do."

Fortaleza Hidalgo
La Gomera

The last of those invited arrived at the dimly lit monastery. Following the other guests, he proceeded from the private helicopter landing area through a network of secret tunnels, before arriving in a private cubicle. Each cubicle was emblazoned with a letter, used to identify people to each other. Few knew the real identity of the others, few wanted to know; too much knowledge could be dangerous. Each cubicle faced outwards to an oval table. At one end of the table sat the Chairman of the meeting, and at the other the Secretary. These roles rotated by meeting and their duties involved ensuring the coordination of the next meeting, when they would hand over their duties to another.

All nationalities were represented amongst the twelve delegates, with no more than one per country. Only the convener and his loyal cohort knew all the identities in the group, and they lived a monastic life in the monastery. Few who actually saw the monastery from the outside would ever gain entrance, as its real purpose was to host the Chamber in its deliberations. It had been that way for well over a hundred years. The influence within the room was sufficient to buy secrecy from those who enquired. The members were elected by each other, but held no elective office outside the chamber. The only prerequisites for membership were wealth and influence.

The mood around the table as they sat down was sombre. The meeting, as always, would be short and to the point. They were people of action and decision. Secrecy was essential, and the dim lighting ensured that they could only see each other in profile. The Chairperson called the meeting to order, speaking in the uniform language of English. The early discussion was on the changing nature of the world's economies, on which many of those in the chamber had a direct influence. Then the debate moved to the organisations activities and the Chairperson attempted to set the scene.

"It is clear," he intoned, "that the competitive nature of the world's economies is changing dramatically. The developing world's economies will drive their prosperity through manufacturing, whilst the developed western economies will be driven by ideas and innovation. We must all recognise this fact in our decisions. Above all we shall not be able to unduly affect this trend; that is not our role." The last remark was deliberately aimed at the last person to join the meeting, who had just taken his seat much to the Chairpersons annoyance. It was a great discourtesy to the other members to arrive late.

"I disagree," said the Teacher. "People will always need leaders; such generalisations as you paint are highly dangerous about nations."

"So what would you do Z?" he asked, referring to the Teacher by his letter code. "Would you control these events like some modern day Stalin? From your recent exploits, this can only be extremely damaging to us all."

"You know my strategy, as you all do here. It will work and will ensure the equilibrium is maintained on the natural order."

"So what disruption do you plan next Z?" came a different voice.

"What you have seen so far is only the start of the changes. My plans remain secret but will become more advantageous to you all as we move forwards. The rights and credibility of those that have passed before us will confirm what. I have told you; we cannot rely on the idiosyncrasies of human events, we must guide them. Learning from the events of the past and improving them will ensure that we all succeed."

"Your ideas are the polar opposite of others here, Z; you are seeking to drive us in a new direction."

"I have the mandate for that," replied the Teacher harshly. "There are enough of you here who agree with what I am planning."

"Perhaps, but that doesn't mean we condone your methods."

"I will decide on the methods necessary to succeed," replied the Teacher angrily. "Do not question my ability to succeed."

"Then see that they comply with our code and our requirements, you know the punishment for contravention."

"It is time to change the nature of this chamber," replied the Teacher angrily. "You have to be more than a talking shop. You will all benefit beyond your expectations, but you have to trust me."

"We will give you licence to move forwards, but do not presume to have total control of our resources, no one has that," said the Chairperson. "That is not our way. I will not have this august group becoming fractured, that will lead to the most terrible of civil wars and ruin everything. We meet again soon colleagues. I trust that when we do Z will have better news for us than last time or we will need to take appropriate action."

The Teacher cursed silently as he walked back down his private entrance to the waiting helicopter. They were a bunch of fools, but unfortunately, he needed them and would have to move carefully. They would have no choice but to go with his plans, anyone who did not would perish. The course of human events was going to change dramatically. His ancestors had prepared him well for this moment, ever since Zhou Wang had en-

tered the chamber in the late nineteenth century. His destiny was
sealed and he would see it through to success, whatever the implications.

EPILOGUE

Bermuda

The sun shone brightly as Guy and Rose scrubbed and varnished the teak deck of *Hidalgo*, getting her ready for the sail back to St Lucia. Guy nodded to Rose as he spotted the now familiar form of Inspector Monty approaching by police launch, his ubiquitous pipe dangling from his mouth. They had parted in the Sierra Nevada a week ago, leaving Monty to tie up loose ends. They had both been very keen to get back to *Hidalgo*. "Good to see you again Monty, I assume you were successful?" Guy greeted him warmly. "Almost," replied the Inspector, climbing aboard. "The good news is that there's a reward for the return of the Tucker Cross. The bad news is that as the Columbus Cross didn't officially exist, we can't give you anything for that," he said handing over a cheque. "Enough to buy another yacht," smiled Guy, looking at the piece of paper. "What's going to happen to the Columbus Cross?"

"There's been an outcry in Spain after the Nasrid affair and the Spanish authorities are keen to hush up the whole event. They feel it's better to deny that the Cross ever had any meaning, and say it was just a fancy artefact. Technically, it is theirs anyway, so it's going into a museum in Madrid. You could say Queen Isabella paid for it, so they will probably give it to the current King Carlos."

"And the Tablet?"

"Probably destroyed by El Hajj as it has little meaning without the Treaty document, and they wouldn't want to be caught with it."

"Vincent and Veronique had the right idea all along, to get rid of the Cross, perhaps they should have destroyed it," said Rose joining them and replacing the tin lid on the varnish can. "They probably felt it wasn't their decision to destroy such an icon," replied Monty. "So they swapped it with the madman Steve's ancestors, for jewellery or other artefacts. Only Steve's family knew of the exact location in the caves and he wasn't going to tell anyone, much to Grasshoppers disgust."

"Only thing that puzzles me is why didn't you arrest Steve before?"

"Firstly, no bodies, for the obvious reason; secondly, because we started to shadow Grasshopper on his frequent trips and realised that there was a link to Steve. We wanted to see where that led us, which was when you arrived on the scene and the whole thing escalated out of control. God knows how those two found each other! It really was a marriage made in hell," continued Monty.

"How is Grasshopper?"

"In jail for many years, I doubt you'll be getting a Christmas card from him. "

"They were a lethal combination," replied Guy, "greed and insanity."

"They fed off each other. Grasshopper will never get over the fact that you found the Crosses right under his nose."

"And Cabbalas's death?" asked Guy, wanting all the loose ends tied up.

"As I said, the Spanish authorities are horrified over the whole thing and have hushed it up. Apart from the nosy journalist who was beaten up by Salboa's thugs at the Alhambra, it seems that the whole Nasrid episode is dying a natural death."

"And the Treaty?" asked Guy.

"What Treaty?" replied Monty, with a straight face, "You burned a worthless piece of leather, as far as I'm concerned; documents like that bring nothing but trouble. The Spanish will never know what they nearly had, and the hole in the Bell Tower has been resealed."

"But you talked of its huge significance," prompted Guy.

"Ah yes, all roads lead to the treaty. A red herring really, only Kristina and Cabbalas thought it was important, whilst in reality it would have been no more than an embarrassment and fuel for a few fanatics, no more. I think this Teacher of yours has other far more important interests."

"But it was important," persisted Guy

"Yes, it was the main reason why a man called Zarco sailed with Columbus," answered Rose. "I disagree with Monty; I think the furore would have been huge, particularly in unstable South America.

"Which is why we had to destroy the copy," continued Monty.

"Copy?" they both started in great surprise.

"The Spanish have the Queen's copy under lock and key in Madrid. Don't worry, I was told to destroy the Moor copy if I found it, which is why I acted as I did with you," smiled Monty. "I wanted you to burn it in front of Cabbalas to kill the thing off forever. There is one other twist; the Teacher has a fake copy that Cabbalas produced. Their problem was that because of the Cabbalas intervention, they couldn't arm Nasrid with the treaty for declaration on television. Ironically, it was located only feet above their heads and Kristina alone knew that, as she had deciphered the Tablet. By the way we found a body in Sicily."

"Kristina."

"How did you know?"

"She was the one working with Grasshopper and Cabbalas, an Unholy Trinity."

"Why would she do that?" asked Rose.

"She was from the same family, Escobar. I heard someone call out her name as 'Eltobar', clearly they meant Escobar. It came back to me in the helicopter, if she had the same name as Cabbalas, there had to be a connection. She was determined to help them for the same reasons."

"What about these Elders and the Teacher?" asked Rose.

"Well beyond me, I'm afraid; it is all is innuendo and gossip. I deal in facts not hearsay," continued Monty. "These conspiracies you keep talking about, I take it you're both convinced of this?"

"Yes, the reincarnation of Nasrid was only the start. I am sure they will do the same again and again," replied Guy.

"How do you know this?"

"Premonitions and deductions; dreams, we both have them."

"As I said before, I only deal in facts, you're on your own with those, I'm afraid."

"What of El Hajj?" asked Guy.

"My sources say he is back in Tunisia, rebuilding his reputation. My advice to you and Rose is to avoid Islamic countries, get away from them all."

"Wherever we go, we'll have to look over our shoulders."

"Afraid so, but you do appear to have a hidden guardian."

"And you've got me for now, Bear," said Rose cheerfully. "To help you spend that money. A proper Charter business needs two boats to ensure continuity and good cash flow."

"What about Beatrice?" asked Monty chewing on his pipe with satisfaction and searching his pockets for a light. "She wants a quiet life in St Lucia; ambition of any form seems to have deserted her. Besides, she has this old cleric to take care of." Rose said mischievously. "Dear Uncle, in a wheel chair but as bumptious as ever! They'll make a good pair," replied Guy. "I take it he has no intention of returning to England to face the music?" queried Monty. "He's a changed man," replied Guy. "The shock of that fall into the Atlantic has affected him badly. He has stopped drinking and is determined to do something useful here in the Caribbean. He's also lost interest in money, or so he says."

"My Aunt invited him to go down to St Lucia," continued Rose.

"Useful, if I need any advice on smuggling," grinned Guy.

"Your new business partner will veto that," replied Rose. "Anyway the new Police Inspector, Cricket, has taken a shine to me; I would be letting him down with such a venture."

"We're planning a big display of the Tucker Cross," said Monty turning to the stern ladder. "To keep you anonymous we've concocted a story about it being found by police divers in the Crystal Caves, which is partly true. Incidentally, we've sealed off the caves where Steve lived, a fitting graveyard for the dead," he continued raising his lighter that he had finally found in his jacket pocket.

"First time I've seen you actually light that thing," said Rose.

"Special occasion," grinned the Inspector. "Where are you heading now?"

"We sail for St Lucia this evening."

"If you are right about this Teacher figure give me a call. Largely thanks to you two I've re-established the credibility of the police force here, so I guess I owe you."

"Feeling is mutual; after my police experience in Hong Kong and with Grasshopper you've revived my faith in Bobbies," replied Guy.

"One other thing, keep those diaries well hidden. They seem to have an uncanny ability to invite trouble."

"They are well hidden," replied Guy.

"Good luck then," smiled Monty, heading to the launch.

"Guess I'd better have a quick nap, as I've got the night shift," said Guy heading to the stern bedroom. Deep sleep came quickly to him, until he felt something or someone in the room. Startled he sat up and saw the monk; or was he dreaming? "What are you doing here?"

"Well done in Spain, but you must never give up and must be ever vigilant," whispered the monk, his face totally hidden by the large cowl. Guy was sure that it was the same monk that they had met in La Gomera. "Why do you come to me? I don't understand?" puzzled Guy, still not sure whether it was a dream.

"It's your destiny; a gift if you like."

"We just want a normal life."

"It is not in my power to explain, but only to help you as much as I can. The Teacher will look for you both, so you are in considerable danger."

"I'm not equipped for such a task, neither of us are, we barely escaped this time with our lives." Guy explained frantically. "On the contrary, you both proved that you can meet the challenges," whispered the monk, turning to go. "The gifted amateur is always very resourceful and always underestimated, so therefore the most likely to stop him. In addition you both have hidden and unique gifts."

"How can I find you, if we need help?" asked Guy desperately.

"I will always find you. There is one other thing, read your history carefully, particularly of a man called Zheng He."

They sailed *Hidalgo* out into the Atlantic Ocean as the red sunset lay before them. Guy pointed her south-eastwards, set the auto pilot, and sat back gazing at the sky, ruminating. "Zheng He, did he say?" asked Rose. "Zheng He," repeated Guy. "I'm sure my father talked about him."

"The name does ring a bell. It looks like we are stuck with each other then, Bear. But, you know, there's one thing that still puzzles me," continued Rose. "The football match; there's something about it that keeps at nagging me. It wouldn't take such a prominent position in the diaries if it weren't important. As with the Escobar notes the diaries are far more significant than their first meaning implies."

"The footballer's names perhaps," pondered Guy, lifting Veronique's French diary down and once more scanning the pages. He looked up triumphantly. "Here it is! In the Spanish team, they had a player called Nasrid, a Spaniard with Arabic parents, according the Veronique."

"Doesn't prove a thing," said Rose.

"Except that there is a link between what is recorded in the diaries and this individual."

"And that Vincent and Veronique realised that. To think, they must have used the same Compass clue as we did to find the caves in Bermuda. There has to be more in the diaries that helps us," continued Rose.

"But where do we start?"

"There were four teams, the Spanish Americans, the Asians, The British and the Germans who all had empires and rich histories, so they may have been selected deliberately to compete."

"Except the Germans," interjected Guy.

"But the German team contained northern Europeans."

"You are missing the Roman and Greek empires, they were the largest," said Guy.

"They were before the time of Zheng He."

"So you do know of him."

"Yes, he sailed the largest fleet ever assembled in 1421 under the direct command of the Chinese Emperor. Perhaps the challenge is the key, not the names of the nations. Perhaps the Elders comprise all these nations and are working with the Teacher to find the long lost treasures of this Zheng He's voyages? Perhaps they have more meaning than just a treasure, which was the case with the Columbus Cross."

"Or perhaps this Teacher is the head honcho, just running his own agenda," added Guy.

"Of course," replied Rose excitedly. "Don't you see that's the point? The Teacher or these Elders are orchestrating it all, whomever it is they are playing with us. Yes, we have solved one of his riddles, but there will be others."

"What others?"

"The prophecies of the Elders," she replied. "The Chinese link, my own people. Something the girl Sabine said when I was listening to them in the Sierra Nevada in the car."

"I thought you were on the Internet?"

"I was using this listening device Monty gave me. Anyway, she said that the Chinese were re discovering their world."

"You've totally lost me."

"Come on Bear, the Teacher is rumoured to be Chinese, so possibly it's him in our dreams."

"Go on."

"What if the Columbus Cross originally came from China? What if it is part of a collection of icons that were sent around the world, long before any of the Western explorers?"

"That would mean that they predated Columbus, Magellan and Cook for instance," replied Guy, realising the significance of his father's message so long ago in Hong Kong. "My God! That's it."

"Exactly," replied Rose. "Maybe, as you said back in St Lucia, your father is right and it's all a Chinese thing; discovering the modern world long before Columbus and the rest. Now, they want to reclaim what is theirs, which is what the Teacher is doing. He wants to bring together these great treasures from wherever they are. This Admiral Zheng He had Vice Admirals who sailed off from his main fleet to discover America, Africa and Australia. Perhaps they left people behind to colonise?"

"And if they left people behind to colonise, then they would have also left antiquities and possibly more."

"Just like the Columbus Cross," said Rose.

"My God! That's what my father meant; he wasn't telling me to study the explorers, he was telling me to go right back to the start," cried Guy.

"Perhaps that's why we are being hunted by the Teacher; he is concerned that we have figured all this out? It could be that his whole secret organisation is predicated on this task."

"Doesn't explain the monk though, does it?"

"Maybe he's a dissenting voice from the Elders."

"Or maybe the Elders disapprove of the Teacher and his plans. After all, they appear to be multi-cultural, with no geographical or cultural bias," continued Rose. "I also have a gut instinct that Veronique's mother, Lady Victoria Silver, and Vincent's father had more of a role to play than is evident at present."

"An out of control roller coaster," replied Guy, tightening the sails as they bit into the wind and turning on the sound system. To the strains of Mozart's Violin concerto No2 in D Major he lifted his head to the skies and let the wind caress his face. "There's another thing, our fathers," said Rose quietly. "Our fathers are dead."

"Perhaps, perhaps not. If the Teacher fears us then maybe that's our destiny to find out."

Thank you for reading
Chasing Columbus

Now read the next in the history detective series
'Bahamian Rhapsody'

Historical References and Acknowledgments

Whilst real characters and events appear in the story, actions and events attributed to them are fictional and in the interests of the storyline.

Three true stories however, are wound into the storyline and are worthy of further comment –

The Tucker Cross

Referred to in the novel, and a major inspiration for the fictional Columbus Cross, did go missing just before the visit of the Queen and to this day remains an enigma in Bermuda. It was highly embarrassing at the time as the substitute, clearly a fake, was discovered only days before Queen Elizabeth's visit in 1975.

The Chinese discovery of new Worlds

In the fifteenth century years before any Western explorer of note is the central premise behind Gavin Menzies book referenced below. He uses scientific evidence, including DNA, to support the hypothesis that Admiral Zheng He did in fact discover all the major undiscovered continents of the World. It remains a hotly contested but a highly persuasive argument.

The Caodoism faith

Is a reality in Tay Ninh in northwest Vietnam and does actually believe in the reincarnation of the souls and spirits of famous people. It remains the only international religion headquartered in Vietnam and it will be interesting to see how it copes with the increasing globalisation of that country.

1421 – The Year China Discovered the World – Gavin Menzies.

Rivers of Gold – the rise of the Spanish Empire – Hugh Thomas.

About the Author

David J Andrews is a leading writer of adventure thrillers. His novels are published on three continents. In South-East Asia, a major Chinese publisher and a significant distribution chain support his work. Currently the leader of a multinational organisation, he uses his insider knowledge of the corporate business world and his extensive travels overseas to ensure authenticity in his writing. Originating from Yorkshire, he is married and lives in rural Lincolnshire, England, where he pursues his passions for sailing and history.

www.ingramcontent.com/pod-product-compliance
Lightning Source LLC
Chambersburg PA
CBHW051240210726
48287CB00002B/335